WHEN I ALIGHT

Book One of

The Essence of the Equinox

CAMILLA ANDREW

For information contact :
contact@aninkwellofnectar.com
https://www.aninkwellofnectar.com

Edited by Molly Rookwood

Cover art & Illustrations by Eeva Nikunen

Drop caps by Megan Wyreweden

ISBN (paperback) 978-1-7393089-0-2
ISBN (ebook) 978-1-7393089-1-9

First Edition: June 2023

10 9 8 7 6 5 4 3 2 1

*For all those who looked at the stars and
imagined themselves among them.*

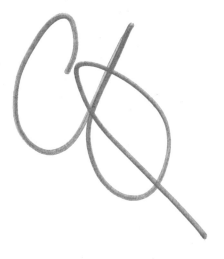

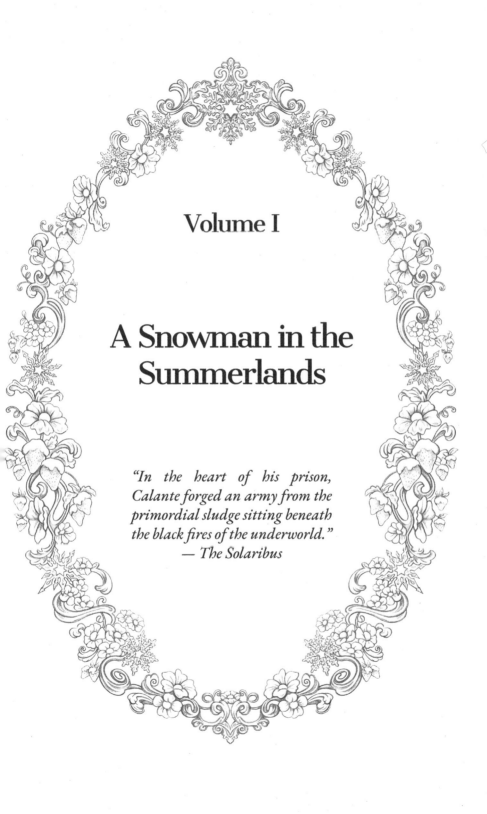

Volume I

A Snowman in the Summerlands

"In the heart of his prison, Calante forged an army from the primordial sludge sitting beneath the black fires of the underworld."
— *The Solaribus*

I

IT ALL BEGAN IN A CLIFFSIDE CITY wedged between sea and sky.

Le Creissant was a sight to behold, lingering sweetly as a daydream. Take a pleasant walk down the promenade, and you would be treated to pastel-coloured storefronts and pale pediments engraved with floral and foliate moulding. Store signs beckoned with gold cursive on frosted glass, promising shade and cool refreshment from the balmy summer weather, while sweet scents drifted from curlicue balconies adorned with wildflowers.

It was a visual delicacy, good enough to eat, but it would leave you feeling immeasurably guilty for doing so.

Château de Rosâtre was the centrepiece—an edifice of dawn-coloured marble fluctuating from pink to orange with the hourly migration of the sun. Within these hallowed halls, star maidens known as solarites congregated in flowing gowns of silk. They governed humanity under their benevolent rule and had been the muses of poems and art and songs for nearly a millennium.

Inside the palace, one solarite in particular was preparing to unveil an item of great importance.

Princess Laila Rose took a few steps closer to the mysteriously draped specimen and bit her lip in excitement. It had been escorted directly to the palace after being fished from the Crystean Sea, one of many items of sinister magical origin she'd catalogued.

"May I, princess?" Antonin, one of her Lightshield guards, asked.

Laila smiled, her face emitting a roseate candlelight glow, before gesturing for him to continue. "You may."

With that, he stripped away the shroud to expose the colossus trammelled inside a block of ice. "Behold—the Abominable Iceman!"

Laila gasped, one hand flying to her mouth. Indeed, there was a creature with the look of a man pitifully imprisoned within the glacial chamber. Yet he was larger than any human male she had ever seen. Freed from the ice, he would tower a little over seven feet, stacked with concrete muscle.

Laila snapped her fingers and gestured to one of her servants. "Quickly! Pass me Calante's grimoire."

The sprite rushed to place the leather-bound tome into Laila's waiting hands. The cover was studded with obsidian and etched with figures alien to even her worldly learning. Even now, Laila still struggled to resist the tome's dark allure—the shameful taboo of its corruptive chaos magic.

She opened to the first page to display an even stranger language complementing this incomprehensible book—made from human vellum and written in blood. As she touched them, the words twisted themselves into her native Soltongue. A useful enchantment.

Laila turned page after page until she found the entry she wanted: "The Perfect Predator". She glanced at the illustration of a tall, muscular humanoid with ink-blotted eyes that resembled the iceman, then traced over a word that jumped out among the rest: "occassi".

"Got you!" Her heart pounded like a child who had discovered their first expletive. A name to the face; what could be better?

She devoured the rest of the entry, learning that the occassi had been given the gift to wield chaos magic, just like the god who made them. This allowed them to, according to the tome, "influence the dark, control the dead and wreak mayhem, malady and misfortune to the fullest extent of their delight."

"Now what am I to do with you?" Laila cocked her head to one side.

She was a solarite; this made him an enemy. Her natural opposite. A monstrosity concocted by Calante's malevolent mind to wreak havoc upon the world he had sought and failed to claim. Or so the myths went, in any case. Yet here the proof was in front of her.

"Léandre, I'd like for you to place our newest houseguest in the Chamber of Chaos with the other confiscated artefacts." Laila explained this without turning, her chin resting on her closed fist. "What shall we call him? He should have a name, should he not?"

Her guard was not so quick to share her mirth. "Would it not serve us better to disintegrate this miserable beast?"

Laila clicked her tongue in mock disapproval. "Now, Léandre, there's no need to be so discourteous. He is still a sentient being, after all, and he looks as if he could use a little warmth." Logic would dictate that she despise this creature out of turn, and yet she couldn't prevent the tender blossom of pity at his predicament. Harbinger of doom or not, surely no one deserved such a frosty fate.

"Your mother will not be pleased with this."

Laila knew this, just as they both knew her frivolity was a thin veneer lacquered over the cracks in her confidence. For some reason, she was unable to show the iceman her back. She was unsettled by the way his eyes appeared to follow her across the room, the way his slitted pupils were so much like a cat's.

She therefore resigned herself to an impasse with the brute, him watching her and her watching him. Her eyes roamed over every rigid line of his rectangular face, every rugged contour of muscle, until he was mapped in her memory. It was her way of ensuring that should he ever move even a fraction of an inch, she would notice.

While this was a ludicrous fear, such an emotion often made a mockery of even the most rational minds, and this titan seemed designed to linger in the primordial corner of the brain that urged one to flee or fight.

Yet it wasn't quite fear that Laila regarded him with. There were nerves, to be certain, that heart-fluttering exhilaration of meeting with imminent danger. But it was the sort that allured rather than repelled. Already she desired to know every inch of this creature—his origins, the breadth of his power, his true nature. She wanted to unspool his brain and rummage through it for study.

She was so distracted she almost didn't hear Léandre's approach. Even in court heels, he had the gentle, near imperceptible tread of a forest sprite, aided by his padded silk armour. With him near, she was able to focus her attention on the grimoire.

"Take this away, too."

Léandre hesitated, what minimal colour there was in his rouged cheeks now evacuated.

"What is it?"

"Forgive me, princess. It is only that..." A light bobble appeared in the elegant column of Léandre's throat as he made a holy gesture. "I would rather not lay hands on such an item, if you'd be so gracious."

4

Laila received this with the arch of a brow, considering if he was serious. Of course she, who had only ever seen temple sermons as an excuse for a light nap, would allow herself to forget how devout forest sprites were to the nation's faith of Caelestis.

"Surely you do not intend to make me believe you are *afraid* of this dusty old tome, Léandre?" Her voice was a birdsong lilt, playful and sweet. Seeing that her guard would not relent, she sighed arduously and packaged the grimoire back into its fine cloth sleeve and clipped its briefcase shut. "There. All locked up, nice and tight."

With the matter resolved, Léandre turned back towards the ice block and regarded its occupant with a sneer. To a pious mind such as his, this was an abomination. Degeneracy could be read from the titan's fiendishly pointed ears alone.

Léandre picked up the shroud and tossed it back over the block in disdain before pushing the cart towards the gilded hallway.

Impératrice Amira Rose was an individual of exacting standards. Perfection was the guideline by which she was ruled, and her heightened senses made it so that she saw possibilities for refinement everywhere. This gave birth to her love of décor, and there was no room in the château that had not been tinkered with to reach optimal conditions.

The Superna was one such room, a private dining hall well-acclaimed by many for the oak dining table set on a gilded mount and veneered with floral marquetry. Amira had it shaped carefully to her vision—a distinguished placement of ecru table linen hemmed with filigree lace, gilt-rimmed porcelain dishes and ornate silver cutlery. Atop the pristine folded napkins were printed menus for the three courses she had selected. A basket of bread smeared with garlic butter and rosemary garnish awaited to soothe her appetite during the interval.

All was arranged as it should be.

That was, apart from the conspicuously empty seat across from her that ought to have been occupied by her daughter. Amira acknowledged this vacuum with an unsatisfied twist of her mouth. Laila's arrival had only been delayed by five minutes, but it was five minutes more than she was willing to allow. Thus, it was not for the first time, and certainly not the last, that she lamented her daughter's shortcomings. Just as she was about to give voice to these thoughts, Laila arrived in a blonde blur before her chair.

"Deepest apologies, Maman," Laila blustered, tidying the unruly curls that had sprung free from her chignon. "I had to see to our new delivery."

Amira pursed her lips, unsatisfied with the excuse. Such efforts she had gone to bring her desired heiress to life—meticulously choosing the mound of kaolin and rosewater that she had hitherto moulded into the shape of a perfect daughter. Yet perfection she'd received anything but.

To Laila's fortune, she did not air such a view, electing only to offer the biting critique: "You missed a curl."

Laila diligently tucked the baby curl behind her ear. Solarite hair was prone to wild, curlicue textures, but Amira kept her platinum locks ironed straight into obedient layers via hot comb.

Laila enchanted her seat so that it glowed with aether and withdrew from the table. "So, what are we having?" She picked up the menu to bring it up close to her face, then hummed in pleasure when she saw a few of her favourites present. "Shrimp and sparkling wine bisque, scallop and orange salad served in a tulip, and peacock confit in burnt honey and lavender sauce with figs. An impeccable feast as always, Maman."

"Why thank you, aurore," Amira replied, the hard line of her lips shifting the merest fraction. "Now, why don't you tell me what this business is with Calante's new... unfortunate deposit to our doorstep?"

Laila explained her findings and helped herself to a few slices of warm bread. By the time she had finished, the bisque had arrived on floating dishes also glowing gold with aether. Amira always preferred the use of enchantments to serve herself, finding too much margin for error when it came to trusting others.

"An occasso, you say?" Amira's brow arched in interest.

"Believed to be one of Calante's most deadly creations, judging by the entries in his grimoire." Laila dipped her bread into her broth and swirled it absently. "Apparently they are to be his underlings upon the event that he returns to unleash havoc on the world. I took the time to verify it with the passages in the *Solaribus*, and it's believed that a sighting of occassi is meant to herald the first signs of impending doom."

"That's just ludicrous," Amira said once she'd taken a spoonful of bisque. "Astrologists have been bleating about the end times for a millennium. Now all of a sudden with the appearance of a carcass in the ice we are expected to panic?"

Laila couldn't help but agree. She had little use for superstition but would concede that a race of creatures forged from chaos was certainly a threat worth investigating. "While I am no sooner willing to invest in the threat of Calante than you, Maman, what we do know at the very least is that occassi exist. What if this creature is not a lone case? If there are more out there, lurking somewhere, should we not investigate?"

"I do suppose that is worth confirming," Amira conceded. "The question then becomes: How do we approach? I wouldn't want to spare too many bodies in case it all ends up being a fruitless endeavour."

"I believe there are scholars who specialise in the study of chaos who may be of some use to us. With your blessing, I am happy to make contact with them."

Amira nodded, taking another spoonful of soup.

"But, Maman, I must ask, supposing that there *are* more occassi... what ought we to do about it?" Laila ran her tongue over her lips. "If Calante truly did leave measures in place to bring about a doomsday event—"

"Don't be absurd," Amira said at once. "Asemani made certain that her son would no longer belong to this realm. Even if there are creatures that might have been born of his power, that does not go on to validate any apocalyptic prophecy. Let us confront one manic human theory at a time, shall we?"

"As you wish, Maman."

"And what have you done with this occasso?"

"He has been left in the Chamber of Chaos along with the other artefacts."

"Good. I should like to see this creature." Amira dabbed her lips with her napkin. "But not until tomorrow. Today, I shall have to host talks with the Magisterium and seek their advice."

II

DR AKIRA ISUKA STEPPED FROM her carriage onto grounds in summer-smitten bloom hemmed with bushes of gold roses.

"Goodness! What sweltering weather it is!" she said, enchanting her paddle fan and closing her eyes in pleasure to the cold zephyr provided. The conveniences provided by her air magic served her well here, for Soleterea had always been several degrees too hot for her northern blood. Odaka, the country whence she hailed, had a much milder climate suited to the studious minds it often spawned. "I feel as though I could be fried like an egg on the pavement. Don't you agree, Emica?"

Dr Hariken's head wilted over the briefcase on her lap. Dark circles bruised beneath her eyes and her limbs slackened with ghoulish unrest.

"Emica?" Dr Isuka frowned as she leaned over to nudge her friend's arm. "We're here."

Dr Hariken sprung to life with a splutter. "Hm, what? Oh yes! Of course. Just give me a moment!" She groomed herself instantly at the sight of Rosâtre's ivy-strangled columns, straightening her spectacles and smoothing the imperceptible wrinkles from her floral-patterned robes.

A summoning to an audience with the Soleterean princess was not something she'd ever dreamed to experience! Even after laying hands on the rose-scented stationery with its official gold wax seal, Dr Hariken had needed pinching several times before she was able to comprehend its meaning.

"For the love of Asemani, stop fussing!" Dr Isuka scolded. "Your robes look perfectly suitable."

Dr Hariken blushed before exiting the carriage, and the two scholars found themselves approached by one of the sprite attendants.

"Well, hello there!" Dr Isuka said brightly. "I believe you'll be escorting us to the princess?"

The sprite nodded and beckoned for them to follow.

Dr Isuka continued to harass the escort with endless queries on the nature of the meeting while Dr Hariken silently cringed beside her. This questioning continued long into their journey towards the audience room, and it was only when they were met with the opening of those gilded double doors that Dr Isuka's voice faltered.

For there was Princess Laila Rose seated on a settee of green velvet. Under the encroaching sunlight from the windows, the diamond stars in her hair seemed to glitter nearly as much as she did. Her ivory satin gown emphasised the warmth of her brown skin, the gold embroidery matching the intricate giltwork spanning from ceiling to wall.

The gold was woven from the thread of sunlight, custom-made from a Soleterean boutique where seamstresses shot needles into the sky and used them to weave frocks from the fleece of clouds and the iridescent threads of celestial beams.

What followed was this—a pause, a swallow, a quick drawing of the breath—all the involuntary little impulses one does when faced with something too vast and unfathomable to take in at once. Mortals weren't often exposed to the fleshly form of a star.

"Your Radiance," called Antonin, "if I might present to you Dr Emica Hariken and Dr Akira Isuka of Azora Institute."

Dr Hariken's throat bobbled like a frog's as all saliva (and ability of speech) receded from her tongue. Only the incessant tugging from Dr Isuka at her sleeve prompted her to set her briefcase aside and kneel.

"Your Radiance," they said in unison, prostrating themselves before Asemani's holy agent.

Laila gestured. "You may rise."

Dr Isuka was the first to straighten. "On behalf of myself and Dr Hariken, I would like to thank you for receiving our company, Your Radiance."

"Please, the honour is mine, Dr Isuka." An even brighter beam graced her voluptuous lips. "Thank you for coming to my call so swiftly."

"Anything at all for such a beatific being!" Dr Isuka said.

"Do sit. Make yourselves comfortable. The impératrice sends her regrets that she couldn't be present for such an occasion."

The latter half was a lie that they need not know—a silk-spun web to keep the favour of academia ensnared.

The scholars approached the settee, admiring the off-white studded latticework intertwined with gilded roses on the inner back. Soon after, a sprite arrived with offerings of fragrant jasmine tea and Seraji coffee served with macarons on a porcelain étagère. The princess's special request was delivered to her on a tray of frosted glass—almond milk and orange blossom honey.

11

"Now, as we're all sitting comfortably, shall we begin?" Laila took a sip from the glass and picked up a macaron.

"Oh, please do." Dr Hariken flushed, looking briefly to Dr Isuka for the nod of approval. "We are most eager to know the reasoning behind your summons."

"Well, it's of a rather delicate nature, you understand." Laila's eyes swept low in a show of demureness, as though she were about to gently broach a topic of vulgarity. "But I am aware that the pair of you are dedicated scholars of the chaotic arts?"

Dr Hariken choked violently on her tea.

Dr Isuka slapped her hard on the back before speaking on her behalf. "Forgive us, Your Radiance. Your interest has come as quite a shock. Indeed, Dr Hariken and I have dedicated our lives to the field."

"Quite a controversial subject." Laila dipped her macaron into her milk. "And while I'm certain there are enough scholars studying aeromagy, why would you involve yourselves with something so malignant?"

"Well, for years now we have taken a specialised interest in Calante—"

"So it's the Adversary you're after," Laila said with a knowing smile. "I'd have thought you two would've known better than to give those poor religious folk in Odaka a fright by poking into the god of chaos himself."

"It was our faith that led us right to him," Dr Isuka said. "We were warned young to prepare for his eventual return and reclamation of the world. We wanted to do our part in stopping him."

"You are doomsday believers?" Laila couldn't help her tone of surprise. Not many would expect an academic to entertain religious doctrine.

"I know that it is an unpopular prophecy in solarite circles, but why else would Asemani deliver you to us if not to forestall Calante's return?"

"To steward humanity in her stead, as we have always done," Laila replied, munching her macaron. "But while we're on the subject... there is something I must ask of you that relates to your expertise on the Adversary."

"What is it?" Dr Hariken perked up in interest.

"Have either of you ever heard the term... 'occassi'?"

The two scholars flinched in fear. The word clanked like a pin-drop echo through a sudden silence.

"I take it you have, then," Laila said grimly. She set down her glass of milk. "That certainly makes things easier."

"Why, of course." Dr Isuka shuddered as though chilled. "Such creatures are considered to be Calante's most heinous creation. As significant a spawn to him as the solarites are to Asemani."

"Then I impart this knowledge not to alarm you, but because I require your aid. It appears that we have discovered a creature that bears a likeness to the occassi described in Calante's grimoire. If possible, we would like to confirm if this is a lone case or if there are more we should expect." Laila moistened her lips. "Would you be able to assist?"

Dr Hariken smothered a nervous whimper. She hadn't bitten her fingernails in years but found herself sitting on her hands to resist the urge. "There is something we have that might be of use to you."

"Oh?" Laila's eyes brightened.

"I have put together a cryptograph to communicate with dark forces," Dr Hariken said. "Any question I ask of it, the instrument answers. I could inquire the origins of this occasso, but I suspect if there are more of them, they will be found on Calante's dwelling place."

"The mountain concealed inside a land of ice and fire," Laila recited, for cultural osmosis made the tale of his downfall well known.

"Give us until tomorrow, Your Radiance," Dr Isuka said with conviction. "We'll have an answer for you then."

After they'd left the château, Dr Isuka sat down to lunch with her assistant, Hana Oto, in their modest lodgings to inform her of their meeting. The two indulged in the famed Soleterean delicacy of hibiscus and sumac shrimp étouffée served with roasted plantains and yellow rice, followed by a rich helping of raspberry tart.

Dr Isuka was the first to put down her fork, belly full and heavy, when she noticed that Dr Hariken's seat was still empty.

"Where is she?" Dr Isuka huffed in annoyance. "She said she'd be down to join us half an hour ago."

"Shall I go fetch her?" Hana asked.

"Yes, Hana, that would be very helpful," Dr Isuka said, a touch gentler, before she launched into an aggravated mutter. "Honestly, what is wrong with that woman today? Had we waited any longer the food would've been stone cold..."

Hana took this moment to gradually slip out from her seat, knowing that Dr Isuka's rant wasn't meant for her ears. She approached the lift lobby and tapped the button eagerly, bouncing on one foot to the next until she heard the ding.

She gave a little titter at the noise, having never tired of it during her stay. So many oddities to be found in this sophisticated country. So much glamour and excess. This was a modern world for a modern woman; far away from the Odakan village she'd left secluded in the mountains that her mother—and her mother before her—had never been brave enough to leave.

Hana rode to the second floor, retrieving from her pocket the ornate iron key that denoted their room number. She entered the main sitting room, a quaint affair of fading floral wallpaper and sinuous wood panelling. The chairs, upholstered in canary yellow, were the only splash of vibrancy in the room.

"Dr Hariken?"

Hana glanced towards the bedroom door and tried there next. Behind it, the darkness was a still wall of gelatine; each window had the shutters drawn like lids over tired eyes. A cocoon ready for slumber.

Dr Hariken sat on the edge of the bed, her bleached blonde bob a mimicry of a solarite's sun-kissed ringlets. She had her head bent over a bronze device that delivered a series of clicks and whirs, suggesting she was once more communing with her cryptograph.

The dial spun rapidly, needle scratching over several eldritch symbols in continuous sequence. Nobody knew how to interpret them besides Hariken herself, and to do so she had to train her mind to take on a certain concentration. She'd called it "dipping into the abyss", for the sensation was akin to descending into oceanic depths until her skull almost cracked from the pressure of it.

As Hana watched her, she felt drenched in shame, as if she had intruded upon her naked. There was something inherently vulnerable in observing her mentor having stripped herself of all the little nuances that made one an individual—one with thoughts and opinions and feelings—to become a blank slate for chthonic forces to write upon.

"D-Dr Hariken?" Her voice was soft and uncertain, so frustratingly *young* to her own ears that she swallowed and made herself speak more firmly. She stepped closer to the doctor and tapped her shoulder. "Dr Hariken?"

Dr Hariken's head drew upwards with the lethargy of being pulled by strings. "Yes, Hana?"

"I—" Hana cleared her throat. "Apologies for the disturbance, but Dr Isuka was wondering when you might join us for lunch."

15

"I have much work to do," Dr Hariken responded. Her lips lifted into some crude imitation of a smile. "Tell Akira to allow me more time."

"Perhaps you should come back to the cryptograph another time," Hana continued, unwilling to abandon her objective. "After all, I'm sure it would be much easier to concentrate on a full stomach."

"He likes it better when I am empty."

Hana stared at her, bewildered. "He?"

"I think you'd better go now, Hana," Dr Hariken said, smile stretching taut to snapping. "There is much work to be done."

"Yes," Hana replied with a gulp, retreating backwards into the wall. She winced when she met it, hand clasping for the doorknob. "Yes, I think it will be better if... Dr Isuka discusses this with you instead."

With that she fled, leaving Dr Hariken as serenely seated as before.

Once Hana had left, Dr Hariken rose from the bed and closed the lid of the cryptograph, placing it on her desk. Then she withdrew one of the drawers to take out a pen, a pencil... absently letting them clatter onto the desk before she found what she sought.

The pen knife was a slash of silver in the darkness. Dr Hariken inspected it, dragging the cool metal lightly over her bird-boned wrist. She inclined the knife to a point just before her vein, pricking until it offered up a small blot of blood. A tribute. She drew a thin, hard line as her flesh split apart with a wet laceration. Her blood spilled forth, red and vibrant and vital.

She continued to illustrate herself as the symbols commanded, indifferent to the warm slither drizzling down her elbow as it trickled red rain onto the carpet.

III

LAILA AWOKE WITH A GASP, her lemon chiffon negligee entirely drenched through. She feared it was saliva, though as the claws of her nightmare receded, she would understand it was from sweat.

In her dreams, she was plagued by visions of herself as a blonde rabbit being eaten alive by a large black wolf. He had eyes like a limpid sky, a long tongue like a sash of red velvet. The wolf ate her slowly, his red tongue slathering over her warm flesh, lapping away at the blood. She could feel the moisture of his hot exhalations as he savoured each chewy squelch of fat and hollow crunch of bone. All the while her pink nose flared and her legs kicked until softly, almost sweetly, she fell away.

She squeezed her eyes shut, trying in vain to cling to the soft oscillations of shallow consciousness. But it was too late. The sun pierced through her eyelids and hauled her into the saturation of morning with all its screeching demands of colour, scent and texture.

Laila whimpered softly as she burrowed into her lavender-scented pillowcase before confronting the distinct, intuitive sense that she was no longer alone in the room.

One of her guards stretched out on her bed beside her, ankles crossed, a long braid of pale, diaphanous hair resting on her shoulder.

"Good, you're awake," said Lyra de Lis as she thumbed through the pages of the grimoire. She was not in her Lightshield uniform. Instead, she wore a purple satin coat and breeches with a floral-printed vest. "You seemed to be having a rough one."

Laila scoffed. "Away with you, Lyra. I haven't the time for your nonsense."

"How cruel you are to me when you *promised* we would visit the iceman today."

Occasso, Laila's mind corrected, its true name burrowing into her brain like a maggot.

"Yes, but only when the scholars have arrived." Laila propped herself up on her elbows, her face a picture of princess petulance. "What time is it?"

"The clocks have struck their first quarter."

"Then we have hours before then!" She picked up her pillow to thwack Lyra with it before she glimpsed the grimoire. "Wait—you can touch that?"

"Of course I can touch it." Lyra's brow arched as she flipped a page. She waved the book for effect. "I'm doing so now, aren't I? Though for an ancient and creepy spellbook, it is a surprisingly dull read. Necromancy, body possession, familial curses, plague conjuring... how pedestrian!"

She twisted the book to and fro, as though hoping for more oomph to be found within.

18

"Well, it is only that your uncle would hardly go near it. You should've seen the look on his face when I held it out to him; I'd never seen a sprite so pale!" And their colouring was lacking enough as it was. "It's why I brought it here with me."

"His concern isn't misguided. There is a very strong... essence that isn't quite like aether." Lyra's brow furrowed. When handling items of magical origin in the past, she could always count on her sprite senses to detect the aether it exuded like a perfume. The grimoire was scentless. But more than that, it appeared to be deliberately pulling its energy from external sources around it.

"I can't describe it, but it's almost like I'm holding the abyss in my hands. Though it doesn't affect me much so long as I only skim." Lyra glanced over at her in concern. "How have you been feeling since you've had it in your presence?"

"Strange." Laila recalled the faint tendrils of her nightmare. "There's almost a compulsion it holds, like the more you read it the more it wants to be read."

"Best to put it away in the Chamber along with the others, then," Lyra advised. "There's an anti-magic field around it."

"I'll see to it later." Laila waved a hand in dismissal. "For now, I am famished. Come, join me for breakfast."

With that, Laila peeled away the silk cocoon of her sheets to slide her feet into her velvet slippers waiting at the edge of her bed. She went to her serving bell next and rang it to alert the kitchen to serve breakfast.

On sultry summer days like this, she always took breakfast on her balcony, and after her night terror, she found the current spread being set across her table to be a welcome sight. Soleterean pastries vied for attention beneath glass domes, enticingly smothered with powdered sugar, lavender honey, and rosewater cream while coils of white steam exhaled from silver pots of coffee and drinking chocolate.

Laila helped herself to a raspberry-and-rose religieuse and took a large bite, indulging in the mélange of flavours—the tart berries, the delicate wisp of rose crème that melted so lightly on her tongue. For a solarite, a meal was to be a sensual experience, and they would often give their food the same meticulous attention to detail as they would all else.

She told Lyra of her nightmare whilst eating.

"Well, that's certainly disturbing," Lyra said, taking a sip of her frothy coffee. "Have you considered going to the oneiromancer about it?"

"What do you think?" Laila replied, her upturned nose wrinkling in distaste. She had stopped attending consultations with the oneiromancer when she realised the contents of her sessions would always end up finding their way back to her mother. "No, I shall spare myself that ordeal. Besides, I'm not entirely certain if it *means* anything. It may only be the influence of the grimoire. In which case, locking it away should remove the initial cause."

"Still, being eaten alive by a large black wolf..." Lyra tapped her ringed finger absently against the porcelain. "Do you not suspect it may have something to do with our... What did you call it again? Occasso?"

"That is what I fear," Laila admitted. She took another bite from her pastry, her bow-shaped lip coming away smudged with fondant. "Other than my nightmare, I could barely sleep a wink for thinking he would break through the ice."

"Perhaps we ought to break it out." Lyra's brows waggled with daring. "See if it'll move."

"Lyra."

"Come *on*, don't tell me you aren't in the least bit curious?"

"I am not a slayer like you, Lyra," Laila said with a sigh. "My first thought when I hear the word 'monster' isn't one of conquest."

"Then perhaps you ought to broaden your perspective," Lyra

teased, her blithe laughter echoing generations of swashbuckling sprites that preceded her and died bleeding for their hubris.

Dr Isuka arrived when the morning was still new, ushered in by a fine layer of sea mist that rolled up from the shorelines. She exited the carriage alone, having rushed an injured Dr Hariken to the healing springs the night before.

The wounds Hariken had inflicted on herself had not been severe, and she thankfully hadn't lost too much blood, but the morning after had seen her bedridden with fatigue. She'd been delirious, cheeks flushed with fever, ranting about how *He* had requested her blood and body in order that she might be worthy of being his cartographer—to map a path to the Shadowlands.

"*Rest*," Dr Isuka had insisted, dispelling any requests her friend had made to come with her. She had not seen that level of mania in her before, and the sight of Hariken's sunken cheeks and black-patched eyes still permeated long after she'd left.

Princess Laila was already awaiting her in the audience room when she arrived, Lyra beside her. The princess wore a tulle dress in aqua blue fastened with ribbon straps at the shoulders, a plunging neckline baring her glistening skin to the sunlight.

Dr Isuka greeted her with a bow. "Your Radiance."

"Hello again, Dr Isuka," Laila said, looking briefly behind her shoulder. "Only one of you today?"

"Yes, Dr Hariken has been taken ill, I'm afraid," Dr Isuka said, before adding with feigned mirth, "I suspect it was something she ate."

She kept her expression as poised as possible, having heard rumours

21

that solarites could detect an untruth. Fortunately for her, such a power could only function under physical contact.

"How terrible. Please send her my regards." Laila and Lyra exchanged a look. "I'll have to send you away with a little something to see to that."

"Thank you, Your Radiance. You are very gracious."

"Please," Laila said, her smile steady. "But if you'd like to follow me, we can discuss this more on the way to the Chamber of Chaos."

They moved from the audience room into the stuccoed hallway, where a gaggle of giggling starlets in swishing silks darted past them.

"Did Dr Hariken at least have a chance to look into what I asked?" Laila asked, stepping swiftly out of the way of the younger solarites. She watched them as they passed, their wildness instilling her with a certain longing. Her mother would never have allowed her to run amuck in such a fashion.

"Yes, we did," Dr Isuka said, "and as it turns out, there are indeed more occassi than our lone case."

Laila's brow raised. Clearly that was not the answer she had been expecting. "Could you tell me more? How many? Where might they be found?"

"Dr Hariken will need time to fully translate what she's been told."

"Let us hope she reaches much healthier spirits, then."

Dr Isuka swallowed as she thought back to Hariken piecing together that crude invention. Perhaps she ought to have paid better attention. Perhaps she ought not to have let it get this far. "But to answer one question: We do believe we've discovered a map to Calante's dwelling place. Odds are the occassi originated from there."

"How is it that you intend to uncover these lands?" Lyra asked.

"Well, we were hoping we might request your permission to charter a voyage north."

Laila gave it some thought. "I am most certainly curious enough to want to see what is truly going on out there. I'll discuss it with my mother."

"How was it that you even became involved with all of this?" Lyra asked.

"My mother was a priestess," Dr Isuka revealed with a shrug. "I grew up in a very devout sect of Caelestis. Throughout that time, we would hear prophecies of Calante's doom and how to best prepare for it. Dr Hariken and I were raised together, and when we came into our aether sensitivity, we both showed proclivity for aeromagic, the element of our home country."

"And the interest in chaos magic?" Laila asked.

"That came later. We were never able to shake our upbringing in that regard. Dr Hariken handles the artefacts; I was always more interested in monsters."

"Monsters are for slaying, Dr Isuka," Lyra said sternly, "not for study."

"Spoken like a true forest sprite," Dr Isuka quipped in response. "However, even you cannot deny studying monsters makes them that much easier to be slayed."

"On that, I would likely have to agree with Dr Isuka," Laila said, despite talk of slaying unsettling her. "Though surely as a woman of academia you cannot possibly believe in prophecies?"

Dr Isuka closed the cryptograph and slid it back into her pocket. "I see no separation between my faith and my education, Your Radiance. For me the two are very much intertwined."

Laila acknowledged this with a nod. "Fair enough."

"Though, as a woman of academia, I have learned the merit of proof as a means of validating my assertions." There was nothing like spending years amongst intellectual sceptics who thought themselves more rational than thou to grow a thicker skin. "For that reason alone, I do hope some heliographs or perhaps even some biological material akin to our iceman can sway you more."

They reached the antechamber, where a hidden lift resided—the only means of accessing the lower levels. Laila cast an enchantment upon the wall to reveal it, and the three of them huddled inside as it delivered them into the bowels of a pristine white hall.

Dr Isuka blinked blearily before it, like she'd been exposed to pure, naked sunlight.

"Beyond this point, there will be an anti-magic field until we reach the vault," Laila explained as they walked through the hall. No aether would be able to thrive inside the meteorite wall panels, nor the unknown dark matter that settled amongst the artefacts. "You may therefore feel slightly disoriented."

The walk to the bolted door was mercifully a short one. Lyra stepped forward to steer open the bolt lock, and the sealed door opened with an audible gasp.

Dr Isuka found herself unprepared for what lay inside. She walked in with her mouth agape, eyes starred like a child in a toy shop whose fingers were spoiled for choice.

The Chamber was an underground vault where sprites and solarites alike catalogued various items of suspected chaotic origin. It had since become home to prohibited grimoires, cursed objects and even unidentified corpses of those with the misfortune to have contact with corrupting forces.

"My goodness..." Dr Isuka exhaled in surprise as she surveyed the tomes and ornaments beneath their glass cases. "Where did you find all of this?"

"From various places scattered throughout the continent," Laila said. "I'm currently in charge of overseeing its curation, but this collection has been building for centuries before I was even born."

"Some of these items I wasn't even sure existed," Dr Isuka exclaimed, stepping near to view the crystal decanter labelled *distilled ectoplasm* and an hourglass full of black essence labelled *reservoir of the abyss*. She brought out a spectacle case that held a pair of amber goggles, which she promptly slipped on.

"What are those for?" The sudden apparition of Lyra behind her caused Dr Isuka to jump.

"Please, ser, have some consideration for this human heart," she cried, adjusting the goggles on the bridge of her nose. "These goggles help make aether visible to the naked eye. Perhaps not necessary to a sprite or solarite, but for us—"

Dr Isuka lifted up a hand and saw the charged golden particles that surrounded it. Aether gathered around every living thing and settled in higher concentrations around those who were magical. Though none were so enveloped in it as solarites, who, as celestial beings, emitted aether themselves. Before the lens of the goggles, Laila had all but disappeared from Dr Isuka's view, swathed in golden light.

"That's fascinating," Laila said, left once more in awe at the resourcefulness of humans.

"That's not all they do, either." Dr Isuka turned back to the display cases and saw that the objects, too, were enveloped. Though instead of aether, there were black particles that swarmed like flies. "They also show me the dark matter that surrounds all objects of chaotic origin."

"Ah, that explains why I couldn't sense it earlier," Lyra said, eyes alight with understanding. "Chaos magic doesn't use aether; it's an entirely different essence altogether."

"Precisely." Dr Isuka raised a finger for effect. "And that is precisely what frightens me so much about it. All magic we use relies on aether, all of it, from elementalist to solarite, and yet here is a type of power that is more maverick—that doesn't abide by our rules." She stepped over to the velvet shroud draping the occasso and tugged it free. Inside, he was obscured by blackness, in almost complete contrast to Laila. "It's why I think our iceman is still alive in there."

"What—" "—*Alive?*" Lyra and Laila cried in unison.

"It's only a theory, but aether doesn't surround the dead, and if we were to look at one of the corpses presented here"—Dr Isuka moved next to one of the mortuary chambers and withdrew one to look at it— "you can see here that there are no dark matter particles surrounding it, either." She took off her goggles and held them out to Laila.

Laila received them with caution and slid them over her eyes to confirm Dr Isuka's supposition. She turned back to the occasso and saw the black miasma that surrounded him. Her lips parted in awe as she reached out towards the particles, watching the way they repelled against her golden dust like the meeting of opposing magnets.

"How is this possible?" Laila wondered aloud. And what was more, what was she to do with such information? To leave a corpse suspended in eternal captivity was one matter... but a living being? Even if he was, for all intents and purposes, a malignant one?

"We should inform the impératrice of this," Lyra told her.

"Yes." Laila scrunched her lips to one side, uncertain. If her mother knew there was even the slightest possibility that the occassi lived, she would not hesitate to have his body destroyed.

"It's what's best for everyone involved, Laila." Lyra rested a hand upon her shoulder, already sensing her thoughts. She knew her friend had a strawberry heart that was too tender and too soft, too predisposed to bruising at any sign of hardship. "What would be the alternative?"

"You're right." Laila nodded, swallowing thickly. "I shall have an audience arranged so I can inform her of our findings."

Dr Isuka's back went straight as a rod in alarm.

"We should probably depart," Laila said, removing her goggles to hand them back to the scholar before she turned her attention back to the occasso. She closed her eyes, seeing flashes of her nightmare in a flurry of images like leaves kicked up by the wind. Was it a herald? Some kind of ominous sign of what was to come? Ironic for her to consider, what with her earlier dismissal of prophecy.

Her mind wavered on the ethics of a preventative kill as the entry of the grimoire taunted alongside it. In the end, she knew it was no use. She couldn't kill it, but neither could she spare it from its inevitable fate.

"Well, it seems this is where you and I part ways, my fearsome friend." Laila sighed as she pressed her hand briefly against the ice. The ice crackled in response, and she pulled away with a gasp. "What's happening?"

She took a step back in alarm, colliding into Lyra as she did so.

They all watched in horror as the ice splintered into a spidery web of fissures that slowly, piece by piece, began to crack and fall away.

IV

LAILA REMOVED HER HAND AS THE ICE shed its layers like a thick winter coat and the waters of the occasso's rebirth began to break through.

"Oh, gods," breathed Dr Isuka in horror as tiny jets of water burst free from the cracks. She willed herself to move back but her legs rejected the message. She was stiff as wax.

Laila scarcely had a moment to react before Lyra's arms were wrapped around her svelte waist, pivoting her out of harm's way.

"What did you do?" Lyra cried, her hands cupping around Laila's face. Her opaline eyes were tinged silver as a blade under the ætherald lamps.

"I didn't—" Laila looked to her friend with wide and guileless eyes, shaking her head frantically as Lyra gripped her shoulders. "I didn't do this, Lyra. I didn't—"

There was little time for either to argue the site of blame, for the ice responded with a loud, hollow crunch as soon as the words were uttered.

The two immortals spread themselves away from the ensuing icy slush as the occasso washed out. His body smacked the ground with a wet clap, stiff and unresponsive. They stared at him as though he were a beached leviathan tossed from the abyssal depths of the sea. A subject of myth, now startlingly factual.

Laila's heart thundered in her chest at his arrival. There was a tempest brewing in her, one powered by both fear and excitement—the dread of the unknown and the eagerness to know it. Disregarding rationality, she stepped forward towards the slumbering titan and saw the faint tremors of his coldness. And, in seeing it, was inspired to drape the blanket over his colossal form.

She crouched low before his head and swept away the damp curtain of his hair to reveal his face. He was all sharp angles, not a single softened curve to him, as though his face scorned the mere thought of frailty. Yet with him limp and motionless on the floor, frailness was all she could see in him.

"He's not conscious," Laila said, prodding beneath his jaw with her fingers. Then she looked up at Dr Isuka. "I can feel a pulse."

"How could this be?" the scholar asked.

"A better question might be: how is it that he got out?" Lyra countered. "And what do we do with him now that he's free?"

"That is something for my mother to decide," Laila said. Though, try as she might, she couldn't stop herself from frowning as she said it.

What caused her throat to squeeze so hard at the thought of harm to the titan, she could not explain. To her, he seemed so *pitiful*, like a lion with a nail in its paw. He appealed to her unquenchable fount of empathy.

"For now, I grant you leave, Dr Isuka."

Though Dr Isuka longed to linger to see the end of this affair, she understood well enough she was being dismissed. "Of course, Your Radiance."

Laila turned to Lyra once Dr Isuka had departed. "Help me move him."

Years of ballet and gymnastics had sculpted Laila's body into one of lithe muscularity, and she could easily carry him with her preternatural strength. His height, however, would prove bothersome without aid.

Lyra closed her eyes and pinched the delicate bridge of her nose, praying upon the higher power of the sun goddess and all her celestial might to give her strength. "Are you a maniac?"

"Do you suggest we leave him here?" Laila asked, appalled.

"If you want my genuine counsel, then yes. The Lightshields are more than capable of taking up the burden from here."

Laila looked back down upon the occasso's face with reluctance, watching the faint rise and fall of his chest. "I can't simply allow him to be killed. Not without—"

"Without what?" Lyra asked, her eyes narrowed. "You need to allow the dog to bite you before you're determined to put him down? Do you have any idea how foolish you sound right now, Laila?"

"What if he's not as dangerous as we're being led to believe?"

"Care to stake your life on that?"

Laila glanced up at her, the heart-shaped curve of her jawline hardened.

Though Lyra knew better, she couldn't help the urge she felt to protect Laila. She could too easily read delicacy into her whittled willow limbs, her ripe apricot flesh, and forget the steel core beneath.

"Well, you might be willing to, but I am certainly not." Lyra stood up to full height, at once a pillar of marble.

Laila knew she might have had better luck at talking a pillar down.

While she might hold the crown in this equation, it was ultimately her mother's word her Lightshield would answer to.

It was clear to both this could only end in one way. They would argue, only for Laila to stand her ground, and it would conclude with her over Lyra's shoulder. How amusing to think such a scenario had once thrilled Laila to the point of desire. Now it only reminded her of why any romantic entanglement between them had been so mournfully doomed to fail.

"Fine." Laila rose to her feet. "But I want him remanded in the House of Correction first."

"Must you drag Lucrèce into this mess?"

"I refuse to consolidate my opinions based on folk tales and conjecture alone, Lyra. I *need* more than this." Laila bunched her fists. "I don't expect you to understand. But I need this for me. For my own peace of mind."

Lyra stared at her for some moments, searching as though she hoped to find the strings of the grimoire puppeteering Laila behind her back. A hopeless endeavour, but not one for which she should be blamed. How else was she to reconcile such reckless behaviour with someone she held so dear? But if you could say only one thing about Laila's character, it was that she had been a magnet for danger ever since they were girls. It swarmed her like captivated moths to her open flame.

Realising this caused Lyra to relent. "All right."

Laila exhaled softly, adjusting the straps of her gown as she prepared for her performance. This was her curtain call, and already the adrenaline was coursing through her veins like a river rapid, her pulse erratic, but one might never guess it from the fluid motion of her feline gait.

At this hour of the day, Laila knew her mother would be in the paradise garden, watching her white lions roam. Laila took the quickest pathway there, seeking shelter through the wisteria-covered pergola and its stark marble pillars until the faint purl of the pond could be heard in the near distance.

Amira sat beneath the partial shade of the pomegranate trees, shadows casting foliate patterns along her skin. Before her stretched lush, green fields carpeted with wildflowers and dotted with fruit trees. Amira had designed the garden with care, each plant a meticulous addition to her symphony of scent, harmonised to olfactory bliss.

Laila remembered the awe when she'd first seen this extensive collection of nature's bounty, knowing the foliage would always remain eternal under her mother's power. But after a while, seeing them unchanged through the seasons, suspended in immaculacy, only served to sadden her.

Laila approached her mother and cleared her throat. "Maman?"

"Yes, what is it, aurore?" Her mother's gaze was a radiant sliver of undiluted sun. Laila felt she was being liquefied straight to the bones by meeting it.

"There is some news about the specimen I feel you ought to know." Laila folded her hands in her lap, her heart thrashing against her birdcage ribs.

"Well?" A lone word, clipped and conservative. Amira had always held her words fast between her teeth, as though they were as precious as the pearls that adorned her hair. Laila had always been a beggar for them, rapping her empty cup for a mere sentence, a syllable. Perhaps she never would've grown such an appetite for attention if she hadn't been raised so starved.

Laila pressed her lips together, debating how much she should say. "I am afraid that during Dr Isuka's recent visit to the Chamber, the creature has—he has broken free from the ice." She swallowed, hastening to explain. "But I promise you, no harm has befallen the Chamber or the palace! I had him swiftly apprehended by the Lightshields and detained."

A low growl sounded from one of Amira's wandering lionesses as she prowled forward to rest her head in Amira's lap. Her fondness for the beasts was what had given her the moniker of White Lioness.

"I see." Amira tilted forward to stroke the lioness's head, the few loose canerows at the front of her halo braid rattling with seawater pearls. A singular canerow ran up through the centre, embroidered with a sun pendant—the holy symbol of Caelestis. "And tell me: How is it you allowed that to happen?"

Laila had been dreading this. Others might display their rage in fits of spontaneous rants or violence, but Amira had always been too dignified for such impassioned histrionics. Her rage was a snow-capped volcano—a careful, contained thing that simmered ever beneath the surface. The control she exerted made it that much more unpredictable.

"I—I—" Laila stammered, a litany of apologies tripping on her tongue.

"You are mumbling, Laila."

Laila jolted straight in response—a dormant reflex from when her mother would administer small shocks to her to correct her posture and speech. "I don't know how it happened! One moment we were all standing there, and the next... it was almost as though it was an act of external will."

"Don't tell me you're becoming a doomsday believer?" Amira snorted in amusement. "Spare me."

"Of course not." Laila nibbled softly on her bottom lip. "It's simply the only way I can make sense of this."

Amira parted her lips in displeasure.

"Regardless of whether you believe in the threat or not... it has been confirmed that there *are* more occassi out there." Laila set her jaw firm. "The one in our custody could therefore become a useful subject to study."

Amira's eyes narrowed in consideration. "The creature? Where is it now?"

"I have him in the custody of Dr Mielette."

"Hm." Amira nodded, willing to accept this arrangement for now. "An inconvenient situation, but not unsalvageable. You are fortunate that your incompetence hasn't been too far-reaching in this instance, Laila. For now, I think it's time I see this creature."

Amira nudged her lioness away as she stood, indifferent to the glisten in her daughter's eyes as Laila struggled to suppress the lump in her throat. There was nothing Amira loathed more than to see tears.

She was already walking away when Laila spoke again. "Maman, I beg your pardon. Please forgive me."

"Don't." Amira held up a hand to halt her. "I have no interest in your pleas. They have no use to me. What I most desire—what I have *always* desired is for you to be better. Yet I can see now that is simply too large of a request. So please, spare me your words. There is nothing more for you to say."

Amira resumed her walk, content for that to be the last word.

Laila watched her go, tears aglitter on her cheeks in the clear sunlight before she politely wiped them away.

An entire Lightshield guard had assembled to escort the occasso to their House of Correction. They'd handled his body with the caution of a grenade that had yet to be detonated. Yet not once throughout the entire process did he stir. He was a spectre in all but pulse.

Laila wandered up and down the expanse of the clinical hallway outside the occasso's padded cell. Eventually tiring of pacing, she sat on the tufted waiting chair, kicked off her slippers, and tucked her feet behind her.

Dr Lucrèce Mielette found her like this when she exited the cell, tidying her bundled bun of pearl blonde corkscrew curls.

"Any news?" Laila asked, brightening considerably at the sight of the solarite physician. She'd been a long admirer of her work and had come to see the elder as a mentor and confidant.

"I was unable to retrieve a read on his aura, seeing as our friend has no aether." Lucrèce grimaced in dissatisfaction. "Traditional medicine tells me there is nothing physically wrong with him. He's a little cold but, well, that's to be expected. It's remarkable. You'd never think he was frozen at all. I haven't seen a healing factor this advanced since, well... one of us."

Laila watched him through the observation window. "So he will not wake at all?"

Lucrèce followed the trajectory of her gaze. "I cannot confirm anything of his condition without a lot of time and observation. Should there be any change, you will certainly be the first to know."

"I appreciate that," Laila said. She glanced through the lone observation window again. "May I have a moment alone with him? Before my mother arrives?"

"As you wish," Lucrèce said. "But make it a quick moment."

Laila entered the room before she could be dissuaded and stepped closer to the occasso, skirting her fingers over one of the meteorite inhibitor rings that had been fastened to his wrists. There was another clasped around his broad, sinewed throat, and she could see how he swelled against it with each passing breath.

He seemed larger up close—built like a mountain. Beneath his bedclothes he was pure bulk; his thighs were like boulders. Laila's breath caught as she observed this, the sight of him activating some primal place. She had seen male bodies before, human and sprite alike. But they had been nothing like his.

Her eyes trailed across the dense mass of his beard, the sharp tip of his ear and the aquiline curve of his nose. Though there was fear along with pity in the cocktail of her emotions, what fermented in her most prominently was *fascination*. The desperation to know for certain whether he would be her victim or villain.

She tested his pulse beneath his jaw, as though to ascertain its realness, and came away marvelling at its much more sluggish pace. But what intrigued her most of all was his temperature—only a few degrees below lukewarm, like a bath left to grow cool.

Perhaps he needs a kiss to warm him up, she thought in amusement. She cupped his russet-coloured cheek, debating whether she should try a less orthodox method of breaching the seemingly impenetrable vault that was his mind. In its rawest form, aether was the essence of life energy itself, and thus heat, light, electricity—all of life's base components—naturally branched from it. If she could manipulate the electrical activity in his brain, she would be able to access dreams, memories, even basic motor functions.

Unable to resist, she brushed her lips against his temple in a kiss. She pried open his mind to her, coaxing her way in so she might see his last memories, and was at once flooded with a deluge of images. She saw him caught in a violent storm at sea, his pursuit of a large white whale crystallised by ice, and his daring, if not completely foolish, battle that led to his icy fate.

She could only dip beneath the surface before she had to come back up for relief, too overwhelmed by the depths of him—the black gulf of memories that appeared to have been lengthened by the centuries of his lifespan. Laila drew back in shock, desperate for air, as though she'd been pinned underwater herself.

The occasso stirred violently in his bed, the crackles of her electricity surging through every one of his nerve endings and jolting them to activity. That warmth of affection, it would appear, was all he needed. It ignited a pyre in his rusted furnace core, coercing the machine to life. Within an instant of her touch, he had awakened with a strained, throaty gasp.

His eyes blinked rapidly, scanning about the unfamiliar room and its scant surroundings until he fixed upon Laila. The occasso drew his head back as he regarded her ethereal radiance. Never before in his life had he laid eyes on a creature like her. Her face was a most exquisite torment—the piercing relief of sunlight at the end of a long tunnel.

He struggled against his restraints and, upon seeing his hands were functional, seized her wrist.

"Who are you?" he demanded in a gravel-laced baritone, his slitted pupils darting analytically over her features. His tongue was a rough, guttural sound, unrecognisable to her.

"Unhand me!" Laila cried out, snatching her wrist back from his iron grip.

He stared at his empty hand in puzzlement, taken aback by her strength and speed. Both realised at once that they did not understand a word each had said.

Dr Isuka sighed as a Lightshield escorted her from the lift into the House of Correction. Tales had long been whispered of the House of Correction and the mysteries that took place within its walls, but it would be the first time Dr Isuka would find herself within its waxed wards. The saga with the occasso had developed a new conflict upon his awakening—one that could only be resolved with her knowledge of his tongue.

She arrived outside his cell to find the occasso being attended to by two sprite nurses while a solarite in a white coat observed from the window. One had slathered his jaw and neck with shaving cream while the other was slicking back his hair with pomade. It might have been the most absurd sight Dr Isuka had ever laid eyes upon, but most amusing of all was the narrowed, unsatisfied gaze of the titan as he was forced to submit.

"Dr Isuka, I presume?" Dr Mielette turned to greet her with a smile. "Welcome. I am Dr Lucrèce Mielette. I thank you in advance for your service to us."

"Of course," Dr Isuka replied, "though I am uncertain of how much help I will be. My knowledge of the occasso's language is likely to be a more archaic dialect, and depending on how old he is, I can't be sure he will understand me."

"Well, there is certainly no harm in trying," Dr Mielette said.

"Indeed," Dr Isuka agreed. She cast a glance at the miserable creature. "Is all of that truly necessary?"

Dr Mielette scrunched her broad nose. "I usually wouldn't, but the impératrice is due a visit and she does hate for things to be unsightly."

"The impératrice?" Dr Isuka replied in alarm. "*Here*?"

"Yes, she will be outside observing."

While the scholar digested this news, Dr Mielette surveyed the nurses' handiwork through the window. The sprites had completed their task of civilising the occasso's wild, rugged features and finished off by applying a subtle rouge to his lips and cheeks to give him a healthier countenance.

Dr Mielette gave a rudimentary check for imperfections.

"Will there be anything else, doctor?" asked one of the nurses.

"No." Dr Mielette shook her head. "You both may remove the mouth guard, after which you are dismissed."

The nurse nodded, taking care to hold the occasso's head as the other unscrewed his guard.

The occasso's throat rumbled as the sprites drew near, his canines itching to descend. But having already suffered the indignity of being primped and preened like a prized mount at a country fair, he was willing to accept whatever leniencies he could.

"What was the mouth guard for?" Dr Isuka asked.

"He took a bite of one of the other nurse's fingers," Dr Mielette said in disgust, "and then he ate it."

Dr Isuka's face folded in horror. She watched the composure of the nurses with astonishment in light of this news. After they had tidied away their equipment, Dr Mielette called for them again.

"Ah, my manners." She clicked her tongue. "Some rosewater, please, for myself and Dr Isuka."

"Yes, doctor."

The nurses opened the door, releasing a balsamic musk from the agarwood shaving cream they were using to groom the occasso. After they'd left, Dr Mielette entered the room to pull two chairs up to the occasso's bedside.

"May I ask what the agenda is for today's session?" Dr Isuka asked.

"We're hoping we'll be able to get this one to talk," Dr Mielette said, observing the occasso's calm, almost self-satisfied composure. "Perhaps find out more about him and where he's from."

Dr Isuka nodded, her mind sifting through the ancient texts she'd combed through with Dr Hariken. All of a sudden, she felt keenly her absence, for the other scholar had always been more adept with linguistics. They'd deciphered the language after realising it shared its roots with an ancient Seraji dialect. "And after?"

"Well, that's for the impératrice to decide." Dr Mielette paused, hearing the lift rise. "And here she is now."

The lift dinged before the doors withdrew to reveal an entire Lightshield outfit, followed by the impératrice herself and Princess Laila on her heels. The guards gathered outside of the observation window, parting to let both royals forth.

Dr Isuka straightened immediately in her presence. "Your Luminosity." She saluted with a low bow.

"Good afternoon," Amira greeted, her lilac eyes examining them both. "Dr Isuka, I presume?"

"Indeed," Dr Isuka confirmed, still a little starstruck but quick to recover. She decided she liked Amira's voice. It was a sonorous, earth-rumbling voice, good for preaching sermons and authoring proclamations; it brought her back home to her childhood in the sect. "It is a great honour, Your Luminosity."

Amira nodded in response. "The princess tells me you should be able to close the gap between ourselves and the occasso."

"Yes," Dr Isuka answered confidently, sensing the impératrice would want conviction in her tone.

"Well then, let's get started."

Dr Isuka nodded, opening the door to the padded cell so that she might sit beside Dr Mielette. She wavered as she drew near, feeling a mammalian tingle in her hindbrain at the occasso's immediate presence.

One never lost those primal instincts, though comfort might dull the blade of their focus and civilisation further subject them to rust. But it always struck like this: a niggling itch, a subtle increase in the heart rate which reiterated itself in the twitching of leg muscles to flee or to fight.

Dr Isuka had faced many monsters before this, but she'd at least had the comfort that they'd often been corpses and not nearly as intelligent.

"You can come closer, Dr Isuka," Dr Mielette said. "I promise you he can't bite."

Dr Isuka sat and smoothed out her lap. Not long after, a sprite arrived with glasses of fragrant rosewater, from which she took a hefty sip before she began.

"Greetings, great beast," she said, in an old, accursed tongue. "I am known as Akira Isuka. I call upon you on behalf of my sovereign to seek knowledge of your origin. If you are able to, I pray you answer my questions."

His features shifted with recognition. Still, he said nothing.

"I divine you recognise the language I speak," Dr Isuka pressed, growing irritable.

"Quite," he said, a wolfish smile quirking on his lips. "Many moons have passed since such a tongue has graced my ears. The land whence I hail had long abandoned it to an antiquated age. Only those of the clergy or the highborn still make use of it."

"And which are you?" Dr Isuka asked. "Clergy or aristocrat?"

His smile sharpened. "Such knowledge would be much favoured by you."

"Yet you will not tell me?"

"It is wearisome to partake in a dialogue whilst I languish in such abasement." He gestured to his patient bed.

Dr Isuka turned to Dr Mielette and switched back to Soltongue. "Adjust his bed. Seat him upright."

Dr Mielette nodded and twisted the gears of his patient bed so he was in a sitting position.

"Is this more to your favour?" Dr Isuka asked.

41

The occasso shrugged. "I would also care to be released from this vexatious collar."

Dr Isuka repeated the request, to which Dr Mielette shook her head. "The collar remains."

"A pity." His smile vanished. "And here I had begun to warm my tongue for discourse."

"He won't speak," Dr Isuka said.

"Tell the occasso if he will not speak," Amira said from beyond the window, "I will gladly enforce a less agreeable method to extract what I require."

"Your sovereign makes her displeasure well known." The occasso chuckled. "I can perceive it even behind this impenetrable wall our conflicting tongues provide."

"I heartily suggest you do not vex her."

"And I, in turn, would eagerly encourage you not to vex me."

Dr Isuka swallowed, the ferocity of his stare all the encouragement she needed. "I shall not squander such wise counsel. Still, I pray you grant me the benefaction of one answer to my question."

"Speak freely, mortal. Demand what you will. But an occasso bestows nothing without price."

"And what price would you demand?"

His smile returned. "Name your request of me, mortal, and I shall grant it upon reception of a vessel to my lands."

"You know I cannot grant that."

"Then I have no desire to proceed with this."

Dr Isuka clenched down on her jaw, her fingers flexing.

Just as she was about to give in, the light patter of Princess Laila's footsteps entered the room.

"Why won't he speak?" she demanded, glancing at him accusingly.

"He wants to barter," Dr Isuka said. "Apparently that is how they conduct themselves where he is from."

Laila walked over to the occasso's bedside to loom over him. The occasso looked back at her. She was no less radiant to him than she had been the first time he saw her, and her proximity disoriented; the warm, heady dispersion of her perfume was like an opiate.

"Translate for me," Laila asked the scholar. To the occasso, she said, "I am the one who is responsible for your awakening. If not for me, and my actions, you would still be wasting away in your glacial encasement. I would say such a display of benevolence would warrant a payment or two, no?"

"Your Radiance—"

"Tell him," Laila insisted, "the exact words."

Dr Isuka nodded, translating to him as best as she could.

The occasso glanced between the scholar and princess, his face splintering into a smirk, and then a chuckle. "Very well, Glowing One. I will reveal to you, and to you alone."

Dr Isuka imparted the message.

"What does that mean?" Laila asked, eyes narrowed.

The occasso cocked his head to one side, then he held out his hand to her. Laila stared at the large, calloused palm before she accepted and placed her hand in his. The texture of her skin was like velvet, and inside of his own, her hand was unnervingly small—birdlike.

Laila's guard relaxed upon his silent placidity, and she tried once more to open his mind to her.

The connection, once established, was electrifying. A current of white heat swelled from the crown of his head to the nape of his neck, causing him to shudder. He closed his eyes to the feathery tickle of her presence in his brain as she roamed his memories and brought them hurtling to the surface. He felt the bitter winters and wet summers; the

43

taste of suckling pig fat on his tongue; the velvet texture of black feathers from a large, indistinct beast; the satisfying crack of bones beneath his knuckles.

He was still tingling with her power when she eventually stepped away, gasping to catch her breath.

The occasso stared at her with eyes of verdant green. "My debt to you is paid."

She didn't understand but was perceptive enough to nod her head. Then she tried once more to scale the language barrier between them. "Laila." She tapped her chest and enunciated the vowels of her name. "Laila."

His eyes seemed to shift with recognition, and, with careful slowness, he responded in turn. "Dominus."

V

DR HARIKEN TREMBLED BENEATH THE SHEETS, ice-cold beads of perspiration condensing on her fevered body. No matter how she twisted and turned, she could not settle. Her healing skin still prickled as though infested with the spindly legs of insects.

"Hana," she cried out desperately into her pillow. "*Hana!*"

Her assistant burst through the door.

"What is it, doctor?" Hana asked, olive-black eyes glistening with concern. "Are you all right?"

Dr Hariken reached for her spectacles. Then she hugged her bedsheets around her, still feeling a chill. "I need more tincture. Please."

"Of course," Hana said, reaching for the tray of Thalit medicine on the bedside table. She uncorked the bottle containing various herbs and flowers floating in marinade—a miniature woodland. Hana picked up the glass measuring cup, filled it to the brim and handed it over.

"Thank you." Dr Hariken tossed back the amber liquid, soothed immediately upon ingestion. Then she rubbed at her tired eyes.

"You should rest," Hana said, filling the glass once more before straightening the covers around Dr Hariken's shoulders.

"It's nice of you to be concerned, but I'm afraid I cannot. I—" I *do not want to face what will happen when I close my eyes.* She could not bring herself to say it, unwilling to burden one so rosy-cheeked with youth. She could remember being that young all too well, full of fire and verve, convinced that the fate of the world was her destiny to undertake.

"I understand," Hana said. She sat down on the edge of the bed. "I could keep you company instead. If you'd like?"

"You're gracious." Dr Hariken smiled weakly. "But you really ought to think about going home."

"Oh no, doctor, I couldn't." Hana shook her head frantically. "There is still plenty of work for me here, and I'd feel simply rotten abandoning you now you've grown sick."

"This isn't sickness, Hana, and we both know it. No matter how much Akira wants to soothe herself otherwise." Dr Hariken traced the pattern on her wrist. "This work, I've dedicated my life to it. And so I intend to continue. But the danger here is graver than I ever could've imagined. I don't think it would be good for you to stay."

"I am willing to take the risks as they come, doctor," Hana insisted, mouth set firm. "Just the same as you. No one ever told us the battle would be easily won, but I will not retreat. Not now." She reached out to take Hariken's wrist. "We are so close."

Dr Hariken followed the trajectory of her gaze, tracing the symbols. "And yet, what if this is all part of his design? What if he's toying with us? And we are mere rats scurrying about his maze for his amusement?"

46

"What's brought this on?"

"I deciphered the text on my wrist today." She met Hana's judgemental stare with calmness. "Yes, I know Akira warned me away from the cryptograph, but I had to. And this is what it said." She retrieved the piece of paper she'd kept secreted under her pillow and passed it to Hana.

"Tread the course of... what is this?" Hana asked in bewilderment.

"Read on."

Hana devoured the contents of the note:

> *Tread the course of ivory salt*
> *'Til the dragon's lungs exhale*
> *Cross the wound of despair before I entered my lair*
> *Within its innards you shall prevail*

Hana furrowed her brow. "I don't understand."

"They're directions," Dr Hariken explained, "to the Shadowlands."

"How can you know?"

"It took me a moment to decipher, but the 'course of ivory salt' is the White Sea. And 'the dragon's lungs exhale' refers to the Dragon's Breath. The rest I have been unable to interpret for now, but it seems as though Calante wants me to come after him."

"And you believe that you shouldn't?"

Dr Hariken shook her head. "I fear I don't even know the answer. Not anymore, Hana. I feel so lost."

Hana's lips sagged in empathy as she put the note down and took Hariken by the hands. "I would like for you to pray with me, Dr Hariken. To ask for Asemani's guidance."

Dr Hariken squeezed back in response before she nodded. "All right, Hana."

In the midst of their praying, Dr Isuka entered the room, blowing in with the strength of a gale.

"Oh, thank the stars." Dr Isuka clutched her breast in relief. "You're awake."

"What time is it?" Dr Hariken asked. "You're back much later than we expected."

"The sun is in its third quarter, and I'm afraid I suffered a minor impediment," Dr Isuka said. "The occasso has awakened, Emica!"

"He awakened?" Dr Hariken's eyes widened in disbelief.

"Yes. You know what this means now, don't you?" Dr Isuka launched herself at the bed with maniacal glee and seized her friend's hands. "The legends that were once dismissed as merely hearsay are true. Calante *is* out there, and so are his monstrosities. We must act at once!"

"Oh, of course. But—" Dr Hariken swallowed as she carefully weighed her next words. "There is the small matter of my sickness, Akira—"

"Emica, don't be preposterous," Dr Isuka replied in irritation. "You are merely stressed. You have been under immense strain, which, I will admit, I may have had a hefty hand in—"

"This isn't a mere response to *stress*, Akira. I am—" She paused with a glance towards Hana.

"I'll leave you two alone," Hana said, making herself scarce.

Dr Isuka closed the door behind her. "Emica, please. I understand that you must be frightened by what occurred last night. It frightened me also. But whatever it was... it seems to have been a temporary bout of chaotically-induced mania."

Hariken's throat tightened. "Yet how can you know—?"

"We cannot afford to believe anything else." Dr Isuka raised her hand in refusal. "The princess has asked one of us to voyage north to discover Calante's dwelling place. It can't be me. You are the one with the expertise with the cryptograph. But if she hears word of your condition, she may cease funding."

"I see." Dr Hariken nodded.

Dr Isuka's chest grew heavy with sorrow as she looked into her friend's eyes. So big and brown they were, set into a cuddlesome face that one could hardly resist reaching to enclose within their hands. She cupped Hariken's cheek with her palm. "I would suggest you take a brief leave of absence from your studies to rest. After which, if you are deemed well enough, we can proceed with the expedition as planned. In the meantime, I will handle everything leading up to the voyage and be prepared to embark in your stead."

Dr Hariken adjusted her glasses, saying nothing.

"Does that sound fair to you?"

Do I have a choice? Hariken wondered. Externally, she nodded. "Whatever you see fit."

"Emica—"

"I am tired, Akira," she said. "I would like to sleep."

Isuka nodded, remorseful yet relieved to have the conversation over with. She switched off the lamp on Hariken's bedside table and crossed over to her own bed on the other side of the room, sliding off her slippers before she tucked herself in.

Dr Hariken lifted up her wrist and traced her fingers along the indelible pattern. How foolish she was to embark on this torrid love affair with forces so beyond her mortal grasp. She thought back to the years she'd spent pilfering back-alley bookstores, haggling with merchants of questionable wares, and pasting in her journal any newspaper clipping that held so much as a whiff of malevolent phenomena.

So convinced was she that she would be able to leave her mark on the world by fighting evil. Seems it was evil that had branded her instead. The bitterest pill of irony she couldn't force herself to swallow.

49

She decided that she wouldn't. She would face the world and its judgement with her head held high and show them she was still on the blessed and pious path. Her depression ebbed with this conclusion as she pulled her covers up to her chin and drifted off to sleep.

As the night passed, the moon unveiled itself from behind the black swathe of clouds in the night sky, as pleasing to the eye as a pearl. Lunar rays pierced the thin bar between the shutters into the scholars' room and played mournful witness to the events that would unfold.

Dr Hariken slept soundly in her bed until her eyes opened, black and lustrous as wet ink. Her body convulsed violently as chaos and aether warred for hegemony over her soul. In the end, no victor was proclaimed but neither was either ousted. The blight lay dormant in her—waiting for its moment to reconquer.

✎

"Are you certain about this, princess?" Léandre asked her as they entered the lift.

"I am certain it is the only way we'll receive true answers." Laila watched the gilded gates of the birdcage enclose around them before they rose. "My mother wishes for me to extract every morsel I can from the occasso before she... disposes of him. The better to further bolster our intelligence on these creatures should we encounter more in the future. I see no better method to ensnare than the use of honey." She patted her satchel upon the final word.

Léandre nodded, uncertain, but he considered faith in the judgement of his charge to be a worthy investment.

"I want to thank you for coming with me, Léandre," Laila said, her smile unfurling like a spring bloom. "Lyra, she would've—she wouldn't understand what I was trying to do here."

"Lyra only does what she feels is her duty," Léandre told her carefully, as ever serving the role of No Man's Land between their conflict. "She is strong-minded but well-meaning. You mustn't think too harshly of her."

"I don't," Laila said with a heavy sigh. "I just loathe to quarrel with her."

"And so does she."

The lift tolled its arrival as the gates drew open to the sterile white walls of the ward.

"Here we go," Laila said, rolling her shoulders back the way she would before bar practice.

Léandre squeezed her shoulder comfortingly, and they shared a smile. One could always count on Léandre to be a safe harbour in uncertain seas.

They approached the cell to find Dr Mielette awaiting them.

"Did you manage my request?" Laila asked, adjusting the strap of her satchel.

"I did," Dr Mielette said, opening the door to the cell. "I hope you know what you're doing."

Laila tilted her chin in response, entering freely into the wolf's den. Inside, Dominus was still seated upright from before—only now he had full use of his arms and neck, though still clasped with magic-inhibiting rings. Tucked over his legs was a portable table, upon which Laila rested her satchel.

"Hello again," she said in her mother tongue, almost for theatrical flair. "I come bearing gifts." She unbuckled the flap of her satchel and produced a pad of sanded paper and a box of fine quality charcoal. "I elected for something blunt, in case you get any ideas." She flipped to an empty page and opened the lid of the charcoal box.

Dominus watched her with eyes narrowed. He had been hand-reared

51

on self-interest, with nothing ever given without gain. To him, such magnanimity could never come without hidden intent. He was right, though the princess's aims were far less malevolent than he expected.

Laila gave nothing away, only meeting him with the prim lace smile she gave every acquaintance out of courtesy; all sweetness and no substance—one's cup of neighbourly sugar. "Go on." She gestured towards the paper. She'd seen through his own eyes his proclivity for art and seized upon the opportunity to ingratiate herself to him. Hopefully, his art would tell her what his mouth refused.

Dominus couldn't deny the paper tempted him, that the impulse for artistry didn't still stir at the sight of an untouched canvas. But the image he had framed in his mind was not of the home he so longed for, but rather how striking the princess looked with her face suffused in incandescent light. How flatteringly it embraced her smooth brown skin with its constellated shimmer, her golden curls spiralling about her like the corona of the sun. He wanted to contain the image and secrete it safely to paper where the sands of time might never bury it.

He picked up the charcoal, almost fearing it wouldn't do justice in her portrayal. Yet he commenced with his sketch, a stern focus overcoming him as soon as he put charcoal to paper. He drafted with unnerving detail the high arc of her cheekbones, the mountain slope of her nose, the pillow plumpness of her lips. Her hair, especially, was nothing he'd ever seen in his lands—tight ringlets, golden as wheat.

Laila watched him, equally engrossed, marvelling at the speed and dexterity he employed in his craft. It wasn't long before she was able to interpret the makings of her features in his image.

"Wait, is that—" Her voice trailed as it gave way to awe.

Oh, it was her to be certain. That same smile and coy head-tilt, beckoning in invitation. Even outlined in colourless charcoal, she radiated a vivacity that leapt out from the page. For a moment she could only stare, lips parted, wondering how someone purported to be so fiendish could craft such beauty with their hands.

"It's wonderful," Laila said, a rosen warmth blooming across her cheeks.

Dominus swallowed in response, regarding the enticing cherry stain on her cheeks with a deep-bellied hunger. Not the kind to feed, but the kind to yearn. He longed to trail his fingers along the star-flecks on her cheek and map the pattern there. His shoulders shifted uncomfortably as he picked up the charcoal to begin another sketch.

She put her hand over his gently to stop him. Then she raised it up to hover before his cheek.

Dominus glanced at her searchingly, curious if this was the payment she required. Nevertheless, he submitted to her palm, allowing that small spark to trickle down his spine like warm water as she opened his mind.

This time, however, he was more determined to narrow the focus on what she'd see. He pivoted her away from any memories that might further divulge knowledge he did not wish for her to know, closing and padlocking the doors. But she entered one such door before he could reach it, and inside was a lady with hair the colour of autumnal leaves with eyes that shared his hue.

"Your mother," Laila said, withdrawing her hand in wonder. She hadn't expected for a monster of legend to have a mother like she did. Or a family at all. The revelation caused something uncomfortable to settle in her chest.

His gaze was hard in response, annoyed at having left a stone of vulnerability unturned.

Laila turned on her heel, triumphant on her way out of the cell. "Thank you for sharing."

VI

MONTH PASSED, AND WITH IT rolled in the first violent tremors of autumnal chill. It was as though the heavens, having sensed the comedown from the feverish highs of summer, had emptied themselves in a great outpouring of grief for the withdrawal.

Dr Hariken grimaced as she looked upon the downpour that awaited her. This should've been a time of jubilation. She had hoped for sun, and she couldn't help but regard the violent gale as an ill omen. Such thoughts were packaged away with the last of her belongings into her suitcase before she climbed into the carriage.

The early morning drive was a pastel-coloured blur to the harbour of Le Creissant, where the lacquered oak hull of the *S.S. Great Northern* gleamed with new polish, the ship's funnels puffing white vapours into the hazy peach-coloured dawn. The rain had ceased by then, replaced by the sun's lilting aubade dispersing in the breeze.

The carriage drew to a stop before the docks, and Dr Hariken disembarked to see that her crew was awaiting.

At the forefront was a uniformed magician who stood with a soldier's resolve, emanating a smouldering furnace energy that could only belong to a Seraji.

"You must be Commander Mabakir of the Red Dragon company?" Dr Hariken said. Those of the Seraji desert were well-acclaimed for their gift of pyromagic, which made them invaluable soldiers and mercenaries.

"I am indeed." Commander Mabakir bowed her head. Her firedrake was perched on her shoulder—a black iridescent serpent that exhaled a puff of steam in greeting. "I have two dozen pyromagicians ready to be deployed at your service."

"Oh, excellent," Dr Hariken said, intrigued by the saurian creature on Mabakir's shoulder. "I look forward to becoming acquainted with you and the rest of your troop."

The rest of the team exchanged pleasantries as porters descended from the ship to handle the passengers' luggage.

Dr Isuka watched the final suitcases ascend into the ship before she looked back to Dr Hariken, twiddling her thumbs awkwardly. "Well, I suppose this is the part where we say goodbye."

"It's a shame you aren't coming with us," Hana said with a frown.

"Unfortunately, my orders are to remain here," Isuka said, "but I expect detailed letters from each of you."

She glanced at Dr Hariken then, her throat thick as she stepped forward to embrace her. This might be the lengthiest period of absence they'd had since they were girls, when a childish squabble had seen them parted for a mere fortnight before they rushed to reconcile.

"Safe travels, Emica," she murmured into the crook of her shoulder. She stepped back to smile, blinking back tears.

"Oh, Akira, don't look so forlorn," Hariken said, taken slightly aback by her friend's emotion. She wiped the tear away from Isuka's cheek. "Before long, I will have returned. And you and I will have made history."

Dr Isuka nodded in response. Their hands parted slowly.

Dr Hariken gave her a final smile before she retreated up the boarding path into the ship to embark on her long journey to lands yet unknown.

Once on deck, Dr Hariken was immediately ushered into the captain's cabin to be greeted by the woman herself. She was of Malakian birth, her tall, wiry build poured into nautical finery with her dreadlocks tucked beneath her cap.

"Welcome aboard, Dr Hariken. They call me Captain Silveira," she said, hands clasped behind her back.

Dr Hariken shuffled forward awkwardly and straightened her spectacles. Then she held out her hand. "A pleasure to meet you, captain."

Captain Silveira eyed her hand before taking it. "I was hoping to pick your brain on how to chart our course."

"Certainly," Dr Hariken said, straightening in false confidence. "Just point the way."

Captain Silveira gestured to the map unfurled across the table. It showed the landmass of the Vysterian continent along with the archipelago bordering Malakia on the Crysteaen Sea.

Dr Hariken observed the pin implanted on the northernmost body of water, past the ridges of Odaka. The White Sea. "I see you already have our first destination marked. Have you done many voyages north?"

"None so far north as to reach the White Sea—the tales of it always rattled me bones too much—but I've known of others who have ventured this far. Some who returned. Many who did not."

"I see." Dr Hariken ran her fingers across her sleeved wrist, too self-conscious to bear the wound as she leaned forward. Instead, she retrieved the handwritten note from her pocket.

"What is that?"

"Our directions." Dr Hariken unfolded the note as she read: "Tread the course of ivory salt 'til the dragon's lungs exhale. Cross the wound of despair before I entered my lair; within its innards you shall prevail."

"Queer way to offer directions," Captain Silveira said in her heavy accent, a smooth, rhythmic tongue.

"I'm afraid it's all I have." Dr Hariken shrugged. "I at least managed to decipher that the dragon's lungs refer to the Dragon's Breath."

The mention caused the captain's eyes to widen. It was an infamous arctic sea fog that had sent many past vessels spiralling way off course.

"I assume you're familiar with it."

"At least the tales." Captain Silveira unscrewed the top of her flask and drank her coffee. "You can only wander so far north before the Dragon's Breath sets in. Those who entered there—they always spoke of strange sea life: monsters, leviathans, krakens, you know the sort. Do you expect we'll see a real dragon out in these waters?"

"Well, I should certainly hope not!" Dr Hariken exclaimed, straightening her spectacles. While exalted in her homeland, dragons had been long thought to have gone extinct—nothing greater than fossils or firedrakes had ever been discovered. "Though it would be a sight to behold, I'm sure, with lungs this powerful."

"Hm," Captain Silveira said. "Best to keep an eye out, I s'pose?"

"And what of this... 'wound of despair'? As someone more familiar with maps than I, do you think you might know what this alludes to?"

Captain Silveira rubbed beneath her chin as she looked over the map. "My best guess is they be talking 'bout the Calantic Trench."

"Calantic Trench?" Dr Hariken echoed in curiosity.

"Deep pit in the ocean where Calante fell to his defeat. Asemani then scooped him out before she locked his rass up for good. But the Trench remains as proof."

"'Wound of despair'... yes, I think that might be it." Dr Hariken searched the map for the destination before she marked it. "Well, now. I think we have our course."

"And what of the final sentence?"

"Now that I can't make sense of." Dr Hariken sighed in dejection. "Perhaps once we've reached the Trench, we'll be able to reconvene from there."

Captain Silveira hummed softly. "I'll let you know should I need anything further."

Dr Hariken tossed and turned in discontent, terrorised by that same skittering crawl seeping up her scarred wrist.

Emica, it seemed to call to her with cricket whispers, scraping up from her arm to her soft cerebral tissue. *Emica.*

Dr Hariken whimpered as she flopped into an alternate position, smothering herself with her pillow. Anything to will away the eventual vision she knew was about to invade her.

She was barefoot, treading through blank drifts of snow. It was the coldest snow she had ever felt, a cold so intense it burned. She had to keep walking. There was nowhere to go where she could stop. Even as the frost erased every hint of feeling in her toes, her heels, her soles, and left them blackened.

When the base of her feet had been rotted away to nothing, she came across the first body. She would always see it from the blood. Against the white the hue was vibrant—as red as beets in the summer.

It coaxed Hariken onward; she was desperate to put her hands on something live. She dug deep, ignoring the pain as her fingers cried out in protest from the icy burn until she touched fur. She grabbed and yanked until she withdrew the limp, lifeless ear of a lop-eared bunny, petrified by frost. The head flopped pathetically to the ground like a fish with no air.

Hariken stood up in disappointment and saw more lumps laid in her path. Carcasses long buried beneath winter's funereal white sheet. As she moved onwards, the mounds enlarged and the blood grew so hot and slippery it was as though life still pumped in it.

Emica— A raspy caw, followed by a deluge of feathers as a black eagle settled upon an emaciated branch.

Emica— called another, from a neighbouring skeletal tree.

They flanked on both aisles, overwhelming the branches, screeching a chorus of her name that raked her ears and beat them bloody. Hariken smacked her palms over her sensitive drums, crying from her torment, before she slipped and fell into a bloodied puddle. She peeled herself free with a grimace.

When she looked up, she saw him. A man who was not a man. Jet black eagle wings draped along his sides where his arms should be, tapering off into clawed hands. He had the bent legs of a wolf. His spine was curved over his most recent kill—a buck whose nostrils still frothed in anguish.

The eagles had quieted, and a few even gathered on the beast's antlers to observe. Hariken watched with them. She watched the fluctuating arc of his spine as he ate, his long and large wings forming a shroud of privacy during his feast. She only had to take one step before he twitched, darting to face her with his ugly and terrible maw dripping with blood.

He smiled when he saw her, showing many teeth, and then he grew larger and larger, his maw distorting to be replaced with a gnarled beak spiked with fangs. He unfurled his wings to display their prodigious length, then he arched forward before her to call her near.

Emica—

She was powerless to resist. His entire being roared with life from the reservoir of souls he'd devoured. She longed for warmth. Even the eagles had gathered to nestle on him.

Emica— Calante called to her, soft as a caress. —Bring me flesh.

Dr Hariken catapulted upright with a scream.

⤮

It took five days for them to reach the White Sea.

The morning of their arrival, Hana rose with eagerness to meet the new dawn, scrutinising the landscape's natural migration from the limestone cliffs of the Soleterean coast to the frigidity of arctic ice caps.

She stood on the dock, watching the pale waves of the White Sea surging below. Just the sight of it chilled Hana's bones and made her hug her mink coat close.

According to legend, the sea's sickly pallor was due to witnessing an atrocity so vile it shocked all the colour from the water. Many called it cursed, others an unnatural phenomenon, and it had long served as the site of blame for nautical disappearances large and small. Whatever the case, Hana hoped that after centuries of speculation, this expedition would help them find the truth.

"You seem to be deep in thought," Dr Hariken said as she moved to join Hana at the dock.

"I'm exhilarated," Hana said, nose pinked from the cold. "I've heard so many stories of the White Sea. But never once did I ever dream that I would see it myself."

60

"Yes, well, it'll certainly be something to write home about," Hariken said, removing her spectacles to clear the condensation from it. "Though we've been at sea for several days now—I shall be eager to find dry land."

"So will I," Hana said, rubbing her gloved hands together. "What do you suppose it will be like out there?"

"I—" A chill overcame Hariken with a suddenness, so cold it burned. Her mind echoed the creak of skeletal trees—a vestige of a long-forgotten nightmare. She gathered her arms with a shudder. "Goodness, there is a chill in the air. Let us continue this conversation indoors."

She ushered Hana inside to the lower decks, where green tea and rice cakes awaited them in the dining room. They relaxed in the cosseted warmth of varnished oak panels and chairs upholstered with thick blue velvet.

Dr Hariken drank two cups to chase the chill away before she felt human enough to resume. "I must admit I am glad to see at least one of us happens to be enjoying the voyage. Especially for such a dire expedition."

"Well, it's rather silly, but, " Hana mumbled with a mouthful of rice cake, her cheeks dusted with sugar paste, "I've always wanted to be an explorer, ever since I was a little girl. My family can trace their lineage back to the village I am from for several generations. None of us have ever left it. Our family shrine and temple are more than filled. I always feared I'd live my life just like theirs. Never seeing what lay beyond those gates. Withering and dying in the same house, the same bed, as the many grandmothers who came before me. It made me feel... insignificant."

Dr Hariken smiled, finding her reasoning charming. How much of herself she saw reflected in the glistening eyes of this barely woman. "I don't think it's silly." She traced the rim of her cup with her thumbs. "When I was your age I—well. I don't think I would've been nearly so bold as you. Dr Isuka was always the more confident one of the two of us."

"Have you and she always been working partners?"

"I've known her perhaps my entire life," Dr Hariken said, straightening her spectacles. "When we were young, we were always told we'd serve a higher purpose. We'd rise up and save the world from invading forces of evil." Hariken paused with a chuckle. "At the time they always made it seem so grand and heroic, but—well, I wouldn't nearly call us glamorous. I often find myself studying evil more than fighting it, I feel."

"So when you finally reach the place Calante dwells? What then?"

"Well—" Hariken's words failed her.

Bring me flesh— A voice rose from the hidden depths of unconscious memory, soft as satin along her cheek. She shoved it out, blocked it away. She would give no fuel to this writhing void inside of her that hissed and snarled.

"I assume that's the part of the story we shall have to write ourselves."

Dr Hariken heard the footsteps of someone approaching. She turned towards the source with a smile and nodded in greeting. "Captain."

"Doctor." Captain Silveira returned the salute. "It seems we have reached the Dragon's Breath, and my crew's navigation skills have gone a bit groggy. I just wanted to let you know in case we suffer delays from this point forth."

"Thank you, captain."

Hana clambered towards one of the windows and saw they'd been curtained by the tenebrous gloom offered by the Dragon's profuse exhalations.

"Oh my," she exclaimed, turning back in concern. "Do you think we'll get lost?"

"There is a likelihood, but I want to assure you my crewmates are more than capable of weathering a fog. Even one severe as this," Captain Silveira replied, tucking a loc behind her ear. "But I'd suggest you wrap up warm tonight. I don't like the look of this fog, and even northern folk like yourself ain't immune to the chill."

"Yes, of course," Dr Hariken said. "Thank you kindly, captain."

Captain Silveira bobbed her head in response and walked away, crossing her hands behind her back.

However, lurking a two-day journey past the curtain of the Dragon's Breath awaited an even greater phenomenon.

The silhouette of the Calantic Trench was a blot on the landscape, a malignant depression in an otherwise untouched body of water. Should one venture close enough, one could almost swear that the spines encircling the chasm were forming a ring of teeth.

VII

URTHER NORTH ALONG THE WHITE SEA was a cursed isle, full of cursed things, where almost nothing gained life that was not then nurtured to destroy. Many monsters had claimed this isle as their home and polluted it with their existence.

The occassi were the first of these monsters, having roamed and ruled the lands for thousands of years after being excreted like a toxin from a mountain's molten core. For as long as they had been in existence, they had been led by the House of Calantis—a dynasty who claimed direct descent from the demon god purported to have made them.

The black coach of Darius Calantis soared past the circumference of a tawny orange moon. Six hippogriffs kept the vehicle afloat—sleek black beasts with gnarled beaks and a perpetual sneer of jagged teeth. Darius sat facing the window, where, beyond the tinted glass, the geometric towers of Gravissia leered with sharp edges: its penetrating spires, its dour effigies, the cramped cluster of matchstick bodies all buried beneath a noxious alchemical brume.

His coach was destined for the dismal seat of the royal family—sat in self-imposed elevation from the rest of the city that scrabbled at its ankles.

Malborg Citadel was a crumbling edifice of onion-domed towers fretfully held together by buttressed bridges. It had the look of incompletion—as though someone in the middle of a jigsaw puzzle had discovered halfway through that several pieces were missing. From a distance, its thin spires seemed to pierce the spiralling clouds above, threatening to release a downpour from the heavens.

Before the courtyard stretched two large doors of burnished bronze where the souls of thieves and vagrants had been etched into figurines like flies caught on a web. They strained against the waxed barriers of their prison, muscles taut, contorting into increasingly anguished positions that would bring them no escape.

The doors opened for Darius as the coach landed roughly in the courtyard with a quake. Inside, Darius was stone-still, having come to expect it by now. His driver, an antlered ghoul known as Igor, opened the door for him, and Darius stepped out into the obsidian spill of night, tightening the pink silk sash on his golden kaftan.

Awaiting him by the doors of the main building was another antlered corpse servant who stepped out of the shadows like a spider to greet him.

"Good evening, sire," the ghoul rasped, his skeletal visage waxing and waning in the candlelight. "May I interest you in some refreshment?"

"Perhaps later, Grigori," Darius said before he made his way towards the royal apartments.

He strolled through the Portrait Hall along his excursion. The varnished eyes of his ancestors followed him as he passed. The row of rexes spanned one wall, while their reginas occupied the other, both depicted in the finest oil paint and framed in a prideful setting of enamelled bronze.

Occasionally, Darius would stop to look upon his father, dark-haired and dusky-skinned, with grey eyes that always looked on the verge of storm. With even less frequency would he turn to the one that lay opposite—the scarlet-haired occassella whose verdant green eyes matched his brother's and not his.

He reached the stairs soon after and made his way down into the bowels of the building, where his quarters were. His rooms were positioned relative to his social class—a step above the servants but much lower than anyone of royal stock. Only servants and spies ever paid him visit.

He took off his sable-trimmed cloak when he entered and draped it on the coat hanger. Then he approached the end table to lift the lid from the decanter of graviji wine and poured himself a tumbler. He took a brief sip of the golden liquor before turning to confront the hidden presence in his room. In the corner by his desk, there was a shadow that was not a shadow. For unlike the other silhouettes in his room, there was nothing solid to cast it.

"Step forward," Darius said. He smoothed one of the sleek, sibilant waves of his pomaded hair.

The spy unclipped his cape of concealment. "Evening, prefect."

"Balthus." Darius nodded. "Silly mistake, that. You should try concealing yourself within a larger shadow rather than pinning yourself in the corner and hoping someone won't notice."

Balthus made a noncommittal sound. "It's served me well enough in the past."

"Well, I suppose not everyone is ruminating on strange shadows as much as I," Darius said, lifting the lid of the decanter once more. "Can I interest you in a drink?"

"Not at all, prefect." Balthus retrieved a scroll from within his leathers. "Just here to deliver a message."

Darius took the scroll and unravelled it to find it had been penned by one of the watchtower wardens, detailing that a ship was travelling their way across the White Sea. Darius touched his lips in thought, knowing what he would have to do. The same thing he had always done to any vessels that had found themselves stumbling towards his shores.

"Well, another one bites the dust, as they say," Darius said as he dragged a hand down his face, then pulled out his desk chair to sit. A spymaster he might be, but his father had him oftentimes feeling like a glorified gatekeeper. "You are dismissed."

Balthus nodded and reclipped his concealing cape to escort himself out.

After his inferior had left, Darius approached his cabinet of curiosities. Kept within the lacquered walnut doors carved with grotesques were rows upon rows of bottles containing the miniaturised essences of sea monsters. He'd captured them during his mandatory service in the naval force and kept them bottled as weapons to dispose of intruders. He caught his chin between his thumb and forefinger, debating which dire fate was to befall their latest interloper.

The blinking eyes of the trammelled souls followed the movement of his finger in anticipation, each one eager to stretch their gargantuan limbs past the bounds of their tight prisons. Finally, Darius selected an agent and brought out his cauldron from the bottom of the cabinet.

He first uncorked a vial of white seawater to fill the small cast iron pot. Then he added the shark-like teeth of his chosen beast and stuck a wooden spoon into the pot. As he stirred, the teeth swirled around the pot until they aligned themselves into a circular formation.

That was when Darius removed his spoon to observe the spiral of water grow stronger and more rapid, sealing the vessel's fate.

Dr Hariken sat in her cabin in the lower decks, preparing to send a letter to Dr Isuka via paper plane. She waited for the ink to dry on the missive before she began to fold it into its necessary shape and imbue it with the enchantment needed to make it airborne.

A low, reverberating moan soon followed.

"What in the world?" she whispered, unable to hide the tremble in her voice. She approached one of the portholes to investigate, and saw nothing but vast blackness.

It could be a whale of some sort, she reasoned to herself. She'd heard of ice whales in the northern parts of Odaka. They were arctic creatures by nature, and it wasn't outside the realm of possibility that one would pass them by.

She soothed herself with the assumption, returning to her seat. Then a rough collision against the hull of the ship sent shockwaves of turbulence throughout the room. It flung Dr Hariken into the nearby wall, robbing the air from her lungs.

Dr Hariken cried out, struggling to catch her grip on one of the nailed-down pieces of furniture as the ship tilted upright. She lifted a hand to shield herself from the falling debris from her desk, which pelted her with a clatter.

A crackle sounded in the distance. Glass. Dr Hariken peered behind her arm to see what else had fallen. What she saw instead was the insidious growth of fissures on the portholes as the water pressure pushed and *pushed* until a jet of ice-cold water erupted from each one.

Dr Hariken's scream diluted into a gurgle as the sheer force of the stream pummelled her against the door. She palmed against it, desperate to jiggle the knob. Finally, she opened the door into the passageway.

The hall was cacophonous with shouts and rushing water, a

discordant choir of fear. By now, the water was up to her calves and rising, and she waded through thousands of needles pricking hoar into her muscles.

Dr Hariken kept pushing through the rising water, desperate to reach the stairs. If she could reach the surface. If she could just surpass this level. Then she might once more narrowly avoid the scrape of the reaper's scythe.

Dr Hariken kicked hard with her numbing legs, every encroaching millimetre bringing her that much closer to victory. She had just about touched the first step when another swell from the sea came gushing in.

Then the water rose high enough to swallow her.

Her chest and head were too full of ocean for her to gesture for a breathing spell. She could only watch helplessly as those around her choked for their last pledge to life before succumbing in bubbles and foam.

Her mind went hazy and soft. Her lungs filled to bursting, and her limbs went stiff from the cold. But before her tether to the living realm was severed by the reaper's scythe, the blackness inside her unfurled, spreading upwards from her chest to her throat to her mind and polluting the dwindling light in her eyes to oil black.

There were others who escaped. There were even those who fought back. Never let it be said that the human spirit was not one of fortitude in the face of insurmountable odds.

The pyromagicians guarded valiantly against the monster, armed at the wrists with firedrakes that each spewed flaming breath. But this was not the land of sun and sand that the soldiers had so foolishly deserted. There would be no flame hot enough, no light bright enough, to fragment the crystallised carapace that a millennium of frost had given Mortos.

Thus, the soldiers were drowned. The ship was sunk. And the

moment the hull was overturned on its side, it caused an additional surf to rise and bury the lifeboats with it.

On one such boat, Hana Oto paddled faster, trying in vain to swerve away from the incoming onslaught.

"Oh gods, oh gods, oh gods—" were the assistant's final words before the wave landed and the boat was submerged.

⌾

The ocean spat Hana out in disgust.

Hana returned the derisive gesture—emptying her lungs of burning saltwater onto the black sand shore as she wheezed. She circled her arms around herself, trembling pathetically. Then she raised herself up to her feet to look back towards the destruction as the hull of the *Great Northern* disintegrated into the water.

Seeing her last hope of escape sink down into oblivion, she hugged her fur coat closer. The only thing she had left to call company. She was cold, wet and isolated. No combination could be more misery-inducing. Her eyes misted at the thought that Dr Hariken might be lost to the apathetic deep. Hariken was a woman she'd greatly looked up to and admired. She didn't understand how someone with so much knowledge and vigour could be stolen away from the world so quickly when they still had so much to offer.

She searched around the shore in the hopes she might detect something, *someone*, amidst the sweeping indifference of the wind. But there was nothing.

"Hello!" she called, her echo her only response. "Is anybody out there?"

She walked forward on unsteady fawn legs, casting a temperature spell to generate warmth. Along the coastline were fragments of velvet ice blocks deposited by the sea. They glistened under the moonlight with the crystallised clarity of a diamond. So taken aback by this slither of natural beauty was Hana that for a moment she dried her eyes and allowed herself to step closer, studying it.

She saw the shadow of an assailant before she heard their heavy breaths.

Hana turned quickly, her mouth opening to cry out. Dr Hariken stood before her with blacked out eyes and veins bulging into unruly scrawls across her cheeks.

"Doctor—" Hana's plea of fear was muted when Hariken's hands wrapped around her throat and squeezed.

Hana's throat hiccupped for air as she fought against Dr Hariken with all her featherweight strength, her tiny hands scraping red welts into Hariken's ice-cold wrists. No matter how hard she squirmed, Dr Hariken's hold on her throat did not yield. She squeezed harder until Hana's throat was cut off, her face turning blue.

"A death for a death," Dr Hariken told her. Her voice was not her own. "Young blood must be spilled so that she may remain."

She dashed Hana's head against the ice block. Her head cracked like an eggshell, spilling the yolk of her insides against the clouded veneer. Beneath the desaturated gloom of night, her blood was black as ink.

The doctor returned to her body the instant Hana's soul left hers. Her hands shook upon confrontation with the gruesome scene, bile rising in her throat as she acknowledged the broken form of her assistant.

The moon could not hide her from the gravity of her crime, and she regarded her black-stained gloves with an anguished wail. "Oh, gods, no. No. What have I done? What have I done to you? Oh, gods, forgive me. I'm so sorry."

Beneath her, the remnants of whatever life was left in Hana seeped from her before she went hopelessly stiff. Sensing that confirmation

71

only made Hariken sob harder as she cradled the girl, still warm in her pink-cheeked youth.

"Hana? Hana, please. Don't go. Don't leave me here. I didn't mean it. *Please*," Dr Hariken whispered, her body quaking with full-bodied sobs

She was still entangled around Hana when the occasso warden happened across her during his patrol across the sands.

"Well, well, well," he said.

Dr Hariken quivered before him. She knew an occasso when she sensed one. Knew it right down to her bones. It was that ancestral yawp of warning every prey received in the presence of its predator.

She didn't draw back when he neared. His sneer was feral, like a wolf's.

"What have we here?"

⤬

Back in the Citadel, the ghouls set a table for two.

The grand oak table was dressed in crisp white linen, then laid with silver stencilled with the royal seal, polished to gleaming. A table runner of dried red roses perfumed the air with their sweet scent and a soft smoulder emanated from the lit flames of the silver candelabra.

The ghouls set down two cocktail glasses, filling them to the brim with a concoction of polugar and vermouth. The first was garnished with two black cherries on a pick, and the second with Hana Oto's two brown eyes, speared through the pupils. Set beside the pristinely folded napkins were bone porcelain plates containing the main dish— two whole tongues, one lamb and one human, each seasoned with mushrooms and red chrain.

Darius picked up his napkin and opened it with a flick of his wrist.

He tucked the starched fabric into his collar before reaching for his cocktail and taking a sip. He sampled the notes of juniper and bison grass with a satisfactory nod and then removed the toothpick to suck the eyes from it, chewing slowly to savour the texture and absorb the knowledge of every text it had read. Next, he cut a small portion of human tongue and, the moment he ingested it, became infused with every nuance and sound of the languages it had spoken.

He ate with indulgence, sparing not a single bite until the whole dish was consumed. When he was done, he lifted his napkin to dab his mouth, tasting this strange new tongue he could now claim his own.

"So, why don't you tell me all about who you are and where it is you came from?" he asked his guest in perfect Odakan.

Across the table from him, Dr Hariken sobbed and whimpered, too far beyond the reach of any deity she called upon to answer.

VIII

A GENTLE CASCADE OF SUNLIGHT trickled onto Laila from the glass dome overhead, enhancing her skin's natural glimmer. She reclined her head against the edge of her rose quartz tub with a satisfied sigh, swathed in a luxurious soak of coconut milk, raw honey and dried rose petals. Her hair was bundled in a pink silk tignon after being extensively moisturised with gardenia-infused coconut oil and left to steep.

She pointed a finger at a gilt bowl of strawberries on an end table, enchanting them with aether to rise, dip into the sauce dish of warm white chocolate, and swiftly float towards her for a bite.

While Laila bathed, Oriel, one of her starlet protégées, arrived to remove her tignon and cleanse her hair with aloe vera.

"Help yourself to a strawberry if you'd like, Oriel," Laila said with her eyes still closed. She knew Oriel wouldn't simply take one, out of dedication to her training, but Laila liked to think of herself as a lax mistress—so far in contrast to her own, who had been near draconian in her demands.

"Thank you, madame," Oriel replied, graciously enchanting a strawberry to dip into the chocolate. After the cleanse, she rinsed Laila's hair with a porcelain jug of fermented rice water into the matching basin and left it once more to steep.

It had been a couple of weeks now since her last wash, and it remained an arduous affair. Her hair was a beast of its own nature, a thick, luxuriant, near untameable mass of spirals that demanded much moisture and maintenance.

Laila crooked a finger to beckon another fruit. "How are your studies?"

"Well," Oriel replied, taking a bite of strawberry. "Madame Cigne has us learning some new sprite folk songs in preparation for the Fête des Lumières. I shall be playing the harp."

"It's a wonder the Fête will so soon be upon us!" Laila exclaimed, one knee rising to reveal a rosy brown leg covered in petals. "Where has the time gone?"

"I've once heard it said that the older one gets, the faster it goes," Oriel said, rinsing the rice water from Laila's hair. "Until it almost seems no time has passed at all when in reality, you've blinked away half a mortal's life."

Laila frowned. At twenty-eight, she was straddling the brink of both life-states: young enough to see things with mortal eyes, and old enough to feel the assuredness of an eternal life ahead. It still unnerved her to think of how far ahead her years had yet to span, to think she might one day become one of those white-eyed elders who concealed themselves from public scrutiny so as not to blind the mortals who were foolish enough to look upon them.

Laila rose from the tub. "Well, I believe I've soaked enough. Pass me a towel."

Oriel swaddled her in white cotton before escorting Laila back into her boudoir. She had just sat down at her sinuously sculpted gilt oak-and-marble vanity when Lyra entered.

"We have a problem," her guard said.

"What is it?" Laila asked, catching Lyra's furrowed brow in the mirror as Oriel towel-dried her hair.

"Dr Isuka has arrived to seek an audience with you." Lyra's frown deepened, the amber dawn staining her eyes pink. "She fears the *Great Northern* may not return from the voyage."

Laila regarded this with a tinge of dread. "It has been eight weeks since they set sail."

"And not a word has been heard from them since they left Odakan territory," Lyra said, pert lips set into a thin line. "There could be reason to be concerned."

Oriel pumped a rosewater and argan-oil mousse into her hands to condition Laila's curls. She took advantage of the dampness of the hair and braided it into a halo, securing the tail end with hairpins.

Laila watched Oriel fluff out her braid, sticking pearl hairpins in for décor. "Thank you, Oriel." She petted the starlet's wrist and pivoted around on her stool. "Where is Dr Isuka now?"

"Awaiting an audience in the salon."

Laila scrunched her lips to one side. "Give me time to get dressed, and I shall see to this. In the meantime, you keep her occupied."

"As you wish." Lyra bent her head. Then she turned towards the exit.

Laila's stomach knotted in her absence. She hadn't known when to expect the return of the ship, but for them to be gone for so long with little insight to their whereabouts... She forced herself not to assume the worst as she sent Oriel to pick out her dress.

Dr Isuka stared vacantly into her cup of jasmine tea, watching the flower blossom. She was unable to think of anything but Hariken's large, round eyes when she'd told her to go on the expedition. *If only I'd gone with her.*

"The princess ought to be along soon," Lyra said, watching as Dr Isuka slid her hands into her hair.

The tea had been Lyra's suggestion—a futile salve she'd pilfered from Laila's repertoire of social cues. She'd never been adept at handling distress. Or civilians in general. The way Laila did it always made it seem effortless, and Lyra now envied her skill at being able to weave pretty words like adornments into the gaps of silence.

Finally, the doors opened and the princess entered in a blue wool morning gown.

"Thank goodness," Dr Isuka said, springing to her feet. "It's good to see you, Your Radiance."

"Dr Isuka," Laila greeted, noticing the scholar's features had taken a gaunt turn. "You don't look well."

"Oh, I haven't been able to sleep since—" Her voice trailed, as though she truly sought to remember. "Well, never mind that. I must speak with you at once."

"Please, tell me what ails you."

"Last holy day I went to my temple to pray for the *Great Northern*'s safe passage. I decided to procure the services of one of the astrologists there to give me further insight." Dr Isuka smoothed her pleated trousers with broad, rhythmic strokes. "I gave her Dr Hariken's date of birth, and she said..."

"What?" Lyra leaned forward in curiosity.

Dr Isuka swallowed. "She said Dr Hariken had gone beyond the Veil, to a place the gods have forsaken, and thus she was beyond the reach of any starsight."

"Beyond the Veil?" Lyra arched one translucent brow. "You mean ‒‒ "

"We cannot know for certain." Laila cut her off mid-sentence, knowing the fatal conclusion she would draw. Horoscopes and other such divine forecasts could have many interpretations. Though the one Dr Isuka spoke of suggested nothing good.

"But regardless, you can at least agree that such a forecast holds ill fortune?" Dr Isuka was bug-eyed with desperation.

Laila resisted the urge to nibble on her lip. If she showed any signs of uncertainty, it would only increase Isuka's panic. She wouldn't allow any of them to see their princess without her steady poise.

"Your Radiance, I beseech you to take this sign for what it is and allow me another voyage so I might go in search of her."

"Dr Isuka, don't be absurd," Laila said, raising up her hands as though to soothe the scholar from her wild temper. "If this forecast does speak of ill fortune, then the last thing I want to do is send you to meet the same fate."

"If not you, then I'll find someone who will!" Dr Isuka cried, too overcome by rage to remember her standing. "You cannot ask me to sit here and do nothing. I refuse it. I should never have let her go alone. I *should've—*"

Her face crumpled and her hands lifted to shield the arrival of her sobs. She couldn't decide what she found more mortifying—that she had not wept since she was a girl, or that she was about to do so for the first time in years in the presence of a solarite.

Laila did not move to embrace her, sensing the scholar would consider it an affront to her pride. Instead, she took a napkin from the tea set and held it out to her.

"Thank you," Dr Isuka said, grabbing the napkin to dry her cheeks.

"Dr Isuka." Laila's voice was soft as fleece. "Please hear me. I cannot allow you to go on this journey you seek, but that does not mean I intend to do nothing. I promise you, we will find Dr Hariken and escort her home to you safely."

"How do you know?" Dr Isuka asked, dabbing her eyes with the napkin.

Laila sucked in a deep breath. Should anything have happened to the ship, she knew she would be held personally responsible not only by her mother but in the eyes of society. Thus, she would need a grand gesture to show she was earnest in her desire to be accountable.

"Because I will go personally to ensure it."

Dominus tore free a cutlet from his morning meal and gnawed with relish, his large canines shredding it like paper. To keep him docile, the nurses would continually offer him large servings of meat—beef, mutton, pork, even venison if he was particularly fortunate. Today's offering was a sacrificial lamb rack dipped in harissa and pomegranate molasses.

It didn't satiate him as it would have had the kill been fresh and writhing between his teeth, but it would certainly do for now. The meat here was always tender and of good cutting, vibrant with flavour.

After stripping the bone of meat, he chewed his way down into the marrow until he was satisfied he'd devoured the last of it. Then he tossed the bone onto his tray.

Immediately, an orderly arrived to check him for pieces, taking care to flash his weapon before he took the tray away. It never failed to amuse Dominus how carefully they trod around him, always alert for newer tricks.

He still remembered the first time the nurses had become alert to his original mounting bone collection. They'd tried to take it away, and Dominus had rewarded their efforts by turning one of their cheeks to dangling strips of ribbon with his extended claws. The nurse he'd struck fully healed, in the end. Not even a paltry scar remained to mark his dominance.

Since then, they kept themselves armed with ætherald batons that never failed to irradiate him into compliance.

Dominus watched as the orderly carried the tray through the doorway to freedom, then sat back with a sigh. He reached for his sketchpad and charcoals and started to outline a new sketch.

Over the past few months, he'd created many pictures—grand, sprawling reimaginings of black beaches, unruly overgrown forests, and icy tundras, all carefully depicted in crosshatch and shadow. They were joined by strange creatures. Eerie, nightmarish figures that haunted the mind—six-legged beasts with heads full of tentacles, tigers with overlapping faces, stalking silhouettes with mouths in their chests.

There were pictures of Laila too, sprinkled among the other pieces. More than perhaps there ought to have been. The thought of her face consumed him, and though Dominus knew he could not touch her, he at least wanted to commit a piece of her to paper to sustain him through the absences. His hand lingered on his most recent portrait of her as he wondered when she'd return. At least the staff tended to treat him better when she was around to witness.

The thought seemed to summon her; he caught a whiff of her scent in the hallway, heard the light patter of her footsteps on the cold, polished floors. She was not alone, and he soon recognised the additional scent of the doctor she was with. The mortal who'd conversed with him after his awakening.

Well, this will be interesting, he thought as the door opened once more to usher them in.

"How unexpected for you to bestow me once more with your presence, mortal," Dominus said, his mouth crooked into a wry smile. "Am I to understand you simply favour me so well?"

Dr Isuka sucked in an impatient breath as she regarded the occasso. It had been her last desire to be faced with this creature again, and being so close in proximity to one of Calante's own creations filled her with an unreasonable odium. She wanted to rip the air from his lungs until he was choking and pleading.

She saw the irrational impulse for what it was, however, and instead conducted herself with the composure the princess commanded.

"It is with the greatest urgency that I call upon you," Dr Isuka said, "for my sovereign desires to travel to the land from which you hail."

That had him laughing, a dry, hollow sound like the crunch of gravel underfoot.

"What amuses you?" Dr Isuka demanded, dark eyes flashed in anger.

"In truth, it is that I've never seen one so eager to embrace death," Dominus replied, glancing over at the princess. "And you will die, Glowing One, should you be so foolish enough to step foot on my lands."

Laila set her jaw firmly, his mockery grating on her fraying nerves. Though she still had little knowledge of his tongue, she had pilfered some over the months with Dr Isuka's tutelage. "Ask him to tell us what might have happened to the ship."

Dr Isuka repeated the request.

"You demand a great deal and yet offer nothing." Dominus spread his arms wide as though beckoning an audience. "Pray tell me why I ought to aid you while dooming myself to rot forevermore within these white walls."

"It is your way to barter, yes? Then let us barter." Dr Isuka stared at him hard. "Knowledge of your lands in exchange for a more accommodating cell."

Dominus's eyes narrowed. "Do you believe me witless? That I would yield to such inequitable terms?"

"Should he have a better offer I'd love to hear it." Laila folded her arms together in expectation.

"Set your terms, occasso," Dr Isuka told him, "and make haste."

Dominus took some moments to consider his words. "Tell your sovereign I am willing to lend my services to her impetuous mission. Let my strength become her strength. My wisdom, her wisdom. I will be both the sword and the shield that she may use to strike and defend—if only you unleash me from these wretched binds. This I vow. Allow me to set foot once more on the black sands of Mortos, and I shall deliver her there with nary a curl rustled."

Dr Isuka imparted the message to Laila, who turned to look at Dominus, eyes uncertain. To have his aid would be invaluable, and yet she knew she could not trust his word alone. She stepped forward to take his arm, almost gently. Then she infused it with illuminating light.

"*Tell me the truth*," Laila commanded as tendrils of steam arose from the place where she touched him.

Dominus grunted through gritted teeth, the light compelling his tongue to honesty. "The truth is there is no one better to defend you than I, and you'd both be foolish to deny it. I have no intent to lead you astray, nor steer you to harm, for your destination is my only desire"— Dominus faltered, suppressing a groan—"and a word from an occasso is more binding than a pact between a mortal and their grave, I pledge you that."

Laila looked towards Dr Isuka—who nodded—before she released him. "Tell him I shall take his offer into consideration."

With that, she stepped back and pivoted on her heel towards the exit.

～∞～

That same morning in the Superna, Amira was preparing for breakfast. This morning's bounty offered sun-dried tomatoes sprinkled with tarragon, quail eggs trivette, and goat cheese–stuffed hibiscus flowers. A separate dish of beignets steamed in the centre of the table, and a bottle of white peach juice and sparkling esterre wine had been left to cool in a gold bucket of ice, stencilled with the Soleterean rose.

Laila caught the wafting aroma the moment she entered, and it stirred a hunger deep enough to offset the anxious nausea she felt.

"Well, look who's early today," Amira said, her bee-stung lips broadening into a rare smile. "Come, sit. Don't let it go cold."

"Breakfast looks lovely today, Maman," came Laila's early morning chirrup as she seated herself at the table and unfolded a napkin into her lap. She ran her tongue over her lips in anticipation as she reached over the table for a beignet. Her mother's dour stare halted her mid-pursuit. She had never been a dainty eater when it came to beignets, and her mother had never shied from making her displeasure clear.

Laila retracted her hand and picked up a hibiscus flower instead.

Amira's beignet remained untouched, and Laila's gaze lingered with a lustful intensity on the golden pastry snow-capped with sugar. She wondered if her mother had laid it out on purpose just to torment her.

Laila twiddled the flower between her fingers before clearing her throat. "While we have a moment to ourselves, Maman, I was hoping to discuss something with you."

83

"Go on," Amira said, compelling the bottle to open and fill two flutes while she waited for her daughter.

"Well," Laila swallowed as she watched the froth rise to a peak. Truly, there could be no more fitting analogy for her nerves. "The *Great Northern* has not yet returned home from its voyage, and we have received little correspondence from its crew or passengers. Dr Isuka therefore fears that there may have been some foul play involved."

"Hm," Amira said, taking a sip from her flute. "That does sound troublesome. How long has it been since the voyage set sail?"

"Eight weeks," Laila said, after eating her hibiscus, "and the last we'd heard from them was when the ship passed Kumori."

Amira took a sip of her beverage to digest this. "If they've ventured far north to reach the White Sea, this will not have been the first vessel to have been lost to its waters."

"I am aware," Laila said, cutting herself a portion of trivette. "But it is the first voyage I myself have chartered, and thus I feel responsible for its wellbeing. It doesn't reflect well on us to ignore the vessel's disappearance. There are the families of the passengers to consider—the crew. The humans look to us as symbols of protection and guidance, Maman. They will expect me to act."

"I suppose you are correct," Amira said, helping herself to a hibiscus. "Still, I am curious what it is you expect me to do."

"Allow me to send a unit of Lightshield chevaliers to track the vessel," Laila said, hastening to add, "I will not require many. Merely a handful. And I think it would look better if I am the one leading the charge."

"The valiant solarite princess embarks on a perilous voyage to rescue her missing ship," Amira said, swishing the words around on her tongue as though sampling their bouquet. "It has decent narrative potential, I'll give you that. Though I will expect you to have Lyra and Léandre close at hand to keep you out of trouble."

"Of course!" Laila said, her chest flaring with exhilaration. "I will merely exist as a figurehead—an embodiment of the Crown itself! I promise to stay well out of harm's way and allow the chevaliers to perform their duties."

Her mother stared at her with the nebulous irises of all solarites—patterned with fragments of infinite stars and space matter. "Then I will allow it."

"Oh, thank you, Maman! You are gracious!" Laila sprung out of her seat with rosy gaiety as she rushed to embrace her.

"Laila," Amira warned. "Not at the table."

Laila deflated immediately, arms lowering to her sides. "I beg your pardon, Maman."

Amira made a dismissive gesture in response.

"Though there is just... one other thing I might request of you, Maman," Laila said sheepishly, lip bitten between her teeth.

"Oh?" Amira set her glass down. "And what is that?"

IX

DARIUS RECLINED IN HIS ALCOVE-BACKED LEATHER SEAT. For the past hour he had been discussing matters of the kingdom in the Eyrie, the affectionate term for the council chamber, for it perched like a bird's nest at the top of a stone spiral staircase. To scale the steps was a perilous affair of abrupt curves and bends at ankle-twisting speed. Wrought iron balustrades on either side were adorned with bronze-carved eagles, ever-vigilant, with a lacquered twinkle in their eye, to any catastrophe that might befall.

Behind brass-barred oak was the chamber itself—a room of varnished ironwood panelled with particle-dusted plaques. Stained glass windows dressed in velvet drapes depicted the sextuple-headed eagle of the royal insignia. With the soft-toned lambency of cavorting chandelier flames and the sweet smoke pluming from the fireplace, the room appeared intimate. Yet lingering beneath the deception was a frigid ambience that seeped into Darius's bones the same way whisky diluted on ice: slow to settle but once there, impossible to shift. It kept his spine rigid so he'd never think to get comfortable at the pinnacle of the social ladder he'd scaled, when he could be so carelessly knocked off.

His father, Lanius Rex, paced around the ironwood table with his prefects before him. The firelight bounced along the virile mane smoothed atop his head with pomade, half-tamed with a gold hair-cuff, the rest permitted to flow lavishly down to his shoulder blades. He stood while the others were seated, his face delineated in the gyrating flames. The light seemed to eclipse him, erase him; he looked almost a spectre. His obstruction of the fireplace enlarged his shadow and darkened the rest of the occupants until only the unearthly gleam of their eyes remained.

"Well?" Lanius asked. Having recently concluded matters of their isle once more being breached, they had now moved onto food and agriculture. He waved for a ghoul to pour him a goblet of gold wine from the diamond decanter.

Claudius Orlovis, his prime prefect, cleared his throat to go first. "Recent forecasts have warned of a significantly harsh winter this year, Your Majesty. One fraught with violent storms and a stubborn frost. With such conditions, there is cause for concern that our game and livestock will be affected."

Throughout this report, Lanius's eyes were vacant, his expression bloodless, every last ounce of emotion having leached from him the moment he'd had his heart removed from his chest. Darius wondered whether he had it with him now—guarded inside that egg of lapis lazuli with gold cagework.

Lanius ran his fingers down the aquiline bridge of his nose. "How severe?"

"The figures vary, sire, but they do not look hopeful." There was a pause as Claudius debated whether to broach this next topic. "Perhaps if we ask for aid from the Vidua Nocte—"

"No." Lanius held up a hand definitively. "I have no intention of ceding any more power to those hags. They were downright unbearable the last time we haggled. The less influence they hold in this time of crisis, the better."

Food production had long been caged inside the black talon grip of the Vidua Nocte, a faction of blood sorceresses to which Darius's mother belonged, and market domination always made them uppity. Much to Lanius's dismay.

"Your Majesty, if I may," interjected Delanus Levitis, prefect of the treasury. "I no more want another blood sorceress at court than you do, but I have seen the numbers Prefect Orlovis has forecast, and if we do not act quickly, this may lead to famine. Many will most certainly starve."

A plea to empathy that would fall upon indifferent ears. They all knew it. Yet such a foregone conclusion did not dissuade them from the belief that they might be able to stir their monarch.

"Starve we may, Prefect Levitis," Lanius responded, hands clasped behind his back, "but perish we will not. We have survived famines before and we will do so again. This is a hard land, but we are hardy people. The beasts in the forest may be poisonous but we still have seas full of fish, provided we run those lupari mutts off the coast first. Plenty of meat to be had before the storm arrives."

Delanus flexed his jaw, clearly unsatisfied. "Your Majesty, I must pray you see reason—"

"You must?" Lanius challenged. His tone was calm, almost toneless, but there was the finest shard of vexation.

"Do forgive me, Your Majesty," Delanus said, swallowing down his defiance. "I spoke out of turn."

"No, do continue, prefect." Lanius took a step closer, one heavy brow arched. "Speak your mind. After all, the only thing worse than an insubordinate worm is one who lacks the spine to follow through with his conviction. So, tell me"—Lanius rested a hand on Delanus's shoulder and squeezed firmly—"are you a worm, prefect?"

Nobody dared speak or breathe, for they had seen an encounter like this before and lived in fear of what followed. The last dispute between the rex and one of his prefects had ended with the latter's spine removed and cast into the fireplace.

Darius cleared his throat and moved to speak. "I am sure Prefect Levitis meant no offence, Your Majesty."

"You will speak when you are spoken to." Lanius tossed off his words with indifference. His attention then narrowed back onto Delanus. "Well?"

"No, sire," Delanus stumbled over his words, practically as white as his hair. Small beads of sweat now studded his forehead. His pupils nearly eclipsed the golden irises entirely. "No, I am not a worm. I only meant to say I think you are making too hasty a decision by refusing to entertain the Vidua Nocte's aid."

Lanius regarded his prefect for a long pause, his manacle grip tight. Then slowly, he loosened it.

"I will take your counsel into due consideration," he said, a shift arriving in the corner of his lips. Not a smile; it looked more like a fissure splintering on a slab.

Delanus exhaled the moment he was released, as though his throat instead had been within Lanius's pincer grip.

The rex approached a polished wooden cigar cabinet standing nearby, firelight reflecting on bevelled glass doors and brass handles. He took out a stick of luneleaf and ran it across his nostrils, gesturing for a ghoul to light it before he inhaled.

"You are dismissed," Lanius said, his nostrils frothing with smoke like a disgruntled beast.

The prefects rose from their seats with a stretch of long legs and broad shoulders. So vast were their bodies, the earth couldn't help but tremble when they moved.

"Not you, Darius," Lanius said, just as he was about to join them.

Darius returned to his seat. "Your Majesty?"

"Did you handle that little problem I tasked you with?" Lanius asked on the edge of an exhale, smoke encircling around his manicured beard like tusks.

"Yes," Darius replied. "I have made certain she will no longer be a nuisance."

Perhaps not the way his father would have expected. But certainly, the hapless scholar was unlikely to be heard from again.

"Good," Lanius said, stubbing his cigar on his backhand. The stub sizzled on his swarthy skin, blackening it to char. "Keep it up the way you have been, and you may prove yourself worthy of a commendation yet."

Such words might have once made his chest lift, but Darius had long ago learned how emptied of substance his father's praise was. Thus, he merely bowed his head in compliance. "Thank you, Your Majesty."

"Hm," Lanius acknowledged, waving his hand. "Now go. Get out of my sight."

Darius nodded, turning on his heel to depart after the prefects.

When Darius reached his quarters, Delanus was already there, having helped himself to a couple of glasses of Darius's polugar. His shoulders were hunched pitifully over his glass as he nursed his wounded pride.

He hadn't come to Darius in such a state for a while—not since he'd gotten betrothed—but Darius sported a blasé air as he closed the door behind him.

"I shouldn't have said anything," Delanus sputtered the moment Darius entered. "God, I'm such an imbecile."

"Calm down," Darius said, lifting the lid of the decanter to pour himself a glass. He swirled the wine around before he sipped it. "He'll have forgotten about it tomorrow."

Delanus refused to be consoled. "I almost feel as though I can't say anything right around him anymore. He used to regard me so well and then..." An exhale of bitter laughter. "Well, they don't call him heartless for nothing."

"Since Dominus's disappearance, he's been rather... tempestuous," Darius agreed, though as the primary target of his father's capricious moods, he often failed to tell the difference. "But you ought to have known better than to mention the Vidua Nocte to him directly after the last incident that occurred between him and the emissary."

"I know, I know." Delanus pinched the corners of his eyes. "I thought enough time had passed for him to have gotten over that little altercation."

"You would think so, wouldn't you?" Darius chuckled, revealing two rows of perfect teeth. "Sadly, while becoming heartless may have excised my father of most emotion, his pride appears to have only swelled to make up for it."

"And I'm sure your mother being appointed their most recent leader hasn't helped."

Darius's hooked nose wrinkled. He didn't often like thinking about what his mother had cast him aside to achieve. "Don't remind me." He swallowed the rest of his drink. "The only good thing about that is it'll offer me a little more sway when I go to visit Katerina myself."

"After all this time, you still have your old dalliance on the hook?" Delanus asked, his mirth distorting his features into something feral.

"We keep in touch," Darius replied, unbuttoning his cream kaftan to unveil the sheer rubakha that clenched tightly around the contours of lean, sculptural muscle.

Delanus sat up immediately in discomfort, eyes everywhere but on him. He'd almost forgotten what a slight dip of a waist Darius had. The way his hips lengthened into generous thighs.

"One blood sorceress will certainly not be enough to resolve the entire crisis, but at the very least she'll keep the city fed where most of our race is concentrated. What to do about the qarna tribes in the hinterlands, well... the enforcers will have to manage that." Darius placed his hand on the obsidian mantelpiece and drummed his fingers against it. "All of these are merely temporary measures that distract away from the real issue. What we need is new land, fertile land, that is less prone to famine or frost than ours."

Delanus snorted into his glass, grateful for the liquid distraction. "And we all know what the rex thinks about that."

"Indeed." Darius twisted the signet ring on his little finger.

Lanius's insistence on maintaining the brutal isolationist principles of his predecessors had often perplexed Darius. He knew his father had a stomach for conquest, something two centuries of unchallenged domination over Mortos could more than attest to. Though after the war for racial supremacy with their competing neighbours had been won, the appetite had long waned. Another consequence of his now heartless state.

"Perhaps what we need here is a new perspective." Delanus raised his glass in salute. "Or even a new leader."

Darius chuckled as he shifted from the mantelpiece to next to Delanus on the divan. "Not an easy task to manage when you have half

92

the kingdom willing to dismiss you out of turn for being a bastard and the other half scared witless to move against the monarch." He crossed one leg over the other, relaxing into his seat. "But I've been biding my time, and it seems Dominus's disappearance may have presented something of an opportunity. You might say I've been finding myself strange bedfellows as of late."

Delanus tensed upon Darius's proximity. "Oh, of that I'm certain."

Darius responded to this with the slimmest smirk, allowing his hand to slide into Delanus's lap. "Though I think we've had enough talk of politics." He stroked his hand along Delanus's thigh. "Let me help you relax."

Delanus swallowed, his mind aswarm with the alcohol and the dark, intoxicating scent of Darius's perfume so enticingly near. He placed his hand over Darius's own. "We shouldn't."

"You always say that," Darius said, deftly unwinding the sash of Delanus's kaftan. "And yet, you come here anyway." His hand wandered leisurely to his trousers next, undoing the button and slipping between the folds.

Delanus grabbed his throat, squeezing hard. A warning, perhaps, but Darius only took it as enticement.

"Would you like me to stop?" Darius asked, leaning daringly into Delanus's grip. His blue eyes were bright as a beetle's carapace, alluring in the way of all things poisonous. He was far too pretty to be a predator, and this only made his strikes more deadly when they came.

Delanus held Darius's throat fast in his hand as he regarded his softly flushed cheeks, the lips that appeared so full and pink even in the dimness of the room. Those lips, especially, had haunted him through many a stressful night.

Delanus closed his eyes with an exhale, opening them to reveal sclera blackened and veins bulging. But the smirk that overcame his features was one of carnality. He pulled Darius into a rough kiss, tongues and teeth clashing.

Darius moaned softly into his kiss as his fangs descended, parting to litter bites and kisses down the expanse of Delanus's throat. He slid down onto his knees to stroke his hands up Delanus's thighs, one final glance given beneath boyish lashes before he sank down into his lap and gave Delanus what he'd been wanting since he came into the room.

When Delanus had long left, Darius parted the curtains to his alcove bed and stepped out into the night. His body was still bruised from Delanus's rough handling, his throat especially. But the post-coital clarity provided by a good ravishing always stirred him to inspiration.

It took a few moments for his eyes to adjust to the darkness, though the colours were a ghost of what they ought to be. He debated briefly on a lantern and decided against it, pulling on a rubakha and a pair of trousers from his oaken chest before closing it softly behind him.

From there, he crossed towards the large bookcase of calfskin tomes and touched the heftiest, manoeuvring it until it clicked. The case yawned open to a hidden passageway, where a rugged wooden staircase ran down into a cellar. He took the widely spaced steps one at a time, his footsteps wool-soft against the creaking dark wood.

The tunnel at the bottom seemed to lead on forever, but finally he stepped into light again inside a laboratory. The room was in impeccable order, pristine as a picture. With its scintillating apparatus and lacquered workbenches edged in gold, it was a motionless landscape—until Darius wandered into the foreground and transfigured it from still art to animation.

He passed beneath his ceiling dome bookcase, the skeletal figures modelling deformed shapes, and the walls papered with labelled diagrams of unidentifiable creatures hybridised from several sources. Here stretched over a century of his research into chimera production, where he'd made a slow, if not steady, progression into the mutagenesis of organic matter.

Over the years, he'd made great use of his surgical knowledge and lithe embroiderer fingers to vivisect the beasts of many classes that roamed their lands, sewing them together in a means that would adapt them for warfare. Such pursuits had borne him little fruit thus far, and it wasn't until a little foreigner filled with dark magic landed into his lap that he received the catalyst he didn't realise he'd been missing.

His footsteps paused before her now as he smiled, reaching towards her. She was all bones, whittled down to nothing. The pitiful remains of her limbs had been bound to a gurney. The only thing that kept her suspended from the release she so begged for was the intravenous drip of chaotic essence, slowly invading and subsuming all of her blood, muscle, and organs.

Her body was changing, mutating. Into what, one could not say. Each of her veins had become sullied from blue to black, jutting out with a twiglike protuberance. A notable leakage had seeped through to her fingers, giving them the impression of having festered and charred to coal. Her nails had overgrown, equally black, curved like sharpened scythes that spasmed with soreness.

But most noteworthy of all were her eyes.

Gone was the clear-eyed health of spongy white sclera—now filled to overflowing with the tar-like substance of chaos. Though she could no longer blink, each time she wept, the heavy coating on her eyes would wobble and glisten, spilling over into inky streaks across her cheeks.

"I want to thank you, Emica, for your contribution. Without you,

I never would've made it this far. Being able to study you has been a rare gift indeed."

Darius slid his hand down the damp, matted hair of Dr Hariken, who swallowed weakly and parted her lips with a plea. "Please... let me die."

Darius tutted, shaking his head gravely. "I'm afraid I'm far from finished with you yet. Not to worry, though—I can promise that your suffering will be in the service of something very, very grand."

He removed the empty canister of chaotic essence and replaced it with another. As the blight poured into Dr Hariken's withered veins, her ailing body rippled with another sob, contorting to the pernicious effects of foreign magic.

No longer did she resemble anything like the scholar that had haplessly stepped foot on accursed soil. The only thing that could be said for certain was whatever tether she'd still held to humanity had now been lost.

X

AILA GLANCED OUT OF THE WINDOW OF HER AIRSHIP, *The Stellaria*, watching as the sun-soaked shores of her homeland slowly disappeared from view. Her heart duelled between excitement and wariness, for though she had explored the continent of Vysteria extensively, she had never before travelled so far north. In the past she'd avoided the cold with prejudice, but she'd decided she would not pass her eternity without experiencing at least one good bone-rattling winter.

She fiddled with the collar of her white rabbit fur coat, its conditioned strands soft against her jawline. The garment had been a special order from her favourite couturier, lined with pink satin, and it complemented splendidly her matching mittens.

How greatly it contrasted to her Soleterean wardrobe full of sheer, flimsy fabrics that often left her feeling more naked than if she were bare.

Solarites had particular sensitivity to the cold, and thus she'd reluctantly traded in her silks and chiffons for the more substantial furs and fleece.

She'd agreed with her mother that air travel would likely be safer than braving the treacherous waters of the White Sea. Thus, after performing a quick aether-tracking spell to trace the exuding imprint of the *Great Northern*'s magically crafted hull, they were now well on their way to its last known destination.

Laila took off her mittens and picked up her ætherald detector to feel its humming pulses. As she watched the throbbing glow of the crystal, her nostrils were tickled by the lavender, bergamot, and mint notes of Lyra's fougère announcing her arrival.

Her friend took a seat across from her and propped up both ankles on the table with an exaggerated sigh. "Not even a week we've spent airborne, and already my limbs want *off* this accursed ship."

"Be patient, now, Lyra," Laila playfully scolded, tossing one of her two thick canerows, threaded together with gold cording. Her journey to a cold, brittle climate had demanded her delicate curls be styled into something protective. "The signal I have on the ship grows ever stronger. It shouldn't be long before we find land."

"Let's hope so, lest I feel inclined to start picking a fight," Lyra said, revealing her teeth in a vixen grin befitting her fox fur coat.

Laila didn't need to guess who Lyra's first target would be. Seated in the adjoining room from them was Dominus, closely guarded by two Lightshield chevaliers who never left his side. Their gilded meteorite cuirasses were engraved with the sun goddess Asemani's likeness, burnishing brightly over their white wool tunics with epauletted shoulders. Around Dominus's neck was a golden collar designed to inject him with an electrical current severe enough to stun an elephant with a single word spoken. One of her mother's precautions.

"Well, if you are in need of a relaxant..." Laila unclipped her sterling silver flask chased with repoussé leaves and flowers, her initials monogrammed in the cartouche on the front. She unfastened the hinged cap and took a swig of Malakian white rum, then passed it over to Lyra. "I managed to swipe some before we left."

"You absolute star!" Lyra exclaimed in delight, snatching the flask with relish to take a long gulp.

"Steady on, you lush." Laila's laugh was warm and silvery. "Remember you're still on duty."

Lyra cringed at the strength of the liquor. "The one time I envy a mortal's delicate constitution. This'll put a fine fire in my belly, but I'll need a great deal more to be fully bladdered."

"Pass it back here, then!" Laila received the bottle back into her care. "What do you think it will be like? Out there in the north?"

Lyra sat back in thought.

There had always been myths about the land of ice and fire prophesied to have been the place where Calante had been imprisoned for his insurgency against Asemani. The Shadowlands, they'd called it. Little more than a campfire tale to send spritelings off to bed with.

"Besides being rather cold and gloomy?" Lyra smirked before her mirth evaporated. "I can't say, but if the tales are true, we may well be travelling straight to our certain doom."

Laila shivered as though she could feel the sharpness of winter chill in spite of her many layers. Dominus's ghoulish pictures were still tucked away in the drawers of her memory, and it seemed the closer they came to the shores of Mortos, the more ominously they rattled.

"Not to worry." Lyra took Laila's hand. "If nothing else, I can assure you I'll be with you all the while. To the gates of the netherworld and beyond."

The two laced their fingers together, sealing their pact.

As night settled, Laila started a new journal entry, not wanting to skimp on a single minor detail along her travels. Once done, she hoped to publish it as a memoir, or at least have an appetising array of soundbites to relay at her next cocktail party. The faint scratch of her fountain pen was all that accompanied her before the swell of music outside her door disrupted her trance.

Curious, she deserted her task to step out into the passageway, where she heard the tender strumming of lyre strings followed by airy, euphonious vocals singing "Oh Morning Star". The voice was entrancingly nostalgic and soothed in the way a palm cradled at the back of a babe's neck did. Laila found she was powerless but to follow in pursuit of its source.

She traced the enigmatic echo up the stairs into the lounge, where she found Léandre seated, one ankle propped up on his knee as his lithe fingers made exquisite work of a silver lyre's gossamer strings.

Laila crept forward on the balls of her feet, waiting patiently until he'd finished the last verse to make a sound of appreciation. "That was beautiful."

"Thank you, madame," Léandre said, a shell-pink blush staining his cheeks beneath long, ivory hair. "Shouldn't you be resting?"

"I couldn't sleep a wink." Laila pulled up the chair beside him. "And you?"

"I volunteered to take over watch for this one." Léandre nodded towards Dominus, transfixed in the corner by the window. "Who, it appears, doesn't ever sleep."

"You know that's not what your duties entail," Laila scolded lightly, though her smile was kind. "You're too considerate."

Léandre merely shrugged in response. "Fancy another tune while you're here? If nothing else, he seems to like the music. Or, at least, he hasn't made too much of a fuss."

"I thought you'd never ask." She rested her chin in both palms. "Do 'My Radiant Warden'; that was always one of my favourites."

"As you wish." Léandre strummed the opening of the ballad on his lyre and permeated the room once more with the limpid beguilement of music.

Laila listened intently, funnelling out all sounds but the mellifluous croon of his voice until the song ended. Then she gave him hearty applause. "Wonderful! That troupe you used to travel with truly suffered a loss."

Léandre chuckled. "Thank you, princess. I haven't thought about that troupe in years. Still, it felt nice to play."

"Do you think you might ever return? When you retire from your Lightshield duties?"

"Perhaps, one day." He placed down his lyre. "I ought to be returning to my coffee though." He lifted the cezve to fill his cup. "Would you like some?"

Laila's nose scrunched in dismissal.

"Ah, of course," Léandre said. He reached for the milk jug. "You are welcome to whatever is left in this. It's powdered goat's milk, I'm afraid, but it is warm and we even have some honey."

"Please," she said, laying her hands upon the jug and the honeypot with relish as she filled herself a cup. She took a sip, eyes wandering over to Dominus.

"You can ask," Léandre said, inferring her question. "Though he seems content as he is."

Laila poured an extra cup of coffee anyway, negating any cinnamon or salep, thinking it advantageous to appeal to his better nature. Having his cooperation might well mean the difference between life and death for the passengers on this ship, and she wanted them to have the best fighting chance.

She rose from her seat to approach Dominus. Standing by the window, he looked inhumanly still, poised like a sculpture, his skin shifting from copper to bronze under the moon's silver glow.

Laila almost hesitated to near him as she presented the cup—an offering. She tilted her head coyly to one side, eyes large and inquisitive. "Would you like some?"

Dominus acknowledged the gesture by arching one thick brow, his pupils eerily lucent. He couldn't understand how the same creature who had ruthlessly shackled a collar to his throat could look at him so sweetly with alms shyly extended. He decided he preferred it back home, where such cruelties were not slathered in dulcet honey coats.

He grunted in dismissal, turning away from her.

Laila sighed heavily as she tapped the cup with her fingers. "I thought you could use this to keep you awake." She scrunched her lips to one side. "If you sleep at all, that is."

Dominus kept his eyes to the window.

"You must be excited to return to your home," Laila continued, leaning her hip against the wall. "I couldn't see much about your family, but I know you have one. Your mother, especially. She seems to love you most fiercely. I wish my mother—" She stopped, for these were thoughts too embarrassing to voice even to someone who could not comprehend. "Never mind."

She pivoted to turn away, but Dominus's hand caught her arm.

Laila turned back slowly in confusion, meeting his gaze.

Dominus stared at her with an intensity too acute to hold, but before she could inquire at his motives for stopping her, he reached out and claimed the cup from her hands.

It happened so fast Laila almost couldn't register it. For it seemed one moment she had the warmth of the coffee against her palms and the next she did not.

She shook her head slightly with a bewildered smile. "You're welcome."

He guzzled the drink down without so much as a pause at the scorch in his throat, finding he liked that as well. Only when finished did he pause to let the brew linger on his taste buds—the rich, earthy notes and bitter afterbite.

"What witchcraft is this?" he asked in astonishment, now eyeing her with the suspicion that she might have handed him some malignant concoction under the guise of hospitality.

Laila didn't understand the remark but noted his appreciation. "If you like it, there's more where that came from." She pointed in the direction of Léandre.

Dominus glanced over at the guard, concluding against poison when he saw Léandre drinking liberally from the same pot. He looked down into his empty cup with longing.

"Come on," Laila said, tugging firmly at his arm so he was forced to join her against his ambivalence. She seated him down at the table next to her, filling his cup before she sat.

"Princess," Léandre cautioned as he watched her fill Dominus's cup to the rim. "I would advise against overwhelming the occasso with coffee on his first try."

"Oh, Léandre, don't be such a worrywart," Laila scoffed in response. "What's life without a little indulgence?"

Dominus slurped happily in agreement from his cup, making noises of appreciation.

Laila tittered behind her palm, suppressing it into a smile. And for the briefest moment, Dominus smiled, too.

Darius skulked through the bronze-tiled hall of the Citadel, his shadow magnified beside him like a spectral colluder. From surface to surface it slithered alongside him, matching Darius's furtive gait as he weaved through the corridors until he found the place he sought. The clocks were all striking midnight, having unlatched their throats to cry the hour, the full moon making even more a giant of his shadow than its original shape.

He stepped into a warm patch of darkness, where his shadow bid him a brief farewell, and pressed his hand against an unsturdy panel on the wall. With some nimble manoeuvring, the panel clicked open to grant him entry, and Darius climbed the steps of rotten wood all the way up to the Observatory.

He moved with a careful foot, for the tower had long become a vampire bat dominion, and they didn't take kindly to visitors. As he rose higher, he could see the red-dotted eyes of his nocturnal companions as they watched him. They swarmed him in a maelstrom of flapping wings, their screeches echoing throughout the night.

Despite its name, the Observatory was not employed for purposes of observation from a vantage point. Instead, it served as the command post for several watchers strategically placed throughout the kingdom in the form of grotesques and gargoyles. These grim statues would observe all from their decorative stance, inscrutable to the average passersby but capturing the tawdry conclaves they unwittingly engaged in. This would be collected and then projected in front of Darius via an obsidian ball, should he choose to access it.

Darius approached the column where the ball sat upon its throne of raven skulls. His reflection stretched and distorted over the globe the more he leered.

"All-seeing eye, I command you to show me the one who dares to trespass across our sky," Darius invoked, watching carefully as the ball lit up with a ghastly white glow and projected an image of the sky. There he saw it, floating like a cloud caged in brass. The flying ship.

"So Balthus *wasn't* spinning me a tall tale."

For a long, indulgent moment he allowed his gaze to linger in fascination at the contraption, curious as to how such a thing was crafted; how it remained airborne. His fascination soured to disappointment when he realised he would never find out.

He sighed, massaging his temples. There was every chance this flying ship was sent out in pursuit of the last he'd wrecked. If so, it would need to be dispensed with. Regardless of his own personal stirrings of intellectual curiosity.

But a more subconscious impulse stirred—one deliriously seductive to a creature of chaos. Being so close to the edge of discovery emboldened Darius in ways he no longer thought possible. He almost felt he could turn away, allow the ship to arrive with the same surgical detachment he took with his experiments and observe what it would do next.

The impulse was so strong that it took a brutal dousing of clarity to turn him away from it. Regardless of his desires, his father would know he'd failed to dispose of the ship, and any benefit he could reap from studying it would be offset by the penalties from his rage.

Knowing this, Darius lamented his next actions as he reached into his pocket to retrieve a vial of cold fire—a blue-white essence, extracted from the innards of a prehistoric draconid, that burned hotter and more lethal than regular red-yellow flame.

He uncorked the vial and summoned the fumes with an elegant dance of his fingers, muttering a few malignant words that caused the bats to screech in excitement as they swarmed him in a black vortex as his chants grew louder. With the final word uttered, a jet of blue-white vapour ascended through the oculus of the Observatory in a geyser, provoking the clouds to gather in preparation for a great and terrible storm.

∽∞∽

The storm brewed after most of the occupants had retired to their bunks for the evening.

Laila slept on the top bunk, that much closer to the sky—as though every subconscious gesture of her earthbound life sought to elevate her back up to her origins. Thus she scaled stairs, storeys, and social ladders, adorning herself in her weight's worth of diamonds that sparkled near as much as stars do.

She shifted from her stomach to her side, curved like a cat, entirely ignorant of the cataclysm now rapidly gathering outside her ship's aluminium husk. The wind howled like a wolf on the hunt, the lightning booming like explosives. Its shockwaves rattled the walls and sent Laila catapulting upwards in alarm.

She stretched herself awake with a soft moan, pushing up the lace eye mask that blocked the light. "What in the world?"

She shifted out of bed and scaled down the ladder to slip on her clothes, watching as Lyra remained snoozing. Merely a guise, for Lyra could awaken at the sound of a pin drop, and thus any slumber she was in was feigned for continued rest.

Laila decided against disturbing her and looked out of the window.

Usually the arrival of a storm excited her, for she couldn't help but find them eminently powerful and, oftentimes, erotic experiences. Lightning, as with all sources of electricity and incandescence, had only ever been a solarite's natural ally. But this lightning was distorted—a wintry ice blue as opposed to the divine white she was accustomed to.

She drew back from the window with a clenched chest and went to shake Lyra's shoulder. "Lyra? Lyra, wake up."

Lyra made an indistinct noise into her pillow.

"I think something is happening outside."

The note of consternation in her princess' voice was enough to awaken her. Lyra rolled out of bed to join Laila by the window. "What is it?" She peered outside the window. "You woke me up for a *storm*."

Her lack of amusement was evident.

"Not just any storm," Laila cried in protest. "Last I checked, lightning doesn't tend to be blue."

"We've recently passed a pure white sea, and a little off-colour lightning is what's got you all hot and bothered?" Lyra rubbed at her tired eyes. "I'm going back to bed."

Then they heard the explosion.

An alarm wailed through the ship as the husk rumbled, causing both to go rigid in fear.

Laila acted immediately by grabbing Lyra by the shoulders. "Go wake your uncle, quickly."

"Wait, what about you?" Lyra called.

Laila blurred out into the corridor too fast for her to answer. She frantically sought out the source of the rupture. At the same time, the first spark from the lightning plumed into a mushroom-clouded flame.

The flame trickled down until it reached hydrogen, ballooning into an inferno. It engulfed the tail of the airship, churning directly into her path as a blue-white lake of fire.

Laila acted on instinct, erecting a field of aether to suspend the flames with a golden barrier.

"Fire!" she called out over the torrent of the weather, hoping the others might hear in time to escape.

Her warning hit Lyra's ears first, and she wasted no time hammering on the doors to wake everyone up. "Come on! Up and at 'em! It's time to go!"

"Lyra." Léandre appeared at his door with heavy eyes. "What is the meaning of this?"

"There's a fire." Lyra grabbed him by the hand and hauled him into the corridor. "It's time for us to go. Now."

Laila's holler and Lyra's quick action soon had the passengers of the ship scrambling in a panic. Lyra and Léandre herded them down to the airlock to usher the sprites, one by one, into the open sky high above the sea.

Laila gritted her teeth against the force of the fire, digging her heels into the floor to catch her grip. She refused to be conquered by whatever demonic conjury had attacked her beloved ship; nor would she let it have her crew.

However, her resolve weakened, and she could feel the beads of her perspiration seeping down her brow. She couldn't tell how much longer she could hold before the fire subjugated her and resumed its consumption. She could only hope that by then the rest of the inhabitants would have evacuated.

Once the last of the passengers had descended, Léandre and Lyra looked at each other.

"Someone has to get Laila," Lyra said, the fierceness in her eyes showing she'd already determined it to be her.

"Absolutely not," Léandre said.

"We don't have time to argue this, Uncle—"

"Quite right, we don't." He leaned forward to kiss her forehead. "I'll find you on the ground."

"No, wait, Uncle—" Her cries of protest were halted as he pushed her off the ledge. She reached for him instinctively, catching air, her stomach plummeting as she fell. She watched as his silhouette shrank further and further away.

"Uncle!" was Lyra's final cry as she plunged down from the heavens.

Laila descended to one knee as her legs buckled, fatigue wearing away at her arms. But before her shield could deplete in exhaustion, a pair of arms encircled her.

"Let's go," Dominus told her, picking her up and speeding towards the airlock. *Nary a curl rustled*, he'd promised, and he wasn't about to break pacts now.

He launched them both out of the ship with his arms around her, their bodies plunging down from the heavens.

The ship was engulfed within a heartbeat.

And then Laila was falling, falling, falling as she had done in her celestial life before. She fell like a fledgling from a nest still fumbling to find her wings, tucked into the arms of the monster who ensnared her.

Laila could scarcely decide what she found more treacherous—the hungry ocean that awaited beneath or the embrace of her captor. Her situation, however, left her with little option to protest. And so, trapped between a demon and the deep sea, she closed her eyes, held her breath, and allowed the ocean to take her.

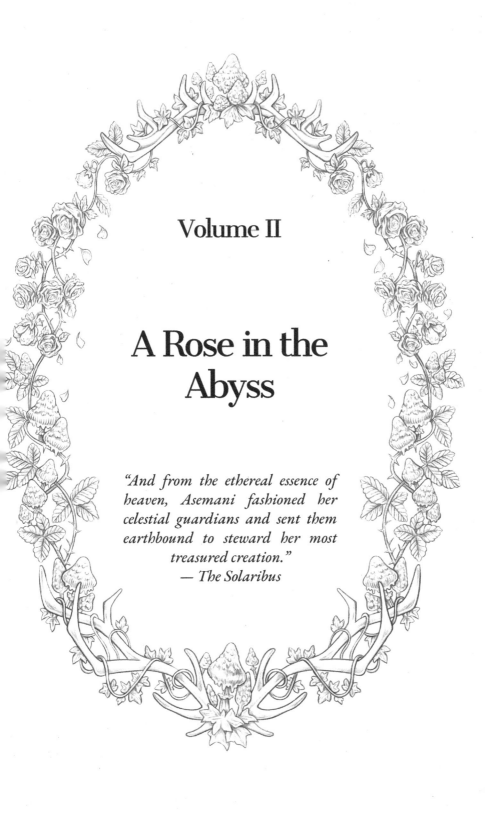

Volume II

A Rose in the Abyss

"And from the ethereal essence of heaven, Asemani fashioned her celestial guardians and sent them earthbound to steward her most treasured creation."
— The Solaribus

XI

"**L**AILA!"

Her name echoed through the tunnel of her subconscious, close enough to hear, too far to reach. She recognised the voice, its gentle timbre, the tender nuance it used to address her.

"Léandre!" Laila shot his name like an arrow through the distance, hoping it was caught. She was swathed in fog, her vision obscured, but she could see him in front of her—a vague apparition, gradually gaining opacity in small increments. "Thank the stars you're alive!"

He had to be. She wouldn't be able to dreamwalk to him otherwise. It was always a lot trickier when the recipient was dead. And his Lightshield bond was still present, stretched taut between them like a thread of glistening gossamer.

"*I'm pleased to see the same of you, princess.*" Léandre smiled, his opalescent eyes shifting with colour. "*Where are you?*"

"*I don't know yet. But for now, that's not relevant.*" Whatever had become of her body, she was certain to know soon. For now, she refused to let herself panic. "*Did everyone else make it off the ship safely? Did Lyra?*"

"*She's fine. Hale and hearty. We all are,*" Léandre assured her. "*She put up a great resistance, but I made certain everyone left before I did. I had intended to come for you, but... the occasso...*"

"*It wasn't your fault,*" Laila said, her heart lightened with the relief that they had both escaped. "*I'm only glad I didn't lose you.*"

"*You still have yet to find me, princess.*"

Laila swallowed, recognising the truth in his words. "*Use the bond to locate me. In the meantime, I will try to find a safe place to wait for you, and then... we will have to figure it out from there.*"

"*Stay safe, princess. We'll find you soon.*"

"*I know.*"

She awoke in a cave.

The cave was dark and dank, like the inside of a throat. Moisture dripped in the distance, as though it were salivating for its newest arrivals. Laila hugged her damp furs to her and tapped into the reserves of stellar energy in her body to warm herself, a radiant glow expanding from her like the inflation of a bubble.

The orb of light emanating from her body brightened her surroundings until she could see the rugged outline of Dominus sitting across from her, watching. A fire was crackling between them. She saw the eldritch glow of his pupils before the rest of him, shadows clinging to the gauntness of his cheeks. He seemed to fit inside the cave like a natural extension of rock, unbothered by his wetness.

Laila suspended her glow, uncertain, before deciding to expand it so he was dried too. Then she opened her mouth to speak.

He was on her in an instant, covering her mouth with a brutish paw, another finger pressed against his lips. He gestured his head to one side so she might look to the opening of the cave where Laila quickly realised: they were not alone.

Shambling along the black sands of the beach were pale figures that had the look of men. One might easily think they *were* men if not gifted with the keen eyesight Laila and Dominus both shared. There was something wrong about these creatures. Their eyes were too beady and spaced apart; their limbs long and gangly; their skin a roughened hide that crinkled around the gums of their lipless mouths.

Those mouths bared their endless rows of teeth, stained pink from their most recent kill.

Laila held her breath upon the sight of them, her heart squeezing like a closed fist. *What are those things?* She dared not ask.

"Bilken," Dominus revealed quietly, then he gestured to his ears to indicate the creatures' strength—hearing. He gestured next to the front of his face and then the back of his head before shaking it.

Laila nodded in understanding. Keen hearing but limited eyesight. These were things her arsenal of light tricks would allow her to work with.

She gestured for Dominus to watch her as she stood and then, slowly, refracted the light around herself to make her imperceptible to sight. She could make herself intangible too, but that took far greater concentration, and she lacked the practice to apply it to anyone but herself. She released the enchantment to bring herself back into full view and held out her hand to Dominus.

He took her hand and marvelled as it disappeared from sight. He'd never seen anything equivalent to this without the use of a concealing cloak before. He kept hold of her hand, and the two of them edged out from the throat of the cave onto the shore.

Laila couldn't help but hold her breath again once they were exposed, an anxious heat thrumming in her body that threatened to unravel her focus. She timed her breaths in the way she was coached—*inhale firm, exhale slow*—anything to keep from focusing on the way her heart was pounding on the door of her sternum. She had to move, she *had* to. Discovery by these creatures was not a possibility she was willing to risk.

But the moment she took a cushioned step forward on the black sand, a lone bilken turned, restlessly seeking meat, and shuffled away from the crowd with a congested snuffle.

Laila stiffened, her legs turning numb. Beside her, Dominus regarded the bilken with indifference as it put its nose to the air with a flex of nostrils, each sniff sounding more and more obstructed. As though it fought for entrance.

The bilken soon relented with a suffocated wheeze before returning to the waters whence it came for a hydrated breath. The rest of them soon followed.

The solarite and her invisible companion took their chance to escape up the cliffside, travelling further up the steep path, slippery with frost, until they were delivered to safety.

Laila leaned in relief against a large stone that might have once, if one squinted just right, resembled a statue of some sort. Though any traces of distinction had long eroded into obscurity.

She rested both hands against the side of her head and craned forward, breathing until she no longer felt like there was a paper sack around her head.

Dominus observed her distress with an arched brow. If an encounter with one monster provoked such an excessive response, he feared she might prove a liability. The night was host to far deadlier guests than the bilken.

In a dark debate, he considered leaving her there and retreating into the night. He found himself preparing to do just that, but after the first few steps his legs would move no further, unable to abandon her. He couldn't fathom why, knowing the bargain he'd made with her had long been fulfilled. He'd escorted her here safely; he'd said nothing of what would happen once they'd arrived.

Dominus grunted, shrugging off his guilt and marching onwards into the snow.

"Wait," Laila cried, darting quickly to obstruct his path. "Where are you going?"

Dominus met the force of her gaze as he sidestepped her. She mirrored the movement.

"You can't just leave me here."

Dominus snarled, taking a daring step forward.

She'd almost forgotten how much larger he was than she was. He towered over her like the bole of a hateful yew twisted cruel by age; his stubbornness deep-rooted. He seized her by the arms to deposit her out of his way before resuming his desertion.

Laila watched him walk away from her with indignation and resentment, a fury burgeoning in her that he would dare leave her to rot in this wasteland. However, he was forgetting one crucial detail—she was the one with control over the shock collar.

She didn't let him make it far before she activated it with a mere utterance: "*Déclencher.*" Then she watched as the collar ignited with several coils of electricity that had Dominus prostrated in the snow.

She approached his side after, arms crossed expectantly over her chest. How vindicating it was to see this goliath felled by a girl, the loathing in his eyes as he looked at her through his frenzied convulsions provoking not even a flinch.

She crouched beside him once his body had stopped shuddering, then reached out a hand to him. "You are not leaving until you escort me somewhere safe. Understand?" She reiterated her point through a projected image into his mind, watching as his lip curled in distaste.

⌒∞⌒

Dominus escorted her through the ossified frames of coniferous trees into the thick of the taiga. The air was stiff as a corpse. No traces of wildlife remained beyond the lumps of dead animals that had struggled and lost against the snowfall, frozen in their final fleeing pose.

Laila's heart tugged at the sight of them, eyes following the trail of every creature great and small. The last victim perished just before finding shelter within the aisle of trees ahead. With each step she took into the snow, the crunch of her boots echoed unreasonably loudly in the slumbering silence.

The winter had claimed everything and wiped it clean. Not a shimmer of gold could be detected by her aethersight. Even the red berries had been encapsulated by drooling icicles like trails of saliva, sharp and glinting as fangs.

Laila hugged her arms as she followed Dominus, eager to find a safe haven to await the arrival of her Lightshields. The bond between a Lightshield and their charge was always stronger from their end, and while she could likely try to track Léandre halfway, her instincts told her it was better to let them come to her.

The night was an inkwell toppled, spilling its tenebrous pigment over the woods like a river. Laila was solar-charged and leaking luminosity through her pores, shoving the shadows back to their corners with the expanding pulse of her glow. But the night contracted with the elasticity of muscle, creeping on the heels of the starlit Laila like a murderer with a knife in the bushes, ever shunned by her luminescent shield.

She glanced up at the sky, hoping even the slimmest blade of light

118

would penetrate through the wiry penitentiary of branches. If she could only make it through the night unscathed, then her odds of survival would be better in full daylight.

Dominus stretched his hearing wide, feeling his way across the rough bark, the wind's soft baby breaths, until it skidded across the faint purl of a river. He knew this river—and that a village was not far ahead of it should they keep walking through the night. Part of him wondered whether Laila could handle the excursion, but he soothed himself with the knowledge that the sooner he could be rid of her, and thus this infuriating collar, the better off he'd be.

So they marched onward, even as the tree roots grew larger and more intricate, giving rise to mangled shapes that clawed their way out from the towering oaks.

One such root gave Laila quite the fright when she nearly stumbled into it, thinking it alive. Her mind soon assured her of its insentient state, and she sidestepped it nervously without turning her back.

Dominus kept charging until the trees relented and backed away from him into an opening—a grim triumph for his foolish persistence.

The river lay ahead, steaming with a vapour that slathered all the trees surrounding it in a sugar-glazed coating.

Laila moved towards it, intrigued by the phenomenon. She'd never seen anything like this before. Soleterean winters were often mild and seldom saw snow but she'd travelled far enough north in Odaka to know a river ought to be frozen in the winter.

She watched the clear current pass her by, rippling like a dress of fine satin that gathered into tulle-like foam at the cascades. The sight enthralled her and filled her with a longing for home, for the satin slips that had been cruelly set ablaze on the ship she'd been forced to abandon.

Laila crouched down and traced her gloved hands over the water in awe, almost wanting to dip her fingers into it, bathe in it. Anything to cleanse her body of the saltwater still clinging to her skin. She lingered long enough to let the steam caress beneath her clothes before Dominus grunted at her, nudging her along again.

Thus it was with water to one side of them and forest to the other that they continued, the dozy rise of the sun dipping everything in broad strokes of twilight blue and obscuring the beast walking alongside them.

It was all muscle and sinew, deep purple veins pulsating along its cadaverous frame. A long, forked tongue lolled between its giant canines in a hiss before it retracted; a pair of gleaming eyes bulged from its skinless visage.

Dominus could sense it before Laila did, and he slowed his walk, predator senses twitching. Laila caught onto the sense of being watched not long after, but not before the beast sprung out from the trees with fangs and claws bared, knocking Laila off her feet and into the snow.

Laila's head smacked harshly against the sleet, stars swarming her vision. She could scarcely perceive her assailant but for the white gleam of fangs and a hollow maw lunging for her.

A frothing snarl exuded from the back of his throat as he bit her shoulder, releasing a spurt of her delicious ichor, golden as the dawn.

Laila cried out as the beast tore hungrily at her succulent flesh. She released a pulse of electric discharge, enough adrenaline surging through her to have displaced her leg-numbing fear.

The monster squealed in pain, muscles seizing in convulsion long enough for Laila to try and squirm free when another opponent entered the fray.

It was Dominus.

Or at least a creature with a likeness to Dominus, for his face had degenerated into something unsightly. Gone were the verdant green eyes and the stoic calm in his features, which had transformed into his *true* monster face: inkblot sclera with glowing irises of garish green and a writhing protrusion of veins beneath them. His fangs had enlarged and latched into the carotid of the beast, tearing it free, coating her face with a warm arterial spray.

Laila swiped it away quickly, revulsion rising in her fast.

The beast collapsed clumsily to one side—whatever demonic energy that possessed it before suddenly extinguished.

Laila let out a whimper. She had been pummelled with tidal waves of horror and relief and gratitude and anxiety, each layer of it piling onto her one by one until she was submerged. She didn't know whether to laugh or weep.

Dominus peered down at her as he lapped his tongue along the black blood staining his jaws, looking no less bestial than the creature that had had her in its clutches.

Laila whined softly, wrestling with her tongue for the invocation to his collar.

Dominus leered at her, fangs bared in disgruntlement before he drew back, his face returning to normalcy.

Laila didn't realise she needed that until she saw it and, in turn, loosened her tongue and let out an exhale in relief. A tear slid down her cheek, and she moved her fingers towards it, paused, and switched to wipe it with her clean backhand. Then she discovered with a start her veins were blackening.

She rubbed frantically at her backhand as though it might scrub away the blight, but the colour only spread, snaking its way up her wrists on both hands.

Her stomach roiled with nausea, revolting against this insidious contamination, trying to root it out, out, *out*. Her vision blurred the further her body sickened, and through the disjointed chaos of her senses, she could see a hand reaching towards her.

Dominus observed the last flashes of Laila's consciousness before she went limp in the snow. He knew it wouldn't take long for the disease from the monster's bite to claim her, and seeing an opportunity for escape, he decided to let nature take its course.

He didn't make it far before hesitation once more set in. There was something about the thought of some other stray beast gnawing at her beautiful face that filled him with immeasurable displeasure. What a waste it would be for a vision so unparalleled to end up mere morsels for fiendish appetites.

Thus before he knew it, he had already taken her into his arms and carried her away to safety—determined for this not to be her final resting place.

✧

Dominus sped through the trees, the cold so sharp it pierced like glass in his throat. There were no words for how much he had missed this— having his nose full of the ungroomed wilderness surrounding him. The fragrant conifers and the pungent tang of the beasts who lurked there; the sound of their shaggy coats rustling in the wind as he pushed himself faster, digging trenches through the snow.

Among the natural musks of the forest was the intrusion of the sweet scent of Laila slung like a prize catch over his shoulder, intermingled with the fetor of disease. This alone was enough to keep him pushing forward, for if smelling her so near could drive him to the point of distraction, he knew it wouldn't be long before other predators would be tempted by her too. At least her glow had dimmed considerably, so he was able to run with anonymity.

He kept his nose to the air, using his impeccable olfactory senses to plan a route to his nearest territory. Occassi could stalk game cross-country through scent alone, able to decipher health, age and emotional state from the unique impression of their spoor. Dominus could track locations just the same, though the methods differed, and by the time he'd taken his First Rite, he could travel the land in its entirety with preternatural intuition.

Within the hour he had made it to the snow-smothered porch of his izba. He paused to swallow the full sight of it and digest it for inspection—the webs spiralling the windows and the relentless strain of lichen. He concluded the lodge had aged some, but it was not in total disrepair. He was, therefore, able to determine the length of his absence hadn't been too extensive. Useful knowledge to store for his future movements.

He held Laila in his arms as he climbed the steps to the door, pushing it open with his back turned. The door swung open on its hinges, unleashing a hoary exhale flecked by snow that dusted the threshold.

He settled Laila onto the divan before he hastened to close the door. Then he turned to the stove and fed it blocks of moon wood and pinecones to build a warm winter fire. The flames flickered to life with youthful vigour, expelling the room's corpse-like chill.

Dominus then pivoted his attention back to Laila and her slowly worsening state. He had not decided what he wanted to do with her yet, but he knew he needed to do it quickly. With the fire warm enough, he decided to unwrap some of her layers—first the soft rabbit furs, the fuzzy fleece jumper, the thermal vest—until only her silk slip remained. He found that the infection on her shoulder had spread—her veins had become rigid, black, twiglike protuberances, and her golden-brown skin had taken an ashen pallor.

It would be easy enough to keep her comfortable to pass naturally, and then her body would become its own treasure trove. From her blood, a viscous honey gold, he could make a fine pigment, stretch her soft skin for parchment, and turn all that coarse, luxuriant hair into excellent bristles for his brush.

And that was only the beginning.

Growing up as a child of occasional subarctic austerity, he had been continually drummed with the merits of conservation—nothing good could go to waste. He would ensure that nothing of her would go to waste at his hand, either. All would have its purpose, its utility.

As he resolved himself to the inevitability of her death, something else niggled at him in a manner too prominent to mute. For each time he considered how her death might serve him, he was intruded upon by memories of hot coffee and rich charcoals and tender meat drenched in pomegranate juice.

Gifts that he only could have received due to her extending her hand to grant him life.

Dominus swatted such thoughts away in scorn and touched the collar on his neck. He watched the frail death rattle of her chest as it rose and fell, and he knew he could easily choose to do nothing. That he could sit here and watch her breathe her last.

The moment he withdrew with finality was when he heard the unexpected cough and splutter from a Laila who didn't appear ready to give in.

"Well, well," he said in marvel, listening to the frantic war-drum pulse of her fighting heart. "You really do not wish to die today, do you?"

He tested the temperature of her clammy forehead with a sigh. Then he vacated the lodge in search of the ingredients he hoped he held to preserve her.

Laila awoke to find her body swaddled in furs, her limbs stiff and embalmed at her sides. The haze of just-woken dew had not yet lifted from her vision, but when she tried to move—*anguish*. This was not how it was meant to be. Solarite bodies were supposed to heal flawlessly from every scrape, every wound. But this pestilence that invaded her and declared her body its colony was a stubborn strain not easily ejected.

Laila nudged at the furs inch by inch until an arm was sprung free. She lifted her limb towards her clearing vision and saw the black trail marks along her veins. She rolled the furs down to explore further and discovered that she had been defrocked. She set that concern aside for now and examined the scrawls that defiled her beige skin.

Though she was no physician, this seemed like no natural symptom of infection that she had ever encountered. It seemed like magic. The wicked sort. The kind one could expect to brush shoulders with when they embarked upon a journey to a cursed isle.

Perhaps I had that one coming, she thought, and she shifted her legs with the same careful slowness until they reached the ground. She had to stop then, for the pain that surged up her legs was so aggressive and unexpected that she thought she would fall if she stood. So for the time being, Laila remained stationary and allowed her eyes to roam around her surroundings.

Dominus had left the fire going, and she could smell faint traces of pinecones amongst the crackling wood. She hugged her furs about her as she glanced around the dusty interiors. The house looked as though it had been long abandoned and only recently revived for use.

She wrinkled her nose, almost wishing she could've been placed in a grander setting to swoon in sickness, when the sound of the door opening snapped her out of her stupor.

Dominus's footsteps were heavy on the floorboards as he entered.

Laila listened as he walked into one room, dropping off a heavy load with a thud, and entered another; his steps grew louder in tandem with her hammering pulse. He stood before her in front of the stove, soaking in all the light that bled from the flames. The light stroked back and forth across his dusky skin and cast half of him in shadow.

She hadn't expected for him to rescue her, much less bring her to his dwellings. And now, met with the full extent of her vulnerability in his presence, she was even more uncertain of how to feel. She decided the best course of action was to make herself seem as meek as a kitten and hope he would take pity.

"Can you help me?" she asked, not caring if he would understand.

Dominus crouched before her and reached out his hand.

Laila stared at this outstretched lifeline, uncertain of where it would lead, but there was something about the stoicism in his expression that made her want to take the chance. She slid her hand into his, and he helped her stand. Her legs were shaking within moments, and she gripped onto his arm for balance; he felt steady as a marble pillar in her grip.

He took her into his arms after observing her discomfort, then carried her out of the lodge and up the stone pathway to a little house sitting on an incline. Dominus opened the door with his back and placed her on a wooden bench.

Laila looked around the room, seeing nothing but an iron stove and a row of herbs strung up on the wall by twine. Her eyes then met Dominus's as he gestured towards her slip, implying that it should be removed.

Laila regarded this with a slight nod, for it bothered her not for him to see her body. Nudity was a matter of pragmatism in Soleterea, and a solarite's body was one of their most versatile tools of expression, specifically built so they might indulge in pleasures of the flesh—food, sex, wine and all other sensual pursuits.

During their Kindling, when one crossed the threshold from starlet to solarite, they were able to build upon the foundations their mothers had first modelled—choosing how best they wanted to present their adult bodies. While many of them favoured the archetypal feminine silhouette, others desired to retain the slim hips and smooth chest of functional androgyny.

Laila had moulded ample curvature in her hips, thighs and breasts to replicate the holy statues of Asemani she had much aesthetically coveted: a shape capable of creating life itself and satisfyingly filling the hands of her lovers. She'd always seen pleasure as something to give as much as gain.

With her arms too weak to undress herself, she allowed Dominus to slip off her undergarments. He handled them with a delicacy she didn't think his hands were capable of as he hung them up by the stove. He barely appeared to look upon her; if anything it seemed he was looking *through* her—beneath the frail sheet of her skin to the blight blackening her veins.

He picked up a jar of salt from the shelf and uncapped it, crunching a handful of the crystals in his hand. The sight of it both intrigued and comforted her, for salt was how they warded against malevolent magic in her homeland. To see it had little effect on him was useful to note.

Dominus scattered the salt along her body until she was mostly covered. Then he added coal to the fire and filled the room with steam so oppressive Laila could hardly breathe from it. She allowed her lungs to stop struggling for shallow breaths, knowing she would suffice without them, and resisted the urge to shudder with every creepy-crawling trail of sweat travelling down her skin.

Dominus took off his clothes and wrapped himself in a towel. Then he sat beside her on the bench, his head reclined, eyes falling closed. For a time he remained so consistently still that she worried he had fallen asleep. But as the fire ran low, his eyes opened, and he lifted her up once again. He carried her over to a wooden tub in another room of the house, plunging her into the water.

"Oh my—" Laila choked in shock as Dominus dunked her head beneath the cold water. The water felt newly melted, glacial and clear, like it had been fetched from the sterile bowels of an iceberg. Pure water was another ward against dark magic where she was from, particularly when blessed. She resurfaced from her unholy baptism with a gasp of disgruntlement and discovered that the water had been sullied.

Laila lifted her arms in puzzlement to search for dirt, realising that it was her veins that had been disinfected. She turned her hands back and forth to examine the emerald fjords that had grown anew over the sickly black earthworm burrows.

Laila turned towards him in gratitude. "Thank you."

Dominus grunted, an evasive sound. He used a wooden bath spoon to wash through her hair and down her neck.

He took her out of the bath afterwards and whacked away whatever remnants of the infection were left with a birch branch. This part of the process was something she was less than familiar with, and Laila gritted her teeth in preparation for each blow as he struck down, feeling her body mending with every sweep of the leaves.

She plucked the branch from his hands when he was done and gestured until he showed her his back.

Their eyes met for an extended pause, but show her his back he did. She lifted the branch and lashed between his shoulder blades.

They retired back to the lodge, where she wrapped herself in the furs he gave her. Dominus poked and prodded at the dwindling fire and fed it new logs to burn.

He went into the kitchen next and unwrapped the seaweed from the lobsters, shrimp, and oysters he'd managed to pilfer along his excursion. He set a pot to boil on his stove, adding sprigs of dill, salt, dill seeds and beet sugar. He dropped the live lobster into the broth and watched it succumb to the heat before he removed it with a pair of tongs, adding the next.

Once both had been cooked and left to cool, he split them in two and gutted the claws for additional meat, arranging them into the shell. Then he smeared the meat with dill and chive butter.

The shrimp he arranged inside a glass filled with a sauce he'd prepared with his haphazard ingredients. The oysters he poached and garnished with pickled cucumber and roe.

He served them all on a platter of seaweed. The fruit of the underworld. The platter was served alongside glasses of tisane in a metal holder that he'd brewed from a samovar.

Laila sipped it, tasting mint, and set the glass over to one side. She tried not to question why the mint tasted so fresh or where he was able to get such large hauls of shellfish. She could recall seeing no gardens or villages here.

She took his glass of tisane and set it aside on the table before reaching for his neck. "I want to express my gratitude to you."

Dominus moved back in suspicion of another mind invasion, and she paused, her hands hovering just out of reach. Her eyes met his, the unspoken question left lingering.

She reached for him again, and he didn't pull back, didn't move away. She put her hands on his collar and murmured a few words of enchantment. The lock sprung open with a click, and she withdrew the collar and placed it on the table.

"You're free," she whispered, hopeful this gesture would establish trust and inspire further benevolence.

Dominus touched his newly bare neck in disbelief. Then he caught her hand and kissed the inside of her palm.

Laila giggled softly, allowing her hand to rest inside his. "Can I stay?"

She raised her hand to his cheek and shared the image of her request. Though not her original plan, she was no more eager to brave the wilderness having experienced a taste of what awaited. Léandre was sure to be following the link of their bond, and until they reconvened, she would make the best of her situation. At least here she had shelter, warmth, food and someone she could influence to provide a steady supply of all the above. Neither she nor her magic would last long without it.

Dominus nodded in understanding.

"Thank you." She smiled. Then she nestled against his chest and lifted one of the oysters from the tray to share with him.

XII

THE SKIES WERE LINED WITH SNOWFLAKES large as coins in the coming days, leaving increasingly bounteous piles on the ground below. Dominus spent two weeks nursing Laila back to full health under her instruction by keeping her wrapped up from the cold, placing her by the window at dusk to soak up twilight, and catching morning dew in bowls, which he heated to her liking. During this, they traded images between their minds.

Dominus showed her projections of his home in Malborg Citadel—a muddle of draughty halls, secret passageways, and time-worn walls infested with an overgrowth of ivy, submerged in a dim stagnation of candlelight. He showed her that he was a prince away from home, long absent after his fateful battle with the ice whale that led to his imprisonment. How he'd only ever seen the feasts and finery as four iron walls that he'd vacate for periods of pristine peace among the natural world, where he could live like his bestial ancestors.

Laila showed him projections of Soleterea—a land of wild strawberries and apple-green fields drenched in sunlight where not a single thing was unworthy of being touched. She showed him the gilt halls that she dominated with her coevals and the fountains where she snuck away to kiss sprite-maids. How she also was a princess eager to go home, away from the treacherous temperaments of this foreign land, where she could live like her celestial ancestors before her.

They showed each other this whilst entangled in the furs he had skinned from the hides of rare beasts, their bodies outlined in the red and orange glow of the fire as it coughed out purple smoke. Dominus would often provide her the warmth of his arms in these moments, but little else beyond that.

Her continued mental unions with him had allowed some of his language to seep through into her mind, and she hoped she'd be able to sustain it to get what she needed from him.

"Look," she said in Mortesian. She shared a series of images with him depicting the airship and the storm.

Dominus thought for some moments before he answered. His mind recognised the hue of the flames as coming from the stomach fuel of a draconid. He shared an image of the fuel being bottled and kept in the cellars of the Citadel.

"Your family?" She frowned in disbelief. "Why?"

"To remain hidden," he explained. "It's been the way of things for centuries. No one gets into Mortos, and no one goes out."

"So I cannot leave?" she exclaimed. The concept horrified her.

"I can send you home," he said, resting his hand on her cheek. "But for that... we will need to meet my father." He showed her an image of an occasso with a feral likeness to himself.

Laila shuddered before his image but kept it in her mind for the event Léandre would reunite with her.

⚬≈⚬

They went hunting in the mornings.

Dominus woke her early so they could trek through the vast oceanic snowdrifts. They continued onwards side by side until they found a hidden patch of paradisal green cradled deep in the bosom of the wood.

Laila couldn't believe what she was seeing. The snow seemed to halt abruptly at the glade's entrance, as though it had met the lip of a doorway and could venture no further.

"What is this place?" she asked.

Dominus shook the birds from his shoulders.

He would not often step foot so near to the Widowlands, but the blood sorceresses' spells ensured the grounds were kept fecund, and he knew he would find good elk here. Ones that had been fattened by black juniper and ripe cranberries. He'd eventually pay the necessary blood toll—twelve souls sacrificed for twelve days of access. A hefty price to be certain, but they knew he was always good for a bargain.

They found a shaggy-haired herd in the near distance, nostrils frothing with alertness. They were two-headed and sprouting mushrooms like cysts, a mutated distortion of their regular counterpart, like all else here.

Dominus crept through the wood with canines and claws exposed, hiding in the shadows. He would disappear entirely into the silhouette cast by one tree before he emerged in full again. He pounced on an elk like an animal, crunching its spine with a well-placed bite. He came away grinning, his beard stained with festive cranberry blood, hauling his prized catch over his arm like victory.

Laila liked the pursuit more than the catch. She liked to startle the herds into stillness, struck as they were by her like deer before any light, before they started running. They ran fast and hard, their little hearts clinging to the knife-edge of survival. Laila would skim close, nicking the back of their legs before she let them loose again.

Dominus caught another elk for her in response to her hesitation. She cradled the catch softly like a babe.

They brought both elk to the lodge and laid them out on tables. Dominus taught her how to skin and gut their kills and saw the antlers off. How to salt and treat the meat so it stayed fresh. First he gutted the elk, cleaned it, wrapped the offal in a bag for later. Then he stuffed the loins full of nuts and berries and rubbed a coating of honey on the skin.

He made sure they used all of it: the antlers for decoration, the skins for leather. That this was what was fair.

She still could not get used to the blood on her hands.

They practised craft in the evenings.

Laila took up sewing by the fireplace, using the pelts of the beasts Dominus had slaughtered to create hunting gloves and stockings embroidered with flowers, berries and thorns.

The needles were dotted with her ichor, golden as honey.

Afterwards, she would stay in the sauna for hours and imagine herself back in Soleterean heat. She rubbed peppermint oil on her braids and scalp, allowing the steam to treat it until she emerged glossy and refreshed. She ran a stiff brush over her scalp, used beeswax to combat dryness and taught Dominus how to do the same. Then she oiled his beard and placed winter blossoms in it for decoration.

Dominus gathered the charcoal left from the fire and forged a stylus out of it. He drew her several times, capturing the images she sent him through projections. Then he would make sbiten with the lingonberries he had gathered from the Widowlands so she could have a taste of summer.

The glasses were smudged by his fingertips, black as char.

They cleared a space in the lodge to display them all: her stockings hanging on the doors, his drawings on the mantelpiece. Laila adjusted the curtains to let in the light, started to smile often and laugh even more. Her laughter banished the cobwebs from the corners, brought the sweet robins back to the branches. She and Dominus awoke to birdsong and fell asleep tracing the constellations she taught him in the stars.

He still could not get used to the flowers in his beard.

Then one frosted morning, after a new snow powdered the earth, two visitors arrived.

They moved like sylphs through the snow, just as pale and near as translucent. Lyra led the charge while Léandre remained vigilant behind her. They were all that remained of the original party, having lost all others to the ruthlessness of the country's flora and fauna.

When they approached the lodge, Lyra took out her lightning rifle and loaded its first five charges.

"This is the one," she told her uncle, pumping the rifle for action.

Léandre glanced sceptically at her weapon. "I would caution against charging in with arms ablaze, Lyra. At least not until we've had a moment to assess our surroundings."

"I respect your counsel, uncle," Lyra said, readying her engraved silver rifle for action. Dangling from it were the canines of the last beast she'd slaughtered. "But I'm not taking any chances."

Léandre sighed heavily in relent. He knew better than to talk his niece down when she was in the midst of a hunt with blood still fresh on her nostrils. He only hoped an altercation wouldn't reap the worst results.

"Cover me," Lyra said, and before a word of protest could be spoken, she'd marched over the porch and taken the door down with one swift kick from her boot. She entered rifle-first, her eyes sweeping across the room in search of targets and finding none.

"Laila?" Lyra's boots creaked the floorboards as she entered the kitchen and then the living area. The rooms were dotted with small signs of occupancy: stained glasses in the sink, a dwindling fire, a basket of unfinished knitting.

The knitting was what Léandre had paid particular attention to, raising one of the scarves in progress and feeling his way along the pattern of stitches. He'd recognise the delicacy and precision of Laila's hand anywhere.

"They've been here."

"But they're not here now." Lyra lowered her rifle in disgruntlement.

That was when she heard it. Laughter. Airy and enigmatic. Coming from far beyond the walls.

"Did you hear that?" Léandre asked, his chest rising in hope.

Lyra nodded and vacated the lodge in pursuit of the enchanting melody. The vapour of mirth grew louder, enticingly remote and yet soothingly near.

The sound led from beyond the rooftop of the lodge to the clearing up ahead, where Laila and Dominus were at play.

Laila chased Dominus over the snow, beneath the spikes of icicle-pronged branches. She scooped up a ball of snow and tossed it at his head, watching it explode into icy cinders.

Dominus responded to her with a slow, menacing pivot as he

scooped up much larger balls in his hands and chucked them with alarming speed.

Laila dodged them with her lightspeed, tossing another ball, and soon they were in full-scale battle, chasing each other around the ice-glazed grounds. Her laughter decanted sweetly in the air like a vintage.

Eventually, Dominus tackled her to the ground and kept her pinned with his brutish strength. Laila squealed and squirmed beneath him as Dominus bared his fangs and made play that he was going to bite her.

It was at this unfortunate moment that Lyra intruded upon the scene and, in seeing their compromising positions, abandoned all prior knowledge of the laughter she had trailed. All she saw was a monster lunging at her mistress, and the method to act accordingly weighed heavy in her hand. So she raised her rifle, lined the shot in sight, and fired.

Laila screamed as a bolt of lightning speared Dominus through the chest.

The shot sent him staggering into the snow where he flailed and convulsed before going entirely still.

Laila sped to his aid immediately, taking his face carefully in her hands and checking his pulse before sighing in relief when she felt it thrumming. Then she turned in the direction of the assailant with her body humming like a livewire, enough voltage going through her to shock, scald and subdue. Her furrowed brow softened upon sight of Lyra, rifle still at the ready to implement another debilitating shot.

"No, wait!" Laila cried, launching herself into Lyra's path, as much for her own safety as for Dominus's. "Stop! I order you to stop!"

"Laila..." Lyra's eyes were wary and uncertain. As a forest sprite, a steward of nature, it was her divine duty to dispose of monsters, and here her mistress was telling her to spare one. "Step out of the way."

"He saved me," Laila said, as though she could condense the past two weeks into one easily digestible phrase. She turned and made her way towards Dominus.

He had overcome the initial shock of his attack and was now growling, his features grotesque. How did one reason with a beast when all they saw was raw flesh shambling towards them?

Laila cupped his face in her hands.

His snarl only deepened, his upper lip curling back to display more of its piercing gleam.

"It's all right," she soothed, then she turned back to Lyra. "Lower your weapon."

Lyra sneered back at Dominus, her expression no less fierce, but she obliged.

Léandre came running into the fray shortly after, his own rifle raised. "I heard a shot fire."

"We're all right here," Laila assured him as she helped Dominus to his feet. She dusted his clothes of snow. "Everything is fine."

She walked towards Léandre and flung her arms around his neck, taking a moment to inhale his familiar scent before she embraced Lyra. "It's good to see you both." She exhaled in relief, then looked around. "What happened to the others?"

Léandre could only gravely shake his head.

Laila ushered them all into the lodge for warmth and hot sbiten, which Dominus brewed and served without a word.

Léandre explained the fall of his comrades along their journey. They gave them shallow graves due to the ice and filled their mouths with nuts they'd scavenged as currency to pay the gatekeeper of the Astral Realm.

138

"May their spirits have a safe ascent." Laila recited the common sprite condolence, squeezing Léandre's hand in comfort.

Lyra had not taken her eyes from Dominus since she'd sat. The tension between them was taut as a wire waiting to snap. "The only question is, what do we do now?"

"I propose we abandon the mission, leave this place," Léandre said. "We can tell Dr Isuka our search was sadly unsuccessful."

Laila shook her head. "We can't leave."

"What do you mean, *can't*?" Lyra's eyes narrowed in suspicion.

"Princess, I must beg you to see reason. This land is too dangerous. I think our numbers are more than proof of that." Léandre's face softened. "I'm sorry to say it, but every sign indicates that the *Great Northern*—and everyone aboard it—has long perished."

"That's not what I mean." Laila sighed, then took a sip of her sbiten to offset the bitterness of her next words. "While you were searching for me, Dominus and I grew closer. He shared things with me. Personal things. Bits and pieces of his past." She lifted her glass for another sip. "It turns out that he is not only an occasso, but also of royal blood. A prince. He also told me that the storm was not a natural occurrence. It was orchestrated to destroy our ship, as is practice for anyone who enters their territory."

"So we came all this way only to have it confirmed that the *Great Northern* has almost certainly wrecked." Lyra palmed her forehead as she shook her head gravely. "Well, wasn't this an utter waste of time."

"It may not have been," Laila said.

"And how do you figure that?"

"Because with Dominus by our side, we have an opening here. To negotiate. I believe he might be exactly what we need to grant us further immunity from harm."

"And you honestly believe you can trust him?" Lyra snorted in disgust. "Uncle, are you hearing this nonsense?"

"I have been with him for weeks, and he has never once harmed me," Laila replied tersely. "Don't you think if that was his intent, I would already be dead? We have an opportunity to broker an alliance here, and Dominus is our insurance. We would be foolish to waste this chance."

Lyra scoffed and vacated the room in distaste.

"Give her time," Léandre said.

"So you believe me?" Laila asked, hopeful.

Léandre cast a glance at Dominus. "I believe he has had ample opportunity to turn on us and hasn't. That isn't to say I trust him, princess. But I am willing to follow your lead."

"Thank you, Léandre." Laila heaved a sigh, reaching forward to kiss his cheek.

She turned to Dominus next to rest her hand on his cheek and project the image of the Citadel.

He glanced up at her in silence. Then he uttered the first word he'd ever spoken in her tongue: "Come."

He led them down to a village in the distance.

It was a small, somnolent place tucked into a cliffside, populated by coastal docks and broad-shouldered wolf-women carrying nets of squirming fish. These were the last dregs of the lupari tribes, pushed out to the coasts after almost being stamped from existence during the occassi's brutal conquest. The sight of their shaggy hair and lupine features put the sprites on alert. Lyra kept her hand on the butt of her rifle.

One of the lupare dropped her net the moment she saw Dominus, a stark fear causing her canine snout to froth as she descended to her knees in deference. She spoke rapidly in a language Laila still couldn't quite decipher, but it sounded like she was pleading with him.

Dominus didn't budge from his austere stance; he was broad as an oak and seemed just as unrootable. He spoke a few subtle words and commanded the lupara to her feet. They exchanged more complete sentences before she pointed in the direction of an inn with one shaky, knobbled claw: *The Rex's Arms*.

Dominus nodded to her in gratitude and then gestured for the others to follow him.

The debossed wooden sign of the inn whined and creaked in the winter wind as Dominus shoved open the door partially ossified by frost. It cracked open like the seal of a bottle top and allowed a raucous fizzle of noise and laughter to burble through the doorway.

The slickness of slush-soaked wood greeted their boots as they entered. Dominus allowed that to tinge his judgement for the rest of his establishment, though the interior showed much the same meticulous skill of Mortesian architecture. Spinal arches bridged the way between the grim figurines that appeared to be lurking from inside the walls.

Laila's eyes swept across the room in fascination, having never before seen interiors quite like this. The furniture, along with the architecture itself, looked carved from bone. She felt as though she were standing in the stomach of something ancient.

The moment they entered, another white-haired lupara behind the countertop dropped her ale mug in surprise.

"Oh!" She quickly wiped down her furry paws on her apron and hobbled out towards Dominus. "W-welcome, good sir." She made a slight dip on her crooked knee. "What an honour it is to have such a magnificent creature patronise our establishment. W-what is it that I may do you for today? Could I fix you a room?"

"She's terrified of him," Lyra whispered in her uncle's ear, though she couldn't decipher what was being said. She let her guarded stance relax, remorseful that she could say nothing to ease the creature's mind.

"That won't be necessary," Dominus replied, pulling on the edge of his glove. "What I require from you is merely transportation. I notice you have a hippogriff stable out back. I would like to relieve you of them. Carriage included."

"O-oh," the innkeeper replied, snout flexing and ears peeled back. "That's quite a request, sir. It's only—"

"Will there be a problem?" Dominus asked.

The innkeeper swallowed hard. One never refused a request from an occasso and lived to tell it after. That had been a creed long passed from mother to babe, and she wasn't about to be the first to tempt her fate. "Not at all, sir. Please make yourself comfortable and I'll—I'll speak to my mate."

"But of course," Dominus said, a smile ghosting across his lips.

Laila observed the interaction with unease. It was as though the kindly creature who, with such care and attentiveness, had aided her survival through this unforgiving wilderness had vanished and the shadow of the brute in the padded cell had stepped into his place.

But as soon as she'd thought to mourn his departure, he turned to her with all the sharpness in his features blunted. With an arm outstretched, he led her to one of the nearby booths and pulled out a seat for her.

She accepted, hoping this more domesticated version of him was one she could maintain. He might be her sole chance of escape, and she wasn't about to squander it.

Dominus picked up one of the menus on the table to peruse it. "Oh, and bitch?"

Laila flinched.

The innkeeper halted immediately in her tracks. "Yes?"

Dominus reclined in his seat with the imposing spread of someone who believed every square inch of space was his to invade. "I'll desire a couple bowls of your ukha. And some mead."

"Of course, sir. Coming right up."

XIII

 ATERINA COLLAPSED AGAINST THE BED in exhaustion, a sheen of sweat clinging to her skin. She looked like a sea creature swept ashore, her dark hair plastered down like seaweed. "Mm, I needed that."

Darius rose from between the shores of her thighs with a shark-toothed grin. "Happy to be of service." He licked his lips, savouring the faint traces of her salt as he kissed a trail along her jaw. "Now how about we get to the part where you tell me why you're really here?"

"I would've thought the past hour would've informed you of that, Dara," Katerina replied through lips swollen and red, trailing wicked black claws along his sculptural back. "And here I thought you were a learned occasso."

Darius caught her wrist in his grip and brought it to rest softly against his lips. "As much as I'd love to flatter myself that you're merely here for the pleasure of my company alone, you forget I know you better than that by now." He reached over to help himself to the decanter of Mort whisky on the bedside table and poured two glasses. "So come on, out with it."

Katerina sighed heavily with an insouciant roll of her eyes. Then she rolled onto her side, her nude silhouette obscured by the seafoam of sheets. "You'll never guess who recently came knocking on the outskirts of the Widowlands."

"Enlighten me."

Katerina snatched her glass from him with a smirk before taking a lengthy sip. She ran her tongue over her lips as she held the glass, expectant.

Darius released a soft exhale of laughter before he shook his head. "Does his name start with an A?"

"You're close." Katerina's eyes, amber as her whisky, were alight with mirth that he'd conceded to play her game. "It was none other than your dear lost brother, Dominus."

Darius halted stiffly before his glass could reach his lips. It wasn't often someone shocked him, and he was eager not to display it. He lowered his glass with another smile. "That's very amusing, Katya. But come now, who was it really?"

"Oh, I'm quite serious." Katerina bit her lip, ever the brazen minx, but her eyes betrayed no sign of falsity.

"Katya, you can't honestly be implying—" Darius trailed off, struggling to infuse the same careless flirtation in his voice to dull the edge of panic. "I mean my brother, he's—"

"Clearly no longer missing." Katerina clinked her glass with his. "And what splendid news indeed. I'm sure your father will be thrilled."

Darius forced a swallow through a throat tightly clenched. "Well, now. Isn't that something? Unfortunately, I'm afraid this means I will have to bring this rendezvous to a premature end."

"I've upset you," Katerina pouted, head tilted to one side. And part of him had to wonder if that hadn't indeed been her intent.

"Not at all," Darius said as he shrugged on his shirt.

"Dara," Katerina sighed, draping her hands along his chest to undo the buttons he'd fastened. "Come now, I hadn't meant to ruin the mood. Let me take your mind off of it."

"Katya." Darius's reply was terse as he detached her arms from him. "You've been lovely, but it's time for you to go."

Katerina extended her bottom lip in displeasure once more, but the message was received. She began rummaging for her undergarments on the bedroom floor. Then she sought the glint of the golden talisman that decorated her sorceress frock and slipped it on, reaching to clasp the belt.

Darius's hands were on hers before she could do so, and she let him fasten her frock just as deftly as he'd originally discarded it. Then she pivoted round to peck Darius on the lips. "You know where to find me." She stepped past him towards the door before she stopped, remembering something. "Your mother sends her regards."

And with the flicker of a feline smile, she vanished out the door.

Darius took off from the room shortly after her once he'd dressed, an unyielding linearity in his trek towards the Observatory. Once past the hidden doorway, he conquered the steps three at a time until he reached the centre of the room and the obsidian ball that lay within.

It had been five years since he'd seen hide or hair of Dominus. A mere blink of an eye in his centuries-long lifetime, to be certain, but significant enough to infer this wasn't another in a long line of his spontaneous woodland recesses before he came slinking back to court.

The last Darius had seen of him, he'd been high on hubris in the dining hall, belting out how he would be the first to capture the elusive ice whale. It had been a fool's errand, and Darius had told him as much, but there was no dissuading Dominus once he'd gained a craving for a kill. And so, with deep disapproval, Darius had seen him off at the gates, and that had been the last of that.

His last knowledge of his brother's whereabouts had been taken from his obsidian ball, in which he saw Dominus as a block of ice lost at sea, his prediction confirmed. Though rather than gloat about his foresight, Darius had instead quietly concealed the intelligence from all interested parties. Not that there were many.

To say Darius hadn't been spending the last lustrum in a tumult of never-ending guilt and despair would, therefore, be quite the understatement. In truth, Dominus rearing his head couldn't have come at a more inconvenient time for his plans. His arrival threatened to ruin all the meticulous schemes Darius had carefully drafted in his absence, leading him upwards from the doldrums of the castle basement to a much more elevated seat.

What was he to do?

Darius tented his fingers and pressed them to his lips, stepping forward to loom over the obsidian ball with his request. "All-seeing eye, I command you to show me where my brother now resides."

The orb glowed and projected above it a sight Darius recognised as the rugged outskirts of a coastal village.

There he saw Dominus exiting an inn. He tossed a silver coin towards the driver of a hippogriff carriage and climbed inside. It'd be impossible to mistake his monumental build for another, and yet there was something about seeing him so definitively that took Darius aback.

"Already homeward-bound, are you, brother dear?" Darius asked, stroking his chin between his thumb and fingers.

He was not alone, it appeared. Others Darius didn't recognise were coming along with him. Two fair-haired individuals of near identical builds were climbing into the carriage. They weren't like anything Darius had ever seen before, gallant and pale as a pearlescent pillar in the daylight. They could almost be twins, with their translucent hair and delicate features.

But the first of his brother's companions were only half the spectacle of what awaited him. He saw the glow of her first, spilling her soft candlelit residue onto the threshold of the inn. The golden girl appeared next, a halo of curls teasing her shoulders.

Darius stopped to wonder if she was some form of vision, but he found his throat sapped of air and moisture when he motioned to speak, as though he'd been exposed to the naked heat of the desert. He could even feel, with some confusion, the cool pinprick of sweat forming.

"Get a hold of yourself, Darius," he scolded, shaking himself free of his stupor. Still, his gaze snapped like a metal to her magnet, to her curvaceous figure as she embraced Dominus outside the carriage doors.

Laila stared out the window of her carriage, clearing the fog from the glass so she might look upon this haunted city. The buildings leered at her as she passed, sharp-edged towers carved with dour faces—a dead echo of activity.

Gravissia was a labyrinth—all spindly structures and constricting venous walls that bled a fiendish orange glow, needle-pointed roofs sharp against the molten red skyline. The occassi seemed to build their cities as though they were aiming for the heavens, seeking to pluck the stars free and grind them to dust beneath their heels.

Laila could barely comprehend this hybrid of ancient and alien. Everything was suffocated beneath a blanket of snow, even the gargoyles. The flakes clogged the streets and the gutters, deteriorating into liquefying slush befouled by filth.

Even with her window cleared, the atmosphere was curtained by a dank fog. It seemed in Mortos, even the air could be toxic—it wouldn't harm her, but it didn't make the place pleasant.

She observed several Mortesians lumbering through the cobbled streets. They wore their stoicism like an enamel coating on their already chiselled visages. A few stared at her as she passed, an amalgam of wary hostility in their eyes. Laila wasn't certain if their ire was directed more towards herself or her carriage; either way, it made her feel as frail as brittle porcelain.

"Are you all right?" Léandre asked as he took her trembling hand. He was the anchor that kept her moored from the asphyxiating ocean of her neurosis. Lyra seemed far more concerned with polishing her rifle.

"Yes, I can do this," Laila replied, fighting to keep her breaths from shallowing. She would not be conquered. She would not be overcome. She would face down her fears with the same unflinching valour she always had.

On the opposite end of the spectrum was Dominus, who embraced his surroundings with a quiet sense of nostalgia. Part of him wished he could've postponed this a little longer, staying lost in the depths of the wilderness with Laila in a world of their own design. Such things were children's fantasies. He knew the call to duty would inevitably come knocking and that he wouldn't be able to resist when it came. He could only hope, when he stood before the rex once more, that it would be the relief of a father he would be met with rather than the wrath of a monarch.

The silhouette of Malborg Citadel loomed through the pea-soup fog, a foreboding emblem. Its structure seemed to melt down the slope like wax from a spilt candle.

When they reached the tall bronze gates and saw the figures writhing within the lacquered metal in spiritual anguish, Laila's breaths grew painful. The tide had risen, evicting the air from her lungs with prejudice, keeping her limbs submerged.

The gates opened into the courtyard, where an entourage of servants awaited to greet them. They were all animated flesh, walking expiry, and they moved with startling dexterity to open the doors, their putrid visages nightmare-inducing with rotting flaps of flesh and calligraphic gnarls of antlers jutting from their heads.

"We've been expected," Dominus observed, one brow arched. Of course, he'd anticipated that Darius would foresee him coming long before he arrived. He'd never been one to miss a mark.

"Laila?" Léandre was looking at her calmly.

"I can't move," she said, for her limbs had calcified to the spot. Her eyes widened in panic, moving frantically. "Help me."

Léandre took out an amethyst amulet and fastened it around her neck. He pressed the gemstone to the pulse point between her breasts and allowed it to infuse her with its calming essence.

"You're okay, princess," he assured her, his hand soft on her curls. "You're okay." Léandre soothed her with gossamer strokes, murmuring sweet words in her ear until her rigid limbs softened and the rising tidal wave of nerves subsided.

Lyra couldn't help but sigh. It vexed her sometimes, how coddled Laila was. She'd faced worse horrors alone since she'd taken her oaths.

Dominus was the first to exit the carriage, stepping out into the open air with a deep breath.

"Welcome home, Your Mightiness." A ghoul stepped forward to greet him with worn and weathered vocals. "His Majesty awaits you."

Laila wondered who he was before he came to this fate, what his soul might think of his current state. Necromancy had always been a forbidden art in Vysteria, and gruesome besides.

"Igor." Dominus returned the greeting with a nod. "My father has been expecting me already?"

"Oh yes," the ghoul confirmed. "And Her Highness has been especially eager."

Dominus couldn't help the shift in his chest at the mention of his mother. It would be good to see her again. "Well, then. Lead the way."

The ghoul folded his hands behind his back and turned in the direction of the Citadel. His dead coevals soon joined him.

"I don't like this country," Lyra said in a whispered undertone of Soltongue. "The land is strange and unnatural; the earth is dead, but the buildings roar with life."

Laila couldn't help but nod in agreement.

"Corpses," Lyra sighed in disgust. "They use corpses as their serving force. We all know the rightful place for a cadaver is in the soil. To see one before me now, talking, walking, or at least making a good show of it—"

"Lyra," Laila interrupted, "I understand this world is foreign to you, but I must strongly advise you to disguise your attitude from here on. Let us not forget we are guests here."

At that moment, Dominus turned back towards the carriage and gestured for them to follow.

Laila took Dominus's hand as he helped her down to the splintered ground. It felt warm beneath her feet, even through her boots—perhaps one of the most disorienting parts of Mortos. The land beneath them was a dormant inferno, a thousand dozing volcanoes poised to erupt.

The hall was like a gaping maw, spanned with a tongue of red velvet. Laila nestled close to Dominus as waves of moist, sweltering air rattled over them at regular intervals. She took in the skeletal beams of vaulted ceiling suspended from above, stretched taut like the spine of some prehistoric beast. The mere sight of it had dread inflaming the back of her throat like the afterburn of whisky.

The audience room was lacquered in ivory, walls of tusks and teeth so white they induced a chill at the sight of them. Alabaster pillars shouldered the pearl vault ceiling, glittering chunks of black diamond running through their veins.

Lanius Rex was waiting on a dais of preserved skulls, onyx and garnets gleaming in their eye sockets. His throne was just as macabre, and yet he reclined upon it comfortably as though the seat were made of silk or velvet, and not the skeletal remains of past adversaries.

It was an image fit to fill the contents of nightmares, to jumpstart a heart to acceleration. Dominus could indeed feel his heart peak with alarm when met with the sheer majesty of his father's presence. Yet only reverence, rather than fear, could be seen in his eyes as he stood before the rex and knelt.

"Hello, Papa." He bent the knee as low as his station required him. He was a wolf tamed, a humbleness compressing his giant shoulders into something more tractable.

"You may rise, my son," Lanius said. Then slowly he stood up from his throne and descended the few steps with his arms outstretched. "Ah, let me look at you." He took Dominus's face in his hands with a chuckle. "My boy." At his height, Lanius somewhat had to stretch to reach his son, but he still laid claim upon him with an overbearing possession.

"Never a day has passed where I didn't pray Calante would return you to my side."

"It's good to see you too, Papochka," Dominus replied with a warmth of good humour in his voice. "It's been a moment."

"Indeed it has." Lanius stepped back to observe, with an imperious stare, the others who stood behind him. "And who might be the individuals you present before me?"

"These are my saviours and my favoured guests." Dominus beckoned Laila near. "If I might introduce to you Laila Rose, Crown Princess of Soleterea and Espriterre."

Laila kept her curtsey light.

"Well, well," Lanius said, his eyes growing so ferocious in response that Laila immediately stepped back. A prey instinct. "My boy disappears for a lustrum and brings himself home a foreign princess, does he? Well, then. Any saviour of yours is a welcome guest here. I shall have the ghouls arrange rooms for this Princess Laila, and then you can explain to me more of your adventures in the drawing room."

Lanius snapped his fingers to beckon a ghoul to action. "Ravenna, please escort our newest guest to the regina's wing." He stopped to glance over Laila's garb. "And find her a suitable gown so she may join us for dinner tonight."

"Yes, Your Majesty." The ghoul bobbed her head in deference and turned to Laila's entourage. "Follow me, princess."

Laila dithered at the ghoul's words, playing the fool at comprehension. Her knowledge of Mortesian was still intermediate at best, but she decided to conceal even her minor understanding for now.

"It's all right," Dominus said in a clumsy attempt at mimicking her Soltongue. He made a gesture towards the rooms upstairs and Laila's clothes.

"All right." Laila nodded in understanding. It would be good to see herself out of these winter garbs and into a hot bath. And a room would provide her the privacy she needed. She hoped the amenities here would be adequate. "I'll see you soon."

"See you soon," Dominus replied.

She held his gaze as the ghoul led her away.

XIV

ANIUS HAD ARRANGED A FEAST to be laid out for his bronze warrior's homecoming. The hall was decorous and darkly opulent, with polished granite and ornamental moulding chiselled from brass. Under typical circumstances, there would have been an array of meats put on display until the table was overflowing—a few whole chickens, a suckling pig, several haunches of venison.

However, winter had dwindled them down to a more modest offering: hot blood soup served with onion and flecks of putrid cheese, marrow roasted soft in its bone and smeared with chive butter and a dollop of caviar. The main course had been Lanius's own personal quip at his son's expense—braised hearts from a whale, carefully stuffed with mushrooms, truffles, and fatty goose liver.

The meal had come from Darius's own private deal with the Vidua

Nocte and cost him several pounds of flesh. But with the winter being what it was, there were more than enough starving qarna willing to throw themselves beneath the sacrificial blade. And if not themselves, then they'd as soon offer their sons.

Darius helped himself to an appetiser of blini topped with lox and caviar, directing a ghoul to pour him graviji wine while he sat on a velvet chair.

Vasilisa Regina, his father's bride, sat on Lanius's other side. She was festive in a cranberry red letnik with silver-embroidered lilies to match her elaborate kokoshnik—the traditional headdress she wore. She remained poised like a wax sculpture in a mausoleum, mummified through age, for it was an age she had waited for her beloved son to return to her.

There was a link missing from their royal chain, one Darius could never mould himself to fit. It was as if he were manufactured of different metal than their regal steel. A crude iron, more earthly and common.

Dominus announced himself like thunder, the floorboards rocking with his powerful footsteps moments before he arrived.

Vasilisa was up in a blur to embrace her son.

Dominus lifted her into the air with his bearish embrace, his hold so tight on her he might have cracked her spine were she mortal.

"Welcome home, my son," Vasilisa cried once she'd descended, pinching his cleft chin in her pincer grip.

"Don't crowd the boy, Vasilka," Lanius scolded, appearing immediately after.

Vasilisa folded herself inwards like a fan, stepping obediently to one side with her head bowed.

Dominus turned to his brother next, with his head slightly bent. This was by far the reunion he seemed most nervous about. "Dara."

"It's been a while, little brother," Darius said, a wry smile on his lips.

156

He raised his wine goblet in salute. "Not to worry, I'll withhold my 'I told you so' for a later date."

Dominus chuckled. "Very gracious of you."

"Well now, I want to hear all about your exploits." Vasilisa tugged firmly on her son's shoulder so he might be seated beside her. "Tell me everything."

The ghouls served them wine as Dominus informed them all of his thwarted battle with the ice whale and subsequent icy imprisonment, and then his rescue by a mysterious princess who was to join them shortly. An enigmatic beauty of sunlit hair and evening-violet eyes plucked ripe from the heavens. Even her name seemed to cause Dominus's eyes to become stricken with stars as he spoke it.

Throughout it all, Vasilisa was utterly riveted by him—enthralled with the sort of encompassing adoration only a mother could provide.

Darius watched them the way someone looked at anything as foreign and unfamiliar as a maternal bond was to him: with a soft and subtle perplexity. He'd never had this side of Vasilisa or anything other than the requisite words of cordiality.

Seated all on one side of the table with his father at the end, they were a chain once more linked. While Darius was the ill-fitting spare cast over on the other end, like always.

He took another sip from his wine goblet. "So, just to reiterate, you and this mysterious maiden of yours arrived here how, precisely?"

"By flying ship," Dominus said, stuffing himself with black bread. "And what a magnificent skycraft it was, Dara. I only wish you could've boarded it for yourself. Well, until it was destroyed by a storm, that is."

"Hm, indeed," Darius said, swirling his wine goblet. He could sense the burn of his father's stare upon the realisation of the ship they spoke of and he knew this wouldn't be the last he'd heard of it for the evening. "Such a shame."

"Though I'm sure you know all about that already, don't you?"

Vasilisa glanced nervously between her husband's sons. "Oh, come now, you two. Let's not quarrel."

"Yes, you know well enough what customs we have for trespassers, Doma," Lanius reminded him, his expression stern. "I am willing to make an exception for your little princess, for now. But we shall have to discuss how we are to... handle this, going forward."

"Papa, I beseech you," Dominus said, and never before had such a tenderness splintered through his rock-solid austerity before the arrival of that girl. "Laila is my guest, and it would please me to claim her under my protection. I must ask that you do not harm her."

"Hm," Lanius said.

"Please, Lanius," Vasilisa asked, reaching out to cover his hand with her own. "Show mercy to the girl. I am sure there ought to be some arrangement we can make for the event she returns home. A vow of secrecy perhaps. Or a spell to alter her memories."

"Or we could treat with her," Darius suggested. "See what her country has to offer."

"We require nothing from her realm," Lanius retorted sharply.

Darius kept his expression perfectly neutral. "Still, it wouldn't hurt to explore..."

"Say, where is this new maiden of yours?" Vasilisa asked, abruptly steering the conversation away from the inevitable fracas. "I'd quite like to meet her."

"Still getting ready, I'd gather," Dominus said, withdrawing his seat from the table. "Shall I go fetch her?"

"No need," Darius said, standing before he could. "I'll do the honours."

"You?" Dominus's eyes narrowed.

"Something tells me she'll appreciate one who can speak her language," Darius replied in Soltongue. Then he waggled his brows.

Laila rose from the stone pool with her body dancing with wisps of steam. Rather than bathtubs, the washrooms in the Citadel consisted mainly of hot springs situated in the floors that continually filled and drained themselves.

She had soaked in the water for an age and emerged like an orange skinned of its rind: soft, stark, and rosy with warmth. She wrapped herself in a towel and wrung out her wet hair, feeling much lighter than she had when she went into the water, as though some intangible weight had melted off her back from the steam.

Turning back towards where she'd left her clothes, she rummaged in her boot for the vial of moonwater she'd kept hidden throughout the journey, then picked up a clay basin left near the pool.

She uncapped the vial and filled the bowl with moonwater, watching the liquid affect a reflective silver quality. Softly, she performed a chant and hovered with her hands over the water until it solidified into glass. She removed the glass and lifted it up to her face, observing her damp reflection in her newly crafted mirror.

"Amira Rose," she said.

The mirror gleamed once before her reflection was replaced by the face of her mother.

"Well, it's about time I heard from you," Amira said.

Laila couldn't help but cry out in relief at the sight of her. Not even her mother's formal disposition could counter the elation she felt. "Oh, you don't know how glad I am to see your face." She traced her fingers along the outline of her mother's high-boned cheek.

"Yes, that's very nice, aurore," her mother sighed, "and I am glad to see you still in one piece. Though one would hope you would have something more substantial to contact me about?"

"Yes, yes, I—" Laila nodded her head frantically. "Maman, I've found it. I have found Mortus. The isle of myth is indeed a reality." She bit her lip to conceal her squeal of delight as she bounced on her feet. Before she knew it, she had gushed the entirety of her journey up to the airship crash and beyond while her mother listened intently.

"Dominus a prince? Now that I hadn't been expecting." Amira's lips scrunched to one side. "Still, it is unfortunate about *The Stellaria*; I had been hoping we would've been spared that loss. Are you at least still in the safety of your Lightshields?"

"Yes, Ser Lyra and Léandre are with me and—"

"That's good. I'd advise you to stay vigilant while in the company of these creatures, Laila. At least until we are able to ascertain their true nature," Amira said. "And what of the *Great Northern*?"

"Eliminated," Laila sighed. "Dominus all but confirmed it."

"Yes, what you tell me about how they treat foreign vessels is... concerning to say the least. We shall have to tread carefully in the event we travel there."

"T-travel there?" Laila stammered before coaching herself back to eloquence. "I don't understand."

"I've been having talks with the archwitch of Odaka and we agree that, in the interest of preserving our safety, we ought to look further into these creatures and assess their level of threat. For that reason, I'm going to invest in more funding for the northern expedition."

"You can't possibly be considering sending more people here after everything I've informed you of? Maman, what are you *thinking*?"

"I'm thinking you have wandered right into uncharted territory

160

with exposure to a threat that may endanger us all. I'm thinking I ought to gain the upper hand of this situation before it has surpassed me."

"Maman, the last thing we need is for you to establish hostile contact. Allow me to pave the way first by acting as an ambassador on Soleterea's behalf. I guarantee you I can create an amicable relationship with this country through the crown prince himself."

Her mother stared at her for some moments, her eyes narrowing.

Laila bent her head low in deference. She knew what her mother was, after all: an empty beach of sand where no footprint lingered, a thick bramble of roses no blade could penetrate. Something so unbreachable, so unconquerable, that to even entertain the idea merely exposed the height of one's vanity.

"Fine, I will arrange for you to travel once we've established peaceful contact. But I will remind you, Laila, that being my successor is a privilege, not a given. Should you prove yourself unworthy in the eyes of the Elders, I could just as easily remove you and convene with them to select another. Do you understand?"

Laila swallowed thickly. "I promise you, Maman, I will not let you down."

"See to it that you don't."

The transmission ended, leaving behind only Laila's reflection. She sighed as she hid the mirror among her clothes and then emerged into the bedroom.

Awaiting her on the bed was a peach-coloured frock embroidered with a spray of pearls, and a matching kokoshnik. Laila slid her hands along the material, admiring its cloud-like texture, soft as dandelion down.

"The ghoul left it," Lyra said from behind her. "I had them sent away while you bathed, as I gathered you wouldn't be partial to having them dress you. May I?" She gestured towards the garment.

"Of course," Laila said, removing her towel to put on her undergarments first. She let Lyra help her into the letnik and weave her hair into a Soleterean braid before the kokoshnik was fastened over the top.

She found herself mourning the extensive collection of her toiletries set aflame on *The Stellaria*. Her skin felt conspicuously dry without her cocoa butter. And while she could take advantage of the current damp state of her hair, she knew she would regret the neglect of moisturising in the future when the frizz had time to set in.

"Well?" Lyra asked, awaiting her verdict.

Laila twisted to and fro in front of the mirror with a sigh. "It will have to do." She adjusted her braid. "Where's your uncle?"

"They won't permit an unrelated male into the wing, so he's standing guard elsewhere."

"All right." Laila nodded in response. "I managed to make contact with my mother."

"And?" Lyra raised a brow.

"She has agreed to let me lead for now, but I doubt I will be able to keep her placated for long unless I make fast progress."

"And you're sure Dominus can be trusted to vouch for your safety?"

"Of course he can; he's infatuated with me." Laila adjusted the position of her kokoshnik. Then she held out her arm, head tilted playfully. "Now, join me for dinner?"

Lyra glanced down at it with a smile before she slung her arm through Laila's crooked elbow.

Laila fastened their arms together and rested her hand on Lyra's. "So how long do you think we have before they'll come calling on me?"

"Why do you ask?"

"Because I intend to have a little look around." Laila grinned, then turned towards the door.

Lyra sighed heavily. "Of course."

⌒∞⌒

Navigating the maze-like corridors of the Citadel was easier imagined than accomplished. For several aisles, they walked among macabre tapestries and glistening web-netted corners, finding rows of aged wooden doors caged in rusted iron.

"My longing for home increases with every millisecond I dwell in this miserable place." Lyra grimaced as she swatted away a prominent cobweb.

"Come now, Lyra," Laila said with her trademark youthful buoyancy. "Their interior design may be appalling, but at the very least the place holds... character." Her hands spread as though to encapsulate the stained glass painted in grisaille and silver stain and the savagely hewn furniture decorated with coloured marble before them.

"Ah yes, but whose character is the question." Lyra leaned against the wall, slightly jostling one of the sconces. The wall gaped open into a doorway that sent her hurtling right through before she even had the chance to yelp, righting itself without even the wisp of a breeze.

"Oh, you're funny, you are," Laila said with a laugh. Though it wasn't until she turned on her heel that she noticed the empty spot where her friend should be. "Lyra?" Her brow furrowed in concern as she took a tentative step forward. "Lyra?" Her mirth diffused, eyes skittish and watchful in the event Lyra was trying to trick her. "Come out, come out, wherever you are..."

When she did not answer, Laila opened the first unlocked door available to her and found herself within a library. The bookcases were stacked with dust-sugared tomes preserved in calfskins and swarming

163

with an infestation of bats. They flitted from shelf to shelf with piercing screeches, swooping low to claw at her.

Laila cried out in surprise as a bat launched itself at her, and she quickly swerved out of its path. She clutched a hand to her thrumming pulse as the bat perched on one of the marble bannisters on a balcony, a satisfied gleam twinkling in its many eyes.

"You look a little lost, princess."

She swerved once more in the direction of the voice and found herself facing what could only be another occasso. He stood imposingly tall against the bookcases, lean musculature concealed in a kaftan that matched her own frock.

The sight of him twinged some nervous reflex in her stomach, though whether it was one of dread or relief at not being alone she couldn't say. She couldn't help but notice how exceptionally pretty he was, almost to the point of distraction. Looking at him had the sensation of being at the edge of a cliff and feeling a conflicting medley of excitement and terror at the long drop ahead.

Ah, but she'd never jump, would she?

"You speak Soltongue?" Laila asked, her brow furrowing at the sound of her language on his lips.

Darius shrugged one shoulder. "I happen to be proficient in many dialects." Then he was stalking towards her with his sleek black panther prowl, leaving her feeling pink and exposed. "I assume you are, then? Lost, I mean."

"Oh, not at all I was just with—I was just—" His proximity had her blushing brighter than raspberries in the summer. She held her tongue to keep from embarrassing herself further. "Who are you?"

"Only a mere courtier like yourself. Consider me to be your belated escort," he said, weaving his way around her in a circle to admire how well she wore the court fashion. "I've come to deliver you to dinner with the rex."

"I see," Laila said, swallowing.

She kept pivoting in his direction, not wanting to show him her back. There was something about him she found unspeakably unnerving. He shouldn't know her language with such fluency, but there was a *rightness* in the way his tongue wrapped around the vowels, smooth as ironed silk. His features also seemed familiar in a way she couldn't trace.

"Shall we?" He offered his arm.

Before she could think to respond, a bat descended upon them from overhead with an audible lashing of wings, then landed on a bookshelf.

"Seems unusual you'd keep bats in a library," Laila said, her questioning brow arched.

"They keep the insects from getting at the manuscripts," Darius replied with another shrug. His eyes reminded her of the hidden lagoons in Soleterea, that same pellucid turquoise. "Many of these documents are centuries old, some even older than that. We do our best to keep them preserved."

"Ah," Laila said. "Well, you see, Monsieur Courtier, I happen to already have an escort. I was wondering if you could help me find her."

He smiled at her, his bright eyes scintillating. "Oh?"

"Yes, my Lightshield guard, Lyra, she... was with me right up until a moment ago. Just mysteriously vanished."

He chuckled in response. "Malborg has something of a... trickster nature, shall we say? One must stay vigilant to ensure you don't get swept up in its twists and turns."

His answer did little to soothe her worries. "Well, it seems I had better stay close to you, then."

"Of course," he said, securing her arm through his elbow. "I'll ensure you won't be led astray."

He had the sort of beauty that caused catastrophe in its wake. Still, she let him guide her for now, for whatever turn of fate had allowed him to speak her tongue made him a potentially invaluable asset. One she intended to have on her side.

How ironic, then, for Darius to have made his way towards her under those same motivations.

"You never did tell me your name?" Laila said once they'd descended the steps of the library.

"Ah. Where are my manners?" Darius scolded himself in jest. "My name is Darius Calantis, the Prefect of Defence."

"Defence? So you lead the armies?"

Darius chuckled. "Something along those lines."

Laila filed it away for future knowledge. "Sounds like a fascinating line of work."

"It's a lot less glamorous than it would appear," Darius said. "Now you, on the other hand, have been quite the talk of the table, princess."

"All good, I hope?"

"Let's say our country doesn't see too many visitors. That makes you a subject of fascination. Though I, for one, welcome the new blood. I've always been appreciative of foreign cultures, and the few travellers we've managed to receive here in Mortos I've always enjoyed becoming intimately acquainted with."

"Is that how you became so proficient in so many tongues? Your intimacy with these foreign travellers?"

"You could say that."

"So I would assume, then, that you happen to keep track of all the comings and goings at your ports?" Laila asked. "Ever hear of a vessel known as the *Great Northern*?"

Darius paused, as though he was taking a moment to truly consider her request. "Doesn't ring a bell."

"Truly?" Laila looked sceptical. "Because it was the disappearance of the ship that led me here. We managed to trace it directly to the White Sea prior to the destruction of our own mode of transport. You know nothing of it?"

Darius shrugged one shoulder. "It's an unfortunate truth of our isle that the White Sea is a treacherous creature. A fair few vessels traverse it and survive. You do, of course, have my condolences for your loss. If you'd like, I could look into it a little further, see what I can find?"

"That would be much appreciated, thank you," Laila said, her smile treacle-sweet. Though she trusted his magnanimity little.

The journey brought them across a very disgruntled Lyra, who, upon seeing Laila on the arm of a stranger, tensed in suspicion.

"Ah, there you are," Laila said brightly, rushing to embrace her friend. "Where in oblivion did you get off to?"

"Turns out our hall of horrors has a couple of trapdoors up its sleeve," Lyra said, then jutted out her chin towards Darius. "Who's the giant?"

"This is Prefect Calantis," Laila said, hastening to add, "He happens to be fluent in Soltongue."

"I see," Lyra said, her suspicion intensifying upon the realisation she would have to be more conservative with her tongue. "Ser Lyra de Lis, of the Royal Lightshield Guard."

Darius dipped his head in greeting. "A pleasure."

"We were on our way to dinner," Laila said. "Please, come."

Lyra stepped in line, not needing to be told twice.

Back in the dining hall, Dominus rose from his seat and began to pace.

"It shouldn't be taking him so long," he said aloud as he completed his tenth circuit around the dining table.

"Doma, please, I beg of you to sit," Vasilisa sighed.

Dominus refused to be soothed. He didn't like to think of his brother Darius in Laila's company for longer than he needed to be.

Fortunately, his concerns were soon put to rest as Darius's light footsteps in tandem with Laila's announced their entrance.

Lanius was the first to acknowledge her. "Ah, your princess arrives."

"We had a little impediment," Darius explained in Mortesian, beginning to pull out a chair for her beside him.

Dominus sped forward to beat him to it, holding out the chair for Laila to sit and offering her a smile.

"Oh, thank you," Laila said, one of the few fragments he'd learned of her language during his time with her. She glanced between the occassi, detecting the ripple of tension between them. Only in seeing them together did she realise how much their looks resembled one another, to the point she decided they must be brothers.

"Apologies if I've kept you all waiting," Laila said, her finest smile adorned as she sat. The furniture was much larger and higher than she was accustomed to, designed to accommodate the size of its inhabitants. She could feel her legs dangling above the floor. "Hopefully the food is still warm."

"She sends her apologies," Darius adeptly translated her words.

Lanius grunted. "Hmph. Well, let us not delay any longer."

The servers proceeded to spoon out servings of blood soup into their bowls.

Laila picked up her spoon and nudged at one of the onion lumps with a grimace.

"Is something the matter?" Vasilisa asked, her lips already stained with the hue of the soup.

Laila feigned a state of bewilderment before Darius leaned over to translate.

"Oh, not at all," Laila said, nudging at the lump again. "Is this... blood?"

"Indeed," Darius responded, as though it were silly of her to ask. "An old Mortesian delicacy. This should've been squeezed fresh. Go on, try it."

Fresh from what? she wondered but didn't have the bravery to ask.

Laila swallowed in reluctance, but upon seeing how ravenously Dominus was devouring his bowl, she felt inspired to at least have a sip. She brought the spoon up to her lips and took a small taste; the iron flavour was muted by seasoning, but not by much.

"Mm, it's—it's very distinctive." She took larger spoonfuls from that point, slurping them down regardless of how her stomach roiled.

"You certainly managed that well," Darius said, "though I do wonder how your palate might adjust to our other offerings. Occassi are a carnivorous species; you might find a few of our customs strange."

"I'm open to trying new things," Laila said, dabbing her mouth with a napkin. By this time, the main course had arrived, and Laila stifled a grimace at the sight of the large organ.

"It's a whale's heart," Darius explained wryly. "My father fancies himself something of a comedian."

"I thought I'd allow you a chance to best the beast in dining, if not in combat," Lanius told Dominus with a large guffaw, slapping his back so hard it echoed.

"Seems a rather cruel jest..." Laila said.

"My brother can handle it." Darius shrugged one shoulder.

Indeed, Dominus seemed more than happy to go along with the ridicule, cutting himself a big portion and swallowing it with relish. "Thank you, Papa."

"I see." Laila regarded this with a pursing of her lips but did not speak to it further. "But while we're all here, I was hoping I might open a dialogue with His Majesty. Prefect, if you would care to translate?"

"Of course." Darius turned to his father. "The princess wishes to treat with you."

"Oh?" Lanius asked, a brief flicker of amusement flexing on his lips.

"I was hoping we could seek a peaceful arrangement between our nations," Laila said. "I wanted it to be made clear that we seek no harm towards you and your country and that we hope these intentions might be shared."

Darius and the rex exchanged words before he spoke. "How do you propose we move forward?"

"Soleterea would like to offer an opportunity of trade and free travel. We are a land of plentiful resources and fertile crops. Perhaps you might find we could be of benefit to you."

Darius spoke some words to Lanius, whose eyes grew hard in response. She wondered what she'd said to offend him. Her eyes sought Lyra to see if she noticed it too.

"Mortos has plenty of resources on its own: metal, timber, coal and oil to name but a few." Darius responded in lieu of his father. "However, you make a persuasive argument. Let us discuss this further."

"Well, first things first, I'd want to discuss ensuring safe passage between our nations—" Laila found her train of speech interrupted when a corpse servant arrived carrying a cake tray. She perked up in immediate interest, straining to see if their desserts would be more to her liking.

However, the moment the cake was served, Vasilisa Regina made a show of scrutinising it.

"Do forgive me, but is that poppyseed I see before me?" Vasilisa looked as though the greatest offence had been enacted. Her upper lip curled in displeasure.

"I believe so, Your Highness," Darius said, glancing down at the cake with a swallow. "Is something the matter?"

Vasilisa wrung her hands together, a habit she was prone to do in apprehension. "I specifically requested a black cherry sponge to be served. The kitchen staff were under strict orders that—"

"I thought poppyseed was your favourite?" interjected Lanius.

"No, Lanius," Vasilisa replied. "No, love, you are mistaken."

"Oh, of course." Lanius chuckled in revelation. "It is Serafina I must've been thinking of."

Darius received his mother's name with a physical flinch, his fork dropping onto his plate with a clatter.

Vasilisa's face had darkened, not helped by how invigorated Lanius seemed in the face of her distress. It was as though he were parasitising this for sustenance.

Knowing better than to fuel him further, she smoothed down the front of her gown and turned towards the nearest ghoul to declare: "Take it away."

Darius cleared his throat. "Your Highness, it seems a waste to dispose of such—"

"I said, take it away." Vasilisa punctuated her declaration by removing the plate and handing it to the servant. "All of it."

The ghouls made no hesitation in removing every trace of the offending dessert, and by the time they were done, not even the crumbs remained.

After that debacle, it was decided negotiations would reconvene at a later date.

Once dinner had concluded, Laila was returned to her guest quarters and prepared to dress for bed.

She unwound her long braid before the vanity mirror, catching sight of Lyra over her shoulder. "How do you suppose that went?"

"Could've gone worse," Lyra said, unstrapping her infantry lightning-bolt sword and leaving it by the bedside. "I couldn't help but notice how silent the queen was throughout dinner. He scarcely consulted her at all."

Laila nodded. "It was odd, to be certain. It's clear they do things differently in this country. Did you notice the way he reacted when I brought up the topic of trade? It was as though I'd slapped him."

"Yes, I'd certainly tread carefully around that one." Lyra grimaced. "Though not as carefully as I'd tread around the translator."

"It was strange the way Dominus was reacting around him," Laila said once she slipped into her nightgown—a simple cotton affair. "He seemed almost... jealous. But you're right in saying there's something not quite right about him. I can't imagine where he learned to speak Soltongue so well. Unless more people have attempted a voyage here than we realised."

Lyra climbed onto the bed and folded her hands behind her head. "Certainly provides an answer to all the vessels that went missing in the White Sea prior to the *Northern*."

"Yes." Laila regarded the implication with a shudder. Then she walked towards the bed, practically vaulting herself over the prodigious frame onto the mattress. She swaddled herself beneath the sheets and slid over to Lyra with her head propped on her hands.

"I'll keep you safe. You don't have to worry," Lyra vowed, reaching over to tuck a curl behind Laila's ear.

"I'm not," Laila said. Though she kept hold of Lyra's hand before she was able to pull it away and drifted off to sleep with it in her grip.

As the night lengthened and the activity of the Citadel's denizens slowed into patterns of rest and relaxation, the less corporeal occupants grew woefully roused to awakening.

These long-suffering wraiths announced themselves by a rattle of the windows, causing arthritic creaks to sound between the crumbling boards of wood. These were the spirits of Malborg's prisoners, bound by eternal torment, and they bemoaned their confinement to the stronghold with low wails that reverberated through the gaps of cold stone.

Their breaths strengthened the draught—leaving a chill that lingered long after in oft-neglected chambers—before seeping out into the wind whistling and whirling between the towers and sending the bats off into flight.

Throughout this spectral unrest, Laila twisted and turned, desperate to deafen her ears to the continuous noise of the Citadel. She lifted the pillow beneath her head and smothered herself with it, keeping her eyes squeezed shut to not be lifted into consciousness.

Whilst she wrestled with sleep, a lone wraith rose between the floorboards of her bedroom. It drifted towards her, relentless with despair, placing ice-cold hands beneath the warmth of her nightgown.

Laila sat up suddenly with a gasp, clutching the bedsheets to her. She glanced around in search of the one responsible for the glacial touch.

"Who's there?" she demanded before her eyes settled on the fuzzy impression of the individual at her bedside. She blinked for some moments to make the image clearer, and then she gasped. Before her was none other than Dr Hariken.

"Is this a dream?" She reached forward to clasp the scholar's wrists. "Oh, you're freezing."

"Cold," Dr Hariken agreed, her voice wispy and faint.

Laila used an enchantment to try and infuse heat into her body, but it evaporated just as quickly. "Oh, Dr Hariken. What happened to you? If you had any idea of how much we've searched and searched. How much Dr Isuka has worried "

"Akira..." Hariken's face fell at the mention of her friend. "I cannot be found... Lost... forever..."

"I'm so sorry," Laila whispered tearfully. "If I hadn't let you come here, none of this would've happened. It's my fault, all of it. I should've paid you more mind."

"Lost... so lost..." Dr Hariken's eyes spilled over with tears. They were black as tar.

"Tell me what happened to you," Laila said, gripping tightly onto her wrists. "Please." She could feel Hariken fading in her hands, but still she clutched her tighter, shaking her, her own voice cracking with her desperation. "*Please.*"

"Let me die..." was Hariken's final outcry before she evaporated into the night.

Laila awoke with a sharp inhale, chest heaving. She looked about her room for Dr Hariken but could see nothing except Lyra beside her and the vast blackness of empty space. She lifted her hands and found them trembling, still heavy with the phantom weight of Hariken's wrists. Then, softly and quietly, she began to weep.

XV

ARIUS ASCENDED THE STEPS TO THE WAR ROOM. The room was one of their grandest, ornamented with the keepsake trophies of the creatures they had conquered in the past. On the floor unfurled the black sheen of a luparo's pelt, while suspended above was a chandelier made from the antlers of a qarnun buck.

He passed several other mounted heads on the walls, their eyes numb and fixed but still somehow all-seeing, all-judging.

Lanius stood before the ironwood table, a glass of gold graviji wine in hand. The sun's first blades of light had pierced through the window panes and patterned his body in a fishnet.

He dropped like an anvil into his seat when Darius entered and waved aggressively for his son to move closer. "Yes, yes, come over here, boy, don't dawdle."

Darius edged towards him cautiously and kept himself firmly planted on the opposite end of the table. Then he dropped an amorphous scatter of maps and documents onto the table before his father.

"What's all this?" Lanius asked.

"All the information I have gathered thus far on any intruders who managed to reach our shores," Darius replied. "I would like your permission to look more into this... Soleterea."

Lanius traced his chin with his thumb and forefinger in thought. "Any particular area you consider to be of interest?"

"Anything I can divine, but I think it best to focus in detail on the country's methods of defence, their borders, and the size and structure of their armies."

"You almost sound as though you're looking to go to war," Lanius said in sardonic amusement. "Very well, Darius. I'll let you have your little scavenger hunt. Find whatever treasures might be hidden down south and report back to me."

"You're agreeing?" Darius asked, incredulous. For years now he had been trying to broach the subject of foreign expedition with his father, only to be tersely turned away. What had changed?

"While that little star girl was twittering away, I got to thinking. It may be about time that Mortos did drop the Veil and end our reign of isolationism. For centuries now, our predecessors had us believe we kept ourselves secret to protect ourselves from the outside world. But the outside world is a thriving place, full of wealth and opportunities I never truly thought possible before."

"And you want your slice of the pie."

"I don't deal in slices, Darius. I intend to take it all. But for that I need to know who and what I'm dealing with. Which is where you enter." He stood up from his seat and approached the fireplace, tracing his fingers over the carved jade mantle. "Put that poncey, bookish mind of yours to use."

"As you wish, Your Majesty," Darius said, accepting the backhanded compliment without so much as a flinch. "I assume you don't intend to bring Dominus into the fold?"

"Not as of yet; boy's distracted with his shiny new plaything, and I intend to let him have his fun." Lanius picked up the iron poker and nudged at the gyrating flames. "I shall call upon him when the time is right."

Darius's brow raised in interest. It was near unheard of for occassi to entertain lovers outside of the race. The House of Calantis, especially, was concerned with keeping their bloodline prominent. "You don't mind that he's fraternising with an outsider?"

Lanius removed the poker from the flames and inspected the red-hot end. "I have no intentions for Dominus to marry as of now, so he is free to pursue his pleasures elsewhere should the urge take him."

Pursue his pleasures indeed, thought Darius. A Dominus distracted from taking a wife was one much easier to puppeteer than one with illusions of ascension. With an ambitious wife in his ear, he might be persuaded to have his father disposed of. That would almost definitely spell the end of his reign. A move well-played on his part. But perhaps the solarite had ambitions of her own...

"Very well, Your Majesty," Darius said, already calculating the logistics of which scout he should place where. "I shall get started at once."

"Oh, and Darius?"

Darius paused before the door, slowly pivoting on one foot. "Yes?"

His father moved too quickly for him to be prepared for it. He snatched Darius by the hair and shoved his face into the hearth, immersing him in flames.

Darius couldn't cry out, couldn't move, couldn't think. There was fire in his eyes, in his mouth, writhing down his throat and stealing his tongue. For a moment there was only pain, agonising, blistering. Then there was nothing but heat.

Lanius tugged him out of the fire and left him to snuff out on the floor. "That was for neglecting to make sure there were no survivors."

Darius whimpered softly, every orifice wheezing smoke. His immortal body had already mended enough to restore the feel of his fraying nerve endings.

"Don't ever fail me like that again," Lanius said. Then he stepped over his body. "Now get out of my sight."

Darius retreated to his quarters with a wounded face and a much more grievously bruised ego. Lanius knew how much Darius prized his beauty, and the attack on his features was a coldly deliberate gesture. It would take days for his face to resemble normality and for the searing itch of his skin regrowing to subside.

With a sigh, he entered his quarters to check the progression of his repairing visage, pausing only when he'd found Dominus awaiting him on his divan.

Dominus's back straightened upon seeing him. "What happened to you?"

Darius averted his face from his brother's gaze. "Father took it upon himself to express his disapproval with our newest houseguests."

"I see," Dominus said, acknowledging his brother's burns with a swallow. He'd seen worse in the past, and he knew Darius would soon heal, but he still felt the urge to apologise for his part in it. However, he knew that approaching Darius in a dialogue would be a much more fearsome battle than any conflict he'd stared down with fangs bared and the hilt of a falcata close at hand. "I, uh, I wanted to say it was erroneous of me to have brought up the flying ship to you in his presence. I should've known better than to rock the table like that."

Darius snorted, knowing that was the most feeble attempt at an apology he would ever receive. Dominus and his skyscraping pillar of pride, his corroding shield of honour. "Well, I suppose it doesn't matter to you either way, does it? After all, we both knew it wouldn't be *you* who would incur his wrath."

Such was his plight as the firstborn, the elder-burdened, carrying the weight of Dominus's faults on his shoulders but never his successes. It was to be his fate as a bastard, the physical proof of his father's transgressions.

Dominus frowned, stroking down the bridge of his hooked nose. "I know his measures might seem harsh, Dara. But Papa only disciplines you so severely because he expects the best of you."

"Discipline?" Darius scoffed in disbelief despite the pain it caused him. "Is that *still* what we're calling this? This surpassed any reasonable form of discipline long ago. Father has become a maniac. Has been ever since he performed that accursed ritual, and you know it."

"That's not true," Dominus said quietly.

"How is it for you to say, as if you'd know any better?" Darius retorted, raising an arm in dismissal. "You've been a block of ice for the better part of a lustrum. During all of which, I might add, Father did very little to find you."

"You shut your mouth." Dominus slammed his fist on the table, a spray of splinters powdering the air from the cracked wood.

"Look at you." Darius shook his head in disbelief. "Still his ever-loyal foot soldier. So eager to defend him, even now."

"Because everything we are today, we are because of him. He is the reason why we now have a united kingdom of Mortos. Why we no longer have to spend centuries locked in battle with our neighbours. Why *you* get to fritter away your time sticking your nose in books and chasing occasselle rather than being the warrior that you are meant to be."

Darius rolled his eyes. "Oh, here we go."

"How could you possibly be so ungrateful to him after everything he's done for you? Papa took you in as a bastard, gave you his name, funded every one of your whims while you ran about the country doing your research. And you stand there and you *denigrate* him when it was your mother who tossed you aside and tore out his heart in all possible ways—"

"Don't you *dare* throw her in my face," Darius seethed. "I will not have you stand there and project her faults upon me. If I thought it possible for her to reverse the ritual, I would've marched to the Widowlands this very day and dragged her here kicking and screaming by her hair. But that is simply not the solution we have been presented with. And I truly tire of having to tiptoe around his temper for the sake of your misdeeds."

"What would you have me do, Dara? Would you ask for me to conspire against our father with you again like you did the last time you two got into an altercation? I won't do it. I won't turn my back on him. I believe in him and his vision for Mortos to be the true and correct course. And as long as I do, he will have my continued support. I won't supplant him. Not even for you."

Darius recoiled as though struck. Then slowly he began to chuckle. "That's fine, Dominus. Run off into the woods. Pretend we don't have a problem. You're not the one who has to be here and watch as Father further unravels. I do wonder what it is going to take for you to truly understand the depths to which he has fallen. Perhaps you only will when he hurts someone you actually care about in front of you."

The words were the finishing strike he intended, and Dominus found himself disarmed, mouth gaping without hope of a counter. Thus, he threw out a snarl, his muscles flexing in anger, and with a huff sent the table overturning onto the floor in scattered fragments before he sped out and left.

∽

Laila entered into the Portrait Hall and found herself observing the short line of rexes and their reginas. She could see Dominus and Darius reflected easily in the faces of the portraits: the same deep dusky skin, chiselled bone structure, hooked noses, and the hunger in their eyes, the calculated menace of a born killer.

Since her nightmare, she had grown even more emboldened to explore every part of the stronghold she could gain access to. Even though she knew the *Great Northern* had long met a watery end, she couldn't shift the sense that Hariken's presence in her mind held some significance.

She walked along the aisle from portrait to portrait, examining each one, before her neck prickled with the spidery sensation of having been watched. She turned to find the source of her discomfort—a bronze relief of an imposingly large raptor with six heads leering vigilantly over the room.

The sculpture took her by surprise, and she couldn't help but feel a crazed impulse to get away from it. Instead, she traced the span of a feather with her finger, observing the iridescent shades of colour as she took it in from different angles.

"You like it?" asked someone from behind her in Mortesian.

She turned to see Dominus there, silhouetted against the castle's

181

masonry like one of its rough-hewn pillars had split itself off and began to walk.

"It's quite, uh... large," Laila said, her cheeks flushed with warmth from her limited vocabulary.

Dominus unclipped his cloak and fastened it around her shoulders, mistaking her blush for coldness.

"Oh, that's not, I—" She stopped herself, as he had already adjusted the cloak around her shoulders. It was soft against her skin, the grey silk inline cool while the fur trim tickled her chin, but the black velvet was heavy, almost suffocating. She could see that the brooch had been etched with his royal seal. "Thank you."

He nodded back in response. "There are many more like it around the city. I'll have to show you the one in our cathedral, one day."

"Cathedral?"

"Yes," Dominus said. "The six-headed raptor is the most common representation of our god, Calante."

The name went through her like a chill. It felt so long since she'd heard it last. That elusive instigator of all the misfortunes that had befallen her thus far.

"Are you all right?" Dominus tilted his head to one side. "You've gone pale."

"I'm fine." She hugged his cloak around her shoulders. "Six heads?"

Dominus gestured to the plaque on the wall. "They represent the six features he gave us. We were created in the core of a mountain thousands of years ago and birthed in flame."

Laila read the plaque that described the statue on the wall, followed by each attribute: Tenacity, Austerity, Ferocity, Supremacy, Cunning, and Vigour.

Laila did not know much about Calante besides what already happened to align with the solarites' beliefs. Asemani bore a son named

Calante, who was struck by a wicked lust for the earth she created and so sought to enslave it until he was thwarted and imprisoned within a mountain.

"Birthed in flame," she echoed, wondering what it reminded her of. "Is that like a... uh, hole that spits fire?"

"Volcano," he amended. He shared an image with her of a smoking mountain. "This is Mount Occassus. It's considered to be a holy site."

"Could I see it?"

He shook his head. "It's considered consecrated ground. Outsiders can't step foot on it."

She sagged in disappointment. Though such a thing made sense. Should Calante truly dwell within the isle's crust, his disciples would do their best to keep it safely guarded.

"Poor Dr Hariken," she sighed aloud in Soltongue. All that effort, and she might well not have seen her goal come to fruition in the end, after all. Though her sceptic's mind still rationed that it was just as likely that such a thing was a work of elaborate myth and that Mount Occassus was no more remarkable a sight than any average volcano.

Yes, in spite of all the phenomena she'd experienced, a cosmic entity causing irrevocable doom was still far beyond the bounds of Laila's disbelief suspension.

"So, your god created you to be cruel and, uh... hungry for blood?"

"Bloodthirsty. And that's one way of looking at it. My father says that he created us to be the perfect predators. Swift, brutal, methodical, capable of withstanding anything."

Her laughter was like the ringing of silver bells. "I think I'm beginning to understand."

Dominus smiled back at her, something rumbling in his throat like a seismic movement. "Will you be staying long in Mortos?"

"I don't know," she said.

183

"Well, when you do go back, I would like to come and properly see this Soleterea of yours."

"Oh, you *must*," Laila insisted with an eager bounce of her feet. "It'll be a dream in the spring. Oh, I'll have to show you the gold roses and the lavender fields and —" She stopped herself, realising in her excitement she'd slipped back into her mother tongue. Her chin lowered demurely as she looked up at him through gold curled lashes. "I mean, if you'd like to."

"I would like to."

They traded a smile.

"Though I would likely have to persuade my father into dropping the Veil."

"The Veil?"

"It's a, uh... a thin barrier of sorts separating our isle from the rest of the world. It has always existed. For protection. Or so our predecessors would have us believe. You probably would've seen it as we journeyed here."

Laila rummaged around her mind for barriers seen throughout her voyage and retrieved none. Unless. "You are the ones who created the *Dragon's Breath*!"

"Is that what they call it in your realm?" Dominus asked, not recognising the term she'd used. She projected an image of the infamous sea mist to him, and he nodded in understanding. "Ah, yes, that's it, all right."

"Well," Laila exclaimed in astonishment. That certainly resolved one unanswered mystery.

"Come," Dominus said, holding out his hand for her to take.

He led her out from the hall to the cloister with its pointed arches and left-leaning shadows, the grounds beyond coated in marshmallow frost.

Laila marvelled at the dense cotton snowfall that settled on the jagged spires of the Citadel. It covered the sunken rooftops, the splitting grooves, the abrupt hair-raising edges, making it look as though the edifice had grown a soft flocculent coat—a more docile shroud over its true ferocious shape.

Unable to resist, she stepped out beneath the softly falling flakes and raised her face to the sky, sticking out her tongue to catch a flake.

Dominus couldn't help but feel a simmer in his chest watching her, locks and lashes freshly powdered, palms open to the sky with a laughter warm enough to dissolve the winter glaze around her. He began to wonder how it would feel to taste that mirth on her lips, catch the heat of her breath on the edge of his tongue.

He moved to do so, pulling her body to his by the waist before he joined their mouths together.

The kiss took her by surprise, and there was a moment between the interval of their lips meeting where her laughter was still vibrating in his mouth. The laugh soon melted away as she dithered on whether to return the kiss before deciding she would reciprocate. She closed her eyes and rested her hands on his chest, raising herself up on her toes to bridge the space between their heights.

XVI

DARIUS MADE HIS WAY THROUGH THE SUBTERRANEAN passageways of the Citadel. Narrow corridors extended like ungainly legs throughout the castle's cellars, catacombs and spas. These were ancient, crumbling structures of uneven brickwork, crooked like teeth, ever-moistened by drippings of dew and furred with black moss. Throughout his youth, Darius had made a habit of familiarising himself with its maze-like composition, leaving small, subtle marks along his journey to differentiate between them.

Darius turned into the spa and became immersed within the diaphanous veil of steam coming from the sauna and the springs. The water was plundered from the impassable wall of glaciers that bordered the north. Darius thought it might be the cleanest item they ever produced here, sterile and entirely without defect, and yet even that was as devoid of life as all else.

He stripped himself bare and hung his clothes up on a hook. Then he perched on the wooden bench of the sauna, allowing the scent of resinous herbs and florals to hotly assault his lungs.

Though he was a creature of all that was wild and bestial, he had grown used to certain civilised comforts: a dense steam with aromatic fragrance and a birch bath besom were one among many domesticated habits.

Darius exhaled loudly as he slapped the dried birch leaves against his hewn shoulders until the clenched grip in his back muscles finally loosened.

He wasn't sure what to make of his father's sudden change of heart. Though he was delighted at the prospect of pursuing greenery and glory in newer pastures, he was still uncertain of the nature of these solarites. And Darius was like to loathe anything he was not certain of.

Still, the thought of conquest was tantalising as any fruit from a high-hanging branch, if only one had the initiative to rise up and pluck it. His father had granted that initiative, and Darius supposed it was only right that it should aid his climb.

After his steam, he moved from the sauna to stand beneath the spray of ice water spouting from the stone gargoyle tap. Then he wrapped his lower half in a towel and passed through the cracked marble pillars towards the springs.

He could sense her from several feet away.

Her scent was an insidious intrusion—a golden summer fragrance of pure nectar and limpid liquid light.

He heard the gentle patter of her heart pressed up against the stone, the susurration of water rippling around her body.

He parted the curtain of steam to see her nestled in the distance.

187

She had her back to him, her spun-gold hair spiralled into a bun that displayed the iridescent wet sheen of her back muscles, clinquant with her starry glisten. Prominently displayed was the constellation of a rose that glittered across the exposed wings of her shoulder blades.

Darius traced the smattering of stars with his gaze, curious of its significance.

He moved towards her on silent footsteps, careful not to startle her away. She had her head resting on a makeshift pillow of her arms, and part of him wondered if she had gone to rest in them—until she stirred and opened her eyes with a sudden quickness.

Said eyes widened in astonishment as she absorbed the sight of his svelte torso, finely sculpted with muscle. Her voice failed her, moisture receding from her lips before she sought to wet them again.

"Oh, Monsieur Courtier," she said in Soltongue, her teasing chosen moniker followed by melodious laughter. She found herself grateful for the heat to disguise the source of her blush. "What a surprise it is to see you here."

"Princess." Darius tilted his head to one side. "I see you've been settling in comfortably."

She hummed pleasantly with a nod. Then she drifted towards him to cross her arms on the stones, resting her cheek on them. "Plenty of room for one more if you're interested."

He was interested, and that was precisely his predicament. Dominus would skin him alive if he saw them in this state. Though he was sure she meant nothing but neutral intent with her words, the mere thought of being within touching distance of her nude body made him throb in the worst places.

He had to cease with this indecorousness. He'd seen pretty faces before, had more than his fill, thought himself above being dictated by the bestial yawp of his primal urges. But it wasn't only simple lust that stirred in his blood when he saw her—there was also cerebral interest, the obsessive compulsion of a scholar's need to *study*.

To oblivion with it, he thought. He turned around and slowly unravelled his towel to slip into the water with her.

Laila bit her lip as she watched him, realising too late it had been a mistake to invite him for company. Seeing his bare torso glistening with moisture alone was far more distraction than she cared for. Let alone seeing more of him. She averted her gaze.

"Are enjoying your stare?" Darius asked, once he'd settled in the spring alongside her.

"Excuse me?" Laila asked. Her blush deepened.

"Your stay," he repeated. "I asked if you were enjoying your stay."

"Oh!" Laila forced a laugh. "Yes, Dominus Regulus has been quite the attentive host."

"I can imagine so." Darius smirked, propping his elbows up onto the stones. "Which reminds me, I looked into your missing vessel."

"Oh?" Laila asked, sitting upright.

"Yes, it's just—well, I only wish I had better news." Darius grazed a hand through his hair with a feigned sigh. The best lies, he knew, were wrapped around a kernel of truth. He only hoped this one would be enough to dispel her prying. "A report received from one of the sea wardens confirms your vessel did have an unfortunate encounter with one of our coastal monsters. The ship was sunk. I'm afraid no survivors were recorded."

"I see," Laila said, swallowing, careful to mitigate her reaction to his words. She knew there was truth in it, even if other knowledge denied her ability to accept it as being the full story. And though she had long come to terms with the loss, there was a sad sinking feeling in her stomach with it having been confirmed.

"Would you like me to give you a moment alone?" Darius asked.

"No." She shook her head. "I'm just wondering what I ought to tell the families of the passengers."

"Well, if you require my assistance for anything," Darius said. "Anything at all."

"Anything?" Laila cocked her head to one side, a vixen expression encroaching on her features.

"Within reason," Darius chuckled. "But yes, whatever you desire."

"Well, I'd have to think about that," Laila teased, her lips bending upwards into a wing-tipped curve. "May even have to draw you up a list."

"Should I be frightened?" Darius asked in mock incredulity.

She couldn't help smiling at that one, try as she might to dampen it.

And what a smile it was, like striking a match in a dim room.

Darius had to brace himself a little to meet it. But he soon smiled back, basking in her radiance. It lasted mere moments before it was shattered.

"Hello, brother." The sound of Dominus's Mortesian and his heavy, lumbering footsteps thudding in the distance had Darius immediately straightening to acknowledge him. "Shouldn't you be off doing some spy-related scavenging on Papa's behalf? I wouldn't want to keep you."

It was the most subtle form of dismissal he would ever receive.

"I was about to make my way," Darius replied, slippery smooth. He rose from the water.

"You're leaving?" Laila asked, slightly bewildered. This had been the second time Dominus had unceremoniously dismissed his brother out of turn.

"Afraid so," Darius replied in Soltongue. "We'll continue this another time, princess. I'll be expecting that list."

He climbed out of the spring, making his way towards the exit.

Laila waited until the sound of his footsteps faded before turning to Dominus in accusation. "You scared him away, you beast."

"Trust me, I paid you a favour," Dominus said, landing with a loud splash into the spring. The water thrashed in a wave against the marble floor. "My brother is not someone whose company you wish to keep."

"Why?"

"Because he is a snake of a creature whose very nature is to lie and charm and scheme." He nearly spat the words. "And he also happens to be my father's favourite weapon. He was likely behind the demise of your ship and all the other vessels that came before it."

"You tell me this now?" Laila said in disbelief.

"The moment never arose." Dominus threw his hands up in defence. "But I am telling you this: Stay away from him. He is not to be seen as an ally or a friend."

Laila exhaled deeply in frustration. She could tell there was far more to the antagonism Dominus shared with his brother than he was willing to divulge. But at the very least, she could heed his warning. Even if she had no intention of keeping to it.

"I understand, Dominus." She smiled, stroking back his damp hair behind his ears. She leaned in to kiss him softly before she drew back.

Darius spent the rest of the evening enclosed in his quarters, writing coded letters and sending them off via shadowbirds. The ink he used was enchanted to only appear upon the confirmation of the recipient. Darius scraped his quill against the neck of the bottle before setting it down with a sigh and a tired eye-rub.

He was about to blow out his lantern and retire when he heard movement in the nearby vicinity.

It wasn't often that Dominus dared to darken his doorway, unless it was for the most pertinent of issues. That was why, when Darius sensed his brother's heavy-footed prowl in the vicinity, he was quick to face him in preparation for what would undoubtedly be another migraine-inducing squabble.

"Stay away from Laila," Dominus snarled.

"Well, good evening to you too." Darius tented his fingers. "How nice of you to visit. Though I admit, a little knock before you entered wouldn't have gone amiss."

"I mean it, Darius," his brother seethed. "Stay away from her."

Always so few of words was Dominus, but it at least made these altercations slightly less tiresome.

"It might have escaped your notice, but I wasn't the initiator in that situation. And I have been."

"Good," Dominus said. "Keep it that way."

"What exactly are you so concerned about, Dominus? Are you worried a mere sustained eye contact between myself and your lovely new companion will spontaneously cause her to shed all her clothes?"

Tension mounted in Dominus's shoulders, and Darius knew he'd struck the nerve he'd desired. But Darius was in no real mood to tussle with him, only tease him a little. Though he recognised from past experience with his father that once tempers were risen in a Calantis, a violent detonation was near certain to follow it. So he stood and stepped closer to Dominus, eager to trigger the explosion and get it over with.

"You need to work on your insecurity, little brother; ladies don't tend to find that attractive." Darius's lips curved slightly upwards into something vulpine. "Perhaps that's why they tend to like me better."

That was enough to cause Dominus to reveal his true monstrous visage lurking beneath the otherwise humane exterior. His lips peeled back, fangs bared; all the white in his eyes was sullied black.

Darius chuckled, his mask maintained as he tilted his head in expectancy. "Go ahead." He stood back and held his arms out. "Take your best shot. I dare you."

Dominus leered close, his fists bunched and twitching to strike, but he didn't take the punch like Darius expected. He recognised this flippantly provocative demeanour in Darius, and he refused to give in to what he wanted.

Thus he sheathed his fangs, exhaling the tendrils of his temper. "You have been warned, Darius. Do not make me come back to you again."

Then, to Darius's surprise, Dominus turned on his heel and walked away.

At midnight, the Citadel had been transformed, stained with the tenebrous black of cephalopod ink. The hour beckoned the arrival of the Citadel's spectres, with Dr Hariken at the forefront as she returned to the quarters of the princess.

Laila slept with her hair fanned out like sunset against her pillow. Though in a deep sleep, she had become attuned to the visits of spectres, and thus, when Dr Hariken came to her, she took little effort to rouse.

"Is that you, doctor?" Laila asked.

Dr Hariken remained fixed at her bedside, unresponsive. Then she turned and walked towards Laila's bedroom door before glancing back, once, and phasing through the wood.

Laila moved like a slip of linen in the breeze beneath the desaturated glow of moonlight. She waited until Lyra's breathing had calmed into slow, steady cycles before tiptoeing her way towards the bedroom door.

She barely made it past the fireplace before she heard Lyra speak: "Don't tell me you're off to a moonlight rendezvous without me?"

Laila paused in alarm before she turned back. Her mind rifled through many excuses and names she could cite to cover up her true intentions. "I've decided to sneak into Darius Calantis's bedroom, see what he's up to."

"Are you mad?" Lyra was upright in the bed at once. "The very least you could've given me is some forewarning." Then she sighed, pushing back the covers. "Give me a moment to get ready."

"No, no, no, you get back into bed this instant. I will handle this one on my own."

"If you think I'm going to let you tiptoe into a monster's den without a guard, then you have another think coming—"

"It'll be easier for me to go in and out without you traipsing behind me looking for a fight. This isn't a slaying mission, Lyra, nor is it like the time you and I tried to go hunting for unicorns. I can do this on my own." She folded her arms together decisively, brow raised in challenge.

Lyra met her gaze unflinchingly before she pulled back the covers. "Fine. But if you do not return after a couple of hours then I will come after you."

"Very well," Laila said, then she turned back on her mission.

Before she left, she administered an enchantment to bend the light around her, making her both invisible and intangible. From there she phased through the bedroom door to follow Dr Hariken's lead.

The spectre had been anticipating her arrival outside, and she walked onwards as Laila trailed behind her, leading her to the stairs. Laila kept her footsteps light and soft as they descended, even though they were unlikely to be heard, trying to guess where Hariken might be guiding her.

She knew Darius's chambers were to be found on the lower levels of the royal apartments, just above the servants' quarters. So it didn't surprise her when Hariken stopped at the designated floor and phased through the wall to the rooms that matched his.

Though the rooms were dark, Laila's eyes adjusted to its gloom as a sheer veil of moonlight seeped through one of the windows to magnify the subdued elegance. The furnishings spoke to a character who'd cultivated fine taste in spite of, or perhaps even because of, his standing. Everything was pulled to impeccable order; not even the dust motes dared trespass from their allocated position.

Laila passed a pointed-arch bookcase chiselled with vine-like motifs, tracing it with a finger to begin her snooping. Dr Hariken seemed adamant to remain at the bookcases, though they bore little fruit Laila could see other than calfskin grimoires and other similar volumes chronicling chaotic magic. She lifted the heftiest book, on the subject of chimeras, and then put it down, finding it to be of little interest. If only she'd shifted it a little more, she might have found what she was looking for.

She turned towards the cabinets next.

Laila released a soft grunt of annoyance when she discovered the cabinet locked, and again when she attempted to rifle through his desk drawers. "Where are you hiding the key?"

Her shoulders sagged at the realisation she might need to enter his bedroom.

She stalked silently into the darkened chamber, finding him thankfully asleep. His bed was built into an alcove of engraved black wood inlaid with ivory, its plum velvet drapes withdrawn to reveal him.

Under the influence of slumber, all the sharpness in his features seemed to have been smoothed away, leaving only the exquisite carvings of his fine visage.

She tried not to look too hard at him as she sucked in the breath that had been momentarily stolen by the sight of his beauty. She did not think it fair that a creature so despicable should come in so lovely a shape.

She dispensed with the thought, reminding herself that this was Dominus's brother she was having such ponderings about, and continued with her task.

Prying open the ornate brass knobs of his wardrobe, she nudged along the satin-cushioned hangers holding garments of fine silk, wool, and floral-patterned velvet with curled toe leather boots stringently aligned along the bottom.

She scrunched her mouth to one side, seeing little of note but how tasteful his sense of style was and felt a tugging impulse to admit defeat.

One last area remained—his wooden chest, which Laila approached with caution pricking at her spine, something primal in her knowing there awaited her an object of eldritch origin.

She reached out a hand, snatching it back with the quickness of elastic. She chastised herself derisively for her nerves as she opened the chest to uncover the contents inside. The box was filled to the brim with more calfskin tomes and parchments yellowed from age, tied with velvet bows. She reached inside to unravel one and found handwritten correspondence in Mortesian penned in Darius's elegant script.

The letters spoke of his research into chimera creation and the nature of mutations aided by magical means. Again, of little interest to her. She put it away and reached for a book next, finding it was locked by a strange, vine-like contraption that slithered and writhed when she touched it. The façade of the book was patterned with archaic symbols that she realised were manoeuvrable when she touched one. Slowly, she twisted the carving of an eye, causing the vines that surrounded it to squirm in protest—

"Didn't your mother ever warn you against snooping?"

Her heart plummeted, but before she could think to move, he'd already shattered her enchantment and taken her in hand—pulling her body flush against his.

She dropped the book with a loud clatter onto the floor and braced her hands against his chest. "I wasn't snooping, I was just—"

"Trying to steal my life's work? I'm hurt. And here I thought we were starting to become friends."

Now she was touching him, she realised he was naked but for his drawers. She could feel the flex of his muscles against her, hard as concrete, and it went through her like a shockwave. Not out of fear. Not for him. She knew if she needed to, she could easily immobilise him with a shock.

"Now... what do you have to say for yourself?"

She sent a pulse of electricity through him, feeling him flinch before her power. She would never tire of feeling a body do that. "Unhand me, first."

His fingers sprung free of her arms as he took a step back, his hands lifted in acquiescence.

"My intent was not to steal from you. I was only trying to discover more about what happened to my ship."

His expression shifted through an amalgam of emotions before settling on neutrality. "I already told you what happened."

"As if I'd take your word for it," Laila sneered. "Dominus told me what your father has you do. I figure if you can lie about that, you can lie about anything. I'm not about to look to a monster for honesty."

Darius chuckled dryly. "A monster, am I? How ironic it is for a thief to speak of me with such *derision*." He was genuinely delighted by this as he took a step closer. "And if I'm such a monster, then it is awfully brave of you to venture into my den, alone and unguarded... where no one would have the chance to hear you scream."

He took another step, looming over her, and while there was no trace of belligerence in his features, Laila found that almost made it worse. Anger she could prepare herself for, but Darius's subtle amusement only left her unmoored.

She swallowed, her chest feeling clenched and tight. "I'm not frightened of you."

"No, I believe you aren't," Darius said before reaching out towards her. She flinched in spite of herself, and he smiled as he tucked a stray curl behind her ear. "All right then, you've caught me. The ship was wrecked, but it wasn't an accident. I destroyed it on purpose upon the demands of my father. I did the same with yours. It is simply our way here, you understand. To maintain our secrecy."

Though she'd already suspected it, hearing how blithely he admitted it caused rage to coil within her. "You're despicable," she spat. Her body sparked with electricity, emitting itself as an incandescent glow.

Darius acknowledged her ire with slight caution. "Now I'd think carefully about the action you want to take next. I understand quite well you may be thinking of hurting me—and I wouldn't blame you one bit—but I think you'll find my uses are far more versatile than as mere fodder for your rage."

No matter how she longed to deny it, she knew he was right. She needed to view the bigger picture, even if that meant relinquishing vengeance. Laila sucked in a breath as she reeled in her temper, causing her wrathful glow to dim.

"There we are," Darius said with a smile. "I knew you were a creature of reason."

"Speak."

"As the sole interpreter of both Soltongue and Mortesian, I'd wager you've come to benefit from my presence. I'd be happy to continue this arrangement, maybe even more, should you be willing to... overlook this little incident."

198

"Little incident?" Laila said. "You've *murdered* people."

"You're right to condemn me, but for what it's worth, I'm glad you survived the crash. I cannot pretend to atone for my acts against you, but I am hoping that pledging myself to your goal of negotiating peace with my father will go some way towards it."

"And what do you desire in return?"

"Other than the mere pleasure of your company?" His smile deepened enough to reveal his dimples. "I am privy to a great amount of knowledge, resources and connections in this country. All things I would be willing to extend towards you as and when you need them. In exchange, I would like for you and I to start fresh. Put the matter of the *Great Northern* out of your mind from this point forth. Their deaths, unfortunately, cannot be rescinded. But the living must go on, must we not?" He reached out a hand towards her. "So, do we have a deal?"

She didn't like it. Not one bit. But he had her at a disadvantage, and he knew it. She was vulnerable in this country, the capricious affections of Dominus her only shield, and should she pursue this further, she wasn't sure she could count on that shield to endure.

Laila glanced down at his extended hand, uncertain. "I gather this little arrangement also encompasses not telling your father I was here?"

"It'll be like it never happened."

She glanced into his viper eyes, finding them unnervingly lucent even in the darkness. Making a deal with a demon was not how she anticipated the night would turn, but if it got them both what they wanted...

"Fine." She took his hand.

He surprised her by lifting it to his lips to graze her skin. "Pleasure treating with you, princess."

He stepped aside to let her leave, and she brushed past him, still feeling the fevered burn on her cheeks. She stopped once inside the sitting room and allowed herself a breath of relief.

Her ease faded when she saw Dr Hariken standing across from her, face weary and resigned in the understanding she'd never see true justice. She dissipated into the air before Laila could call to her.

∽∾∽

Once the princess had left, Darius made a thorough sweep of the room to ensure things were still in order. He approached the areas where her scent had permeated most—at his desk mainly, and a few of the bookcases. After a vigilant scan he could discover nothing out of place, but he remained troubled.

What had you been looking for? Darius pressed a fist to his mouth. There was a draft in the air that felt distinctly phantasmal in nature and he wondered if Emica still happened to be restless. He approached his bookcase again to jiggle the heftiest tome and descended into the basement.

In his laboratory, Emica Hariken lay strapped to her bed, though mutation had done its work of making her look near unrecognisable to the knock-kneed human who'd entered. Her limbs had undergone a significant growth and were now far too gangling for her torso. Her skin had tightened over what little musculature remained, gaining the impenetrability of steel.

Darius heard the congested snuffles of her agitated sleep as he edged near. Tenderly, he put a hand on her chest and shushed her. "There, now. My apologies for leaving you alone for so long. I haven't forgotten you, Emica. I promise."

He'd been noting the stages of her transformation in painstaking detail, and soon, he hoped, he would be able to share the contents of his

200

findings with his father. His first successful chimera. And the future of their country's militaristic advancement.

"I'm just going to give you something to keep you calm." He reached for a potion bottle and filled a syringe. "Give you a nice sleep."

When he stuck the needle into her neck, Emica could do nothing but tense in refusal, too starved and weakened to fight it. A soft whine whistled in her chest before she, and her long-suffering spirit, finally went still.

Darius stroked down the length of her matted hair before pulling back. She might be a long way off from becoming the weapon he desired her to be, but he sensed she had the makings to be magnificent.

He made his way back to his main quarters where he was greeted by the scent of flowers. The scent was like a pelt to the nostrils, subtly overpowering. His distinguished nose traced the source of the fragrance to his end table, now newly replaced, where a bouquet of pearlescent blooms were arranged. He knew of this particular type to be night-blooming; by morning they would all have entirely died.

He stroked one of the velvet petals, plucking it loose to bring it close to his nostrils before it browned quickly in his hand.

A card had been left within the flowers, though Darius needn't have looked at the signature to recognise the author's symbolic flower or her fine hand: *Come to my quarters tomorrow morning. —Vasilisa*

He crunched the petal in his hand and took the card from the bouquet, whistling jauntily back to his bedroom as he pondered what the morning would bring.

XVII

ASILISA REGINA SAT IN HER QUARTERS, lighting a bundle of blood-soaked wolfsbane before she left the herb to rest at the edge of a ceramic bowl. The herb coiled plumes of smoke around her in calligraphy patterns and sealed all sound within the walls of the room.

Burning wolfsbane was a small ritual practice she'd taken from her mother before marriage, and she'd learned to burn it before all important meetings she wanted kept secreted from her husband's ears.

The resulting smoke would be masked by the rich musk of the Mortesian Beauties native to her gardens—thick black roses with the faintest tinge of red. She leaned over to inhale the scent of one of her bouquets, fluffing its petals before returning to her seat to stir her tisane of peppermint and poppy.

Darius entered not long after and closed the door behind him. He instantly caught the whiff of wolfsbane and acknowledged Vasilisa with a low bow. "Your Highness."

"Good morning, Darius." She ceased stirring and wiped her spoon lightly at the edge of her glass. "Thank you for coming. Please sit. I hope you enjoy medovik." She gestured to the confection served alongside hot buttered black bread.

Darius took his cue, stepping forward to the empty chair. He curved his hands over the billowing skirt of his deep navy fustanella before he sat. A glass of tisane had already been served for him, and he picked it up with relish.

"You must be wondering why I called you here."

"Well, I assumed you'd get to that."

She took a moment to straighten her kokoshnik, which today was adorned with the horns of a ram—a common custom for married occasselle. According to folklore, the bigger the horns, the more endowed her husband, and, constantly at the mercy of Lanius's mercurial whims, she would clutch at any chance to bolster his ego.

"I was thinking we haven't had a chance to discuss Dominus's return. What it means for the state of the Citadel, for us as a family, for—well—you."

It didn't go amiss to him how he'd been excised from the concept of family for her.

"I wanted to tell you that, well—you may have thought, in Dominus's absence, that is, there might have been a chance for you to transgress your role here. But now that he has returned, I feel required to let you know that will not be the case."

Darius took a long sip from his beverage, deciding how to answer. "I respect your concerns, Your Highness. But I have always been quite thoroughly, *startlingly* aware of what my position is to be in the Citadel."

"Yes, of course, dear; I never meant to imply otherwise." Vasilisa petted his hand gently, following it with a soft breath of laughter. He recalled how he'd always been taken with her pearl white prettiness stretched over periwinkle veins when he was younger, her autumnal locks. She was a Mortesian rose embodied, pale as the driven snow and just as frigid towards him. "But I know you've been hosting private meetings with some of your father's courtiers—wives talk, you know—and I wanted it to be clear that, whatever schemes you may have, I will not tolerate any threats against my son's claim in them."

Darius's saurian smile remained solidified into place. This confrontation didn't come as much of a shock to him, inconvenient though it might be. However, the fact he was currently having this conversation with Vasilisa rather than his father's prison guards told him more than he required.

"Dominus's claim." Darius traced his finger over the rim of his glass. "But not my father's seat?"

Vasilisa sighed. She set down her glass and cut herself a portion of cake. "I tried so very hard for him. Your father. You must understand. I did everything I could to make him love me. Sometimes I wonder if had I been better at it, he never would've gone back to that... to her. He never would've done the ritual. I had one duty, and I failed it."

Darius swallowed, his mood darkening at the mention of his mother. "You don't have to castigate yourself for that, Your Highness. I'm not certain my father has ever been capable of loving anyone."

"He loved her. Or at least obsessed over her enough that he'd never truly gotten over it when she ran away from him. I kept trying. I tried so hard. I thought if I could give him Dominus, then maybe... but even that only pushed him harder towards the ritual. And now Dominus... he's all I have in the world, do you understand? Mothering him was my greatest accomplishment. I couldn't bear losing him. And so I need you to tell me truthfully that whatever move it is you intend to make against your father will be in the interest of seating him on the throne thereafter."

"Dominus will never be convinced to turn against our father." Darius drummed his fingers impatiently against the table. "You know this."

"You let me handle that should the time arise," Vasilisa said tersely, "but do we have an understanding?"

Refusal lingered on the edge of his tongue before Darius swallowed it thickly. He knew the law of the land by now, that bastardry precluded him from any spoils of political warfare. He also knew Vasilisa was equipped to thwart his aims with a mere bedtime whisper—even in spite of knowing she and the rex hadn't shared one since heartlessness stripped him of virility. Still, he would humour her for now, up until it benefitted him not to.

"Of course, Your Highness," Darius said, hollow dimples appearing beneath the sharpness of his cheeks when he smiled. "I think I'll have a slice of that cake now."

Drakalyk Castle was a building of soft-toned masonry reminiscent of gingerbread pulled from the oven, capped with onion domes in slate grey. Contrary to the otherwise romantic architecture, it was ornamented with vulturine statuettes, which tinged the dwellings with an undertone of foreboding. The estate was usually reserved for honouring visiting royalty, but it had recently been granted to Laila on behalf of Lanius Rex to serve as the site of the Soleterean embassy.

Her velvet shoes padded hurriedly around the vicinity as she made clipped, exuberant demands of her servants to rearrange the interiors to her liking. She had Darius acquire many of the fixtures she considered essential in her Soleterean home—from the handwoven silk sheets to the bobbin lace netting.

She rearranged this setting into an exhibition of her innermost self—transfiguring every one of her girlish reveries and fanciful whims into objects, such as a cream chaise lounge that sprawled as dramatically as she did. She took these material things and used them to solidify herself into being: to magnify her presence against the impermeable gloom of the country.

"So, this is going to be our new home for the foreseeable future?" Léandre asked, his hard leather soles clacking against the reflective ivory floorboards.

At the use of the plural, Laila smiled. "It would seem so."

"Well, it could be worse," Lyra called out from her reclined position on the settee. "I mean, the weather is appalling and the people are bleak, but they have good woods here and nice, clear springs, so perhaps all is not lost."

Laila laughed. "I would not have blamed you in the least if you chose to return to Château de Rosâtre."

"And leave you in this frozen nether-hole alone?" Lyra cried in mock-offence. "Perish the thought."

"We'll both be with you for as long as you need," Léandre said, placing a hand on Laila's shoulder. "We came into this accursed realm together, and together is how we will leave it."

Laila smiled, warmed by his claim. Then she put her hand over his with a sigh. "I wish it wasn't only us who will be leaving here."

"I know," Léandre said. He took her into his arms.

Laila rested her head against his chest and exhaled. The letters she'd written to the families of the passengers would soon be making their way, dictated over mirror transmission with Oriel, relishing the ability to speak directly to her starlet protégé back home. Dr Isuka's was the one she had ruminated on the longest, and Laila hoped the scholar would have greater, if not total, peace of mind.

She opened her eyes, moistening her mouth to speak until she saw the clock on the wall, which morphed her next sentence into a shrill gasp. "Look at the time! I need to be at the Citadel to discuss trade negotiations within the hour."

Thus she detached herself from the bustle of her household to take the carriage back to Gravissia.

Darius waited at the gates of the Citadel, looking out for Laila's carriage. He flipped open his skull-shaped watch and snapped it shut again with a sigh. Trade negotiations had not been a great success, and each time he had to find himself censoring for his father's ill decorum. He considered it a fortune that Laila had not learned to speak Mortesian, but he was uncertain of how much longer he could keep the charade going.

He was about to glance at his watch again when he saw her, a blonde blur of lightspeed, as she entered the courtyard and adjusted her skirts.

"How late am I?" she asked, flattening her windswept curls back into place.

"Actually, you are"—he checked his watch—"just on time."

"Perfect."

She swept past him like a breeze and he followed close behind—a lean dark silhouette to her bright beacon body.

They passed the Portrait Hall up the steps to the Eyrie.

Lanius was already there when they arrived. He was seated alone, as was often the case—the self-imposed isolation of a creature who valued the voice of no one but his own echo.

"Good, you've arrived." Lanius cut the edge of his cigar and struck a match. "Let us get started."

For the past few days, Laila and Lanius had been going back and forth on trade regulations. According to Lanius, Soleterea was too rigorous on their import laws and restrictions, which Laila continually argued were set in place for the safety and benefit of their mortal populace.

"I simply do not believe that all this tedium is necessary simply for the sake of trying to scale our way past these borders," Lanius said to Darius in Mortesian. "I wonder if this impératrice guards her knickers so prudishly."

Laila suppressed the urge to react in the face of his vileness, having perfected a neutral expression whilst allowing the rex to speak his truth in his mother tongue. Let him see her as little more than perfect porcelain pleasantness; those who couldn't see past the façade weren't worth entertaining, anyway.

"If I may, princess," Darius said on behalf of his father in Soltongue. "My father seems to believe that these might prove to be too much of a strain on our city merchants, considering our workforce consists mostly of ghouls."

"With respect to you, sir, mortals and sprites would never allow themselves to touch something that was handled by a corpse. They view corpses as unclean and harbingers of death and disease. And they are not wrong," Laila said, sipping from a cup of tisane she'd been served by the very thing she spoke of. "Perhaps you do not view corpses the same way in Mortos, knowing that you will never fall victim to disease. But mortal bodies are much frailer. It will be near impossible for you to trade perishables with us, let alone any other country in Vysteria, under these conditions."

"We are admittedly a lot more lenient in this approach than you are accustomed to in Vysteria," Darius said. "But it doesn't appear to have done our subjects great harm. We have many thriving races here in Mortos. And yes, while there might be the occasional plague or pestilence to dwindle the numbers, they often come back just as strong."

"Can barely cull enough of the miserable bastards," Lanius murmured into his own goblet. As per usual, he was drinking wine. Laila wondered if he ever consumed anything else.

"I respect that," Laila said, trying hard not to react to Lanius's statement and the horror of its implications. "But I do not believe that what's good for the goose being good for the gander. And neither does the impératrice. I am afraid that I must enforce the same regulations as before. You may take them or leave them."

"Like talking to a puppet doll." Lanius smothered a smirk. "One has to wonder if she even has a brain there in that feeble little skull, or if you'd open her up to find her full of feathers."

"My father says he and I will discuss this further and get back to you promptly with a response." Darius stood up from his chair to offer his hand. "And that he hopes to see you at dinner tonight."

"Thank you, prefect," she replied, shaking his hand firmly. "Oh, and one more thing before I go—there is something I'd like for us to discuss in private, should you have the time. Would you care to meet me at the embassy?"

"Why, of course." Darius attempted to conceal his curiosity. "I'll be there tonight."

"Perfect." She wielded her smile like a blade before she turned to leave.

She retired to the embassy that night, where she spent the duration of her evening signing off correspondence with her lip print in cherry lacquer and a newly created stamp of her royal seal. Each time, she spritzed the paper with scent or pressed flowers on them, then sealed the envelope with an electric imprint so that her missives were easily identifiable—a common practice in communications between solarites.

Now that the Veil had been dropped, sending things in and out of Mortos had grown considerably easier, and she'd been keeping in touch with her mother on matters of trade.

Laila filed the letters away into her cherrywood holder and then moved over to her vanity, her willow limbs bent in repose as she disentangled her golden tresses with a tortoiseshell comb. The brittle weather was treating her hair poorly in spite of the peppermint oil and steam treatments, and she decided to bind it into twists for protection.

A gentle knock on the door disturbed her from her endeavours.

"Come in," she murmured, as though the very task of speaking was strenuous.

She heard the click of footsteps she did not recognise. It was not the steady strides of Léandre, nor the light, near imperceptible foot of a ghoul.

Laila glanced into the mirror, saw that it was Darius standing there, and at once stood to attention. "Prefect." She straightened out her clothes. "You've arrived. Thank you for coming."

Darius strode into the room with caution, taking off his feathered kolpak. "It was of no trouble to me at all, princess. A lady's invitation always takes precedence in my list of priorities."

Laila scoffed at him, eyes rising skyward in reproach. "Well, don't get any ideas. It's not that sort of invitation."

"And just what do you believe I had in mind?" He held her gaze a touch too long for comfort, almost daring her to speak it.

"I—" Laila couldn't keep herself from growing flustered. "Nothing."

Her birdlike nerves coaxed in him a feline instinct to taunt, but he soon relented. "I must commend your taste." He gave a sweeping glance about the room. "You've truly breathed life into this decrepit old manor."

"In no small part thanks to you." Laila tucked a curl behind her ear. "But about why I called you here—"

"Yes, please do tell," Darius said, reclining back into her tufted chaise lounge.

"It's about your father." Laila fiddled with the objects on her vanity, rearranging them into perfect symmetry. "You don't care for him much, do you?"

Darius's playful mirth disintegrated. "What gives you that impression?"

"Your exasperation with him during our meetings rings louder than you think," Laila said. "Contrary to his belief, I do not quite have a head full of feathers."

"Well." Darius's eyes flitted with a rare befuddlement. "You are full of surprises, aren't you?"

She kept her prideful smile muted.

"And how long were you intending to keep your comprehension concealed?"

"Long enough." Laila lifted a shoulder. "I wanted to see if I could trust you."

"And does this mean you trust me, then?"

Laila bit her lip, unnerved by his casual comfort in her room. She had never seen anything like him before. His features were diamond sharp, even reclined in the chaise lounge, cast in shadow. He had all the elegance of a predator, relaxed but alert. "No, but I believe if our aims are aligned we can help each other more," she replied.

"Sound reasoning," Darius said. "I must confess, I find his short-sightedness aggravating." He sighed, nestling into the seat. "Mortos needs more of Vysteria than it needs more of us. With that in mind, it's sensible to play by the rules, so to speak. But my father hasn't been sensible for a long time. He is a creature built for war, not diplomacy, you understand."

"So it seems," Laila said. "Why is it that Dominus hasn't succeeded him yet?"

"Ah, so he hasn't told you?"

"Told me what?" Laila asked, with an inquisitive sparrow tilt of her head. Too curious for her own good.

"Well, it's an intricate tale, but I'll let you in on the abridged version. After Dominus was born, my father procured the talents of my mother to make him heartless—and therefore deathless, for it is only in the destroying of an occasso's heart that we perish. Now my father keeps his heart somewhere hidden, guarded in a lapis lazuli egg. It is the reason he has such a... charming disposition. My father was never kind, but removing his heart made him even harder. One can never remove something so essential to themselves without it taking something else in turn."

Laila's spine prickled in repugnance, and she fought to disguise how much his words disturbed her. The tale clung to her in a way that she knew was bound to follow her to bed at night. "You were right, prefect. That is quite the tale."

"Truth be told, for all his faults, Dominus would probably make a much poorer monarch than my father. He's a lot more... malleable, easily led, and that makes for a weaker country. Though... perhaps that's why you'd want him."

Laila said nothing, allowing him to draw his own conclusions. "I can't help but notice that no one refers to you as a prince. Are you not also in line for the throne?"

Darius chuckled. "Now *that* is another story in and of itself. The mother I mention in the tale isn't the same as the one you might have had in mind. Vasilisa Regina is Dominus's mother, not mine. My mother was never regina, and thus I can never be rex."

"That matters?" Laila's brows bent in questioning.

"Quite a bit, as it would happen," Darius said wryly, though there was a bitter edge to it. "Do you not have similar customs in your land?"

"I am my mother's sole child," Laila asserted pridefully, "but such a thing doesn't make me an heiress by default. We have a Council of Elders to decide that. An impératrice's reign lasts for a hundred and twenty years, and as soon as it ends, she must choose a successor to take her place."

"How fascinating," Darius said. He would have to make a note of that. He rose from the chaise. "Well, I won't outstay my welcome in any case. Though, before I forget, I also wanted to give you this." He reached into his pocket and produced a small tin.

"What is it?" She plucked it from his fingers.

"The beeswax you requested."

"Oh, of course," Laila said, brightening immediately. This would be the perfect addition to her hair regimen. "I must say, I'm amazed by your resourcefulness. I think you managed to check off everything on my list."

"I can't keep all the praise," Darius said, hands folded behind his back. "Your list was very detailed, and in many ways quite specific. It also helps knowing the kingdom as well as I do."

"Well, thank you," she said. Then, without thinking, she leaned upwards on her toes to kiss his cheek.

The gesture took him by surprise, and he became hyper-aware of the proximity of her mouth to his, the feel of her kiss lingering close behind like a chill. As she drew back, his expression was imperceptible but intense in a way that made Laila's body feel languorous as a sultry Soleterean afternoon—the kind of warmth one shed their clothes to.

She bit her lip as her eyes flit briefly to his mouth and then met his gaze. The moment went through them both like a pulse, electric. She had to remind herself that he was a monster, that he was untrustworthy. She shouldn't be imagining what the taste and feel of his mouth was like.

The moment splintered as Darius cleared his throat. "Pleasant evening, Your Radiance."

Then he departed from the room in a blink.

XVIII

WEEKS PASSED, AND SPRING ARRIVED TO BREAK the siege of frost at Mortos. The ice splintered and released the isle from its lacquered hold, allowing the trees to unbend from their protracted pose, the fish to taste the surface of their rivers.

This was a period of celebration for the denizens of Mortos, heralded by their traditional holiday of Callemas—the birth of Calante's first son, the sire of the entire Calantis bloodline. It was marked, as were all Mortesian holidays, with feasts and fighting and festivals in the streets.

Laila was in her bedroom, sifting through several frocks in search of something to wear. She was due to watch Dominus participate in the arena games with the rest of the country's elite warriors, and the prospect both intrigued and unnerved her.

Vasilisa had deposited several dresses made by her seamstress for

Laila's perusal, and she rummaged through them with increasing disdain before eventually setting them aside, finding them to be too matronly for her tastes. Soleterean fashion could not differ more from the way the occasselle obscured their bodies like shamefully guarded secrets.

"Ugh!" she declared in defeat as she shoved away yet another ill-fitting frock. She collapsed dramatically on the bed and threw an arm over her eyes as though to shun the world in upset.

"Would you like some help?" Léandre asked from the doorway, observing her fit of temper with a rumble of laughter in his voice.

Laila peeked out from beneath her arm and sighed. "I'm supposed to be picking out a dress for tonight's festivities. The regina suggested wearing something red or green to symbolise fertility. I only wish these weren't so"—she gestured towards the high necklines and straight silhouettes—"constricting."

"Let's see if I can be of some assistance." Léandre stepped towards her wardrobe to rummage through the frocks. "Well, now, this one is pretty." He retrieved the gown he spoke of—a length of green velvet lush as garden grass embroidered with gold thread.

"Hm." Laila scrunched her lips to one side. "Perhaps if I lowered the neckline somewhat and slit those sleeves." She caught her chin between her thumb and forefinger. "And let out that underskirt beneath. Léandre, do we have any sewing tools available?"

She leapt up from the bed and approached her chest of drawers, rummaging through the shelves until she found a small wooden kit.

"Have a spark of inspiration?" he asked.

Laila grinned in triumph as she retrieved a pair of scissors and infused them with an enchantment to animate them. "Well, it's as they say." She turned towards the dress, sticking her tongue out of the side of her mouth. "If you want something done, right, you're going to have to do it yourself."

Gravissia truly was a city that never slept. Beneath the ancient and indecipherable veneer lay a breeding ground of constant nocturnal activity that rumbled with the discordance of circus shows and bloodsport. This further sprouted an underworld of vice and vulgarity offered in an enticing exhibition to the corrupted souls that converged. Establishments cajoled on every street corner, both dens and public houses practically perspiring with luneleaf and cigar smog.

Laila glanced between the red velvet drapes of a black carriage to see the tidal surge of bodies as they flowed, rose and fell back again. Tonight she wore a palette of leaf-green and wheat-gold, the colours that winter craved. Her plump lips were hued berry-red with an artful smudge, ripe as if for eating, for kissing, for all pleasurable pursuits of the mouth, and in her hair were the scrunched blushing buds of spring blossoms.

The carriage parted the sea of the crowd to enter through the theatre's gates. From there they were escorted under the ghastly leer of the grotesques to a prime seating booth near the very top.

Laila sat beside Vasilisa, who regarded her state of dress with shock. "Goodness! You must be catching your death in that frock. There's hardly anything to it."

"Oh, I'm quite well." Laila smiled. "I thought, seeing as the weather seems to be on the turn, I would take inspiration from my hometown's fashion."

"I must say, is that truly what they have you wearing down south? I couldn't imagine being so bold."

Though it was said gently, there was an edge of disapproval in her tone that reminded Laila uncomfortably of her mother. She almost felt the need to apologise for herself. Physically, Vasilisa couldn't be more her opposite—where Laila was brown-skinned and brazen, she was the picture of pearlescent poise with skin like the pink-tinged hue of apple blossoms. She had the same imposing build of her son but, her bulk, while muscular, was broader in the hips, with a heavy bosom.

"I think she looks exquisite," Darius interjected with a smile. He wore a red kaftan sprayed with an arterial spatter of rubies that glistened each time he moved.

"Thank you, prefect," Laila said, finding it hard to meet his gaze with how intensely it fixated on her. Nonetheless, she was ever hungry for praise no matter the source; it nourished her better than mother's milk. She took her seat between Vasilisa and Darius, feeling warm upon his proximity to her. He exuded a darkly alluring aroma of rose, oakmoss and ambergris that persuaded her body to lean closer. "You're not participating tonight?"

"I prefer to watch," he said. There was something tigerish in the curve of his smile. One could imagine him as a spectator, with the same inquisitive detachment as a child frying worms through a magnifying glass.

The arena came alive before them with a blaring of horns, followed by fire dancers swinging their poles of flame in mechanical synchronicity—heralding the arrival of the umpire on his bronze chariot.

The umpire stood with arms raised, beckoning the uproarious cry of the crowd as he descended from his chariot and made the first round of announcements.

Laila was transfixed as the games unfolded and the occassi poured in from the skies on their black hippogriffs, performing acrobatic feats she would never have thought possible on a mount, let alone airborne. Her hand gripped her seat in horror several times as she watched warriors perform stunts that seemed unfeasible—only for them to accomplish it with untroubled skill.

As the events progressed, her heart became a gymnast of its own calibre: belly-flopping with dread at the airborne mounted archery, somersaulting with delight at the levitating ring jumps.

Just when Laila thought her heart could take no more excitement—there was Dominus riding in on his tar-coloured steed, clashing with his opponent as they attempted to wrestle each other to the ground.

There was a subtle throb in her chest at the sight of him in his element, oil-slicked and sweat-sheened as he tussled in the sky with his competitor. It reminded her of times she'd watched Lyra dominate the arena back in Soleterea with that same vigorous bravado.

The throb blossomed the more she watched him, sliding lower to take root in her stomach before seeping further down between her thighs. She squirmed in her seat, her breaths quickening, an unbearable heat puddling deep within her core. She felt flushed and exhilarated.

"You seem to be enjoying the show," Darius whispered low in her ear, and it travelled right to her toes like a bolt. She looked at him and he looked back. The tiger look was emphasised. It amused him to see what this was doing to her.

Her eyes travelled back to Dominus, who had emerged victorious, knocking his opponent down with a well-aimed strike. He fell to the ground with an echoing crackle, bones dislocating and emerging like spines through the skin. She couldn't tell if the sight horrified her for how much it thrilled her or thrilled her for how much it horrified her.

He was not dead. His body had already engaged a skeletal hex to slide each dismantled jigsaw bone back into place—though this process seemed exceedingly more painful and was nauseating to watch. Dominus swooped down beside him once he'd healed. They shook hands.

The umpire announced Dominus champion and presented him with the champion's ribbon, from which hung a solid gold eagle egg—a symbol of Callus. He was next presented with a wreath of Mortesian

Beauties, which he hooked on his arm as he swung his leg back over his hippogriff and took to the skies.

The audience held their breath as he ascended, and there was nothing audible but the laceration of the hippogriff's wings as it slashed the open air, bringing him right to her. Dominus hovered before Laila with a smile as he presented the wreath to her.

Laila bowed her head, stretching the swan arch of her neck forward as he crowned her. The audience erupted.

⚮

She found Dominus on a street corner after the excitement died down.

He had refreshed himself backstage, newly showered and oiled, his hair a dark slick against his velvet-covered shoulders. His emerald-green kaftan was practically bursting at the seams, the velvet rippling like water each time he moved.

Laila ran to him, her wreath dripping petals of black rain as she launched herself into his arms and crushed their mouths together. His lips were full and soft, his beard a pleasant tickle against her cheek as she inhaled his scent of cedar and pine.

His hold on her back was near spine-crushing, but to him, he was using no more force than a feather in the breeze. He was more cautious with his mouth, ghosting every shadow-movement of her lips against his as though he were always a little uncertain of it.

She sucked lightly on his bottom lip. "Let's go somewhere."

He set her down, and they weaved through the thickness of the crowd in search of a covert location. He turned towards his carriage, which was stationed on a much less cramped and crowded area of the street, then slammed her up against the door with enough force to shift it onto two wheels.

He kissed her more forcefully this time, taking initiative as she hooked her legs around him for something steady to grip. He was like an iron hull against her soft beach sand. She wanted to pin him down and grind on him into oblivion.

He handled her with ease as he manoeuvred open the door with one hand, tossing her inside the carriage with the other and closing the door behind them.

She'd never taken a male lover before. She had never felt inspired to in the past. And though she was no untouched flower in the ways of intimacy, there was a little shiver that crept down her spine as he slid on top of her, his mouth ravenous against her neck and jawline.

Dominus's face had changed; his true monster visage rose from the abyssal depths to claim possession of his features. He tugged at the front of her dress, tearing away the fabric, too eager to reveal her body to him.

A small sound of affront rose at his carelessness. That soon dissolved when his mouth was on her neck again, leaving a trail of raspberry welts that bloomed into violet bruises as he descended down her collarbone to her sternum.

She reached up to unfasten his kaftan, slowly uncovering the masses of his body layer by layer, and let her hands roam along the rugged contours of muscle.

Now they had each other bare and vulnerable beneath the moon's all-seeing eye did they stop to stare at one another, a softness dulling their savage lust from before.

Dominus raised a hand to cup her cheek, his thumb sliding across the curve of her bottom lip. His thumb slid down her chin and over her throat, pressing into the fluttering pulse there as the rest of his hand cradled her neck. He slid his hand down to her chest before moving it to grab her hip. Large hands, strong and bestial; how easily they fit on a waist, a breast, a throat.

He pulled her to him by the hips and aligned their bodies together.

Laila tensed as he sank inside her and she squeezed her eyes shut, a sharp gasp drawn in from the shock of it.

Dominus buried himself as far as she could take him, shuddering from the tight caress of her around his shaft. He jerked his hips with impatience, plunging deeper with a hard pump that caused Laila to cry out. He mistook her exclamation for pleasure and rammed forward, making Laila grit her teeth.

"Stop." She braced her hands on his chest, trying to keep him at bay. "It's too much."

He ceased mid-thrust, eyes questioning.

"Let me," Laila said, grabbing his shoulders to try and ease him in slower. But whether it was the tension of her mounting anxiety or some physical mismatch, she simply could not make it fit right. She closed her eyes again and exhaled a quiet whimper, her face contorting with pain she was not accustomed to receiving. She was used to eager fingers and mouths, or a body part to move herself against. "I—I can't."

Dominus watched the tension in her face with uncertainty. He hadn't expected her to be so new at this. He took her chin in his hand and shook his head. *No?*

She nodded back at him. "Let's try something else."

He let her switch their positions as she decided to try an alternate part of his body that was less unnerving and settled on his thigh. She found an optimal position wherein he ended up pressed against her stomach as she grinded on him with abandon.

Her earlier anxiety melted from her shoulders as she established a rhythm, a moan working its way up her throat as the firm sinews in his muscle slid over her exactly right.

He palmed his shaft, stroking himself, and as their eyes met there was a pulse, a surge of some powerful source that she realised had originated from her power. He slid his hands between her legs to feel how slick she was, and he coated his shaft with it, his other large, calloused hand curving against the small of her spine. He brought her close to latch his teeth onto her shoulder, his fangs descending in a bite.

Laila gasped in surprise as his fangs sunk further and further in before the pain was soothed by the feel of a tranquilising substance entering her bloodstream. Occassi venom. She heard him groan as he bit her, his body trembling with relief. Her muscles wilted before the poison in her veins, her initial shock quieting to calm.

Her head felt lighter than a cloud as he rocked against her, his tongue gliding over her shoulder before he bit down again. The next bite brought him over the brink as he climaxed, and Laila clutched at him, raking her nails over his spine. He pulled away, his mouth and beard gold-smeared with her ichor.

She staggered off of him, still disoriented, looking at her tattered dress on the floor with a sigh. She used a renewal enchantment to repair it. "A little forewarning would be nice in future, if you decide you wish to mishandle my garments." She touched her wounded shoulder and examined the bite. She'd never been treated roughly during intimacy before but figured it to be another among the occassi's bestial habits. "And savage me like an animal."

He at least had the grace to look apologetic, but she held her princess pout firmly until he dragged her down to his chest and kissed the top of her head. She was too serene from the venom to scold him further as she nuzzled his chest and stroked the dense sprawl of hair there.

"Will there be a future?" he asked.

She tilted her head up to face him before shifting to cradle his face in her hands.

"I have to go back to Soleterea for some time," she said, for she would need to deliver the news of Lanius's final decision regarding

223

trade, whatever it might come to. "But I would like for you to come with me, if you would. Soleterea is unearthly in the spring."

He kissed the edge of her wrist. "I would like that."

XIX

OLETEREA WAS SWELTERING WHEN THEY ARRIVED, the kind of heat so dense it was fit to swim in. Laila watched the residents walk by with their sun-soaked glisten, the heat fluctuating around them in waves, like she was observing the fish in a tank.

Dominus sat beside her in silence, his shoulders hunched. He had been crouched uncomfortably in the carriage for hours now due to his stature and the sight of him kindled pity in her.

"It shouldn't be much longer," Laila told him in an attempt to soothe. She had come here to escape from the winter, and yet she had brought a slice of it with her. It pained her to watch her abominable snowbeast melt. "Would you like to use my fan?"

Dominus grunted negatively in response. She had gradually become fluent in his non-verbal cues.

"All right," Laila said, opening it up to fan herself. She stuck her hand out of the window and felt the light ocean breeze drift between her fingertips. She took her hand away from the window and placed it on the silk brocade of the carriage chair, sealing a fray in the fabric with her aether until it was good as new.

"Now, I have made an annotated brochure of activities that I think you might enjoy while you stay," Laila said, pulling out a little booklet from her purse to hand to Dominus.

He accepted it with wary interest, flipping briefly through the pages.

"I can already sense your misgivings, but you need not despair: I had a ghoul assist me to make sure there were versions written in both Mortesian and Soltongue. And, oh"—Laila slapped her hand down on the page to halt his flipping—"there are even little illustrations I had peppered in to appeal to your artistic eye."

He looked up at her with a brow arched. She beamed beatifically in response.

"Thank you," he said, lifting up the pamphlet higher to his face to squint at it. "What is... opera?"

"Oh, you absolutely *must* see the opera at least once in your life. It's rather like theatre but more... majestic. It's something that needs to be seen to be explained."

"We're here," called out Lyra, who had been dangling out of the window.

Laila poked her head out of the window to see the golden gates of the château opening to receive them. The carriage drew to a stop in the courtyard before the chauffeur went to open the door for her.

Laila stepped out, head tilted towards the sky to receive the sun's warm kiss on her cheeks. She heard the carriage jostle as Dominus came lumbering out next, stretching himself once more to full height.

The atmosphere shifted immediately in his presence. Among his peers, it was easy to forget how imposingly enormous he was, even for his race. Here, he eclipsed all who were near him by at least a foot.

"Come," Laila said, taking his hand and leashing him to her, an assurance of his safety. "Before we enter, I want to make sure you are fully aware of what to expect from my mother."

"Yes, I know, Laila." Dominus sighed wearily. "We have discussed this several times."

"Apologies, it's just—" Laila straightened the lapels of his kaftan. "You are aware she is a very... particular individual. And while I know we've discussed it, I think it is best to let me do the talking—not that I doubt your abilities at etiquette. It is just... well, you'll see."

Dominus nodded, grateful to be relieved of the opportunity to talk.

Laila led Dominus through the gilded stuccoed walls into the salon, where her mother awaited. Amira sat on a green velvet armchair ornately carved in the form of a garden trellis with flowers and foliage.

"Hello, Maman," Laila said, dipping slightly in her presence. "I have returned from Mortos with a decision from Lanius Rex, as you've requested."

Amira took a sip from the froth of her cappuccino before setting it down without so much as a smudge on her lip. "With company, I see."

Laila glanced towards Dominus. "Yes, you've met Dominus Regulus."

"Your Luminosity," Dominus said in Soltongue, descending to one knee.

Her mother stood. She circled him like an inspector, her gaze clinical in its examination of him. "What brings you back to Soleterea?"

"I thought he might like to have a taste of the country," Laila said for him. "We discussed it immensely during my stay in Mortos."

"I was asking him, not you," Amira said; she framed the side of her face between her thumb and forefinger. "Well?"

"It is... as your daughter said," Dominus murmured, scratching behind his pointed ear. "I have an interest in seeing your country better. I do hope my stay will not be unwelcome here."

"Well, of course not," Amira said, her smile sharp. "You will have the pleasure of attending my daughter's cocktail party. She's been planning it for weeks in advance for her return. Though I would assume you knew that."

"She has informed me, yes."

"I see." Amira gave Dominus another once-over. "And how would you define the current status of your relationship?"

"Maman—"

Amira held up her hand. "Let him answer the question."

Laila's head whipped round to Dominus, watching intently the way his throat bobbled and shifted.

"She is—she is"—Dominus cleared his throat—"a valued ally to our country. Something I hope to solidify during my visit."

Laila deflated in relief, her chest lightening with hope that her mother might find his answer satisfactory.

"Well enough, Dominus Regulus. I am sure you must be worn down from your long journey." Amira snapped her fingers towards one of the sprites in the periphery of the room. "Please escort Dominus Regulus to appropriate quarters and make sure he is settled."

The sprite nodded before ushering away Dominus, who could only glance lingeringly at Laila before the door was closed behind him.

Amira's eyes flitted over to Laila. "Why have you brought him here?"

"I thought perhaps some exposure to our country would help to endear him towards it," Laila said.

"You mean you thought it'd endear him towards you." Amira sighed. "Why have you entangled yourself with this creature?"

"He has his uses. I doubt my time in Mortos would've been nearly

228

so successful without him. I don't see where the harm is if I happen to establish a cordial relationship between myself and the next heir to the throne..."

"I am assuming then you have not had good news from Lanius Rex," Amira said, once more seated.

"I tried my best, but quite frankly, he is impossible," Laila said, sitting down on the chair across from her mother. "For now we have reached an agreement of trading goods that would not be subject to our more rigorous checks, such as foodstuffs, but I don't know how long that will placate him."

Amira took a long sip of coffee. "If you are experiencing difficulties handling the Mortesian rex, then I am more than happy to send someone else in your stead—"

"It's fine, Maman," Laila interjected. "I am handling it. I wish for once you would have more faith in my abilities."

"I am not a faith-based individual, Laila; you ought to know this by now. I make judgements based on evidence. When I have evidence of your self-proclaimed abilities, then I will cease in my scepticism. Until then, I consider your position as a diplomat to be tenuous at best."

"Yes, Maman," Laila said, swallowing the lump that formed in her throat as she stood. "May I please be excused?"

"Yes, you may continue entertaining your new beastly companion."

Laila had a smile for every occasion, carefully arranged on a retrievable spectrum of brightness. The one she retrieved to accessorise her now was pathetically muted and barely held, but she maintained it long enough to make it to the nearest powder room.

Her mouth collapsed the instant she caught sight of it in the mirror. She spun the taps and ran one of the hand-towels under the water until it was damp, and then stuffed it into her mouth so those outside might not hear her loud, undignified scream.

They gave Dominus a room with an ocean view, the coast's breath cool on his thick winter hide.

He decided to take a shower.

Dominus stood beneath the gelid spray on the coldest setting, head bent to receive direct contact on the burning nape of his neck. He felt like the weather was thawing him out, leaving him soft and boneless as a piece of berg melting on the sea.

He heard Laila enter the shower with him. She placed her palm on his shoulder. "I hope you don't mind, but I took the initiative of having a trunk delivered with clothing better suited for the weather. I had them tailored especially to your measurements. If you'd like, I can help pick out an outfit for you to wear today."

"Ah, yes, the, uh... cocktail party." Dominus turned to glance at her wryly. "With food tasting, I think?"

"It won't be anything too large, just a cosy gathering of the most important people. There are many who are curious to finally meet the infamous occasso, and I thought having a chance to sample some of our finest delicacies would sweeten the ordeal for you."

"You know, in Mortos, there is a certain custom we have during harvest season. Every hunter brings out their most prized catch to be displayed amongst our peers for amusement." His lips quirked upwards. "I assume I am to be this season's most prized catch, yes?"

"It's not like that," Laila said, stepping forward to slide her hands along his chest. "You're not my trophy, Dominus. You are"—her voice faltered through lack of a better term—"you are very dear to me. And I want you to meet my friends so they might see how dear you are to me too." She brought his face down to kiss him. "Now, I was thinking white linen. Perhaps with a green ascot to accent and bring out the colour of your eyes."

"Whatever you think is best."

"I'm being fastidious, I know, but I want you to give off the best possible impression." Laila leaned her head against his russet chest, inhaling his warm campfire scent. "You won't be used to the way we do our hunting out in Soleterea. Everything is a little more... sneaky, more guileful. I don't want you to be caught out unprepared."

Dominus chuckled. "Perhaps you ought to have brought my brother here with you instead."

She laughed, perhaps too hard, as Darius's face flickered unbidden into her mind's view. "I happen to like the one I chose just fine." She brought him in for another kiss, her tongue soft against his.

He strung his arms around her waist to pull her closer, lifting her up to press her against the wall for better access.

Celebrants converged from all over at the château's hallowed grounds to see their beloved princess returned to them, delivered into their waiting arms from across the phantasmal sea.

The lemon grove was warm and honey-soaked in the late evening sun as partygoers danced in swishing skirts of silks and chiffon. The grounds were bedecked with enchanted white chocolate canaries that flitted from table to table to escape the delighted squeals of hunting children. Strings of ætherald crystal lights hung from citrus trees, and a sprite ensemble played melodies for the masses who paid attention to nothing else.

Laila danced barefoot to the strum of the oud and Soleterean guitar, her body twirling like a candle flame. Like all of the solarites, she was garnished in tiers of white lace, her neckline receding below her shoulders to display the faint glimmer of stardust across her light brown skin.

Her solo dance was interrupted as Lyra joined her. Their hips were loose and undulating as they bumped, grinded, and teased each other in sensual rhythm to the music. Laila slung an arm around Lyra's neck to draw her near, losing herself in this—in the languorous haze of heat and music and intimacy as Lyra's hands slid lower and lower down her spine.

"Gods, I've missed this," Lyra murmured into the crook of Laila's neck as she spun her around so they were back to chest.

"It is good to be home," Laila said coquettishly over her shoulder with a silvered trill of laughter. Then Lyra spun her again until they were back facing each other.

She had missed the sun on her back, the sea breeze on her shoulders, the mellifluous cadence of Soltongue on her ears. She'd missed making love and swooning asleep without fear that come dawn she'd awaken into Mortos' icy clutches.

Laila shivered, and not for the first time that day. She reminded herself it was Lyra's arms that held her in her strong archer grip, drawing her near like the string of a bow.

The music soon came to an end, beckoning for them to part. She sent Lyra to get her a drink while she mingled, greeting and charming and kissing as she went, delighting in her once more unshakeable position at the pinnacle of her social ladder.

Despite the congestion in the garden, the world had slowed to a languid drizzle in her presence—as though one couldn't help but orbit the descent of her footsteps like a heart awaiting its next pulse. There were too many faces old and new, all eager for her. She was more than happy to quench their thirst before her throat ached to quench her own.

Afterwards, she diverted her attention to Dominus, whom she found lurking in the shadow of a lemon tree in the near distance.

She smiled, swaying her hips towards him as she slung her arms around his shoulders. "Come dance with me," she pouted, lifting his arms to encircle them around her.

Dominus remained stiff against her gyrating hips. "I don't really know how to move like—"

"You just listen to the music." She clutched his hips and tried to make them roll with her. "Let it guide you, come on."

Dominus swallowed uncomfortably. His body was like cool granite. Laila sighed in defeat before a hand touched her shoulder.

"Your drink, as requested." Lyra held two flutes of nectar in hand, one of which she gave to Laila.

"My heroine, as always." Laila received the glass of nectar fizzling with fairy floss and clinked it against hers with gratitude.

"At your service," Lyra replied, with a sly smirk forming on her lips.

Laila took a sip of nectar, the sweet fluid soothing her parched throat and frazzled nerves. She took a longer, deeper sip until the glass ran dry, and then she took Lyra's.

"Steady on," Lyra protested.

"I'm celebrating, remember?" was Laila's witty rejoinder. She took another swig of her drink and handed Lyra the empty glass. "Another, if you would."

Lyra sighed heavily as she shambled off again.

She was immediately replaced by the arrival of Laila's ladies, Oriel and Astrid.

"Looks like it is time for the inquisition," Laila muttered to Dominus before brandishing a smile. "Pleasant evening, ladies, I hope?" She kept the kisses brief and the introductions even briefer, knowing it was unlikely Dominus would be able to digest all the names before the night was done.

"So large..." Oriel observed, reaching out before Laila could dissuade

233

her to test the width and density of his biceps. "What are they feeding you over there?"

Dominus glanced over at Laila first, almost as though asking permission, before he shrugged. "Elk, boar, moose. The occasional seal. Once, I have even consumed an entire whale tongue."

That caused a round of shocked gasps to ripple through them.

"What about other foods?" Astrid asked, fiddling with her pearl necklace. "I hear Mortos has an array of unusual delicacies. Have you ever had anything more... sapient... on the menu?"

"Astrid," Laila censured, though it was said lightly. She couldn't deny she had missed them. For these precious girls, these starlets, were as much treasures to her as any gown or jewel. And, oh, what was it to be a light without these shadows that clung so stubbornly to her heels.

"I was only asking out of interest," Astrid protested. "I have no intention of passing judgement on the cultural practices of others."

"If you are asking if we eat, uh... people? The answer is no."

"Oh, well that is reassuring." Astrid brightened. "But still you have a castle run by corpses, do you not?"

"All right, I believe we have had enough questions." Laila clapped her hands together. "Come along, Dominus."

"But we haven't even asked him for a demonstration of his powers!" Oriel said. "I was looking forward to it all evening. I have never before seen chaotic magic up close..."

"Perhaps later." Laila dragged Dominus over to the serving tables, where the chefs crafted intricate delicacies for the delight of the audience.

She kept passing him dishes in apology as they came: small towers of saffron risotto, figs wrapped in cured ham, heavenly cheesecakes topped with red berries and pansy flowers.

"I'm sorry about that," Laila told him sheepishly as she passed him a rosewater meringue on a rose petal plate. "They're just curious."

Dominus grunted in acceptance, consuming every offering she gave with one bite, as though he didn't even pause to chew.

"Don't vacuum it," she scolded, holding back her next appetiser from him. "These flavours are meant to be *experienced*. Savoured. Here, let me show you."

She took up a bowl of one of her favourite desserts: banana flambéed in cinnamon and brown sugar syrup, doused in coconut rum and served alongside a helping of vanilla ice cream.

"Take a bit of banana onto your spoon and dip it into the ice cream, just so. Now, eat. But don't swallow immediately. Let the ice cream melt a little on your tongue, contrasting with the warmth of the banana, the spice of the rum. Can you taste it? This is the rhythm of Malakia dancing on your tastebuds. You feel how smooth it is? How sensual? It is one of the reasons the country is my favourite place to travel."

Dominus chewed softly, swallowing slowly as he ran his tongue over his lips. "Can we go there next?"

Laila's face creased with a chuckle. "We'll see." She took a spoonful of the dessert next, then fed him the bite that came after.

"Laila." She heard the familiar croon of Céleste, her old flame, white cream cocktail in hand.

"Céleste!" Laila exclaimed in mock delight, kissing both cheeks, as was custom. "Oh, it's so good to see you. How long has it been?"

"Well, just over a year. You are quite difficult to reach now you've been so busy with all this Mortesian business... and now I see who it is you have been busy with."

Laila forced a smile; a hand draped protectively over Dominus's arm. "This is Dominus Regulus."

"So I hear," Céleste said, wielding her dagger of a smile upon him next. "What a pleasure." She held out her hand for him to take. "Hm, strong handshake. Not that I'm surprised, after all, with arms almost as large as my head."

"Nice to meet you," Dominus said. "I assume you are another friend of Laila's?"

"Well, you could say that," Céleste simpered politely. "But I really must dash. Laila, good to see you again, as always. Do feel free to call upon me for a little tête-à-tête when you are available... I feel it'll be a very enlightening one." She cast another scrutinising glance upon Dominus before she brushed past them with a lingering scent of lilac left in the air.

"She seemed nice," Dominus said, stuffing a meringue into his mouth.

"Trust me, Céleste is far from nice," Laila scoffed, taking a long sip from her cocktail. She gathered she was probably here to size up the competition. Literally.

Dominus raised a brow in interest. The customs here grew even odder to him the more he learned. "If you do not like her, why smile and kiss her cheek?"

"Because she is a dynasty solarite, like myself, and her family owns the royal opera house. If I do not make nice, then there will be no VIP tickets for me and you." She dug her spoon deep into her dessert and took another bite in frustration.

"Your customs here are intriguing. If it were me, I would simply ask to settle our enmity in combat."

"Well, not all of us can afford to resolve our issues quite so... directly. Like I said, we do our hunting a little differently in Soleterea. More honey than vinegar."

She scooped a spoonful from the honeypot and drizzled it on her dessert. Whilst taking a bite, there was a parting in the crowd, as Dr Isuka made a warpath towards them.

"Dr Isuka!" Laila exclaimed, so thrilled to see her she forgot to notice the rage on her face. "What a pleasant surprise. I hadn't—"

The scholar halted her by holding up the letter of condolence she'd been sent. With one swift tear, she had it in two. "Is this the best you could've done?" She dashed the paper to the floor and scrunched it under her foot. Then she spat at Dominus. "Vermin."

Laila recoiled in shock, watching as a Lightshield seized Dr Isuka and hauled her off of her feet.

"Count your days, occasso!" Dr Isuka snarled. "I will have my divine justice yet!"

Laila inhaled shakily as the scholar was carried away. She was about to pursue her when someone seized her arm.

"Let me see to this." It was Lucrèce Mielette, leaning close to whisper in her ear. "Too many eyes on you to make a scene."

Laila glanced around to notice the hushed murmurs and concerned stares. She swallowed and composed herself, putting on a reassuring smile for Dominus who barely concealed his murderous ire.

Laila spent the following days showing Dominus all the haunts of her youth. She walked him through the forest of white unicorns, where she picked strawberries among the foals, down to the pristine white beaches skirted by an azure sea.

They took Le Creissant next, startling the hordes of doves on the pavement. Laila dragged Dominus into every building as they walked through the city: museums and art galleries and temples built for worship. She asked his opinions on artists he could not name and traced her fingers over alabaster busts, marvelling at how someone could take an amorphous mass of stone and chisel life into it.

But it was this she wished to show him: all the life and the beauty and the artistry that awaited him outside of the secluded isle he called home. Where even the stone could have life. How it always seemed so new and exciting, even to her, to watch her city's ever evolving growth.

Dominus couldn't say he appreciated it with anywhere near the same amount of fanaticism, but he found a renewed respect for this strange summer world, so far from his own, that he otherwise wouldn't have entertained.

On their final day, Laila took them for ice cream sundaes in one of the pastel-coloured parlours on the beachfront. She tossed a coin to a sprite guitarist so he might play a song for them while they indulged.

She ordered them both the special—orange ice cream garnished with candied lavender almonds, orange peel and violets, and flakes of gold leaf, drenched in orange brandy liqueur and spiced syrup.

Laila helped herself to an indulgent spoonful, her lips coming away flaked with gold. "I think it is the food I will mourn most when we return to Mortos."

Dominus grunted in agreement. He tapped his spoon against his sundae glass. "Would you like to return?"

"Why do you ask?"

He looked up at her contented face. The orange sunset on the horizon had painted her skin honey. If he could have drawn her at this moment he would have, with the dying dregs of sunlight framing her gold-limned locks.

"You seem happier here, among your friends and family. In Mortos you seemed... dimmer. Less vibrant."

She twirled her spoon between her lips in thought. "It was a difficult adjustment to make. But I do wish to return with you."

She smiled reassuringly. He remained unconvinced. She was like him, blessed and cursed into godliness. Swaddled in privilege and doomed to cripple beneath the weight of the universes they carried on their shoulders.

"Do you think you will ever regard Mortos as your home?"

"What's brought this on?" Laila asked, apprehensive of his answer. She set her spoon down inside her melting dessert.

Dominus laced his fingers together, the correct words alluding him. He'd only experienced this sort of encompassing devotion once before in his immortal life but, he'd been once bitten and twice shy. He didn't want to pluck his heart out for the offering if it was only for her to refuse.

"Nothing."

"Dominus?" Laila put her hand over his.

"Another time," he assured her, deciding this was a topic better left unbroached for later.

XX

DARIUS SLUNG HIS CLOAK OVER HIS DESK CHAIR before he sat at the table. Over the past month, he had gathered all he could on the topic of solarites—a vast chronicle detailing their voyage from the rosy skies to the iridescent shores of Soleterea—which he had combined inside a journal for his own personal perusal.

He had become obsessed with unravelling the intricacies of delicate stitching so he might separate the simple facts from embroidered myth. The facts being their first arrival to in an asteroid nearly a millennium ago, their exclusively female forms, and the cores of their bodies, powered by stars.

It fascinated him how different their story was from the chthonic origins of the occassi, how they held a mastery of life in comparison to the occassi's of death, light in comparison to their dark, creation in comparison to their chaos. Almost as if some higher, incomprehensible force had seen the occassi and erected their natural opposite as a challenge.

Regarding defence, his scouts had left no avenue unexplored. While solarites were formidable on their own terms, they also had allied forces with forest sprites who were adept in the ways of combat and hunting— in particular, monster-hunting, which they had long adopted to be their divine purpose.

The mortal countries, in comparison, were far less threatening and thus less compelling. In each of the countries, there were witches with magical abilities that pertained to the four base elements of fire, water, earth and air. The countries had industries to reflect these proclivities, and most were rather mundane.

However, in Seraj, the arid fire nation close in proximity to Soleterea, they wielded firedrakes that could spew balls of flame at speeds and distances that made a mockery of even the finest archer. Fire was one of the few things occassi were not impervious towards; Darius gave this information the appropriate disquietude.

Darius doubted his father would like the conclusion he came to, which was that this was a mission best left abandoned. At least until they could have time to gain an upper hand. And Darius felt he knew exactly how.

However, he also knew this would be the point of contention most likely to rouse his father's unpredictable rage. So it was with caution that Darius prepared himself to go to the Eyrie to inform Lanius of his findings.

Lanius was standing before the fireplace in wait for him, the fluctuating smoulder having made a skeletal mask of his features.

"This had better be you arriving with the information you sought." Lanius's voice, low and sonorous, had become ominously slurred.

241

Clutched in his fingers was another in a long line of whisky tumblers he'd downed after dinner.

"I have it," Darius answered, notably cagier than before.

"Well then, out with it, boy," Lanius said, his whisky sloshing in his grip. He didn't often drink to the point of inebriation unless he needed to soak away the oppressive bouts of numbness due to his heartless state. Violence and vice were the only things that ever roused him anymore.

Noting this, Darius treaded carefully as a church mouse among traps. "From the information I've collated from various sources, I'm going to have to put forward the suggestion that a war with Soleterea may not be the most sensible course of action."

"Stop mincing around with your riddle talk and say what you mean, Darius." His father's eyes were now hooded with a menacing gloom. "You mean to say you think we are too weak to win this fight."

"Weakness has little to do with it, Soleterea is simply too equal a match for us. To go up against them now, in light of this, would be near suicidal."

"Suicidal." Lanius barked the word with a hollow bone-crackle of laughter. "You seem to forget I am deathless now, Darius, courtesy of that venomous pit-snake you have to call your mother. There is very little now that can overcome me, destroy me, defeat me. Let the solarites come with their little sunbeams and thunderbolts; I'll tear them all apart limb by limb and still be left standing long enough to eat the throat out of that uppity wench Amira as she screams for me to stop."

"Your Majesty, you are not listening to reason." Darius sighed; he could see his father was too far sunken into the pits of his madness to be reached now. That crazed, manic look in his eye only made an appearance when it was time to fully abandon ship. "Deathless as you may be, that doesn't extend to your warriors. How many of us must you sacrifice in pursuit of a goal that may not even be realised? Will you edge us near to extinction merely for the sake of your ego trip?"

"You've had your head stuck in the books for too long, Darius." Lanius glugged down the rest of his whisky. "But it's my fault for not beating that miserable habit out of you sooner. You've forgotten what it means to be a warrior; you've forgotten how to adhere to the chain of command." His voice lowered as he stepped forward. "Perhaps I ought to remind you."

"Striking me down will not lessen the legitimacy of what I'm saying to you, and you know it," Darius countered, his own rage simmering beneath the still waters of indifference he carefully displayed. "But if you would just listen to me, you would hear that my books and I might have an alternate solution for you."

"Oh, and what's that?"

"You know how long I've been studying chimera creation and mutagenesis. I'm nearing a breakthrough." He thought of Emica undergoing metamorphosis in his laboratory, still hatching from her chrysalis. Soon. He just needed more *time*. "If you'd allow me more funding to pursue it, then I might be able to craft us mutated warbeasts for the express purpose of surpassing Soleterea's arsenal."

"No."

"*No?*" Darius challenged.

"How long will it take before your inventions are even near serviceable? Decades? A century? I've told you this once before, Darius. Swords and sorcery. That is how we win our battles. All this artificery nonsense is for lesser beings, beings that do not know how to fight for themselves. I simply refuse to cower behind a piece of weaponry and allow it to do the fighting for me. When I fight wars, I fight them with my hands."

"Then you will lose with your hands."

It was the wrong thing to say.

Darius knew it the moment the words vacated his lips, and his father's bestial visage burst through the seams of his face. Lanius blurred towards him and smashed his glass into smithereens on Darius's nose, dragging him by the hair to slam his face against his kneecap before he punched him to the floor.

Darius took each blow as it came, knowing it would be better to wait it out than to fight back, to let his father release his steam.

Lanius rammed his boot down on Darius's side, smirking as he heard the satisfying crackle of ribs beneath his sole. He moved his boot to his son's throat next, pressing down hard. "I should've ripped out those smart little vocal cords of yours years ago."

Darius choked beneath him, but still refused to give up his poise. He wouldn't give his father the satisfaction of begging him to stop.

Lanius cracked his knuckles before he hauled Darius back up onto his feet, about to ready himself for another strike when a voice in the room gave him pause.

"*What* is going on in here?"

There stood Laila in a whirlwind of curls, having phased through the door upon the sound of commotion. She'd been searching high and low for Darius to greet him after her return from the sunny shorelands being, unbeknownst to her, at that moment hotly debated. How unfortunate that her timing had delayed her from being privy to such a crucial discussion...

Her eyes widened in horror at what she saw. Darius broken and bloodied, splints of glass pushing out from his nose as his wounds attempted to heal while his father loomed ferally above him.

It might be the truest image she would ever see of them, stripped back of their cultivated airs to the undomesticated barbarism beneath.

Lanius turned towards her with a hiss, his fangs full on display. "Leave."

But Laila was deafened to this danger, either too brave or too blundering to recognise Lanius's hair-trigger restraint. Instead, her attention was all for Darius as she reached for him, up on her toes, touching his shoulders.

"Are you all right?"

How strange to be on the receiving end of such unburdened empathy, no terms or conditions necessary, no dangling strings. Just a gentle touch on the shoulder and a crease of concern on her forehead— Darius wanted to melt within it.

"You should do as he says, princess," Darius said.

"Yes, fly home, little birdy," Lanius sneered, lip curling back in disdain. "I wouldn't want to see your pretty feathers ruffled."

Laila removed her hands from Darius's shoulders and turned to face Lanius with a look of utter dismissal, like he was something to scrape off the edge of her embroidered shoe.

"You are not even worth the energy I would expend dignifying your response, you sad little creature."

Darius understood it. Lanius did not.

However, Lanius did not need to be fluent in Soltongue to realise an affront when he heard it, and he responded by smashing his fist into her face.

"Have you taken leave of your senses?" Darius exclaimed in alarm as Laila crumpled to the floor, stunned more than pained. Her lip had pierced to seep a golden rivulet of ichor. Darius crouched before her to survey her face for more damage before turning to his father in disbelief. "Are you trying to cause an international incident?"

His concerns fell on deaf ears as his father took another trembling step forward in provocation. Darius turned back to Laila, expecting fear, bewilderment, even upset—only to find she was *smirking*, of all things.

"I shall let you have that first strike, Lanius Rex. As a greeting gift. But should you raise your hand to me again, I'd best warn you: you'll be in for quite a shock."

That usage of Mortesian was all the catalyst Lanius needed to step forward.

Darius rose to barricade him. "Don't," he warned, holding out an arm to enforce it. His fangs were itching at his gums to descend. "Go and sober up, before you do something you regret."

Perhaps it was the threat of an obstacle to his violent pursuit—or whatever rational portion remained of Lanius's mind—catching up with the weight of his actions, but he desisted with a snarl and took off out of the room.

Darius heaved an exhausted sigh before he turned back to Laila, holding out a hand to assist her. "Well, that was foolish."

She stared at his hand in puzzlement for some moments before she accepted it. "I heal fast."

"I can see that," Darius noted in wry amusement as he seized her chin and tilted it up. The cut had healed, leaving only the glistening smear of her blood on her lip. He withdrew his handkerchief with a flick of his hand and used it to dab her.

"That doesn't seem like the first time he's hit you; does he do that often?" She took his wrist in her hand to still it. "Does he hurt Dominus?"

He could feel the radiant warmth of her hand, paired with perhaps the *softest* look he had ever received. He wondered if this was even a fraction of the potency she looked at Dominus with. If so, he could understand his brother all too well now.

"Some stones are better left unturned, princess," he said, realising that, despite himself, his thumb had started easing its way over her chin in delicate strokes. He dropped his treacherous hand into his pocket, slid his handkerchief away with the other and turned to depart.

"Why do you always shrink away from me in fear?"

Though he knew it shouldn't, her words halted him. He pivoted around with a chuckle. "I'm not afraid of you."

"Then why does it seem every time we are around each other, you can't find a quick enough excuse to leave?"

She inched her way towards him until the minimal distance between them was closed.

He stared down at her, matching her daring with his own immovable stance. "You should walk away."

"Why?" Her head cocked to one side.

It would be so easy for him to close the distance between them a little more, take her cheek in his hand and—ah, what a reckless fool he was! Wanting to scavenge her for crumbs of affection he could easily get elsewhere, should he look. Yet did she not provoke him? Looking so *warmly* at him like this? Someone for whom he could throw off his cloak and nestle beside and feel the comfort of a home for once?

"Because if you don't, then I might be persuaded to do something... foolish."

Laila's throat ran dry. She slid out her tongue to moisten her lips. "Such as?"

He let his eyes fall to her lips, his pulse quickening. It took every ounce of restraint in him to refuse this, to prevent what he knew would only ever be a short-term pleasure leading to long-term pain.

He turned on his heel to depart. "As I said before, princess. Some stones are better left unturned."

Dominus and Vasilisa sat beneath the lambent glow of the brass wall sconces, drinking lingonberry kompot and eating nettle bread. The apartment walls were etched with grotesques built from sleek oak panels used to make casks and coffins.

"Shouldn't the others have arrived by now?" asked Vasilisa, refilling her son's glass.

"I'm sure they won't be long, Mamochka." Dominus took a large bite from his bread. "But while we have a moment alone, I'd like to discuss something with you."

"Of course," she said.

Dominus cleared his throat, scratching nervously behind his pointed ear. "What would you say if I desired to make Laila my bride?"

Vasilisa swallowed suddenly, coughing when her windpipe filled with kompot. She made a gesture of wellness when Dominus reached to support her.

"Goodness, that's—" Her words failed her. "That is certainly—"

"Unheard of, I know," Dominus replied on her behalf. "But I feel right about this. Not only for myself, but for the future status of our nations. A marriage could serve to join us both."

"Doma," Vasilisa sighed. She'd always feared this day would come. Part of her hoped that his first brush with heartbreak would've staved the appetite for marriage off for good. "I can certainly tell you feel strongly about this girl. But Laila, she isn't one of us. You understand? We know so little of her nature. Can she even provide you a son? An heir? In the event something happens to you?"

"I am well aware of our curse, Mamochka. But I wouldn't want an heir off her—at least, it wouldn't be my immediate concern. I wouldn't want Papa to believe I sought to move against him."

Vasilisa's shock took a turn for disappointment. Though she

couldn't blame Dominus his loyalty, it might very well have been that which had kept him alive for so long. "Yes. That is... a valid concern."

Upon seeing her so forlorn, Dominus took her hand. "This wouldn't change much. I want you to know that. Regardless of whoever else I invite into our lives, you will always be my mother."

Vasilisa looked up with a smile, curving her hand over his cheek.

Not a moment later did Laila come blustering into the room. She paused before the sight of mother and son, feeling wrong to disturb them, but she was still shaken from her earlier encounter with Lanius and needed the strength of Dominus's arms around her to moor her to the shore of stability.

"Dominus," she called out to him as though it were the last breath she had to give in her lungs.

Vasilisa looked up first, her expression guarded. There was something fey and uncanny about the gauntness of her features—all that was porcelain and petal-soft in her seemed to drip away like wax.

"Laila?" Dominus's brow was furrowed in concern, but before he could stand, Vasilisa's hand snapped over his like an oyster shell. "We'll only be a moment, Mamochka."

"Is it not enough that she has had you for a week? It seems I cannot ask for more than one hour," Vasilisa said, her tone softly pleading in a way that strummed guilt on Laila's heartstrings.

"I'll come back later," Laila said, turning on her heel. There was nothing that stole the wind from her supercilious wings quicker than the will of a mother, even one that was not her own.

"Wait," Dominus called to her, making her pause. Then he brought his mother's hand to his lips. "A moment, please."

Vasilisa sighed softly as the settling dusk. "As you wish."

"Thank you, Your Highness," Laila said.

Vasilisa dipped her head in response. She seemed almost gracious in comparison to her husband, a gentle giant.

Dominus escorted her towards the doors and closed them behind her before turning towards Laila. "What is it?"

"We need to talk about your father," Laila replied, taking a definitive step forward.

Dominus's brow bent in confusion. "My father?"

"Yes, I went to call upon him earlier and found him with Darius. They were fighting." Laila's hands animated with gesticulations. "But, Dominus, I'd never seen such violence in him like that before. He was *beating* Darius. And then when I tried to calm the situation, he struck me."

"He *struck* you?" Dominus's expression took a barbarous turn.

"Yes, but, I'm fine. That's not relevant as of now. Dominus..." Laila moved towards him to rest her hands on his chest, her fingers in his kaftan. "How long has this been going on? Does he hurt you?"

There was a shift in his throat as he looked away from her, moving her hands down from his chest like he was lowering a weapon. "No, Laila, he doesn't hurt me. But we mustn't speak of this."

"Why not?"

"Because this is a family matter and because I do not wish to."

"Your brother is being beaten and you want me to brush it off as a family matter?"

"You'd do well not to make a victim out of Darius, Laila. Matters between him and my father—they are more complicated than you could ever know." Dominus raked a hand through his hair in agitation. "In fact, I'd advise you against involving yourself in his situation altogether."

"What?" A shallow exclamation expelled at the edge of a breath. "*Why?*"

He did not look at her, almost as though he couldn't. His green eyes were dense and unyielding, an impassable savanna where beasts camouflaged themselves from prey.

She made him face her, her neck craned towards him in demand. "Tell me."

"Because he wants to fuck you."

Her lips opened, closed. Then she parted them once more to speak. "Don't deny it."

She couldn't, and he knew it. Not when her mind was reconstructing all the evidence before her eyes—all the looks, the touches, the tension. Too compelling a case to be anything other than convicted.

"So because he wants to, that somehow means he will?" she said.

"You know, I had a previous lover tell me the exact same words once. Guess what happened? She fucked him. So forgive me if I'm not willing to be made a fool of twice." He took a step closer, looming over her like the shadow of an axe at an execution.

His rage smouldered, as toxic as the black exhaust fumes of a coal fire. She felt suffocated beneath it. This ire. All for the spectre of a lover whose actions were not hers to own.

"Take a step back, Dominus," Laila warned, her body humming with an electric pulse. She would not be caught off-guard twice.

He breathed in deeply through his nose, exhaling slowly, but step back he did. "Tell me you won't be around him anymore."

"He is your brother, Dominus; I can't simply eject him from my presence," Laila replied, her gaze setting hard and crystalline. "But I think it's about time we ended this conversation. Come back and talk to me when you're being less of an intolerable boor."

She dismissed him with a toss of her honey-gold curls and marched out of the room.

251

The morning after had her up early, roused by the trumpeting blare of daylight. The sky was grey and clustered with clouds that threatened downpour at any second. Laila almost hoped it did. She could do with some rain, a shower of needles to pierce this bubble of humidity.

Laila could hear her home in her ears as she brushed her hair with an ornate silver brush. Each stroke of unicorn-hair bristles was the shivering of wind through the palm trees. The sound made her feel strangely nostalgic, and she wondered, not for the first time, if her mother had been correct at not wanting to send her back.

She considered summoning an audience with her through the mirror, but the mere thought of admitting defeat and informing her of what happened with Lanius made her pause, not wanting to face her disappointment.

Outside her door, she could hear the mechanical squeak of trolley wheels and knew Morgana was bringing her breakfast to her. Laila greeted the ghoul at the door and received her tray with a smile.

After she had eaten, she received another servant telling her a visitor had arrived from the Citadel. Laila peered through her sheer drapes to see Dominus. She considered having him sent away but decided it better to go down and face him. Regardless of how she felt about his loutish behaviour the night before, she couldn't risk a row, not when Lanius was still certain to be on the warpath after her.

She made her way down into the courtyard, where Dominus waited on the back of his hippogriff.

He slid down from his muscular mount when she appeared and moved to greet her.

She did not look at him.

"I—" He paused, scratching behind his pointed ear. "I may have been too rough towards you in my conduct yesterday."

Laila gazed at him like she was seeing him for the very first time—as though he'd been solidified into being by virtue of her acknowledgement. "Is that an apology, Dominus?"

His eyes lowered in deference, making a remarkably pitiful pup out of this bestial creature.

Laila sighed heavily as she walked over to the hippogriff and reached out to stroke his silken mane, scratching behind his long, bat-like ear. "Does he have a name?" She longed to touch his feathers, but the moment she reached, the glowing iris of the hippogriff's bloodshot eye dissuaded her.

"Talon," Dominus said from behind her. "Have you ever ridden a hippogriff?"

"No," Laila said. "There's nothing quite like these creatures in Vysteria. Instead, we ride lions or unicorns. My unicorn is named Polaris." Her heart swelled with longing at the thought of him.

"I could teach you, if you'd like," Dominus said, his stoic guard gradually lowering in response to her warmth. "It seems daunting at first, but the trickiest part is getting him to trust you. After that, he wouldn't dare let you fall."

"All right," she said as her hand moved back and forth over Talon's lustrous mane.

Dominus moved cautiously towards her, almost worried she would fragment in his hands if not cradled with the lightest touch. For his hands, while adept at taking things apart, were never adjusted for the task of putting them back together again.

He took her by the waist and sat her astride the hippogriff, making eye contact with Talon as he did so. Then he mounted behind Laila and wrapped his arms around her.

She liked the way the creature's muscles tensed between her legs, how broad and powerful it felt when she clenched her thighs together in turn. There was no bridle, no stirrups, nothing to hold onto but Talon's mane. And so she did, clenching hard, pulling harder, subduing him beneath her will.

"March," Dominus ordered.

Laila's stomach soared as Talon launched forward with ungodly speed, throwing off the binds of gravity as though it had no hold.

"Fly."

He fanned out his wings mid-stride, and the clopping of his hooves disappeared as they ascended.

Laila threw her arms around his neck, clutching him tightly as the manor shrank to a microscopic blemish beneath her vision. She'd flown before, but it never lost the novelty to her anxiety-prone nerves.

"It's all right, I've got you." She could feel the vibration of Dominus's laughter through her back. "I won't let you fall."

They flew far past the outskirts of Gravissia into the more rustic hinterlands that lay beyond.

Laila could see the way the lichen parasitised every surface as they flew above the treetops. It carpeted a dense rug of verdure over every bole of archaic oak. Even the silver birches were shawled with the moss and coiling vines that swallowed every glimpse of the ground below like an infestation of flies over a carcass.

Dominus ordered Talon to descend inside the mire, and their skin grew moistened by the wet exhalations of its pungent swamp smog. Laila wiped the condensation from her brow and noticed a gaggle of antlered maidens known as qarnine. Their arms were weighted with wicker baskets full of mushrooms and berries, which they plucked in abundance to smother into jars and preserves to last them the winter.

It was unusual for her to see so many at once that were not corpses, their antlers luxuriant with vegetation and red mushroom caps as opposed to a deathly bone white. She was struck by how charmingly mundane they were with their loop braids and patterned head-scarves bobbing intimately as they chattered, the hems of their embroidered sarafans crusted with leaves and dry earth.

Only when she saw the moss-bearded remnants of the lodge in the distance did she realise: this was the forest she began in. This was the same forest trail, the same unfathomable trees. How alien it looked to her now it had shed its white winter coat.

Dominus stopped outside the door and helped her down from Talon.

"Why have you brought me here?" Laila asked, tracing her hand against the furry down of moss along the wood.

"I always hoped we would return, one day," Dominus said, scuffing his foot along the underbrush. "I hoped we could go back to the ways things began. When we were happier. At peace. Undisturbed."

"Dominus." Laila breathed his name in a laugh as she moved to place her hands on his chest. "We can't go back to that time. You do know that, don't you?"

"Why not?" Dominus asked, disturbingly earnest in his tone. "Who's to say I cannot sweep you into my arms right this moment and lock us both up forever where no one would find us?"

"They'd find us here eventually," Laila countered. "I'd imagine it's the first place they'd look."

"Then I would slaughter them, all of them, by the dozens, until the forest was soaked black in warning, and we would be the only two left." He smiled at her, and his teeth glinted like a knife. "Perhaps I ought to have done that from the beginning."

"Dominus."

"I just wish we could be with each other, without all of this. Without politics and rivalries and schemes." He took her hands, and there was such tender desperation, such mourning for the expiration of their relational innocence. "Isn't that what you want?"

She looked down at their hands together, then back up into his eyes with a strained smile. "Why don't we stay here for a while? And then we can discuss it after. All right?"

"All right." Dominus smiled in relief. "We can go to the little fishing town down south and collect the supplies we'll need."

∽

The town of Putrich ushered them in on rugged cobblestone streets, the marketplace still haemorrhaging the overflow of its morning crowd. The place was cordoned with distinguished wattle-and-daub houses in black timber frames. Even more crudely fashioned izbas languished away in their shadows from a distance, cast over like a subject of shame no one was meant to discuss.

Laila walked among them, her nose assaulted by the pungent aroma of fish on ice. She purchased a candied apple from an insistent merchant and devoured the layer of warm congealed toffee, her eyes searching for where Dominus had slipped away to.

She found something else instead.

The sight of a large black carriage swelled into her field of vision like a blot of ink as it sped across the cobbles. The driver was going like a bat out of the abyss, momentum near tipping the car off its wheel as it swerved a sharp turn before the residential houses.

Two occassi slipped out, whips and chains in their hands. They went from house to house with methodical synchronicity, hammering the doors with a hollow thud before they opened.

Each time they entered, they emerged with a single qarnun led in

256

bondage. They did not discriminate with their plundering—their haul encompassed male and female, parent and child.

Laila could not take her eyes off of them, her attention tethered to the scene like a snare.

It happened so quickly, so smoothly, as though it were commonplace. Something to shrug off with ease. She kept glancing about her to see if anyone else was noticing, but the sellers carried on selling, and the market-goers went about purchasing their wares with dulled faces.

She herself was about to turn away when a shrill cry of a qarnina sliced through the air and pierced her ears.

"Please, you can't take him."

Laila looked up again with swift deer senses and saw the qarnina running through the door after the uniformed occasso. Her husband caught her at the threshold, pulling her back as she kicked and screamed.

Shivering in the custody of the occasso was a young boy no more than fifteen.

"You know the edict," said the occasso in a blasé tone. "Only three exemptions before we come knocking."

"Mama, don't let them take me!" The boy's face had crumpled with a sob as he reached back for his mother, causing a ripple in the chain link that jerked the arm of his escort.

The occasso snarled cruelly as he wrapped the chain around his wrist, yanking the boy up to the carriage even as he cried and pleaded.

"You fiends, you monsters!" the qarnina cried hysterically, but her venomous curses fell on the ears of indifferent demons. "Let him go. Please, just let him go."

Laila could take it no longer. She stepped forward, intent on putting a stop to it.

"Don't." Dominus had appeared behind her, and he reached out a hand to stop her.

The qarnina's shrieks were a dire sound, and yet the world remained unmoved to her pleas. She tore free of her husband's grip in desperation to launch herself at her child's captor.

The occasso smacked her down as easily as if she were a ragdoll, and she fell, caving her skull open on the cobbles. Her antlers shattered to pieces. Blood and bits of brain swirled out on the stones.

Laila cried out in horror.

"No!" yelled her husband as he ran to her. He cradled her body to him as her broken skull wept its last.

The occasso didn't bother to turn back, flinging the boy into the carriage with the others. His partner retrieved the qarnina's body from the grieving clutches of her husband and carried it, oozing and dripping along the cobbles. He tossed it inside with the others and barricaded the door. Then both occassi slinked back into the vehicle, tearing off into the horizon.

Laila slapped Dominus's hand away with a bee-sting swat. Her body was rippling with rage. "What in oblivion was that?"

"A misfortune," Dominus replied, eyes solemn. He shook his head. "She shouldn't have tried to fight it."

"Shouldn't have tried to fight it?" Laila echoed in disbelief, unable to believe her ears. "They were stealing her child!"

"That was an honour he was bestowed," Dominus said, gesturing after the carriage. "He was the holy hare, a sacrifice made to appease Calante for a fertile summer."

Laila shook her head violently. "I can't believe what I am hearing."

"This is a natural thing," he persisted. "As a shepherd herds and culls his sheep, so do we rule over the lesser beings here. Their deaths serve a higher purpose. But you don't have to worry." He brought his hands to cradle her head. "Remember what I told you? About hunting? None of him will go to waste. We never let the qarna go to waste."

Her chest seized at his words. "Y-you mean—" She thought of Dominus with the knife in hand, cutting away the antlers, cutting away the skin, preserving the meat for later so it did not decay. Only when she looked over his shoulder it wasn't a deer on the slab, but a white wraith that reared up with an airless scream. "The ghouls."

"His suffering will not be in vain."

His words were all too much for her.

She shoved his hands from her head. "I need to leave this place."

XXI

DARIUS ENTERED THE EYRIE TO FIND HIS FATHER among his prefects, a rare sight for him outside of urgent meetings. Most noticeable of all, however, was the absence of Dominus among them.

"Sit down." Lanius gestured to the seat furthest from him on the table.

Darius pulled out the seat with a noisy groan of wood on stone, straining the sound for dramatic effect before he sat. "Good morning."

"I've gathered you all here today to discuss important business." Lanius stood tall, hands folded behind his back. "For millennia we have struggled against the precarious whims of nature, forced to submit to barren summers and famished winters. Well, to this I say no more. I see hope for a new kingdom on the horizon, one where we no longer have to beg from hags and borrow from foreigners. I see hope for a kingdom in which Mortos, and Mortos alone, takes charge of our own destiny. Where we will ascend to our rightful place as the world's superior race, the way Our Papa Calante intended."

Throughout the speech, Lanius's prefects murmured in intrigue amongst themselves while Darius paused in bated breath, praying against all odds this wasn't going where he feared.

"This is why I called you here today, as a rallying cry. For I have set my sights upon this land of greener pasture." He took out a scroll and unfurled it across the table, revealing a large map of Vysteria. "In the land south of us, these star-creatures fatten themselves upon the well of riches of their continent. I say the time has come for a new order, where we take possession of the keys to their castle and help ourselves to all they have acquired."

The others, besides Darius, were all ears, their features grown crooked with their avarice.

"How do you suggest we proceed with this, Your Majesty?" asked Prime Prefect Claudius.

"Soleterea is the beating heart of the continent." Lanius slammed his fist down upon the country. "Rip it out, and the rest will bleed into submission, unable to resist our command."

The prefects murmured in agreement.

"And what of the solarites' means of defence?" Claudius asked.

"What of it? These are pampered socialites who spend their days growing soft and lazy by the sun." Delanus chuckled in derision. "What possible match could these delicate demoiselles be against us?"

"Quite a formidable one, Delanus," Darius interjected, his throat bobbing. Then he outlined the exact same logistics he had to his father, pausing to assess the effect among his prefects.

The once-assured confidence was growing flimsier, he could see, but Darius knew it would take much more convincing to dispel them from the notion that Soletereans were meek-mannered merchants easily thwarted by their martial supremacy.

"Your Majesty, you cannot expect us to go up against such odds and prevail," Claudius said once Darius had finished. "Surely, we ought to listen to Prefect Calantis and bide our time for a more advantageous standing."

"I refuse to hold back any longer!" Lanius roared. His eyes were maniacal with conviction. "The longer it is we wait, the more they learn of us, our strengths and weaknesses. No. I say overwhelming odds are not the same as impossible. Have you forgotten the breadth of power Calante has given you? We can win this. And we will!"

His voice was booming so loudly it echoed, as though Calante himself spoke through him as a vessel of his divine will. He felt stronger than he ever had before, infused with deific might. He would not hear a refusal. He couldn't.

"This is madness!" Claudius rose from his seat. "Absolute madness. I apologise for speaking out of turn, but you're going to get us all killed. I refuse to listen to this any longer." He pushed out his seat with a huff, tearing towards the door.

He barely made it a foot from the table before he was impaled on the end of Lanius's closed fist.

The prefects all stood in alarm, a cacophony of hushed whispers and strenuous gasps.

Lanius sank his hand deep into his prefect's chest, clenching hard around the muscle of his heart before he withdrew with it intact.

Claudius only had time to gurgle before he sank to his knees and slumped over, blood pulsating out onto the floor like a jug of wine spilled.

"No, my dear Claudius," Lanius spoke towards the throbbing heart in his hand. "I am afraid it is you who is going to get them all killed." He let the organ slide from his hand and raised his arms. "Anyone else care to defy me? I have no trouble at all slaughtering the lot of you and replacing you with sycophants more malleable to my whims. Well?"

The silence was so thick it was almost audible.

"Then you are dismissed."

The prefects couldn't leave fast enough, clambering over the body of their fallen comrade as they went.

"Not you, Darius," Lanius said as he was about to join them.

He remained rooted where he stood. "Your Majesty?"

Lanius cut the stub of his cigar and struck a match. "I've been giving some thought to your... tinkering as of late, and I've decided I would like to see one of your weapons in action."

"Under what condition?" Darius asked, sweat prickling on the nape of his neck. "I assume there must be one."

"I have a certain target for you in mind." His father exhaled a ring of smoke. "Consider this your chance to impress me."

Darius nodded, grateful for the challenge. "What would you like me to do?"

"Laila Rose has intentions of resigning her post as ambassador and returning back to Soleterea." Lanius inhaled from his cigar. "I don't intend for her to make it."

Darius's throat seized. "You want me to—"

"Dispose of her. Yes. That ought to send a salient message that the time for negotiation is no more. I want that dim-witted wench erased from existence."

"Your Majesty, I understand your pride might be feeling wounded due to what occurred the other night—"

"I have no desire to discuss this with you, Darius. I have given you an order, and I expect you to carry it out. Or perhaps you'd rather me send you down into the dungeon. Does that proposition lean more to your liking?"

Darius glanced towards the cooling body of Claudius and saw there was no reasoning with him. "No."

"Very well. I have requested the princess attend our annual tarot tournament. You can perform the deed there. Let me know when it's done."

"Yes, Your Majesty."

Darius rose from his seat.

"And Darius?"

"Yes?"

"Do not fail me."

⌀⌀

The evening had Darius drowning his sorrows in polugar.

He brought out his finest bottle of single malt rye, which he'd reserved for a significant occasion. The bottle was a gift from an old lover and was one of only fifty in existence, finely distilled in copper pots and left to age to maturation. He popped the cork, filled the glass near to overflowing, and slumped down on his divan to take a sip.

He closed his eyes, savouring the creaminess of the texture, when he heard a creak in the corridor, signalling someone approaching his quarters.

He put down his glass, not expecting visitors and silently praying it wasn't Dominus. He was unprepared to see Vasilisa appear in his doorway instead.

"Your Highness," Darius exclaimed, not sure whether to be more alarmed by the sight of her face or the sight of her hair. It was court fashion for married occasselle to hide their hair unless they were alone or among relatives. "Is something the matter?"

Vasilisa smiled at him, though he could tell it was only for decorum. "I heard my husband made quite a stir at the council meeting today."

"He's gone stark-raving mad!" Darius gesticulated wildly. Then he scooped up his glass for a long sip. "He *murdered* Claudius. Then he declared war on the entirety of the Vysterian continent and threatened to execute us for refusing support."

Vasilisa silently made her way over to the divan.

"Poor Claudius." Her lips sagged in thought. "It seems we may have to start pushing Dominus sooner than I'd hoped."

Darius scoffed. "You think he'll listen?"

"If the situation grows grave enough, he won't have a choice. We need him to understand the danger his father poses."

Darius pinched the corners of his eyes, realising the truth of her words. "Father asked me to eliminate Princess Laila." He uncorked his bottle again and held out an extra glass to his guest.

Vasilisa dismissed his offer with a wave of her hand. "He did what?"

"He desires for me to kill her at the tarot tournament. I assume it is an elaborate spectacle to declare war." He emptied his glass and filled it once more.

"Well, I suppose that could work," Vasilisa said, catching her chin between her fingers. "Are you going to complete your mission?"

"Why do you ask?" He smiled bitterly into his glass.

"Because I can sense there's turmoil in you, Darius." Vasilisa shifted to one side, her face the picture of motherly concern. It shouldn't have hit him the way it did, seeing that. But the minute shift in her tone was all it took for him to feel his oceans rise. "You're not usually like this."

He blinked back the saline burning his eyes. "Well, I do what I have to do. I always have."

"But you care for her, don't you? This isn't like the time your father asked you to seduce Drusilla."

He wouldn't bring himself to say it, couldn't. The words were too vast and unfathomable for even him.

"And I know Dominus cares for her too." Vasilisa sighed, gathering up her skirts to stand. "I can't provide you with the answer you might be looking for, Darius. But I will say you've always been smart enough to figure out the path that's right for you. I can tell this will be no different, whatever you choose."

She gave him one final sad smile before she left.

Summer swept over the Citadel in the shape of a storm, staining the rain-soaked walls with a dense smear of black ivy. Even in summer, Mortesian weather remained merely tepid at best. The bone-rattling winter chill soon gave way to a stickier wetness—a density that hung in the air, heavy and ominous, like a noose with no neck.

Summer marked the rex's annual tarot tournament, during which nobles poured in from far and wide to gamble riches, relics and even immortal souls on the tables of the royal gambling house.

The Siren, for such the house was named, was fronted by a façade of sea-green marble adorned with chimerical grotesques and geometric ironwork lacquered in gold. It was both nauseatingly garish and darkly entrancing, the sort of eyesore that burrowed its way in through the socket until it was embedded in the soft cranial tissue beneath.

Tonight's tournament was hosted personally by Dominus and Darius, both of whom arrived at the gambling house at the climax of the storm. Lightning plunged its fork into the earth as they entered, splintering the dimly lit interiors into shards of light and shadow.

Darius walked through the crowded hall, his blue kaftan mottled by the kaleidoscopic shards of the stained glass chandelier above. He scoped the room, marking its victims, deliberating on who would be the unfortunate soul he would inflict his diabolical skill upon.

He reached into his pocket for the deck of cards he kept on hand, preferring to use his own. They were antiques, hand-painted and faded with age, and he liked to think they brought him luck. Though it was rare that he would submit himself fully to the raw chaotic magic of chance, he liked a challenge from time to time to see if he could get the hands of fate to rest warmly on his shoulders.

He smelled Laila beneath the smog of sweat and smoke. She wore midnight velvet with a satin bertha, the frock embroidered with climbing roses made from cannetilles and hand-cut organza. Beside her was Dominus, dressed in pale gold, but most notable of all was the vacuum of space between them that ached to be filled.

Darius quickly took the initiative. "Your Radiance," he said, smooth as chenille. "Fancy seeing you tonight."

"Hm," she hummed in response, her cherry-lacquered lips sipping from a diamond tulip glass. "I wasn't intending to, but all the stories Dominus was telling me made me *horribly* curious. And so I decided I would venture out, see where luck takes me."

Darius grinned in response, thinking how much the hare she looked in this den full of foxes. Not far behind her, he spied the silhouettes of Lyra and Léandre amongst the crowd. She'd taken extra precautions. "Does that imply you intend to play?"

"We were," Dominus interjected in brusque annoyance, "before you so rudely interrupted."

"I haven't decided yet, in truth," she corrected, her chin dipped low. "You see, I happen to like having possession of my soul, and I wouldn't quite want to part with it."

"There are a vast number of other things you might part with in its stead." Darius chuckled. He spied the choker of rubies glinting around her neck. "Your jewels, for instance."

"Oh, no, certainly not." Laila's hand flew towards them protectively. "But, well, there is one thing I can think of to place on the table. If you're interested. Dominus refuses to be anything but a dullard about the stakes."

Amused as Darius was by the continued barbs against his brother, he was not fooled by the charmingly unassuming way she tilted her head. "I might be."

"Tell me a truth," she said, "to any question that I put forth."

Darius inhaled sharply. "She drives a hard bargain, doesn't she, brother?"

It was a price far more precious than a soul, more valuable than riches. The truth, under the right circumstances, could easily be more lethal than a blade.

"If you are willing, then I am more than happy to accept," Dominus replied with a shrug. "Should be interesting to see you be forced to tell the truth for once."

"I accept." Darius's lips coiled up like smoke. "But if I win, I expect the favour to be returned."

Laila smiled. "All right."

He handed the croupier his cards. The ghoul looked sceptically at them before replacing his deck and dealing their hands.

Darius was careful to give nothing away as he lifted his, appropriating a tumbler of whisky that was hovering about on a tray.

He kept stealing glances at Laila to find her staring at her hand intently, her brow delicately crinkled. Whether it was in dismay or confusion, he could not yet tell. She was just innocent enough to be illegible.

Laila, on the other hand, was trying to make sense of the cards she'd been dealt. She was no newborn to the art of tarot-playing, though the cards here were unlike anything she'd seen. The numbers seemed to jumble around, leaping from face to face, the illustrations coming to life in ways that deliberately seemed to discomfit her. The fool pulled cruel, mocking faces; death brandished his bleeding flagpole with a sneer.

She closed her eyes, shaking her head in the hopes that this topsy-turvy switch might cease. She looked to both Darius and Dominus and found them gazing at their cards serenely.

Dominus set down his cards, playing to the first trick. They each continued their hand until the round was complete.

The croupier announced Darius the winner.

"Don't feel too bad," Darius said, noticing Laila's pout. "It's a treacherous game, tarot; you might consider the cards to have a life of their own." As he said this, the cards before him fluctuated and shifted like a mirage, a soft sound reminiscent of laughter dispersing through the room. "But it appears you owe me a truth."

"What would you like to ask?"

He bit down on his lip, considering. "I couldn't help but notice there appears to be a bit of tension between you and Dominus tonight." He took a sip of his whisky, savouring the residue on his mouth. "Why is that?"

"None of your business," Dominus snarled.

"Uh uh." Darius tsked in disapproval. "I am afraid rules are rules, brother."

Laila's own expression remained perfectly docile. "He and I are... having a little disagreement, shall we say? A little lovers' spat."

"Regarding what?"

She smiled, her eyes twinkling with mischief. "You only earned one truth, prefect. You'll have to work a little harder for others."

They go another round, this time with Laila coming away the victor.

The switch in her attitude was immediate, every inch of her body erupting into a pageantry of synaptic sparks in elation.

Darius watched this scene with an amalgam of amusement and incredulity that settled involuntarily into a bloom of endearment in his chest. It was times like this he forgot how young at heart she still was. She had not yet aged into apathy. She had not yet hollowed into indifference. She was still living the feverish highs of her summer years, in contrast to his barren autumn.

"I believe I owe you an answer," he said, polishing the dregs of whisky from his glass.

She scrunched her lips to one side. "Tell me about the Culling."

His hand stiffened at his glass. "An unexpected request."

"And yet you promised me truths, prefect. So let's hear it."

He glanced over at Dominus, whose expression had considerably darkened, rage smudged like coal across his features.

"All right," Darius said, for a deal was a deal. "We do one every lustrum. Qarna tribes mark their doors with pig's blood to signal they desire to be passed over; those who don't must make an offering. Each family that makes a tribute that season gets spared the next, though only three cycles may be skipped before the next visit has the local enforcer come knocking. They give over the ugly, the sick, the deviant. Anyone they're willing to spare, the ones that won't be missed. It doesn't matter what afflictions they come with in life, for they all end up the same when undead. Save the damaged or crippled, of course; we require the bodies fully intact. Can't put a corpse to work when it's missing an eye or limb, after all."

"That's barbaric!" Laila exclaimed in disgust.

"That's Mortos," Darius replied, with a lethargic lift of one shoulder. "I feel I am beginning to understand what your lovers' spat might have entailed." He traced his finger over the rim of his glass. "You have *got* to improve on your tour skills, brother."

Dominus's eyes flashed with anger. "You think I brought her there on purpose?"

"*Don't* fight," Laila said, hand rising to rub at her temple.

"On to more mannerly subjects, then." Darius switched gears with ease, holding out his arm. "Join me for a dance?"

"Shouldn't you be on your way—" Dominus began to protest.

"Actually, yes," Laila interrupted, seizing hold of Darius's arm. "Yes, I think I will." She flashed a smile at Dominus over her shoulder—a sharp, supercilious thing.

Dominus's expression fluctuated from red to black to red again. He was a balloon filled to bursting, and Darius didn't wish to be around when he eventually popped.

He led her towards the dancing area, where a live ensemble played melodies designed for a slow, intimate mood. He spun Laila underneath his arm before pulling her close to lock their bodies together with his hand at her waist.

"You shouldn't tease my brother so," Darius murmured in her ear once their fingers had intertwined.

"What makes you think I'm teasing?" Laila asked, resting her free hand on the crook of his shoulder.

"Because if I were with you and I had to witness you two going off to dance together, I'd be furious."

She lifted her chin to look at him as they bobbed in well-timed circles, expecting smugness in his expression. And there was that in spades, for certain. But there was something a little more earnest too, swimming underneath the surface.

"Perhaps what makes him so angry is that you persist in making comments of such nature."

Darius chuckled, unable to refute her words. "You have a point."

He soon fell silent, allowing the conversation between their bodies to take precedence. He was surprised by the affinity in which they moved together, and he found himself enjoying this. Perhaps *too* much. The warmth and vigour of her body against his own was almost too much for him to bear.

"For what it's worth, I am sorry you had to encounter the Culling in such a manner," he said, eager to break the silence.

"I suppose I shouldn't have expected anything different," Laila replied wryly. "I have long known your land to be home to many horrors. What's one more in the grand scheme?"

"Spoken like a true Mortesian."

Laila scoffed in amusement. "I don't think I'll ever belong to this place."

"Yes, I heard you had decided to resign your post."

"A spur of the moment decision, but I've come to recognise when I should admit defeat." Laila sighed.

"You don't sound too pleased about the fact."

"Well," Laila said, "I don't believe my conscience could allow me to stomach shaking hands with a father who beats his child so savagely. I believe that is what truly disturbed me the most about Dominus. I suppose I could understand being indifferent to the plight of a stranger. But the plight of a brother? That I could not accept."

He was so surprised he almost missed a step. "You don't have to feel scandalised on my part, princess. I am long used to my father's dour moods."

"But do you not ever wish for things to be different?" Laila asked. "Why submit to such mistreatment?"

"Well, it is as you said. Mortos is a cruel land, home to many horrors. Perhaps if I were mortal I would feel more immediacy in detaching myself from my predicament. There's nothing like limited time to give you some perspective. But I am not mortal. I am a mere bastard of a king who cannot die. There is no corner of the isle where I could seek refuge untouched by his authority. Where could I turn to escape in such an event? Better to remain close at hand to feed from the scraps of his table. Or at least that's how I've come to see it."

"That is too cruel for me to accept," Laila said. "Living one's life eternally shadowed by an oppressor isn't a life worth living to me at all. What is the use of having forever if not to use that time to access higher planes of joy? Tranquillity?" She rested her hand against his cheek. "Love?"

Darius swallowed thickly, caught in the deep haze of her stare. He was a deep-rooted glacier of direction and purpose. Frozen, deadlocked. But she was the equator striking through him, matching his ice with her fire, and it was too much, too hot: the scorching white heat of her tongue. He steeled himself against the impulse to step back.

He dipped her down low, their eye contact not once breaking as he lifted her up again. "I've never looked at it that way." As much a proclamation to him as it was to her. He suddenly wanted to draw her near, taste the cherry lacquer on her lips. Red and full, like the berries famine often denied them. "Thank you, princess. The world could do with more souls like you."

She received the compliment with the gentlest of smiles. "Thank you for the dance, prefect." She gestured for Léandre to bring her shawl. "But I feel I must go."

Darius swallowed again, loosening the noose of his collar. He didn't understand why his throat constricted so much upon seeing her escorted away.

"Wait," Darius called. He couldn't let her leave. Not yet. He realised this might be the last time he'd ever see her. Talk to her. He wanted to cling onto it a little longer. "Princess, wait."

He followed her out into the unslaked bite of the night air before he caught her arm, swivelling her around to face him.

"What is it?" she demanded.

"At least stay a little longer."

"For what possible reason?"

His mouth floundered. He was a fish without water. How was it that she reduced him to this stuttering fool, trying to scrape words off the ground like stray pennies when he'd had centuries of poetry and prose, of oratory prowess under his belt?

She turned back on her heel in disinterest, marching towards her carriage. Her chauffeur saw her approach and with a smile began to open the door for her.

"No, wait, please don't—"

When the grenade launched and the chasm tore open, Darius lost all sense of reasoning, all sense of self. He flung himself on top of her, shielding her even as debris flew wildly from all corners, striking his back and shredding his clothes.

He felt her writhe in panic beneath him as she clutched his shoulders, but he didn't rise from her, he didn't lessen his grip, he didn't spring upwards in shame or anguish. He kept holding her as the air's new ungodly mouth mercilessly engulfed the carriage into blackness.

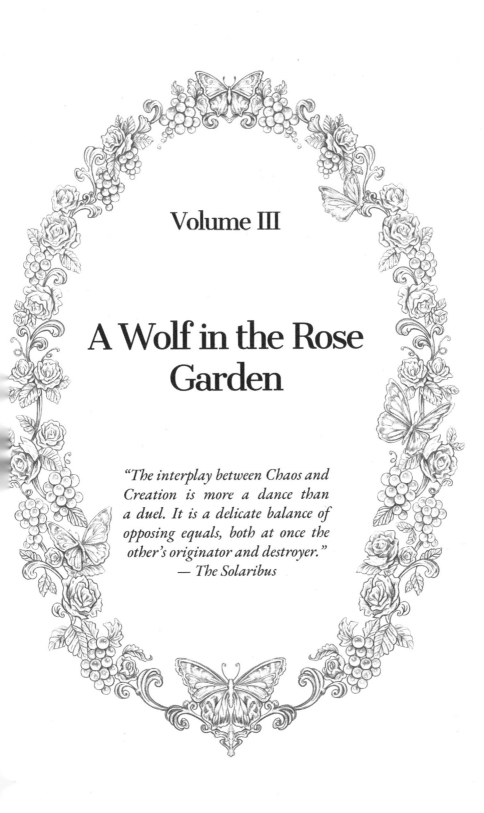

Volume III

A Wolf in the Rose Garden

"The interplay between Chaos and Creation is more a dance than a duel. It is a delicate balance of opposing equals, both at once the other's originator and destroyer."
— The Solaribus

XXII

MIRA ROSE SAT HIGH ON HER SOLAR THRONE, its name reflected in the gilt carvings of sun rays that ringed the head of the ivory chair. Her brown, beautiful face emitted enough rage to outshine the merciless radiance of ten thousand burning suns. Such was the fury she felt towards the accused standing opposite her.

Since word had travelled across the water of the attempt on her daughter's life, she had sent demands for an immediate extradition. While many might consider there to be little in the way of tenderness from Amira towards Laila, she had known nothing but pure, undistilled repugnance towards the one who'd see her harmed. The sheer audacity of anyone attempting to harm her heiress, her *legacy*, was a transgression of the highest order that demanded answering.

Seated beside her was Laila, who shifted slightly on her birch bench as she regarded Darius. He had not put up much of a fight, seeming almost eager to surrender himself to the Lightshields' custody. All the better to escape his father's wrath.

For a creature in chains, he seemed relatively untroubled, wearing them with a certain leonine composure. As though it were he who submitted to this treatment for the comfort and safety of others, rather than being the subject of an arrest.

Laila didn't realise what the sight of him would do to her. How there was *anger* mixed into the cocktail of her nerves. Confusion that he'd simultaneously tried to kill her and yet tried to spare her from her fate.

Amira looked at him with disdain. "Come over to me, Darius Calantis."

He walked over to Amira in brisk, confident strides as he scaled the steps to stand before her. Now up close to the impératrice, the prodigious build that the occassi were known for was even more pronounced. He towered over her like a monument.

"Kneel."

He descended to one knee before her.

Amira hooked her finger beneath his chin and tilted it up to face her before cupping his cheeks in her palms. She held him so delicately. Laila almost thought her mother could've been touching her. Then she saw the light in Amira's palms infuse him, irradiating his skin with a divine glow as plumes of white smoke coiled around his temples.

Darius hissed in agony, but he did not pull away.

"Light illuminates, Darius Calantis; it reveals the truth no matter how you may try to obscure it," Amira said calmly over his strained grunts. "You stand accused of attempted murder. How do you plead?"

"Guilty." The word was extracted from him like she had plucked it from his tongue by force.

"Walk us through your crime."

Darius hissed again as his cheeks ignited with pale light. "I sent for one of my underlings to rig Princess Laila's carriage to explode on the night of our annual tarot tournament. The grenade was a weapon of my own design, built by my own hand."

"You admit, then, to orchestrating the crime, right down to the very weapon you would use to accomplish it. You lured the princess to a public event under false pretences, certain she would not expect such a brazen attack in public quarters. And while you charmed and danced with her, you admit to sending a subordinate to rig her carriage to explode when she returned, unsuspecting all the while. Yet in spite of all this planning, meticulous and premeditated as it might be, you managed to fail in your mission. Tell us why."

Laila's breath suspended in fear of what he would say. She still remembered the weight of his body on hers when he'd shoved her away to safety. The way he'd looked at her with such sheer desperation in his gaze.

"I had begun to develop second thoughts," Darius managed to grunt through his torment, beads of sweat bejewelling his forehead. "Until eventually such thoughts took precedence."

"You mean to tell us you fumbled your mission purposefully out of mere guilt?" Amira sounded almost humoured in her astonishment. "Even in knowing the consequences you must surely reap?" She could not believe him.

"My entire life I've been a bastard," he said. "I'd known my life to have no meaning and thus sought to detach meaning from the lives of others as well. I'd committed numerous grave ills with no remorse, and yet I could not do the same to her. Her life, to me, held meaning." He glanced up to meet Amira's gaze. "I couldn't simply snuff it."

"How noble of you to infuse meaning into the life of one victim!"

279

"I never implied my motivation to be of virtuous cause," Darius replied, his forehead wrinkled, "but my motivation it was."

Laila looked away from him, head and heart too burdened by his declaration. She couldn't understand how a sentiment so polluted by his soot-stained psyche could almost be considered sweet.

"And upon whose orders were you forced to enact this crime?"

Darius attempted to stopper his tongue, straining with fiendish might against the compulsion of Amira's enchantment.

"Whose orders were they?" Amira emphasised every word.

"My father," he cried, his breathing harsh and body trembling. "I acted upon the orders of my father, the Rex of Mortos."

"Well then." Amira settled back into her seat. "Why does your father want her dead?"

"He wants war." Darius looked to Laila. "You were simply meant to be the declaration."

"No further questions," Amira said. "In light of what you've told us, and due to your compliance with your arrest, I see no reason to delay your verdict any further. I hereby sentence you to life imprisonment. You will be committed to the House of Correction. Take him away."

Two Lightshields arrived immediately to extract him from the room, delivering Darius down a long, narrow path to retribution.

Laila walked through the gold-veined marble hallways towards her mother's glazed doors, nodding at the Lightshields that guarded them.

They opened the doors to let her through, and she entered the frescoed hall of her mother's antechamber with its splendid silk furnishings. Amira stood before her gilt mirror talking with Lady Commander Cassia, the head of the Lightshield guard.

Laila remained at the doorway to overhear, realising they were discussing suspicious activity from the Mielette dynasty following the diplomatic mess up north. Laila bit her lip, puzzling over what it meant. She realised their kind had often disagreed, but should there be lasting dissent from a dynasty, political in-fighting was sure to follow.

The conversation ended the moment Laila entered, and Amira drifted over to take her seat on the settee. "Come over, aurore. Sit."

Laila stepped forward into the room in uncertainty. Her mother was always particular about the way she conducted herself in her chambers. She decided to sit in the armchair she always took.

"Would you like some tea?"

Laila shook her head. "No, thank you."

"How about coffee?"

"I'm fine," Laila said, always slightly discomfited in the face of her mother's magnanimity. She knew there was always something less benevolent to follow. "Léandre said that you requested I visit."

"Yes, I wanted to discuss with you what I feel our next move towards Mortos should be." She gestured for a sprite to pour her a cup of cappuccino with a fleur-de-lis in the foam. "In light of what has been said about Lanius Rex, I fear he has become a liability to our country. A dangerous one. One that I feel should be removed before he has a chance to become more of a threat."

"What are you saying?" Laila asked.

"I'm saying that I no longer think your method of diplomacy is sufficient in dealing with this country. It is time for me to take matters into my own hands. If Lanius Rex desires a war, then I shall give him one. Let him see that we will not be so easily cowed by a hulking brute with a god complex."

Laila found herself nodding along, heart cold to the implications of her mother's words. She hadn't felt warm since the assassination attempt; wrath ravaged her insides like a winter famine. "I agree with you, Maman. We have entertained this creature's whims long enough. I want him off the throne."

"Glad we can see eye to eye on this," Amira said approvingly. Her voice was warm and golden, like a slow-drip of nectar. "The only question is who to install in his place." She took a sip from her coffee. "You believe Dominus to be a more amenable candidate?"

"He will certainly be resistant to ascension; he is greatly loyal to his father." She shifted uncomfortably in her seat. "How loyal I have yet to test."

"You think his loyalty to him will supersede his feelings for you?"

Laila swallowed the unease swelling in her throat. "I guess I shall find out."

"Well, we'll need to move quickly. I have our naval forces ready to deter any invasion from Mortos, and should there be any sign of assemblage, I have given them strict orders to invade on their own. It appears the only language these creatures understand is that of violence. And fear and intimidation and cruelty. We are merely translating to suit their needs."

Laila nodded in deference. Her mother was right, and she knew it: if Lanius was not stopped, then his aggression towards their country would only escalate. He was a monster. Just like Darius was a monster. She'd extended her hand, and they had bitten her for it. Perhaps it was time to change tactics. Perhaps it was time for the monster to be slain.

XXIII

PRISON LIFE ENDED UP BEING ABOUT WHAT DARIUS EXPECTED—long stretches of impenetrable ennui interspersed with pockmarks of interest. He saw his life emptied of all the material comforts that once brought him solace, and within a few days of it he'd grown to mourn all the books, the fine clothes, and the gourmet meals he'd taken for granted.

Yet in spite of all that, he knew this emptiness, this harrowing void of irrelevance he'd found himself in, was preferable to what awaited in the bowels of the Citadel dungeons. For that reason alone, he sought to be a model prisoner, playing the part of the domesticated monster until an opportunity arose for him to sink his teeth into. He memorised his routine for lack of any other way to pass the time, from the circulation of nurses to the exact minute of the hour his meals would be served.

As a full-grown occasso, he required, at a minimum, six meals per day with carnivorous options—though he'd always been most partial to fowl and fish. He liked the elegance that came from ensnaring them. How the process seemed cleaner, neater, than the foul-smelling, blood-soaked mess that was hunting down an elk. He'd dirty his hands should he need to. But should there be a choice in the matter, he would always prefer to keep his fingers spotless.

Once his late afternoon meal was cleared, he took to exercising. It was essential to keep his body as sharply honed as he did his mind, and with the absence of possibilities to satisfy one, he'd been driven to overcompensate the other. He'd worked himself into a deep sweat when a break in his routine arrived in the form of a solarite. He could tell her instantly by the bright hue of her hair and eyes, the glistening skin that overpowered under incandescent lighting.

Darius ceased his regimen, standing immediately to attention, predator senses alert.

"Oh, please don't stop on my account," she said from the observation window. "I was beginning to enjoy the display."

Darius quirked a brow in response. "Do you often flirt with your charges?"

"Only the pretty ones," she said with a smile. "My name is Dr Lucrèce Mielette, and I am in charge of this fine facility. Come, let us talk a moment." Then she unlocked his door.

Intrigued, and a little wary, Darius slipped back into his white uniform before he followed her out of the door. He was accosted by Lightshields the moment he stepped foot from his cell, from whose necks dangled a glowing yellow crystal that sickened him upon proximity to it. He would later learn that this crystal was ætherald.

"Come along, don't dawdle," Dr Mielette called over her shoulder, continuing her brisk stride.

He pushed through his discomfort to catch up to her, mirroring her poised tightrope walk. He took this time to commit to memory the journey from his room to their destination: all the entryways and exits, the enclosed stairwells.

Their final stop brought them to the office of the doctor herself, her name stencilled on a gold plaque in bold lettering. Yet another was she in the long line of female leaders he had encountered on Vysterian soil.

A Lightshield opened the door for them before they entered, and Dr Mielette made a gesture to one of the many seating options in the room. "Please, make yourself comfortable."

The chairs were all upholstered with leather in a meek cream, far more pristine than it had any right to be. Darius almost feared he'd sully it through sight alone. He chose the chaise lounge and reclined into the plushness, grateful to take luxury where it came.

Dr Mielette regarded his affinity to opulence with a smile, taking a seat opposite him. "Can I interest you in some rosewater?" She gestured to the frosted floral jug and glasses on the table before them.

"You are gracious," Darius said, offering her his most charming smile, the one that best showed off his dimples. A little flirtation could carry him a long way, in his experience.

The doctor poured them both glasses and handed him his. "I want to apologise for the belated nature of this consultation. Typically I like to catch my new inmates when they first arrive, but things have been rather busy. Have you been settling well?" She raised her glass to her lips.

"Quite well, yes." Darius took a sip, having waited for her to drink first. "For a prisoner, I have certainly been treated with remarkable courtesy."

"Well, I don't quite know how you do it in Mortos, but here in Soleterea we treat criminality with the aim of rehabilitation rather than retribution."

"Sounds rather... soft," Darius said, taking another sip from his drink.

Dr Mielette smiled widely, a small spectacle of light fluctuating across her features. "You aren't too partial to forgiveness where you're from?"

"Forgiveness," Darius chuckled. "I'm sure your impératrice didn't have me sent here in the hopes I could be forgiven."

"No, she sent you here in the hopes you could be reformed. Once you are reformed, forgiveness comes easily."

Darius smirked heavily into his glass. "Something tells me that the opportunity for reform has long surpassed me."

"What makes you say that?" Dr Mielette cocked her head to one side, curious.

"Oh, I've done a lot of very bad things."

"Tell me about them," Dr Mielette encouraged, the oscillations along her skin now a soft and steady shimmer. "What was the first terrible thing you ever did?"

"I—" He almost couldn't think of it, mesmerised as he was by her pulsating glow. "When I was young, Dominus used to have this bird. This little crow he used to go hunting with. I remember it so fondly. It had these ink black feathers, soft as a cloud. Oh, he loved that bird. Used to take it everywhere with him. He'd drive me mad with it. Then one day we were having a spat over something. I don't even remember what it was. And for whatever reason I was so angry with him that night, I couldn't let it go. It reached the point where I waited until he was sleeping, then crept into his room and took the little crow deep into the forest. And I set it free." Darius wet his lips, swallowing thickly. "He searched for it for days after, all up and down the Citadel and on the grounds. Just calling for it. I never said a word."

Dr Mielette sat back in her chair, hands folded. "Why did you do it?"

"I couldn't tell you."

"Yes, you can," she said. Her skin flickered like a dying flame. "You know exactly why you did it."

Darius tried to hold fast his jaw but found he could not control what his tongue was saying. "I did it because I was jealous of him. Because he had a nice thing. Because he *always* had nice things and I wanted to remove it from him so he would know how it felt to have had something so close within your grasp... only to have someone else take it."

"Did it feel good?" Dr Mielette asked. "Taking from him?"

"Yes," Darius said, swirling the admission around on his tongue.

"And what about after? Did you ever feel bad after the fact?"

Darius clutched the glass of rosewater. "I helped him look for a little while, travelled deep into the forest with him as he called and whistled. I knew he would never find that blasted bird again. I just wanted him to have closure with it."

"You felt guilty," she said.

"Does it matter? I still did it."

Dr Mielette leaned closer towards him, her light engulfing the room in a stifling summer warmth. "I want you to focus on that. On your guilt. Your jealousy and resentment, your insecurity with your brother... I want you to let those go."

"Why are you doing this?" Darius asked, stiffening suddenly. "Why am I even telling you all of this? What have you done to me?"

"This is the first step towards your reform," Dr Mielette said, her voice soothingly serene. "Don't fight it. Just let it take you."

"Get out of my head," Darius snarled. His sclera was eclipsed by shadow, the veins beneath thick and writhing. "Get out of my head *right now*." His final bark unleashed his fangs as he lunged towards her.

Dr Mielette barely shifted an inch, erecting a force shield around her that sent Darius rebounding across the room. He hit the wall with a thud, crackling paint and dust.

The Lightshields burst in to her aid.

"Hold your weapons," Dr Mielette said calmly, holding up a hand. His resistance was fascinating to her rather than irksome, and she debated whether he'd be the ideal specimen she'd been searching for. She folded her hands behind her back as she approached Darius. "I have to say I'm disappointed. I had hoped you might be more amenable to improvement than this. No matter. We have all the time in the world to get past this rough start, you and I."

Her smile was so radiant it sickened him.

$\backsim$

The red carriage of Vasilisa Regina ignited like a flame through the greyed moroseness of Mortesian weather, drawing to a stop outside a rain-mirrored building.

"I want to thank you for extending this invitation to me, Vasilisa Regina," Laila said once they'd vacated the carriage and climbed the steps towards the exclusive ladies' lounge owned by Domitia Orlovia.

A ghoul opened up an umbrella for them once they did so to shield them from the torrent of the summer storm.

"Thank you for being brave enough to return here," Vasilisa replied, her rubicund lips upturned in admiration. "Not many have braved my husband's wrath and lived to tell the tale. Let alone be bold enough to step foot on his soil afterwards."

"Well, it took a bit of coaxing, I will admit," Laila said, gathering her cape about her shoulders. "Though it did help knowing he's had his hands too full to truly be concerned about me as of now."

Since Claudius' murder and Darius's subsequent arrest, more and more of Lanius's prefects had been roused into doubting the rex's competency to lead. They vacated court in droves, and those who had not been subject to arrest were currently still in hiding. With the loss of Darius, especially, came the severance of vital intelligence networks the Citadel relied upon to keep the kingdom under heel—a loss, Lanius quickly discovered, that was not so easily replaced.

They paused before the oak-panelled glass doors. Vasilisa turned to Léandre. "I am afraid there are no males permitted beyond this point. There's a local tavern not far from here, if you'd care to join my guards."

Léandre bowed his head. "Of course, madame." He turned to Laila. "I'll be with you as soon as you need me. For now I leave you in Lyra's hands."

"Thank you, Léandre." Laila stepped forward to embrace him before he left.

"Now, shall we?" Vasilisa beckoned to the doors as a female ghoul opened up to receive them.

They entered the foyer, where they were greeted by the sound of faint orchestral music. Haunting, lilting melodies of strings and woodwind suffused the air as their footsteps echoed on the polished marble flooring.

Another ghoul arrived to receive them. "Welcome, Your Highness," she rasped, bowing low in courtesy. She, like all the ghouls, wore a uniform of red and black. "May I relieve you of your capes?"

"You may." Vasilisa extended her arms out like a bird, allowing the ghoul to unveil the fox-trimmed garment from her shoulders.

Laila mimicked the gesture while Lyra remained firmly attached to her outer garment.

"You may, in fact, be the last appointment to arrive." The ghoul gave a rudimentary glance at her guest list. "I shall escort you to our mistress."

As she led them through to the lounge the music grew louder, joined by the subtle interplay of ringing porcelain and silver. Laila took a moment to observe her surroundings, absorbing with slight open-mouthed awe the tall green marble–inlaid pillars and carved dark wood, the sculpted friezes coated in brass. The place had a gloomy grandeur to it, an eerie, mystical quality that seeped down her spine the further she entered.

There were two floors to the lounge and their table was located on the second, nestled up against the mirror-paned wall. The sole occupant at the table stood to attention the moment they arrived.

"Domina Domitia," crowed the ghoul, beckoning to her most recent guests, "the regina has arrived."

"My dearest Vasilisa," Domitia exclaimed in delight, rushing to kiss her cheek. She was square of jaw and tawny-skinned with eyes the same bright hue of lemon rind. "How wonderful to see you; please sit."

The casual manner with which she beheld the royal did not go unnoticed by the others, and the mood shifted to one of relaxed formality as the two were seated.

Lyra remained in the corner, ever watchful, deciding to take advantage of her proximity to the mirror to have an extra pair of eyes on hand for suspicious activity.

"I assume you've heard of Princess Laila by now," Vasilisa said, unfolding her napkin to smooth it onto her lap. "She's come to join us all the way from sunny Soleterea."

"Pleasure to meet you." Laila accessorised her greeting with a scintillating smile. "Vasilisa has told me a great many remarkable things."

"Likewise, Your Radiance," Domitia replied.

"Yes, I've brought Princess Laila here today so she might have an opportunity to sit in on our little niche gathering." Vasilisa gestured for a server to pour her a cup of poppy tisane. "And further discuss our current state of affairs." She reached for a ruby red cake garnished with whipped cream. "Domitia here is an esteemed member of the Golden Owl."

"The Golden Owl?" Laila echoed in curiosity. "That's a fascinating name; what inspired it?"

"Well," Domitia began, sipping from her tisane, "that happens to be me. Our members are all, besides Vasilisa here, proud owners of a gold medal of motherhood. Which means we have each produced eight sons to contribute towards the expansion and prosperity of the kingdom. With such a hefty investment made, it isn't any wonder we have some misgivings about our current monarch as of late."

"I can imagine," Laila said, astonished as she took a sip of warm milk. While motherhood was certainly held to great esteem in Vysteria, she'd never heard anything like hosting a reward system for it. "Eight sons, that's quite an extraordinary feat!"

"Well, seven now in my case." Domitia's face grew embittered upon referring to Claudius. She took a bite from her black cherry tart. "And that's all within the four hundred years of my lifespan. Babes are rarer than diamonds for our kind and a thousand times more precious. So we like to commemorate the event."

"And your daughters?"

"Will never grow to be warriors." Domitia dismissed the question as though the subject bored her. "And thus the rewards are less grand."

That didn't seem right to Laila at all. Surely, in her mind, the producers of the next sons ought to reap far more value. It was like placing a higher price tag on the milk than the cow.

"But on to other matters, it is a shame about Lanius," Domitia sighed. "Pity those hags at the Vidua Nocte became involved. If he hadn't traded services with them, who knows where we would be now. As it stands, something must be done about him. His reign has spanned almost three centuries. It has been a healthy run, all things considered. However, all good things must come to an end."

"Which is why we are here, Domasha," Vasilisa said. "I believe it is time for my son Dominus to take the throne, and Princess Laila has agreed to lend her support. What I want to know is how many of the gentry we can count on."

"Lanius has been making many unpopular decisions as of late, what with how he's been choosing to deal with our weather, his revolving council seats, and now this diplomatic mess. To be perfectly honest with you, Vasya, we'd have seen him off the throne a century ago, but Dominus's reluctance has been a large factor. Has he seen a change of heart now?"

Vasilisa sipped from her tisane to take some time to think. "I have been supporting him towards... an alteration in perspective."

"What a wonderfully neutral way of phrasing it!" Domitia declared in amusement. "Well, regardless, the support is there should he need it. Lanius's base is still strong in spite of his mistakes even now, but Darius's arrest has gotten people questioning whether he is still fully in control. If he can't control his son, how does he expect to control a continent? Though he would be foolish to move now with so many eyes on him over the water. I'm sure Soleterea is on high alert, ready to move in should there be any signs of conflict."

"You assume correctly," Laila said, helping herself to a small red cake.

"Well then, we're at a standstill," Domitia said with a shrug. "But that makes this moment the most critical of all. If you want Dominus on the throne, it's best to move in now, while you can. Before Lanius begins to suspect the worst."

"We're certainly prepared to discuss it with him," Vasilisa said, turning to Laila with a smile. "Aren't we, Your Radiance?"

Laila swallowed softly, taking a moment to stir burnt honey into her poppy tisane. For so long she'd lived in fear of this moment, and in truth she still didn't know with which face of the coin Dominus's loyalties might fall. She concealed this as she always did with the brandish of a smile. "Yes. Yes, of course."

XXIV

DOMINUS RODE TO THE PADDOCK in the early rise of dawn as the sun melted the belligerent chill of the night before. A ghoul attendant untacked the hippogriffs as they shook their shaggy, silken manes and fluffed their spacious wings.

Dominus reached out with a leather-gloved hand to pet the gnarled curve of Talon's beak, then into one of the feeding buckets to toss him a dead white mouse. Talon speared it on his spiked teeth with one quick jerk of a neck and chewed appreciatively at his catch.

Since Darius's arrest, Dominus had acted as expected, absconding deep into the woods for a lengthy getaway. He hadn't wanted to be seen or spoken to, instead burrowing deep into the wound of his anger and disbelief at having watched his older brother give himself away in chains after trying to murder his beloved. It had only been a summon from his father himself that provoked his reluctant return.

He flexed his gloved hand in a subconscious gesture, remembering how right it had felt when he'd enclosed both around Darius's long, elegant throat. He'd watched his face become a deadly shade of cyan to match his eyes as his windpipe constricted. He'd have wrenched his head from his shoulders right there had the Lightshields not been quick to disarm him with a lightning bolt and briskly escort his brother away.

He couldn't understand why his brother would've wanted to hurt Laila, why it seemed Darius *always* wanted to cause ill to anything he happened to hold dear.

He tried to recall when they were boy-cubs and the worst quarrel they'd had was deciding which hippogriff was whose. In the end they'd made a bet at midnight to take turns climbing onto the back of their chosen mount and whichever one was quickest to be tossed off would be declared the loser.

It had gone wrong, though, as things often did, and in their bid to fulfil their petulant childish needs they had soon set loose five hippogriffs. Ten. Twenty. They'd stampeded past the barriers of the stable gates and once free began to soar their way to liberation.

He and Darius had spent the entire night wrangling them, eventually having to awaken the stable master and his attendants to join them in their lassoing and coaxing. Darius had decided to assume the blame in the aftermath, a gesture for which Dominus had found himself eminently grateful. For even though his father had never raised a hand against him, he still lived in eternal fear of his disappointment.

So he had watched as Darius unburdened his shames onto their patriarch with mouse-meek eyes and timid apologies. He should've known that his brother could never talk his father's incendiary rage into a ceasefire, that Lanius would only ever see his son's contrition as a show of soft underbelly. Darius extended a hand, and his father repaid him by crushing it.

His kneecaps next.

Dominus didn't remember all that had happened—when his father had finally stopped beating Darius—but he did remember the way he had cowered behind his knee all the while, smooth and unblemished as a newborn.

Perhaps that had been it then. The sad, cyclical tragedy of it all. His father hurt Darius and so Darius in turn hurt Dominus. And on and on and on it went. He should think it would be good that they were rid of each other now, that his arrest had severed the chain. But all Dominus could think of was all he had yet to say, all the questions he yet needed answered.

He tossed another mouse to Darius's hippogriff, Razer, before his ears picked up the frequency of light footfalls that could only belong to a ghoul.

"Yes?" Dominus asked as he inhaled a breath of mint-refreshing air.

"His Majesty requests your presence in the Eyrie."

Dominus straightened the cuff of his gloves and followed the ghoul.

Once inside, he scaled the steps to the council room in search of his father. What he was met with instead was a blackness so dense it almost appeared corporeal. He blinked a few times to adjust his eyes to the murk before he entered.

"Papa?" Dominus called out. He edged a toe into the room and saw the curtains were drawn, the fireplace long snuffed, the sconces and chandelier similarly smothered.

The room looked long abandoned, and yet Dominus could smell the pungent vapour of his father's sweet graviji wine. He used his predator senses to scan about the room until he found him, a thickened bloat against the wall.

"Close the door behind you," Lanius ordered.

Dominus did as he was told. As he did so, a flame struck into existence with a fizzle as Lanius lit each branch of a candelabrum held within his fingers.

"What is the meaning of all this?" Dominus asked, stepping forward with arms spread.

"Keep your voice down," Lanius whispered harshly. The candelabrum was lifted close to his face, illuminating him with a ghoulish visage. "I need them not to know I'm here." His eyes darted. "Eyes and ears everywhere."

"Papa," Dominus said, struggling to control his volume. "What are you talking about?"

Lanius crooked a finger to beckon him. "They're plotting against me."

"Who are?"

"Everyone. All of them. I know not who I can trust." As he said this, Lanius swung around again with the candelabrum brandished. It was as though, to him, even his own shadow was in on the plot. "Can I trust you, my boy?"

"Of course you can," Dominus said, eyes softly earnest. He hated to see this, his proud father reduced to a skittish maniac afraid of his own voice. A deep anger stirred in him, belly deep, at those responsible for his ails.

"Yes, yes." Lanius nodded to himself. "I have always been able to trust you, haven't I, my boy? You are a good boy." He reached out to grip his shoulder. "Not like that other one." He made a disgruntled noise upon reference to Darius. "A disappointment all the way to his own grave, should the solarites be merciful."

"Yes," Dominus said, swallowing the swell of anger. "I only wish I could understand the inner workings of his mind."

"Well, it was obvious, was it not?" Lanius's brows raised in incredulity that Dominus hadn't reached the conclusion himself. "He was jealous of you. Always has been. He saw you return home with a foreign princess on your arm like a trinket and thought himself entitled to her. He's always wanted what you had, Doma. Ever since you were boys."

"Yes," Dominus said, unable to deny the truth of it. "Yes, you're right."

"If there is one bright spot in all his treachery it is that we are both well rid of him. I beg you to put him out of your mind, son. Spare him no thought. We have other matters to attend to." Lanius brushed past him towards the table and set the candelabrum down.

"Such as?" Dominus asked.

Lanius gripped the table's edge, drumming his fingers against it. "My enemies grow numerous by the day, and it is certain they will soon come knocking. They will first, however, seek to corrupt you against me."

"That will never happen!" Dominus exclaimed in indignation. "I would sooner gut a traitor with my own hands than turn against you. I will only ascend in the event you ask it of me, Papochka. No sooner."

"Of course, of course," Lanius said, chuckling softly. "That's exactly what I wanted to hear. Yes. Still, you will need to be prepared for this. Expect treachery everywhere you go. Don't cede ground to anyone. I simply need to burn a fire hot enough to wipe out this corrupt growth, and once it is ashes"—he brought a piece of paper to the fire and let it ignite—"we can continue to the next step."

"Which is?"

Lanius turned to him slowly, his smile faint. "The conquest of Soleterea."

"Papa?" Dominus didn't know what to say.

Lanius seized his son's shoulders and held him firm. "Don't tell me you haven't thought of it! Don't you see you have the opportunity to benefit most of all? You want to take the star princess as your bride, yes? Do you think she would ever relinquish her right to rule to join your side? This way you don't even have to ask, you may simply take. You cannot tell me such a thought has never once occurred?"

Dominus's mouth floundered, wordless. Should he ever have cast a thought to conquer her homeland, he knew Laila would never forgive him.

"What do you say, son?" Lanius bared his teeth like a shark. "Join me in the makings of our empire."

Dominus opened his mouth, closed it again. He was adrift with no anchor.

"Of course, this is overwhelming," Lanius said, his grip softly receding. "I'll give you time to think about it. But I expect you to be at my side, my son. As you always have. I trust you will not fail me."

Dominus paused after a swallow. "Yes, Papa."

He retreated to his mother's quarters. There she and Laila sat, awaiting him, bloodied wolfsbane left to puff smoke on the fire.

"Doma!" Vasilisa exclaimed brightly as soon as her son darkened the doorstep. "Oh, thank Calante you've arrived. We've been waiting for you all morning."

"I've just gotten back from speaking with my father," Dominus said, scratching behind his ear before he took his mother's hand. "I strongly feel he is unwell, Mamochka. You should go to him at once."

"That is what we were hoping to discuss with you," Vasilisa said, guiding him towards the divan.

"What do you mean?" he asked.

"Well, it is as you say, Dominus," Laila said, reaching for his hand.

299

She realised it had been the first in an age they had ever touched each other. "Your father is unwell. Deeply unwell. Several in the kingdom have begun to fear for his health to the point where—"

"What is this?" Dominus asked, snatching his hand away. "What are you talking about?"

"Doma, please," Vasilisa said. "I pray you listen."

"No." He burst up from his seat. "I see what you mean to say. You believe he is unfit and thus should be forced to abdicate." He paced around the room, rubbing his temples. "You know, he did say I should expect treachery from every corner, but I had not expected this."

"Dominus—" Vasilisa chastised.

"No, Mother," Dominus roared back. The taut sinews in his neck flared. "You are supposed to be his wife. You pledged yourself to him. An eternity of loyalty and devotion. And now you go behind his back and conspire against him?"

"Don't you dare speak to me this way!" Vasilisa cried, voice shrill and eyes blackened. "I have done nothing but stay steadfast by his side for *centuries*. Even while he constantly sought the ghost of another in my face. I was a *good* wife to him. Loyal and devoted and true. But I have seen the way that he has degraded, Doma, even as you remained adamant in blinding yourself to it. I have seen whatever was salvageable in him depart as he slinked further and further into cruelty and indifference. And my only fear, my *one* consideration, was that I cannot sit back and wait until he turns on you. So yes, I turned from him. Because the only thing that might surpass any duty I feel towards him is the love I carry for *you*." Her voice broke, face rippling into sobs.

Dominus knew he couldn't face her. He loathed nothing more than to see his mother's tears. Yet his father's own words still dug their claws into his mind, and whatever guilt he might feel for hurting her, he could not let himself be stirred to treason.

"I can't hear any more of this." He turned on his foot, making haste towards the exit.

"Dominus." Laila got immediately to her feet. She blurred past him until she was obstructing the way. "Listen."

He took a step forward, looming over her. But she remained rooted.

"If you won't hear your mother, then at least hear me. I know you and I haven't been on the greatest of terms as of late, but... please"—she took his jaw in her hand "if you have any softness in your heart left towards me, I am asking for your help."

Dominus's throat bobbled as he saw the quiet desperation in her gaze. He began to look away.

"We can be together, you and me, on the throne in Mortos." Laila turned his face to her. "We can face your father together. Stand up to him, for once. Just please, help us." She closed her eyes and projected a reel of images of them together in the audience room's blanched white chill, seated on their thrones of bones. Him dour in black velvet, her in festive red by his side. A mirror of his parents. "*Please*," she said again, pulling back to look up at him with tear-clouded eyes.

"Laila." Dominus exhaled softly, leaning against her forehead. "You know I'd do anything for you, but I can't do this."

"Yes, you *can*," Laila said. "Your father has already tried to order my death once before. If he isn't stopped, there's no saying when he will attempt it again—"

"What do you mean, he ordered your death once before?"

"Darius told me that—"

"Darius." Dominus chuckled dryly. "Oh, and you believe him?"

"He was under oath and illumination enchantment," Laila said, indignant at his mirth. "He couldn't lie to us."

"I think my brother has proven he's more than capable of overcoming enchantments."

"And I suppose your father was the one who told you he acted alone?"

"Yes," Dominus snarled, "and I trust him a great deal more than my snake of a brother. I can tell you that."

"Then you are a fool."

Dominus recoiled from the words as though struck. "Insult me if you wish. Cry if you desire. The fact remains that I will not help you. This isn't what I want, Laila. I don't want to be rex. I've never wanted it."

Her entire body went cold, her tears freezing mid-spill. Then she lowered her hands from his face. "Then you and I have nothing more to say to one another," she said, her tone sharp and clipped. Whatever flicker of tender feeling that might have remained for him became inexorably snuffed.

"What does that mean?" he asked. But she wouldn't answer him. He ensnared her by the wrist to shake her like an empty tin, hoping for the words to fall free. "What does that mean, Laila?"

"It means that I'm through with you." She was crystallised composure, each of her words glazed with a thin sheet of ice. And where did this coldness come from? Dominus wondered if she'd always been this cold beneath it all and he'd been conned by her veneer, her sun-warmed surface, taking the plunge before he had time to grow wise to the frigid depths that awaited beneath.

He could only step back in disbelief, bitten by her frost before a volcanic rage burned through him in denial. "You don't mean that."

"Oh, yes." Laila gave a dry laugh. "I do." Then the mirth melted from her face, giving way to indifference. "Get out." She laid her hands flat on his chest and shoved him. "*Get out.*"

He snarled back at her with his monster-blackened eyes, claws unsheathed as he embedded them in her stomach, yanking her towards him.

Laila had no time to recover before he sank his fangs into the side of her neck and emptied a shot of venom into her bloodstream that caused her muscles to languish. Her body acted on instinct, igniting with a voltage high enough for him to go limp and lifeless in her grip.

She peeled him off of her like a leech and deposited him to the floor, sterilising the venom still lurking in her bloodstream. That was the thing about light: it wasn't all pageantry. It could blind, blister and *burn* too. She put a hand to her wounded neck, feeling it mend beneath her touch.

Lyra appeared a moment later with her rifle at the ready, pressing the muzzle of her firearm into his neck, her foot on his back.

"If you ever put your teeth on me again," Laila sneered, "I'll put you down like a dog."

XXV

AILA SOAKED IN HER ROSE QUARTZ TUB for so long she thought she might wither inside it. There was a part of her that wanted to dissolve into suds and salts and seep out through the drains to the ocean. She imagined it would be peaceful there, in that swathe of velvet blue. That it would smother her in the sweetest drowning.

She rinsed her arms in the water, watching as the rose petals stuck to her skin. She was so absorbed in observing the petals that she didn't hear Léandre enter.

"Her Luminosity has insisted that I see to you."

She shook a rose petal off of her palm. "I'm fine, Léandre."

"You are not fine, Laila. And don't tell me again that you are," he said, his brow creased in concern. He sat at the edge of the bath. "You never talk about what happened before we left. I know how much you cared for Dominus—"

"Stop it."

"I feel it would help if you would discuss it with someone."

"I said *stop*." Her body pulsed dangerously with a current. The lights stuttered. "I don't want to talk about Dominus with you, Léandre. In fact, if you desire to keep your post as my Lightshield, kindly do not utter his name in my presence ever again."

He sighed heavily, rising from the bath. "Her Luminosity has requested that you join her for breakfast once you are ready."

Laila sank down until the water was to her chin, a wordless dismissal. She waited until he had withdrawn from the room before she rose and squeezed the water from her hair, letting her hand drift down to her neck as her fingers scraped against the spot where Dominus's teeth once lay.

She shuddered as she closed her eyes, feeling the indentations as though they were still there. Fresh. But there was nothing but smooth skin when she tested it again. It was always the psychic wounds that were the most stubborn to heal.

She vacated the bath to find it was dawn, and she decided to dress and take breakfast with her mother. A practice she had been increasingly performing the further she became estranged from the concept of sleep. Not usually prone to early rising, Laila found she'd always been fondest of that liminal space in between waking and awake. Those enigmatic hours where she could watch the world shake itself of its slumber and pretend that she might be the only one alive.

The garden was saturated in a thick, honey-lacquered gold from the lethargic rays of the rising sun. She and Amira seated themselves in a little nook underneath an untamed shrub of wisteria, its heavily perfumed branches offering them shelter from the penetrating rays. The wrought iron table was neatly laid with offerings of mild goat's cheese, fig and lavender galettes and warm spiced brioche, and an ornate tea set of decoratively frosted glass and gilded rimming.

Laila helped herself to a honeycomb from one of the plates and took a bite, the sweet nectar oozing into her palm the moment she touched it. She finished it messily and sucked her fingers, fully aware of her mother's disapproving stare as she did so.

"You couldn't have picked something less messy for breakfast?" Amira critiqued with a cluck of her tongue before wrapping her coral-pink lips around her teacup. "Just look at what you've done to your chest."

Laila glanced down with a slightly vacant look at the trails of honey that had slithered down her neckline. Then she shrugged. "I think my breasts caught the worst of it."

Amira made a disgruntled sound. She'd noticed her daughter's turn towards carelessness as of late and had taken it both with understanding and impatience, hoping it wouldn't be a lasting change. She unfolded one of the rose-shaped napkins with one swift flick of her wrist. "Hold still."

Laila was used to having her mother puppeteer her like a marionette. So hold still she did as her mother diligently cleaned her chest of honey before choosing for her daughter the much cleaner option of sliced brioche to slather with lemon jam.

Laila chose not to protest the forcefulness of this gesture and took a small, appeasing bite out of the corner of her brioche. "I've been thinking about what our next move ought to be with regards to Mortos."

"Have you now?" This surprised Amira, for she had tried to evade the subject of politics with Laila upon her return. She'd never been suited for sympathy and she feared broaching the topic of Mortos would provoke an emotional outburst.

"Yes," Laila said, taking a sip from her tea. "But I'm afraid it's going to involve something you won't like."

Amira sighed as she placed the sullied napkin to one side. "Why do I feel as though you are about to bring up the name Darius to me?"

"He is the last hope we have, Maman." Laila put down her cup firmly. "He is known to us, appropriately connected, and he even claims descendancy from the bloodline they so favour. We are not going to find a more suitable candidate."

Amira cut herself a portion of galette. "I suspect you are expecting a full pardon from me for his crimes."

"I think that will be a small price to pay in the grand scheme of victory." Laila picked back up her cup. "I don't like it any more than you do, Maman. But we are out of options. Dominus will remain quiet about our previous conspiracy so as not to endanger his mother, but that means I can no longer use her." She slid closer on her chair to take her mother's hand. "Allow me to speak with him at least."

Amira met her daughter's gaze, tapping her glass with one finger. "All right. I'll allow you to move forward with this plan of yours. Let us see if Darius Calantis ends up being the saving grace we need."

That same morning, Darius was taking his own breakfast, lifting a cup of peppermint tea to be puffed cool. Dark circles lined his eyes and the gauntness of his already sharp northern features had intensified during his stay. He'd been spending his nights trying to disentangle the effects of Dr Mielette's influence during his sessions. He had been slowly building up an unbreachable mind-fort, the doors of which would be impervious to even the subterfuge of her psychological trickery.

Unfortunately, this only made him a more intense subject of

interest for the doctor, and she was erecting newer and crueller ways to whittle down his barriers until an opportunity might occur for her to slip through his weak spot. For that reason alone he was prepared to stay vigilant, keeping his mind fiercely guarded for anything she might use against it.

He took another sip from his tea in the hopes it would give him clarity, and then the elusive patter of light-footed steps had him twitching to alertness. He caught the scent of her before he saw her—always that warm heady aroma of white florals and vanilla. She appeared as a vision in green floral-patterned silk layered atop a white underdress, remaining cautiously at the observation window.

"Your Radiance." He bowed his head in greeting. "To what do I owe the pleasure?"

It had been far too long since he'd last laid eyes on her, and he found himself desperately roaming the contours of her face to memorise what he could. She'd changed her hair again, he noticed. Today it was half-pinned with the rest let loose in pretty tendrils.

She stepped closer to the window. "Hello, prefect."

"It's been a while since someone has called me that," Darius chuckled, gesturing to the interior of his cell. "Won't you join me for a moment? I believe the tea is still warm."

"I think I'll stay here, thank you." Her refusal was spoken with grace, though her smile was razor-edged. "I was actually arriving with a proposition for you."

"Is that so?" Darius took a seat on a nearby chair and crossed one leg over the other. "Please, enlighten me."

Laila dithered on her words as she observed his cool steel composure, searching for the right thing to say. After so long, she'd thought herself grown immune to this, but he still managed to disarm. "I can see prison life isn't treating you well." She grappled for a weakness, any weakness in which she could gain a foothold. "You look... fatigued."

"You almost sound concerned." Darius put a hand on his chest. "But it seems we are diverting from the important subject at hand here."

"Yes, indeed." She scrunched her lips to one side. A lock of his hair had fallen loose and snaked around his eye; she wanted to brush it back into place. "I'm sure you'll be interested to know that Mortos' circumstances have increasingly worsened since your departure. Your father grows more unstable by the day and there are growing signs of civil unrest."

"That is interesting." Darius tented his fingers in front of him. "Shame I can't do much about it from here."

"Yes, well, I tried asking Dominus if he would be willing to join forces, and he refused to budge an inch."

"Steadfast until the end, my foolish brother." He cocked his head to one side. "Still, it does shock me to know that Dominus ignored your plea. I would've thought for certain you were the nudge he needed to finally make his move."

"Well, clearly you miscalculated. What made you think I would even have that measure of influence over him?"

"Well, it's just... if I were with you, I couldn't imagine not giving you anything you wanted."

Her chest seized the moment the words were uttered, and had she not coached herself to remain cold, she would've sworn the fever of a blush began to take hold.

"Perhaps I'm here to take you up on that offer," she said.

"How do you mean?" His eyes narrowed.

"Since Dominus has proven a liability, we will need to turn our attention to a new candidate to depose Lanius. I see no better suitor for the role than yourself."

"And what do you want in return?"

"What you just said," Laila teased, a secretive smile appearing on her rosy mouth. She looked at him with large, rounded eyes that were improbably doe-like, tinged in a cornflower hue, making it easy for anyone to want to invest in her innocence. "For you to give me everything I've ever wanted."

Darius couldn't help but smile in response. "You want a puppet installed for Soleterea's whims. I see. You make a tempting offer. One I'd be a fool to refuse considering my current predicament. But you see, if we are to work together there are a few demands I desire to make myself."

"Such as?"

He gestured to his surroundings. "Let's start with a more comfortable abode than this. You have given me comfortable amenities, I will admit, but I don't like the idea of collaborating with someone keeping me prisoner."

"I shall take it into consideration," Laila said. "Anything else?"

He took some moments to consider this. "My father's heart. You can dispose of the rest of him any way you wish, but his heart belongs to me."

A disturbing request, to be certain, but not one Laila was willing to argue against. "Very well."

She adjusted her features into an expression that set aglow the entirety of her face, and he understood once more how Dominus had so easily been made a fool for her—being on the receiving end of a smile like that. "Until we next meet, Prefect Calantis."

She removed herself from the window, smoothing down her skirts of tulle before departing from the room with one last furtive glance at him.

Laila and Lyra circled one another, their bodies synchronised in perfect precision—surrendered to a subliminal trance that made their limbs malleable as liquid. They moved beneath a sun trained on them like a spotlight, like their bodies were hosting a performance for celestial eyes alone, something purer and perfected than any offering from the earthly realm.

With startling swiftness, Laila kicked towards her opponent. Lyra caught her leg, spinning her around to catch her in a chokehold that Laila smashed through.

"Good, you're getting better," Lyra said as Laila ejected her leg in another kick that sent her staggering backwards.

Sprite-dancing was a sacred art form that shared more with dancing than with fighting. It demanded fluency in the language of one's physique, requiring you to make a quick study of your opponent's next movements from a flex of a muscle or quick jerk of a limb. The result was something far more delicate than deadly, an elegant collision of bodies that appeared to have shrugged off gravity.

Soon they were tussling again, arms and legs blurring at a speed imperceptible to sight before Lyra swept forward, curled her leg around Laila's, and flipped her over onto her back.

"Stay focused," Lyra said, and she nudged Laila with a foot. "Don't let me catch you off-guard." She reached out to help Laila to her feet.

Laila accepted the offer graciously, but once her grip on Lyra's hand tightened, she took her chance, snapping her legs around her neck and twirling them both to the floor.

"Seems that I am not the only one being caught off-guard," Laila chimed in her songbird lilt, her voice pitched higher as she stopped to taunt. "Your focus has gotten sloppy recently, Lyra. I may have to go browsing for your replacement."

She tightened her hold around Lyra's neck with her thighs until Lyra tapped out. "My focus is sound as a bell; you simply lack scruples."

They disentangled from one another, their chests heaving and sweat-sheened.

"There is no honour in warfare," Laila said in sardonic mimicry of a previous sprite instructor she'd had. She tucked away a curl that sprung free from her unruly braid.

Lyra rose with a pant, flushed and rosy with exertion as she picked up her bottle of mint-infused rosewater and chugged it. "Since when are you so desperately into sparring anyway?"

Since Dominus tore into her innocence with his teeth and swallowed it whole, leaving a splinter on the margins of her psyche that only sealed upon contact with near-peril.

"I want to be prepared," Laila said, picking up her own rosewater bottle to drink from it. "There's no saying that war won't ever come to Soleterea, and after what I've experienced in Mortos—felt what an occasso can do—I refuse to ever be caught unaware again."

"Well, you're not wrong," Lyra said, beginning her cool-down stretches. "After all, we've already been infiltrated."

By this she meant Darius.

"I still don't know what to make of him," Laila said, her lips scrunching in thought.

"What's there to make?" Lyra huffed as she stretched. "A hound on a leash is still a hound and capable of biting something fierce if not appropriately muzzled. I don't think it was your wisest choice to join forces with him."

"I can't disagree, but—well, I suppose I was curious." She joined

Lyra's stretches, feeling the tension in her muscles ebb away with a feline unfurl.

"About what?"

"About what he will do." Laila undid her braid and shook out her vibrant mane of curls. "Unlike Dominus, he at least seems willing to cooperate, and... well, should we succeed in overthrowing Lanius, we will need to install a leader to replace him."

"And you think Darius ought to be that leader?" Lyra asked, tearing the gauze from her hands to unravel it.

"I don't know," Laila admitted. "I admit I haven't thought beyond the initial goal of removing Lanius, but if Darius proves himself trustworthy, then he's sure to be a better option than installing one of our own."

Lyra nodded before wrinkling her nose. She had never been one for discussing politics; it was too cloudy and obscure for someone who had always seen the world in clear monochrome. "You know what I want to have right now?"

"Éclairs?" Laila asked with a touch of knowing.

"Éclairs," Lyra confirmed. "Let's rinse ourselves off in the showers and then we'll go to my chalet."

"I'm assuming you'll want to *share* again," Laila sighed, knowing how often she and Lyra ended up in a battle for the same spout.

"Don't pretend you don't enjoy it."

They rode beneath the gossamer rays of late afternoon sun to the apple-green hills in Espriterre: the land of the forest sprites.

Laila rode her unicorn, Polaris, a purebred with a platinum horn and hooves of palladium; an occurrence so infrequent it was the subject of myth. Unicorns were well known for their skill at evading capture, and solarites were the only creatures capable of luring them near enough to be tamed. As with most earthbound creatures, unicorns were irrevocably drawn by a solarite's supernal essence. For even beasts look to the skies for stars and will hunt for them when they disappear behind the wood.

Laila could recall her shrill and whimsical delight when Léandre first presented Polaris at her débutante ball, a giant silk bow around his neck. They'd been practically inseparable ever since. She nudged her heels into his metallic white coat to urge him to travel faster, firmer, his nostrils frothing with exertion.

Lyra rode alongside her on a gold mare, racing her on the leaf-covered trail as they travelled through Bluebell Wood towards the village of Lis. As it was summer, the underbrush was carpeted with the bell-shaped blooms, flanked on either side with lithe blondewood boles that were hollow as bird bones. With each slim wisp of breeze that rustled through the trees, the branches made sweet music like silvered chimes.

They stopped outside of Lyra's chalet and left their mounts to graze on the fields. Her home was inside the stout bole of a sycamore. Such was the nature-loving way of the forest sprites: they sought to immerse—not invade—themselves in the earth.

Lyra shared the home with Léandre, having lost her late mother to a monster-hunting quest to kill a basilisk—a subject she seldom discussed. She kicked open the front door and stepped beneath a low-hanging wood beam. The inside of a sprite's house was as earthy as its exterior. Furniture consisted of carefully contorted structures grown from willow trees, upholstered with large leaves and petals.

"I'm home," she declared with gusto, then paused for an answer. When there was none, she turned back to Laila with a vulpine smile. "Appears we have the place to ourselves."

Lyra opened a cabinet bearded with moss and brought forth a box of

Soleterea's finest éclairs garnished with nuts, berries and edible blooms. Every morning, Lyra had a box delivered from the local patisserie for breakfast and saved whatever was left for a late afternoon snack.

She put her clay kettle on the fire to boil and spooned rosebuds into the broth to make tisane. "Take your pick."

Laila did so, deciding on a whimsically decorated pastry with raspberries and rose petals. She took a greedy bite, sighing in contentment. "Just as good as always."

"Oh, yes," Lyra said, setting out a tea arrangement on the dining table coated with flowering ivy. She poured them both glasses and sat, propping up one leg on the edge of the table.

They ended up going through the whole box and splitting the last pastry after measuring it with a knife. By the end, even the crumbs had been demolished as Laila licked them hungrily from her fingers.

"So, hypothetically." Laila capped her fingers with the raspberries and ate them off one by one. "Say you were intending to bring a highly dangerous, deviously intelligent, potentially treacherous monster into your castle. Where would you put him?"

"Are we still discussing this?" Lyra groaned. "You're obsessed."

"I am not obsessed," Laila protested, cheeks flushing in affront. "I am merely... thinking ahead."

Lyra snorted. "Your mother would be proud."

"Just answer the question."

Lyra smiled upon seeing her friend's fixed jaw and petulant pout. "The Moon Tower." She sucked fresh cream from her fingers. "It's isolated, it's secure, it's perilously short of exits besides the entrance and a long drop out of the window. I'd put him in the Moon Tower."

"The Moon Tower," Laila echoed, nibbling on her bottom lip in thought. "Yes, I think that should do nicely."

XXVI

THE MOON TOWER WAS A SLENDER COLUMN of pale marble on the outskirts of the main palace structure. Though an insubstantial building at first blink, its primary attractions came in the form of its lofty height and endless rows of staircases that were enchanted to transfer directions. This made it so that however far the occupant spiralled down, they would always be redirected into their room. By day, it was stained pink with the hue of a newborn's flush, while the evening dyed it violet through the circulatory migration of the sun's cycle.

Darius was escorted by his Lightshield entourage, who delivered him in chains to the top of the tower, unlocking him only once he was safely installed within its rooms. Once freed, Darius massaged his wrists and looked about his surroundings. The furnishings had been finely carved from mother-of-pearl and chiselled with celestial motifs.

It was a beautiful setting, one much suited to opulent tastes such as his own, and he heaved a sigh of relief that he had seen the end of incarcerated austerity. The first thing he did upon receiving his new dwellings was request a change of clothes—for a good predator should always seek to camouflage amongst his surroundings. He would embody monstrosity in its most subtle form, the kind even hunters couldn't perceive until he was upon them.

He chose a suit of wine-red velvet with a corseted vest. The tailcoat was embroidered with gold roses, the same that blossomed in the pavilion not far outside of his window. Pleased with his meticulous façade, he sprayed a few puffs of perfume, indulging in the subtly citrus aroma before he moved into the sitting room to await Laila's arrival.

He found he was not prepared for her when she did.

She ascended the steps in red charmeuse draped in a black overdress of jet-beaded point d'esprit with a neckline that drooped from her shoulders. She entered with one brow quirked towards him in appraisal, her gaze taking a lingering journey down his form.

"Well, don't you look fetching," Laila said, reaching up to adjust his cravat. "Soleterean attire suits you well."

"I could say the same of you."

She released a soft breath of laughter as her hands rested briefly on his chest before she removed them. "How are you liking your new abode?"

"Quite well, thank you." The corner of his mouth inched up wryly. "You have chosen an impeccable setting for my confinement."

"I know this may seem like an unconventional arrangement, but you are not a prisoner here."

"You have a habit of locking up your guests in towers?"

"That is only at my mother's discretion until we can ascertain your reliability. I'm sure you can understand." Her tone had taken on a serrated edge to the otherwise pristine primness. "And speaking of—she has asked that you join us for dinner tonight."

He hadn't expected to meet the impératrice so soon. He fiddled with his cravat in apprehension.

She held out her arm for him to take. "Shall we?"

When she turned he could see her dress was similarly low-cut at the back, adorned with a red velvet ribbon and displaying the delicate framework of her shoulder blades.

He slotted his arm through her elbow as they walked down to the bottom of the tower.

Laila breezed past the guards with a nod of acknowledgement before steering him past the rose bushes to a candlelit setting prepared for their arrival.

"It's such a lovely night out. I thought we'd enjoy our meal in the gardens," she said, approaching the table to pull out their chairs and re-scatter some of the rose petals that had clustered at one corner of the lace tablecloth.

Darius certainly wouldn't disagree with her assessment, for in contrast to the frigidity of Mortesian climates, Soleterean nights were sultry events that left one gasping if not accustomed to the rise in temperature. Even their darkness made him want to strip himself bare.

"Why not?" he said, taking a seat near the faint purl of the fountain in the pond where the light breeze could cool the nape of his neck.

Not long after did the impératrice herself arrive wearing iridescent blue silk.

Laila burst out from her seat to receive her. "Good evening, Maman," she said, bright as a bell as they exchanged kisses on both cheeks in Soleterean custom and began to speak rapidly in the liquid speech of Soltongue.

Darius was content to listen to them. Soltongue had a pleasant cadence to one's ears—like dripping honey on the skin.

Laila parted from Amira to introduce him. "Maman, you've met Prefect Darius Calantis."

"Indeed," Amira drawled in response, looking none too impressed with what she saw.

"It's a pleasure to be in your company again, Your Luminosity." Darius bowed low in deference. He peeked up at her from beneath his lashes. "I hope I can make a better impression on you than our prior encounter."

"That remains to be seen," Amira said, impervious to his charming looks. She took a seat at the table and unfolded her napkin. "So tell me about yourself, prefect. Why is it that my daughter seems to believe you to be a suitable replacement for our current Mortesian menace?"

"Let's say I have become accustomed to a certain lifestyle afforded by a peaceful nation and I would like to uphold it where possible," Darius said as a server arrived with their drinks—soft pink cocktails misting with froth and rimmed in crystal sugar, bearing cocktail sticks of speared strawberries. Love potions, they were called.

"So you would be willing to maintain an allyship should you ascend?" Amira swirled her cocktail stick around her glass.

"Yes."

"And the trade agreements?"

"Will resume as before." Darius took a sip from his glass. "Hopefully with some re-negotiations to be made in the future."

"Hm." Amira regarded his compliant nature with suspicion. "What makes you so amenable to treat with us in a way your father and brother couldn't before you?"

Another platter arrived, this time an appetiser—bruschetta topped with sheep's cheese, sliced pears and pansies.

"As my father's bastard, it has been my lot in life to be overlooked and disregarded. I have watched for centuries as my younger brother took every opportunity life afforded him and chose to squander them. This arrangement is about as good an opportunity as any I will receive to take what I feel ought to have been mine to begin with."

"You've been thinking about that for a while, haven't you?" Laila said, a smile soft and teasing playing on her lips. "Ways in which you might accomplish a usurpation."

He gave her a blithe shrug. "When you have an eternity to live you start to daydream a few things."

Amira quirked a brow in amusement, taking a bite of bruschetta. "I assume daydreaming isn't all you've done over the centuries?"

"Certainly not," Darius said. "I have been amassing names and contacts during my brother's brief absence who would be willing to come to my aid. It's a significant enough number of the gentry, though still small—my father was greatly feared, you see. But with your support we are certain not to lose." He helped himself to a piece of bruschetta. "Though I feel I should be asking questions of you also, Your Luminosity."

"As you wish."

"I assume Mortos shall retain all of its sovereignty in the event I ascend?"

"I see no reason to argue against that." Amira crooked up her lips. "Let Mortos be your sole playing field. The role I see Soleterea playing is... supervisory at best."

Her specific word usage did not go unnoticed by him. "So what is it that you want in return for this gesture? *Just* my loyalty?"

"Loyalty shall be all I require from you," Amira said. "Anything else is simply additional. You are not the only one who has become accustomed to a peaceful lifestyle, prefect. The easier it is to uphold, the better. And I will do whatever I can in service of keeping that peace."

The threat beneath was veiled, but widely heard all the same. She wouldn't hesitate to act against him should he disturb their tenuously held peace.

"Then it seems we're all in agreement," Darius said, gesturing to them both. "The next step, I would gather, is to talk strategy."

Laila's knees collided against his, not for the first time that evening, but he'd tried hard not to notice it until now. He stole a glance at her as she took a bite out of bruschetta and saw her cheeks had gone roseate from all the alcohol she'd been drinking, her lip rouge enticingly smudged, and he wondered again if this was how she might look after being kissed.

He swallowed the thought away with another drink from his cocktail and transferred his attention to Amira, whom he engaged in an intense intellectual back and forth until the main course arrived.

A platter of deep-sea delights was set down with one focal centrepiece—butter-poached lobster served with seaweed tartare, borage flowers, and sparkling nectar wine sauce. The lobsters were an iridescent teal blue to match Soleterea's waters. Darius had never seen it before.

"I hope you don't mind seafood," Laila said, chasing away the sensual memory of her and Dominus's first meal together with a sip of cocktail.

"Actually, it happens to be one of my favourites."

"Any particular reason for that?" Amira asked, swirling her half-full cocktail, "I would've thought an occasso would prefer something bloodier."

Darius's smile did not falter. "It goes back to my time doing mandatory military service in Mortos. It is required of every male who comes of age in my country to select a particular branch and do a full seventy-five years before we are able to discharge. I managed to put mine off for a bit, attending university instead, but it soon caught up with me, so... I chose to join Squalons, which is our naval branch, and spent a lot of time out at sea guarding our waters and slaughtering sea monsters."

"Do you miss it?" Laila asked. "Being in service, I mean?"

"Calante's wrath no, it was *awful*." Darius took an oyster from its neatly arranged platter. "I do, however, miss the sea terribly. I would spend hours in the water, catching all the food I could want and exploring the depths of the ocean. You should see it for yourself sometime, Your Radiance; it's a whole other world down there. Entire civilisations built to suit the sea—carried on the backs of whales that span centuries older than even myself."

She bit her lip, her finger winding tightly inside a curl as he spoke. "That sounds fascinating."

"Oh, there are all sorts of things I could show you," he said, sucking the contents of his oyster shell and licking his lips. "Sunken ships, secret treasure troves, underwater caverns full of giant squid. But my favourite, and the one I think you'd like best, is the show the sirens put on every year during Midsummer. They turn docile, and their scales go entirely bioluminescent as they perform their ritual mating call to lure a partner. It's... hypnotic, hearing their voices. It's something that has to be heard to be explained."

Laila angled her body towards him, her chin resting deeply within her palm as her eyes glistened with interest. "Oh, I'd love to."

"Perhaps one day I'll get to show you," he said, fixing upon her with his eyes of aqua blue—as depthless and dangerous as the ocean itself.

"Oh, I—" she said softly, clearing her throat. She tilted her chin down, tucking a loose curl behind her ear. "Perhaps."

The last course of the evening was a lemon pound cake glazed with vanilla. Darius curiously helped himself to a slice, having never been exposed to citrus, and surprised himself with how much the sour, piquant flavour stimulated his taste buds.

At the very first bite he made a soft, orgasmic sound, and he filled himself with several slices by the time the night was through, much to Laila's amusement, before Amira polished off the last of her drink and rose to depart.

"I think it's about time we all retire for the evening," she said, setting down her empty glass. "Laila, I trust you will handle the prefect getting to his room safely?"

"Yes, Maman." Laila understood perfectly the words behind the words. Amira wanted to ensure he didn't have a chance to slip away.

"Then I shall bid you a pleasant evening." She smiled towards them both. Then she was on her way, disappearing into the swathes of pastel-coloured rose bushes and leaving the two alone.

"You can thank me any time now," Laila prompted, her head arched in slight mischievous glee as she grinned at him.

He found himself smiling back at her, unable to resist being infected by her insidious jubilation. "Thank you, Your Radiance."

She scoffed, sidling over to him on her seat. "Oh, come now, '*Your Radiance*'." She rolled her eyes. "I think I deserve a warmer thank you than that."

"Thank you, Laila," he amended, his tongue tracing carefully over the vowels of her name as though he almost couldn't believe he got to say it.

She paused in response, a blush rising on her cheeks. "Hm, that's better." Her features settled into something hazily soft. "You know, you can be nice when you let your guard down. Quite charming, in fact."

Perhaps *too* charming. In the span of one evening she had almost forgotten herself, going as far as asking him to say her name just to hear it on his lips. She had to rein herself in. She had cast the net of her charm to keep *him* ensnared, not to become entangled within it.

Laila traced the rim of her cocktail glass and polished off the final dregs. "I think I shall escort you back to your quarters and then retire."

Darius had nearly forgotten his freedom was but a temporary arrangement, and it was with growing disappointment that he was led back to the Moon Tower. The Lightshield guards awaited to welcome him inside.

Before he entered he turned back to get a final glance at Laila, finding she had already paused on her own journey to look back at him. Beneath the moonlight, her skin was opalescent, and she looked even more befitting of her supernal origins.

"Good night, Darius," she said, her final vowels floating in the breeze before she turned away. It was the first time they had exchanged names on such an intimate basis, and it was as carnal a sensation as if she had kissed him goodnight.

∼✦∼

The next morning had Darius glancing out of the lone window in the sitting room in search of a shred of entertainment. He had become so desperate that he even began to fantasise his escape from the tower and dedicated his mornings to plot out how he might do so.

He peered out of the window to survey the tower's structure and noticed the skirts of ornate corbels jutting ever so slightly out from the main marble bricks. It didn't take him long to conclude that simply climbing out would only result in the inevitable shattering of every bone in his skeleton.

However, should he be able to utilise his mathematical aptitude to his advantage, then it was very possible he could calculate a method in which he could jump from corbel to corbel in such a way to avoid certain (temporary) death. However, even with the numerical machinery of his mind on the task, he saw he couldn't avoid a perilous drop from the last corbel skirt to the ground below.

In simpler terms: he was going to have to break his legs.

He winced in psychic anguish from the predetermined injury, for even though he could repair such damage with the use of a skeletal hex, the sheer anguish endured from contorting his fractures back into place did not appeal to him. He'd had enough of that growing up in the Citadel.

Even more bothersome was the idea that he should accomplish this whilst avoiding being spotted by the patrolling Lightshields. He'd already taken note of their shifts and the changes within them. He knew what the best times of day and night were to strike. All that was left to him was pure chance, the chaos from which he was reared.

With a heavy sigh, he propped his elbows against the window ledge and let his gaze travel across the palace grounds. He saw the solarites going about their days, their fair tresses in opulent hues of gold, platinum and pearl.

He tried to locate hers among them.

Perhaps a difficult task due to the relative uniformity in their appearance from afar, but he'd already memorised enough of her to recognise her catlike gait when he saw it—the lively bounce in her step, the fluid movement of her hips and the particular uptilted way she held her head.

He located her eventually in a daisy meadow drenched in sunlight, wherein her carefree walk was more frenetic than usual as she prepared a parade float. If he focused his hearing enough he could just about decipher her high, clipped tone as she dictated orders to her subordinates:

"Could you straighten out those flowers over there? They're looking a little crooked..."

"I want to make sure there is ample space for the ballerinas to perform their entire dance without peril..."

"No, no, no, not like that. Rosewater fountain here, rosewood thrones there. Need I present to you the design sketches again..."

He chuckled to himself, not envying those on the receiving end of her perfectionism, a trait he did not doubt was inherited. Still, he could admire her artistry and fastidious attention to detail as the float—a part of the annual Day of Enlightenment festival, he'd heard—was certain to be nothing short of picturesque.

He decided to watch the transformation as Laila eventually departed from the meadow, satisfied with the outcome. What he noticed most, however, was that positioned away from the eyes of those surrounding her, she had let drop that perfectly constructed façade she'd been emitting for the past several hours and allowed her face to look sombre, conflicted. He wondered about the person lurking behind the rosy veneer who could emit such a dour look, and he decided he would stuff it away for later study as a secret all to himself.

XXVII

AILA STEPPED BENEATH THE PAVILION to find her mother awaiting her on one of its alabaster benches. The pavilion was one of Amira's favourite places in the palace. Laila's too. The princess had read many books on the bench her mother now occupied.

"You wanted to see me, Maman?"

Amira severed one of the gold roses from its bush and lifted it to her nose. "Yes, I wanted to see how your plans for the Day of Enlightenment were coming along. You are aware we have quite a lot resting on this event, as I intend to use it to gather everyone to discuss the coup d'état and I want to ensure it goes impeccably."

"Of course, Maman," Laila chirruped sweetly. She had been anticipating this. "Everything is going splendidly."

"You have taken care of the parade float?"

"Yes."

"And you have made everyone aware of their respective agendas for the night?"

Laila watched her mother's fingers and how they made quick work of depriving the rose stem of its thorns. "Yes."

"Well then, aurore." Amira's voice was soft but her smile was sharp as the thorns she had plucked. "It is certain to be an eventful evening." She lifted the rose to her nose. "Let us also hope your intuition with Darius Calantis has not been misguided and that he will do what needs to be done when the time arrives."

The last thing Amira wanted was another case of family loyalties causing cold feet.

Laila swallowed, feeling a tight constriction in her chest as though she was being wound tight in a vice. "I believe he will, Maman. He seems to want the throne more than anything."

"I'm sure." Amira's jaw tightened as she snapped off a petal of the rose, finding it imperfect, and let it flutter to the floor in disdain. "He seems to be quite taken with you, doesn't he?"

"I—" Laila hadn't expected for her to say it outright. "I suppose he is."

"No need to be coy about it, aurore." Amira smiled that much wider. "As with Dominus, that's something we can use, and at the very least his infatuation appears to... influence outcomes far better than with the former."

"Maman." Laila shifted uncomfortably, a blush unfurling on her cheeks like ripened red buds. The prospect of flirtation seemed different than with Dominus, more threatening to her, though she couldn't fathom why.

"I mean, he did allegedly defy the wishes of his father to save your life. I don't much care for your chosen romantic entanglements, and when given the choice I will always rely on a much firmer hand when it comes to negotiations... but a softer touch doesn't go amiss, here and there. I trust you will make note of that."

Laila nodded. "Of course, Maman."

Amira allowed her enough time to reach outside the pavilion before reeling her back.

"And Laila?"

Her shoulders solidified as she made a slow turn. "Yes?"

"Consider this your last chance to correct your mistakes."

"Yes, Maman."

Laila staggered away on unsteady fawn legs, making it halfway through the wisteria-covered pergola before she had to stop. She collapsed pathetically against the frail shrubbery to drag air into her wanting lungs, her body trembling like a leaf in autumn wind.

She wasn't sure when she found it safe to move again, but soon her body began to right itself—the blur in her vision clearing and the nausea dissolving away from her stomach. She recovered the strength in her legs to continue through the grounds.

She spent the rest of the morning in the palace vineyards among the nectar grapes, watching the field workers rummage vines for translucent pink berries to fill their baskets. Grape season was in full swing this time of year and she wanted a decent selection of bottles for the upcoming festival. No bash would be complete in Soleterea without its famed sparkling nectar wine.

Laila plucked a berry from a vine and put it in her mouth, the skin bursting the moment her teeth touched it. She closed her eyes and hummed in pleasure as she was soaked in the dreamy languor a nectar grape always provided its consumer. It was part of what made their wine so sought-after.

She tugged one of the branches to take a grape-cluster into her mouth and devoured more of them. Then she wiped the corner of her mouth daintily and heaved a satisfied sigh, walking through the fields of resplendent golden vines.

While she walked, she noticed the fragments of a figure between the gaps of the gilt leaves and moved closer to investigate, parting two vines to find Darius being escorted by two Lightshields.

Laila had a burning urge to talk to him and decided she couldn't wait until he was safely restored within the tower. So she created a diversion, sparking an orb of pure electrical power within her fingertips that grew in force and intensity until she tossed it.

It ignited with a crackle of writhing, spidery legs in the near distance.

"What was that?" called out one of the guards as the other pivoted to look in the same direction, prompted by her partner.

Laila parted her way through the vines and seized Darius by the wrist, hauling him through the opening and resealing the plants. She placed a hand over his mouth as the Lightshields turned and, on seeing their charge had escaped, sounded an alert.

"Come on," she said, taking his hand and transporting them to the other end of the vineyard with quicksilver speed. "It should take a while for them to find us here."

"Not that I don't appreciate it, but"—Darius straightened out the sleeves and front of his tailcoat as he plucked a stray vine leaf and flicked it away—"is there a reason for this abduction?"

"My mother still has some misgivings about you," Laila said, hands clasped behind her back. "I was hoping we might find a way to put her mind at ease?"

He narrowed his eyes in disbelief. "That's it?"

"I've put a lot on the line, helping you, what with everything you've done." She tapped her foot impatiently with a sigh. "I would just like some reassurance that I didn't risk it all for nothing."

"Well, you needn't worry your pretty little head about it, princess," Darius said. "I'll be sure to put any doubts you have to rest the night of the coup. My circle doesn't extend far, but it is loyal and I've spent enough time amassing it. I know where every piece of the board will be set, right down to my chosen council."

Laila nodded softly before biting her lip. "Do you ever think about what's going to happen when this is all over? To your father? To... Dominus?"

The soft lambency in his expression dimmed. "It has crossed my mind."

"And you're okay with it? You have absolutely no reservations about how this is bound to end for them?"

He said nothing for so long she didn't think that he would answer.

"I've made my peace with their losses long ago; it has to be done." He looked down at her, his eyes ablaze with diabolical interest. "But the real question is... have you made yours?"

"I—" Her tongue turned to lead in her mouth, her words seeming hopelessly insufficient. "I'm just trying to understand what it is that went so wrong between you that you would need Dominus dead."

"It's not about us, it's not about hatred or bitterness... it's just our ways. If I could count on Dominus to step down without a fight, perhaps my tactics would be different, but I know that he will not, and thus I must not." He slipped his arm through hers as they walked. "You remember how we choose monarchs in our culture?"

"Yes, when a rex takes the throne, you rule for as long as you see fit until you abdicate or are slain by your kin."

"How many rexes do you think ever stepped down willingly?" His brow arched in irony. "I'll give you a hint: not terribly many. Killing each other for a throne is something deeply embedded within our bloodline. It's practically family tradition. I think both of us know that, deep

down, regardless of me being a bastard. It's why we were never closer—
it's harder... when you're close." His throat bobbled with a swallow as he
choked down any rising regret with a smile. "Shame we don't have any
wine to offset such a dour conversation."

She held up one finger and reached into one of the vines, producing
for him a small pile of nectar grapes. "It's not quite the same as when it's
vinted, but it's the best I can offer right now."

She put a grape to his lips.

He paused in bewilderment at such an intimate gesture before he
opened his mouth and accepted the offering of fruit.

Laila ate one herself, indulging in its sweetness, before nudging him
playfully with her shoulder.

"Though if we're trading motivations, it's only right I ask the same
of you," Darius said, taking another grape from her palm. "You never
did explain why you chose me."

"I didn't think you would take well to being told you were a
substitute."

Darius chuckled, eating a grape before he continued. "No, you are
quite right. That would be a blow to my ego. Still, I'm used to it by now.
And at the very least I can thank my brother's abysmal decision-making
for providing me with this opportunity."

"Which is?"

"Being able to stand here with you under the sun." He halted their
walk to face her and traced his fingers down the incline of her high-
boned cheek. "Not having to feel any reservations about doing this."

Her breath suspended as he took a loose curl and slid it through his
fingers, all the while looking at her with that glacial blue stare that froze
her to the spot.

She shouldn't be letting him do this. Regardless of their aligned
status, he was still a monster, after all, like all the rest. But curiosity

overrode, and she found herself wanting to indulge in what she'd been forbidding herself from.

"Or this." He slid his finger down her cheek so slowly, merely luxuriating in the silken texture of her skin. He curled his finger beneath her chin and tilted her up to face him. His breath was tantalisingly warm against her lips as he exhaled, and she could still smell the mint tea he had consumed for breakfast.

Laila swallowed thickly as she looked at him, remembering the phantom of her mother's words. The lingering confrontation with Dominus and all the ways he had hurt her in it. And she knew that this would hurt him. More than any physical injury she could inflict.

"Or this." He leaned in too cautiously for either of them, but he'd been waiting so long for this and he wasn't about to rush it now. So he let their lips ghost tantalisingly close before sealing them with a kiss.

Laila's eyes fluttered to a close as she leaned in with a feather-soft sigh. The kiss was a simple meeting of the lips; there were no roving hands or eager tongues, and yet she felt it—oh how she felt it—all the way down to her toes. There was a stirring in the pit of her stomach like she'd plummeted off the edge of a long height and was about to meet the sweet relief of landing. She lifted her hands to his chest, winding her fingers into his shirt to hold him closer.

That was all the provocation he needed to grow emboldened—one hand in her hair while the other slid low on her hip to press his body to hers until not even a scrap of sunlight could seep between them.

He coaxed her mouth open to deepen the kiss. He took his time, the kiss slow and attentive, unable to bear pulling away from her when he eventually parted for breath. His lips were back on hers as soon as he'd inhaled, dragging a small sound from Laila as she melted into the embrace.

However, it was here she realised where she was, *who* she was, and the threat of impending discovery forced her to part them with a whimper. "Wait."

"Too much?" he murmured against her lips, sliding his hand through her hair.

She took a moment to catch her breath, resting her nose against his. "Far too much."

"I had to do it at least once." He nuzzled her gently before he pulled away. He refused to regret it, no matter how her thoughts might evolve on this moment in the future. He withdrew with reluctance to look down at her face, to capture the sight of her cheeks still flushed red from him before he stepped away.

She snatched his arm before she could stop herself. "Come to my boudoir tonight."

He glanced at her with enigmatic intent. "You're sure?"

She slid her tongue over her tingling lips, knowing she wouldn't be able to live with answering any other way. "Yes."

His chest lifted with hope, lips parting to speak as he stepped forward to gather her back into his arms.

The moment was shredded by a sudden call in the distance—"Cressida! I believe I see him! Halt, occasso!"

He sighed heavily in annoyance, glancing towards the guards before back at her. "And how do you suggest I get out of the tower?"

"I'm sure you'll figure that out," she said, and with a coquettish smile launched in his direction, she walked away, leaving him to the mercy of the Lightshields.

The night was marked by the vehement roar of a storm and a wretched wind that whistled through the towers of the château. Raindrops

334

battered the walls of the marble palace like beggars seeking entrance only to be cruelly turned away.

Such an event would seem an ill omen to anyone but Laila, who instead became energised by the tumult of the weather. She let open her balcony doors, allowing the charged breeze to inflate the silk gauze of her curtains and dance along her back.

She had always loved storms. There was something about them that she found so eminently sensual—the way the sky would excite itself into a violent collision of acoustics and light like it was building towards the margin of some powerful climax.

The air was sticky against her bare shoulders, causing her skin to shudder with a pleasurable chill. As the hours ticked by and the storm reached crescendo, she started to wonder if Darius would not come. Part of her hoped that he wouldn't. That she had managed to narrowly escape consequence for her spur of the moment request. Though she was curious, too. To see if he would manage to escape the tower like she suspected.

She decided not to dwell on it as she sat down to loosen her hair from her floral garland, the corona of her curls a truer crown than any circlet. She moisturised it with her gardenia and coconut oil, scooping it into a pineapple bun. She was reaching for her ribbon when she saw a figure invade her mirror, and she turned with a start.

The tenebrous silhouette of Darius appeared with a flash of lightning behind the billowing drapes that veiled her balcony. For a moment she just stared at him, waiting for her pulse to settle. He looked dishevelled, hair slickened from rain, his loosely buttoned blouse now drenched to reveal the musculature of his torso.

Laila bit her lip as she let down her hair and rose from her vanity to approach him through the parting in the drapes, almost uncertain

335

he was real. Who could blame her, when he seemed designed to have wandered from the confines of one of her erotic novels?

"Aren't you going to invite me in?" His stare was intent, looking right through her frock.

She became aware of the flimsy garment of satin and lace that was her nightgown, and she folded her arms around her chest. She shouldn't let him in. She should alert the guards with haste on his escape and have him escorted straight back to the tower. Or so her mind told her. What her body wanted was a different matter.

"Come in."

Laila watched him stride into the bedroom, his buckskin breeches clenching the thickness of his thighs. She closed the glass doors behind him and turned to find he was closer than she anticipated. He pinned her against the door with his body in moments.

Her breaths shallowed as he looked at her, her chest becoming unbearably crushed and tight beneath his weight. Cold moisture seeped through his shirt. As he loomed above her, she couldn't help but think of the last time Dominus had her trapped this close, how differently it sparked a frisson of energy through her body.

"How did you get out of the tower?" she asked, looking up at him through a gold canopy of lashes.

He touched a spiral coil of her hair, tucking it behind her ear before tilting her chin up to face him. "I had to break my legs."

Laila released a soft moan into his mouth the moment their lips met, her legs slackening with relief.

The kiss was slow at first; hesitant. Until Darius wrapped his arm around her waist to pull her closer, his hands sliding low on the small of her back. Then the kiss grew deeper, more fervent, as his hands hooked beneath the backs of her thighs to lift her up against the wall.

Their lips parted for a brief moment during the transition, though as he pulled away Laila hooked her fingers into his shirt to pull him back to her. He was getting harder as they kissed and Laila could feel the urgency of it pressed into her thigh—the movement of his hips against hers making her inconceivably wet.

Reluctantly, she pulled back with a whine to catch her breath.

"Having second thoughts?" He exhaled raggedly against her mouth as he searched her face for uncertainty. Never let it be said passion made him predatory. He wanted her to want this as much as he did. To want him.

She responded by bringing him in for another kiss, long and indulgent. Her hands deftly unbuttoned his shirt to slide her hands along his skin. "The bed," she murmured insistently against his lips.

He obliged, carrying her over to lay her on top of the mattress. She snaked her legs around him as they kissed again, and it was a marvel how they'd managed to keep from doing this with each other thus far when it felt this good.

She flipped their positions, sitting upright on his lap as Darius slid his hands up her thighs to maintain contact. He hooked his hands beneath the hem of her nightgown and lifted it over her head, her ample breasts coming free with a bounce. Then he let his hands rest on her waist, moving them downwards to the swell of her hips.

"God, I've wanted this for so long," he said in a low rasp. His eyes blackened with lust, the veins beneath them swelled with calligraphy patterns.

Laila bit her lip to hide her smile. "Do you intend to stare at me all night?"

His throat oscillated with a swallow. "Come here."

He pulled her into another kiss, and a shudder went through her as he slipped off her undergarments and stroked along her thighs, so gently it was almost hallucinatory. One wouldn't think it possible for hands like his, tools built for battles and bruising, to have such unbridled tenderness within them.

She shoved away his shirt, wanting to feel more of his skin against her as she kissed down his neck and along his collarbone. Her hands made quick work of his lower half, stripping him of his boots and breeches.

Laila slid his drawers down and swallowed, looking towards him for guidance. "I'm not sure what to do next—" Her breath caught when he slipped his hand between her thighs.

"Tell me what you like," he murmured with eyes intently focused. "I want to know how to touch you."

Laila put her hand on his, interlacing their fingers and slowly guiding him up to her clit. "Stroke it. Along the sides."

He hummed in understanding. "Like this?" He took her clit between his thumb and finger and massaged it between them.

She moaned as a shudder went down her legs. "Softer."

He touched more lightly, parting her folds to slip two fingers inside her and pump them back and forth. His were thicker than hers, longer, and she whined as he spread her further, crooking his fingers, every thrust adding an oddly pleasurable stretch to her muscles.

"Does that feel good?" Darius asked.

Laila couldn't muster any response but to nod.

He withdrew his hand from her and replaced it with his tip. "What about this?"

Laila winced as he pushed inside, discovering this was far more imposing than his fingers had been. "Stop."

His smile vanished. "What's wrong?"

"I don't want that... It—it's too painful."

"Hey, it's all right." His expression shifted to something unreadable before he gently touched her cheek. "Look at me. Did Dominus hurt you?"

"Yes." Laila swallowed. "Sometimes. It was never on purpose."

Darius closed his eyes to conceal his anger on her behalf. "Well, I can assure you it doesn't have to be painful. If done right it should be rather enjoyable for you." Still he pulled back from her. "However, there are plenty of other acts if that's not what you want."

His hand enveloped his shaft, stroking himself. There was something intensely erotic about seeing him do that. "What would you like to do with me?"

Laila received his request with a shiver, finding it hard to catch her breath at his stare. She pinned him down onto the mattress, positioning herself so that her clit was against the head of his cock. They released a moan into each other's mouths as Laila anchored him with her hips, rolling against him at a languorous pace.

The sensation was so warm and slick that a chill went up his spine as she moved along the length of him even faster, even firmer, until he almost couldn't take it.

She reached her peak long before him, her back arching to push her breasts into his face. He lavished them with kisses, tongue swirling over the nipple as her next release came in rapid succession.

Darius almost spent himself three times as she grinded on him. But he suspended it, wanting this to last a little longer before it was over. He put his hands on her hips, fingers digging hard enough to bruise as their movements grew more frantic until he finally let himself climax.

Laila released a shaky moan as she braced her hands on his chest. Her skin was roseate and the afterglow had left her with a radiance that was almost unearthly. She paused briefly to nudge her nose against his while sliding her fingers through his hair. It had grown wavier now that it was no longer plastered down with pomade, coiling into loose, romantic locks.

She drifted her hand over his stomach, cleansing it with an

enchantment, before she broke away slowly. Her breaths were heavy as she chuckled at him. "I hope that was worth breaking your legs for."

He matched her mirth with something even more bestial. "Not finished with you yet."

He pulled her back to him.

She lost track of the hours they spent exploring each other's bodies. They kept waking each other up, indulging in their desire to bring the other to satiation every time. As with most things, Darius was meticulous as a lover, and he traced every part of her with the same deep-abiding fascination as a cartographer with a map. With such a fine performance, little doubt remained as to why the princess ended up preferring him to his junior.

They lay spooned together in the aftermath, their legs entangled from when she'd taken him between her legs to massage his tip against her and he had rubbed himself off between her thighs, their moans muffled between kisses shared over her shoulder.

She dozed with his arms clutched around her, one breast still eclipsed by his large palm as he lazily brushed his thumb along her nipple. She trailed her fingers up his forearm, thinking it was exactly this that had been missing from her bed during all those sleepless nights. She was already halfway swooning when the gentle graze of a claw scraped along her spine.

"What are you doing?" she said sleepily, her back arching in reflex as his claw provoked a frisson of shivers down her spine.

His claw travelled in a rhythmic motion, his touch careful and restrained to avoid pricking. It was only as she lifted herself from the dense heaviness of near-sleep that she realised he was tracing a pattern.

"I'm tracing a constellation," Darius said, as though the answer could not be more obvious.

Laila tilted her head ever so slightly over her shoulder to catch a glimpse of him drawing over the dynasty marque across her shoulder blades. A rose, in keeping with her family name.

"How is that you have this? Does your body just know, or are they assigned?"

She shrugged one shoulder. "We all receive one based on our bloodline. It appears when we reach maturity."

"That's fascinating," he said, genuine awe in his voice.

She shivered as he pressed his lips between her shoulders before kissing down the arc of her spine. Such a thing might have enticed her to let him stay until morning, but she knew better than to get swept away by this whirlwind lust. One night was all she'd allow herself, and with the morning light on the horizon she knew this temporary insanity had reached its end.

"It's almost dawn," she said sleepily, a faint smile on her lips. "I'll have one of my ladies escort you to the tower."

"I'm quite content where I am," he said in a blended timbre of gravel and silk that slid with ease to the pit of her stomach. Then he kissed the corner where her neck met her shoulder.

She rolled over towards him until she had situated herself on top. "If my guard finds you here, she'll have you dragged out in your skivvies."

"Let her." His lips curled in mirth as he pulled her into a kiss. "I bet I'd put on one mighty show."

"You're silly," Laila murmured softly into his mouth.

He smiled back, reaching to tuck a loose curl behind her ear. Rare was a time that he'd felt this—a deep inner peace of both mind and body. He found himself craving more. "I want to see you again."

It was a request spoken without presumption or demand; he knew he'd no right to have either, but the desire was palpable all the same. And there was no language Laila knew better than desire—the mother tongue of wishes. As a star, she'd been nourished on them, all the hopes and prayers of the earthbound with their lips aimed toward heaven. She was the physical incarnation of every *I wish* woven into one being.

Laila looked at him and saw his eyes were still heavy-lidded, shaded soft beneath boyishly long lashes. It was difficult to deny him when he looked so tempting like that, but she maintained her resolve. "I don't think that's such a good idea."

He frowned. "Why not?"

"I think it's best for us to keep this as a one-night event. It'd only complicate things otherwise."

"Complicate things?" he echoed in derision. "What do you mean?"

She slipped away from him to reach for her sheer peignoir, desperate for a barrier to wrap around her skin. "Darius, come on." She perched on the edge of the mattress. "You didn't really expect anything more to come of this, did you?"

The words landed like a blow, stunning him to silence. He suddenly couldn't bear to look at her, let alone touch her. To think moments before he'd been on high, fuelled by the foolish giddiness of a schoolboy. What a lovelorn imbecile. He ought to have known it would mean more to him than it did to her.

"I see," he said. He withdrew from the covers to reach for his clothes, dressing in silence.

Laila saw the hurt in his eyes before he could shield it. "Oh." She spoke again, desperate to salvage her earlier words. "Darius, I didn't mean to—"

"It's all right, Laila. You've made your intentions towards me perfectly clear. Please allow me the grace of leaving with at least some dignity intact."

She watched him walk towards the balcony doors with her robe clutched in her hand. "Darius—"

"Have a good morning, Laila."

Then he continued on his pathway out of her bedroom.

XXVIII

NE OF THE MOST COVETED EVENTS OF THE YEAR, the Day of Enlightenment observed the first contact between mortal and solarite and was thus marked by a yearly parade and festivals in the streets.

Parties detonated in the streets in an effervescent fizz of laughter and drinking. The nectar was free-flowing, sparkling in the fountains like spilt diamonds. Decanters fountained with it as the ringing chime of clinked glasses echoed from rooftop to rooftop. The streets were littered with blood droplets of rose petals. There were fireworks and ribbons and macarons stuffed with ripe cherries. Stores embellished their doorways with sweet musk roses and brugmansia.

Laila watched the festivities unfold from the safety of her bedroom window as Oriel picked up the plump reeded glass bottle of her perfume, spraying a few puffs to her throat. Then she stained her lips with rouge lacquer made from crushed rose petals, adding a touch of gold paint to the bow of her upper lip and canthi.

"I thought we'd agreed after Dominus: no more occassi," Lyra said. She reclined on Laila's cream tufted leather chaise lounge with one foot atop the knee of her other leg, bouncing her ankle rambunctiously.

"It's not that I meant for it to happen again, Lyra," Laila huffed as Oriel spritzed her face with grape water for a dewy finish to her skin's natural glimmer. "It was just... he was there and he was saying all the right things and... I've been having a really difficult time recently with Dominus and my mother, so I could do without your judgement."

She turned to Lyra and jutted out her bottom lip petulantly, hoping she looked pathetic enough to take pity upon.

Lyra sighed. "I'm not judging. Much. I'm just concerned about you. After what happened with Dominus, I'm sure you can understand why I hesitate to watch you crawl into bed with yet another monster."

"Well, you needn't be," Laila replied flippantly in the mirror as Oriel fixed a crown of pastel pink blossoms with tinges of yellow on her head. Her dress was of a similar hue, with bouquets of her nominal flower sewn into the skirt. "What happened with Darius was... a singular event. It shan't occur again."

"Oh, of course, Laila. That is until he starts giving you those eyes and saying the right things and then, oh! Suddenly you've misplaced your underwear..."

"Lyra!"

Her friend merely intensified her knowing stare. Oriel struggled to suppress her giggling.

Laila scoffed as she slipped on her mask. "I am perfectly capable of containing myself around Darius Calantis. I am not some ditzy little daisy, allowing myself to wilt before any pair of pretty eyes and silver tongue."

"Well, I should hope so!" Lyra exclaimed in response. "Need I remind you that he almost had you killed and he has every reason to catch you with your guard down. I suggest you remain vigilant."

Laila nodded, though her lack of confidence unsettled. Tonight would be the first time she would be thrust into the occasso's presence again after spending every moment since that night trying to avoid him. She could only pray her resolve would keep.

"Well, I'm ready." She rose from the vanity to smooth the skirt of her dress.

Lyra let out a low whistle in approval. "Look at you."

Laila crossed one ankle over the other, spinning all the way round to give Lyra a full view. "All prepared for the parade float. Let's hope the rest of the night goes off without error."

She slipped her hand through the arm of her guard and found herself marvelling briefly at the firmness of wiry muscle. Laila knew she would be more than safe under the thrall of Lyra's protection.

"Lead the way," Lyra said as the two took towards the door to enter the festivities beyond.

Every year on the Day of Enlightenment, the ten dynasties of The First Who Fell put together a float to represent their namesake. Though it had become somewhat difficult to maintain originality during the centuries of the practice, many tried all the same.

Laila sat beside her mother on their parade float, which she had fashioned in the style of a music box. The box, when wound, sprung open its gilt-edged pink lid to reveal a composition of sprite ballerinas all dancing an esteemed adagio from one of her favourite ballets in the Aureate Theatre, La Rose D'or, while fragrant jets of rosewater surged from ornate spouts. She kept waving beside her mother on their twin thrones carved from rosewood lacquered in gilt to match the edging of the music box.

Eventually, the parade drew to a close and she was mercifully let down from the float to join the ensuing celebration. Enlightenment wasn't her favourite holiday—that honour would always go to Midsummer—but it was among them and it was always this part she liked best: when she could walk among the streets of her people as they peddled solar-inspired food and watch fireworks ascend into the air with a spidery fizzle.

Citizens set up stalls of fried and celestial-shaped goods that enticingly coaxed in a mélange of flavour and colour to all who passed them. Laila helped herself to some beignets at one stall while the firework shows proceeded in an elaborate spectacle around her.

Her attention was as fleeting as the beat of a hummingbird's wings, and she did not linger long before her mind began to dull. She searched for something sharper to renew it. She soon found it when she located the more "underground" festivities—a lambent jazz club fogged with body heat and desire where the gradual theft of one's sight led to reliance on more primal senses: the throbbing bassline of the music's rhythm, the aftertaste of sweat and perfume or the wandering hands of a dance partner.

Laila slipped into the den of writhing bodies with ease, her hips swaying languidly to the composition of saxophone and bass. The music stirred within her something sensual that seeped deep into the pit of her core and began to spread as she moved, a small, self-satisfied smile curving on her lips as she did so.

Darius entered the fray not long after, moving like a beetle through a field of dandelions. Amira had granted him leave from the tower for the evening, and he had spent it on the hunt, his sharpened senses slicing through the crowd to seek Laila out. He caught her in glimpses. First by the sprinkling of rose petals, then the flash of gold tresses beneath the dimmed lighting—a flicker of sunlight in this dusky setting.

He caught himself mesmerised by the rhythmic gyrations of her hips as she took on a sprite for a partner and wrapped his arms around her waist. Darius's hips subconsciously mimicked her own movements as he considered the collision of their bodies under an entirely different context. He shook off the sensation in dismissal, her earlier rejection of him still acute enough to sting.

Though days had passed since, she still haunted his thoughts. He found himself dissecting every interaction they shared with surgical precision: every touch, every kiss, every time he had made her moan and tremble and she had done the same in turn.

Had it all been lust, then? Just a heightened stress response to the extreme conditions they found themselves in? He couldn't say, and it was the wondering that plagued him, disrupting his thoughts when his mind should be focused on other matters.

He had to wonder if that wasn't the end goal—to keep him so entranced by her that he forgot to keep his guard up. He could almost laugh at how ridiculously easy it had been. Of course she ultimately didn't care about him. For this had never truly been about wanting him, but rather keeping him compliant so he would be a willing pet to the machinations of Amira.

But then he thought about when she cradled his face at the tarot tournament, her hands on his shoulders in the Eyrie, and his conviction wavered.

He decided he couldn't go on like this. He had to confront her. He had to know.

Darius watched on hungrily as Laila traded tiny shots of crème liqueur with the sprite, drizzling it sparingly on her throat before he cleaned it with a light suck. Darius wasn't sure if it was the deep

348

throbbing of the bass or seeing the sprite's lips at Laila's throat that sent blood shooting to his temple, but he found he could watch this no longer.

Laila giggled in delight as the sprite traced his tongue over her neck but found her mirth cut short when the vestige of fangs biting into her neck wormed its way into her sensual memory.

She pulled back suddenly and excused herself with a smile to drown out the feel of his lips against her throat with something stronger. She took a fever pill someone gave her and let it dissolve on her tongue.

While their immortal bodies would never know true sickness, many solarites were partial to the symptoms predicting the onset of a fever: the high temperature, the numbing tingles and the near alcoholic buzz of drowsiness. For Laila, it was the only thing that kept her calm after emotional events, and she could already feel the swelling knot of anxiety deflate as soon as she consumed it.

As the fever thrummed through her bloodstream she made a valiant return to the dancefloor, feeling a new pair of hands grip her waist. She began to prepare herself with a simper and an offer of a dance when the person spoke in her ear:

"You look like you're having a good time."

The voice was like a dousing of ice water down her back before an unbearable heat encroached to take its place. She tried to pivot to face him but he only held her tighter to his chest. She knew the shape of him when she felt it. His height and build alone displaced him as an elephant among ants.

"What are you doing here?" she asked, fully aware he had not let go of her waist.

Darius smirked at her annoyance, his smooth cheek brushing against hers as he spoke. "I was rather enjoying the show."

Laila's heart skipped in spite of herself. This was too much for her.

With his voice low in her ear and his hands on her waist, she could all too easily remember how perfectly her body fit into his.

"Well, I am glad you are enjoying the festivities, prefect. But if you don't mind—"

"Back to that again, are we?"

"I—" she stammered, realising she had slipped back into the rules of propriety when using his name. "I don't know what you mean."

He leaned in closer so that when he next spoke she could feel the hot exhale of his breath on her neck. "Yes, you do."

Laila shivered, feeling his voice travel right to her toes. She sought to put distance between them, not wanting him to sense how deeply he was affecting her. "How did you even find me here?"

"You're quite easy to spot even when you mask yourself," he told her, and she remembered he was a hunter, a predator even. She was not the first he had tracked. "I was hoping that we could talk. In private."

She pressed her glossed lips together before answering. "About what?"

"You know what."

She did, but she refused to indulge him in this. She removed his hands from her waist and slipped past him to allow the crowd to swallow her.

"What are you so afraid of, Laila?"

Familiar words. She shouldn't have let that stop her, but the low, taunting quality of his voice dug its way inside her nerves. She turned on her heel.

"You want to talk?" she asked, taking a few small steps towards him to bridge the space between them again. "Fine. Let's talk."

She grabbed him by the arm and led him upstairs to the corridor of rooms that had been set up for more private conclaves. She picked the first vacant one she found and walked inside, not even waiting to see if he was following her.

Darius stepped in after her, grateful for the seclusion the room offered, closing and locking the door behind him.

"What do you want?" she snapped at him, tearing off her mask and dashing it to the floor.

"I had to see you," he said, slipping off his own mask as he stepped closer to frame the side of her face. "I haven't been able to stop thinking about you since that night."

She broke away from his touch. "Hoping I'll go to bed with you again? I would've thought one night was enough."

"And why would you think that?"

"Let's not pretend this was something profound. We wanted each other and we've had each other. Now we ought to be content to go our separate ways."

She sidestepped him towards the door only to be stopped when he grabbed her arm.

He pivoted her towards him, his eyes boring into hers. She was never prepared for the effect his stare had on her. He looked at her as though, in a sea of smeared greys, she were the one thing vibrant with colour.

"Is that really what you think this is for me?"

Laila swallowed thickly to moisten her parched throat. "We can't do this again, Darius. It's not right. You're Dominus's brother. You're my mother's captive. You're—"

"You're exhausting every possible answer other than the one that truly matters," he said, taking a step closer. "That you don't want me."

Her breath hitched as she looked away from him. "I don't."

"Really?" Darius hooked his finger beneath her chin and tilted her up to face him. "Try looking at me when you say that next time."

He traced the edge of her chin as she looked at him, her eyes flitting briefly to his lips as they drew near. She swerved away from him. "Stop," she said, shaking her head softly. "I understand what you're going through, Darius. I know you're alone here and you're lonely, and sometimes I'm lonely too. It makes sense you'd want to cling to someone for company, but—"

His expression shifted into anger. "That's not what this is."

"What are you talking about?"

"I mean your little condescending speech about my loneliness. That's not what this is to me. I don't want someone, I want you. And I know I shouldn't. And I know it comes with a lot of risks for us both, but still I want you... and deep down I think you want me too."

"Darius—"

"I've wanted you ever since I met you, Laila. And it didn't matter to me that you were with my brother. Or that my father wanted you dead. Or that our countries were at the brink of war with one another. All that mattered to me was the chance, however miniscule it was, I could ever get you to return what it is that I feel. And now I know there is a chance... I can't simply give that up."

Her throat thickened as tears clouded her vision. "You can't do this to me, Darius. You can't just say all of these things and expect me to believe—"

"Look at me," he said, shushing her as he placed his thumbs against her cheeks to wipe the tears as they fell. "It's okay."

Somehow that only made her cry harder, the attempt in itself. That of all the people in the world she could turn to, she had found herself within the arms of a monster and never felt more cherished.

"Laila, look at me," Darius said again, and he took her hand to rest it against his face. "Illumination doesn't lie, remember? If you earnestly believe I don't mean my words, that I'm just out to deceive you or captivate you into bed again. At least this way, you'll know the truth."

She traced her thumb over the fine hair on his cheek as she met his gaze and found it calm, direct. He had clearly not yet forgotten the strength behind illumination; he knew that it would hurt, but he was willing to let her do it to him anyway.

His readiness to suffer for her snuffed away the last lingering doubt this was just another machination from him. So she took his other cheek in her hand and brought his face down to kiss her.

Darius released a sharp breath into her mouth before he returned the kiss, sliding his arms around her waist to bring her closer. So close that they were only aware of the combination of their heartbeats. He walked her back against the wall to press her against it, his hips digging into hers to anchor her there as their mouths continued to collide with breathless intensity.

He kissed her like he'd been desperate for it, for her, not realising how much until their lips were joined again.

Laila's eyes closed as their hips pressed into each other, a pleasurable throb growing between her legs. At once she wished they were both shed of clothes so he could lift her against the wall and have her then and there.

Darius slid his hand down her spine to curve beneath her thigh, hooking her leg around his waist as his lips parted from hers to kiss her cheek, her jaw, working his way along the slope of her throat before he continued downwards.

"Darius—" Laila sighed as he lowered to his knees before her. How did he know this was exactly where she wanted him?

He shushed her as he lifted the skirts of her dress. "Just relax."

She watched his head disappear beneath her skirts as he slid her bloomers down and hooked her leg around his shoulder. She clasped at the window ledge for purchase, feeling his warm exhale against her inner thigh. He started by kissing a trail up the delicate skin before he moved his mouth towards the source of all light and all life trapped between her thighs.

Laila cried out as Darius sucked her clit into his mouth, her legs buckling as he moved his lips in slow, sensuous glides—almost in the same way he'd kissed her. She arched her hips towards his face as she told him to go softer, slower. His moan vibrated against her skin as he obeyed.

Darius dipped his tongue inside her, savouring the little noises of pleasure she made as her taut muscles flexed around him. She tasted divine and it was made all the sweeter knowing how desperately she writhed as her thighs tightened.

What a rare sort of bliss this is. Dominus was insane to give it up.

He kept going until her legs were shuddering and little shockwaves from her power had started to circulate through his body, causing his nerves to twinge in a manner that wasn't at all unpleasant.

Laila's head fell back in ecstasy as the build of her orgasm coiled tight in her core. And she just let herself go—all the doubts, all the fears, all the insecurities. She just let herself go with him.

The Magisterium was located within the Summer Château, about a moat-bridge away from the palace, nestled within a ring of lithe blondewood trunks. It served as the main quarters for the magistresses and active sessions of parliament when they weren't being called to attend court at Amira's whim.

The palace façade filtered the light from the fireworks like a prism, casting a hazy kaleidoscope of soft-toned hues in teal and pink and white.

Laila entered through the marble lobby, signing her name into the visitors' guest-book. She straightened her curls before she entered the main chamber, self-conscious as if her indiscretions had left her permanently marked.

The room was full when she arrived, her mother sitting on the far end of the table in her gold-legged chair, a white lion cub snoozing twitchily in her lap.

"You're late," Amira said, gesturing towards the chair nearest to her for Laila to sit.

"I do apologise, Maman," Laila spluttered as she drew out the seat and pushed herself in, smoothing out her lap. Her cheeks flushed as her mind flickered to Darius's head between her thighs. "I got caught up with something."

She gave a welcoming smile towards the other magistresses seated around her, each of them mortals chosen from the five mortal realms to represent their nation's interests.

Beside her was Magistress Yen Cho, who was wearing her scholarly robes in heavy painted silk. Suspended from her neck was a large astronomical watch of overlapping dials, one each for the sun and moon, with finely illustrated symbols for the monthly constellations in gold leaf. The hourly dial was equally gilded and pigmented with midnight hues of blue to the pink-orange of dawn. Laila recalled a much larger replica in the Celestial Court: a floating orb encased in gilt-brass framework that mechanically rotated in accordance with the current position of the sky.

"What seems to be the matter?" Laila asked.

"We've received word that Domina Domitia has been doing her part to fan the flames of insurrection against Lanius," Amira said, a small smile playing on her lips. "With the tide already turning in our favour, I do believe this is the time to make our final moves."

"Lanius Rex still appears to be sitting comfortably in his Citadel waiting for an attack," said Madhali Azar, Magistress of Defence. "You say the word, Your Luminosity, and I'll send one of my spies to snuff him out like a light."

"Shouldn't we account for Lanius's deathless nature?" Laila asked.

"Yes, Prefect Calantis has made us well aware of that particular quirk," Magistress Cho replied, "which is why I believe we are better off sending in a group of soldiers to detain him and have him brought back to Soleterea for imprisonment."

"It seems a reasonable enough suggestion," Amira said, scratching beneath the chin of her cub. "Though there is the question of what we are to do with the rest of the royal family."

"Either imprison them alongside him or have them disposed of," Madhali said. "I don't suppose I need to make my opinion known on which I'd prefer, Your Luminosity."

"Your preference has been duly noted, Magistress Azar."

"What is to become of the throne should this mission succeed?" asked Lady Commander Cassia of the Lightshields.

"Darius Calantis wishes to install himself as the new rex once his father and brother have been disposed of," Amira said, sipping her wine. "I have therefore agreed to allow him to take up the throne once his country has been subdued."

"Are we to trust this occasso traitor, then?" Cassia asked. "After all, if he is to double-cross one party, who is to say he will not do it to another?"

"I'd not consider him to be an immediate threat," Amira said. "It would be exceptionally foolish for him to strike back at us after helping to significantly reduce his own numbers. In the near future he will be one to watch, but I will have contingencies in place by then to make sure our little beast remains tight on leash."

"Very well."

"What ought to be our next moves, then, madame?" Madhali asked.

"I want a team assembled to extract Lanius Rex from the Citadel. Remove anyone who happens to get in the way of that."

Cassia bowed her head. "As you wish, madame."

XXIX

ARIUS NAVIGATED HIS WAY TOWARDS Amira's quarters. The impératrice had called upon him for a clandestine meeting, and so under the obscurity of the deep violet hours he entered the palace and walked the stairs to Amira's boudoir.

He remembered the last time he snuck into a lady's quarters and how that ended up, though he doubted his encounter with Amira would be anything so pleasant.

There were no guards posted at the ornate doors, so he thought little of simply entering through them.

Amira was awaiting him. She was picturesque atop her raspberry velvet settee, with a glass of red wine in hand, swirling it absently when he arrived.

"Close the door behind you, prefect."

He did so and noticed the lighting was dim but for the waning lambency of candlelight. He walked towards the empty seat across from her and observed the sheer peignoir she had chosen to clothe herself in over the top of her satin negligee.

"You requested me, Your Luminosity," Darius said, hovering over the seat and hoping she'd have the grace to grant him rest.

"Sit down." She took a conservative sip of her wine. She'd have let him stand a little longer, if only to see him squirm, but there were more pressing matters to attend to. "I thought I might inform you on what is happening now with regards to our final movements towards Mortos."

He nodded, having heard little but whispers and rumours he'd attempted to piece together. It would be nice to hear it from the horse's mouth at last.

"I intend to launch a mission to apprehend your father, Lanius Rex, to detain him in Soleterea. Unfortunately, the Citadel remains to be unbreachable, and I am afraid we will need extra help."

Darius inhaled sharply before expelling it. "By that I assume you desire to deploy me on this mission."

"Your intelligence has been valuable to us thus far and your contributions to this mission would be invaluable." Amira swallowed another gulp of wine and lifted the lid from the decanter to top it up. "Who better to infiltrate a fortress than the one who has spent their entire life living there, after all?"

"I would agree." Darius tented his fingers, his mind battling away a horde of unwanted questions clawing into his immediate recollection. "I assume that it is only my father you'll be wanting, then? What is to become of the rest of the royal family?"

"I have given orders to eliminate them, for their survival is not necessary to me. Nor to you, I imagine."

Darius released a wry chuckle, weak on his parched throat. "You would be correct in that assumption."

"If the mission would be too distressing on you, prefect, I perfectly understand—"

"No." Darius swallowed down the rise of dread at the back of his throat. "No, I am perfectly willing and able to do what needs to be done."

"Then I will make sure you have everything you need to prepare yourself." Amira filled another glass of wine and handed it to him. A token of gratitude, and a little pity. "You have done well for us, prefect. I thank you for your service."

He bowed his head, taking the drink. "And I thank you for the opportunity to prove myself, Your Luminosity."

"I'm sure you are looking forward to being home soon, but I do hope you have managed to develop a certain... fondness for Soleterea during your visit."

"It's a very special place," Darius replied without pretence, "full of beautiful things and beautiful people. You ought to be proud of it."

"I am," Amira said, raising her glass in salute, "and I do hope we can continue our productive relationship in the event of your ascension. I notice you and my daughter made quite a pair when it came to appealing your case, without which you probably wouldn't have received your opportunity to prove your worth."

His throat clogged and he sipped his wine to combat it, finding it soothingly sweet. "Princess Laila is... also very special," he said, voice thickening with concealed emotion. "You ought to be proud of her, too."

She looked at him for an extended moment, her eyes searching. "I am." She took a long sip of wine, finishing it to the bottom. "You may go."

He stood, grateful for the chance to leave as he walked briskly towards the door. He opened it, stepping into the clear, unburdened air for a short breath before closing it behind him. Then he found himself face to face with the last person he expected he'd see.

"Snooping again, I see." He observed Laila's mane of lascivious curls pressed up against the second door frame. "Seems old habits die hard."

He walked down the hall to put some distance between himself and Amira's chambers. She followed with pattering footsteps.

"Don't do it."

He paused, turning on his heel. She'd switched to Mortesian, and so he followed suit. "Don't do what?"

"The mission in Mortos to capture Lanius." She walked forward to lay her hands on his chest. "I don't want you to do it."

He sighed, letting himself look at her the way he'd been aiming to avoid. The widened doe eyes, brimming with concern for him, if he wasn't simply projecting too hard. "I have to."

"No, Darius, you don't. Listen to me—" She caught his face in her hands and held him near. "I already have to contend with sending people I care very deeply about off on this mission. I have no idea if I'll ever see them again. Please don't ask me to do the same with you."

"The Citadel is my home, Laila; no one here knows how to breach it better than I do." He took her wrists and lowered her hands from his face. "It has to be me."

"And what if Lanius kills you?"

Strange it was to be wanted like this, worried over, when he had only known what it meant to be aflame with his own desire. He almost couldn't believe it; he had never dared to hope that she might look upon him as anything more than a beast to take into her bed. And yet.

"Have a little faith in me, princess. It's not entirely out of the realm of possibility that I'll make it out alive. And I happen to like my odds.

Either I destroy him or he destroys me. but whatever way it happens, it ends."

"And Dominus?"

Here was where words failed him, confronted with the name he hoped she wouldn't utter.

"It's him or me, princess. I hope you understand."

In that he hoped she would choose him ultimately, irrevocably, in the way that no one else ever had.

He watched her breath hitch, lips parting without words, and it was amazing how long a moment could stretch even after centuries had passed him by in a blur of monotony. But a word, a sign, a mere *syllable*.

Give me something I can carry into battle with me, princess; that's all I'll ever ask for.

"Goodbye, Laila," he said, turning away in defeat. He knew it was foolish to ever expect she would give him more than impartial silence.

She pulled him round to face her and, before he had a chance to react, dragged him down by his face to put her lips against his. He yielded instantly to her as her mouth moved cautiously against his before gaining enough confidence to deepen the kiss.

He closed his eyes, all the wound tension in his body softening as he pulled her close. It would be so easy for him to lose himself in this for how badly he wanted it, wanted her to show him that she cared for him like this.

"Come back to me," she said softly, digging her fingers into the lapels of his coat as though that alone was enough to keep him near. "Do whatever you have to."

"I will," he said, resting his forehead wearily against her own.

XXX

DARIUS ROSE BEFORE THE SUN DID, a residual behaviour of a time long past for him. During training it was common practice for an occasso warrior to learn to sleep lightly, to rouse himself in preparation for a battle in spite of repose.

So he woke himself up in increments, first bodily with all the reflexive instincts of his muscles engaged, further unwound with a stretch. Then the mind, which he coaxed open with an ice-cold shower, herbal tisane and incense smoke.

After that, it was time to prepare.

He sealed himself inside his leather armour, the suit slipping on with the familiarity of a second skin. Then on his back he strapped two falcatas: one of obsidian for killing enemies and one of bone for killing comrades.

The latter an occasso kept in higher esteem than the former, always sheathed in fine sharkskin and silk with an engraved silver hilt. Killing one's fellow occassi was not a decision to be made on a whim, and Calante had designed them purposefully so that it was not a pursuit easily undertaken.

Past the speed, strength, claws and fangs there was also the problem of their hearts: impenetrable as stone with all the smooth, flexible properties of regular muscle. Metal would not pierce them; stone would not scrape them. Only weapons forged from materials once connected to the cycle of life were capable of doing them harm: a wooden stake, a claw, a sharpened bone.

Darius withdrew his bone falcata to admire its fine ivory hue. The blade was pristine, untouched by the black blood it was about to shed. He remembered all he had done and experienced just to hold it. How in Mortos, training to be a warrior was all but ritualised torture. He remembered all the bouts of starvation, the exposure to elements, the beatings and forced viewings of executions—all culminating in his First Rite, where one was sent to fend for oneself in the wilderness. No magic, no weapons, nothing but their own body.

Darius remembered his First Rite well, all the ways he'd survived where others did not.

It was the same reason he knew he was destined to survive what was to come.

It wasn't strength, wasn't speed, wasn't superiority; it wasn't even the breadth of his smarts.

It was adaptability.

"Are you ready?"

Behind him, Ser Léandre stood poised at the door.

"Yes," Darius replied, sheathing his sword behind his back. He followed him out of the tower.

The crew Amira assembled was a small, elite faction prized for their skill at stealth. She wanted this to be a clean extraction with surgical precision. They were to sneak in and attack the Citadel covertly to capture his father without resistance.

To reach Mortos she had provided them with access to one of her starships. Darius glanced up at the silver behemoth stretched out before him with the awe of a child. It would be his first time even getting near one of Vysteria's famous airships and, in spite of the dire circumstances, he was as giddy as a schoolboy.

He met with the rest of the soldiers inside the main deck, where they seated themselves at a table to wait for the crew leader. There was no doubt in Darius's mind that the Lightshields did not desire his presence and trusted it even less, but by now he had surpassed the mood to charm and convince those who dwelled here.

The hushed speculations on his loyalties soon ceased when the door opened once more to reveal the one who would lead the charge on this mission: Lyra de Lis.

"Welcome, all." Lyra strode in in full-armoured glory and deposited a rolled parchment onto the table. "I'd like to thank you for being so brave as to offer yourselves to this mission." Her eyes drifted along all of them with a smile, hardening when they eventually fell upon Darius. "Under the orders of Lady Cassia, I have been advised to seek guidance from Darius Calantis on how best to breach this fortress. So, if you would like to take over, monsieur. I have a map here of the Citadel and surrounding territories."

Darius unfurled the map and gave it a quick glance over. "This map won't do," he said, and then he picked up a pencil and sketched out all the hidden entrances and exits, the elusive scrambled passageways he'd memorised all throughout his youth. Never before had he imagined they would be so useful.

"Now if you'd pay close attention to the places I've marked, I believe the cathedral"—he set a marker down onto the map—"will be the best place to enter. There is a tunnel that connects to the Citadel, through which we escort our dead rexes to the catacombs. It is unlikely he will have too many guards posted in this area, so we will be able to slip in almost entirely unnoticed. The real trouble comes when we enter the Citadel proper. The castle structure is full of traps and secret rooms, which my father will no doubt use to his advantage. Fortunately, I know the landscape of the castle like the back of my hand, and so I am unlikely to be surprised by its offerings. I would, however, recommend caution and for you to follow my lead."

"How convenient for you," Lyra said dryly.

Darius's jaw twitched in amusement. "I mean, you are welcome to try your luck at it on your own terms, Ser Lyra. Though it would be quite upsetting for me to see you as an unfortunate smear on the wall when we've only just begun to be such good acquaintances."

"Ser?" The Lightshields looked to Lyra, seeking her approval.

Lyra glanced down at the map, chin in hand, before nodding. "I approve of Calantis's strategy. We know our orders. Lanius Rex is to be detained at all costs. Everyone else, we aim to kill." She reached into her belt and retrieved a glowing vial of a mystical substance.

Darius's stomach roiled and his blood vessels shrivelled in its presence. "What is that?"

"It's ætherald," Lyra said, "an undiluted strain that is especially potent. I want you to use it to pacify Lanius when you eventually face him. A dosage of that strength would be lethal to anyone else. As Lanius is deathless, however, it should have him incapacitated for a long while."

Darius reached for the vial, but as he did so the hammering pressure in his temples intensified.

"Is something wrong?" Lyra asked, though there was glibness behind it. "Let me help you with that." She placed the vial in a sleeve of material, and at once the oppressive migraine lifted. Lyra handed the vial to him. "Keep it safe."

Darius nodded and slipped the vial onto his person.

The airship flew over a world torn asunder.

The first solarite assault arrived as a dark, portentous overcast along the coastlines of Mortos. Those with eyes as keen as occassi could just about catch a glimpse of one of the ships as a faint silhouette of scintillating silver—a skybound leviathan armed with vaporising bombs of pure light.

Darius observed the devastation wrought as the starship's blinding beams disintegrated the bodies of his comrades into a shadow of charred ash. Those who had managed to survive the initial exposure could be found steaming and delirious as they burned from the inside out, their flesh liquefying off their bones.

He knew then that there was more to light than simply glamour or glitz; there was horror to behold from it, too.

Chaos had engulfed the haunted city of Gravissia, gobbled it down between its serrated jaws and spat it back out deformed. The ground was eating itself beneath them, shattered into a splintering web of fissures, opening into new mouths that steamed with furious plumes of volcanic smoke.

But this ruined landscape and its many perils was only half the horror that awaited as the streets became illuminated beneath the ship's watchful eyes. The world was empty. The solarites had left the imprint of their boot upon this anthill and exterminated them with a pointed twist of their ankle. Nothing but the charred black skeletons and shadow-tattooed remnants of its inhabitants remained. The streets wailed in mourning of their vacancy.

Darius couldn't help but take a hard swallow at the sheer magnitude of the devastation before him. He had seen occassi raze cities to the ground and exterminate villages by the dozen. He had seen them suffuse the air in so much blood one could almost swim in it, string up entrails in festive display, kick skulls around like balls. But never before had he seen *this*—this erasure. Seeming all the more merciless for how it left nothing behind but ash and absence.

Is this what I am to be the king of, then? he dared himself to wonder.

Lyra approached his side before handing him a parachute. "Time to go."

Darius accepted it and strapped it on before the exit door was pushed open and they jumped down towards the city.

They descended to an empty greeting, not that Darius was expecting much of an ambush. His father would likely have given strict orders for everyone to remain inside the fortress, where they would be safe from attack. The castle had been reinforced by an ancient ritual of sealing criminals into the walls, thereby making it impenetrable to any breach, —from natural to manufactured.

Darius led the way towards the cathedral as the bulbous onion domes floated into view from a distance. The steps were littered with the remains of those too unfortunate to reach sanctuary before they met their radiant end.

Darius heard his boot crunch the tibia of one skeleton and watched it disintegrate into black powder the moment he touched it. He made a conscious decision to tread more lightly from that moment, careful not to disturb the rest.

They opened the doors to the cathedral with a hefty tug and a groan of weary wood, walking the aisle up towards the altar where Darius knew the tunnel entrance lay. He pushed the table aside and lifted up the hatch, peering deep into the stomach of the dimly lit cavern.

"Everyone, light your torches," Lyra said, and she ignited her own ætherald light before she descended first into the cavern.

The rest followed her.

Deeper and deeper they went into the tunnels, hearing nothing but the loud, wet drips of moisture until Darius paused in alert.

"We have to stop."

"What?" Léandre asked. "Why?"

"Do you not hear it?"

Léandre paused and strained his ears. "It just sounds like wind."

"Listen closer."

The air rolled noisily around them like a yawn. He watched the other Lightshields glance around them, weapons ready for attack.

"Is someone else here?"

"Turn off your lights," Darius said, "and move slowly."

The words had scarcely left his lips before a pair of hands with gnarled fingers lunged out from the walls.

Darius snatched Léandre by the arm, hauling him out of the way of its clutches. The fingers lashed at the air in spite before withdrawing back into the walls.

"What in oblivion—?" Léandre's voice faltered and then he swallowed. "Thank you."

Darius nodded back. "We've reached the Citadel now. The castle is full to the brim with trapped souls, and they're hungry but they never feed. If they grab you, they're not letting go until they bring you into the walls."

"But we're solid," said Lyra. "So how do they intend to get us in there?"

"They don't," Darius replied, "but that doesn't mean they won't stop trying. Do you understand?"

Lyra shivered in response. "How do we evade them?"

"You hold your breath. And you don't stop moving until I tell you you're safe."

He heard the Lightshields take a deep breath, indulging in their last fresh gulp of air, before they crossed over the threshold of the Citadel.

More hands sprouted out from the walls, wandering, groping, relentless in their pursuit, for they had been left for so long without shelter and sustenance, receiving only the cruel indifference of their sovereign when they sought the Citadel for aid. The closer they edged to escape, the louder the wails of anguish grew, until one realised it was not wind or draft but the beggars' cries that chorused through the tunnel with their pleas.

Please...

Have mercy...

Hungry...

So hungry...

We beg of you...

Please...

We've been waiting so long...

Darius could feel his lungs straining for his next exhale, forcing him to clamp down even harder until the voices fell away with a resigned moan. Another day left unsated.

"We're safe," he said in his exhale, sucking in his next breath like it was something to savour.

"They sounded so sad," Lyra said, her voice clogged. Darius was astonished to see how forlorn she looked. "So alone." She glanced at him and her face hardened. "How long have they been left there? Why don't you let them out?"

"It's not up to me," Darius said. "It's been a practice of rexes of the past for a long time now to trap the souls of thieves and beggars for their trespasses."

"So your people came to you because they were hungry and desperate and *this* is how you treat them?" Lyra exhaled a bitter laugh. "You creatures never fail to disgust me." She walked past him, shoving him hard on the shoulder. Then her foot triggered a slab of stone looser than the others, which opened into a trap door.

"Lyra!" Léandre called out as his niece stumbled into the opening fissure.

Only through sheer reflexes did Lyra catch hold of the edge for grip, clinging to it as though it was life itself.

Darius moved even quicker. "Give me your hand."

Lyra glanced down into the pit, the molten fiery death that awaited her below with its belches of sulphuric air, then up at the hand before she clasped it.

Darius hauled her out to safety and sealed the door shut. When he turned, she was already in Léandre's arms.

"Are you all right?" Léandre asked.

"Yes, I'm fine," she said, removing her arms from him to look over at Darius, her eyes no softer than before. "I'm fine."

"As I said before, tread cautiously," Darius said, "and follow my lead."

He led them through to the catacombs, where they met the first of the occassi guards. Darius drew his sword as Lightshield and occasso dominator alike engaged in an intense dance of blades. The numbers of the occassi were few, but theirs were even fewer. However, Darius did not let that perturb him, did not let fear tip the balance of his mind's equanimity.

He'd never approached combat like a brawler, after all; he approached it like a mathematician. Always with his silent calculations of speed, force and velocity behind his every strike and swing, balancing for variables in his opponent's weight and skill. So he advanced calmly, his mind scribbling the equations needed to make his first strike into the heart of one warrior before he struck off the head of the next.

He maximised his surroundings to his advantage, slipping into the tenebrous sludge of a shadow before he emerged in full again, only to vanish behind the next. Then at once he materialised to pierce his bone falcata through the back of another occasso, a vibrant dispersion of blood and arterial matter exploding in the air.

The more Darius crossed blades with those who were not his father, the more aggressively he succumbed to his bloodlust, trading greater and more deadly blows that splattered black blood onto his leathers as he drew nearer and nearer to what he sought.

He opened the door into a secret passageway leading to the Portrait Hall, where an even more gruesome vignette awaited him. The walls had been freshly painted a lustrous black, the glass frames spattered with streaks and handprints. The portrait's eyes were sorrowful.

Darius could hear a snuffling sound in the distance and readied his falcata. The whine sounded bestial, but he knew they kept no pets here. He sought the source of the sound. Then he leapt out, sword at the ready to slay this undisclosed mutt, and found only Dominus instead.

His hulking figure was bent in anguish as he continued to weep his undignified sounds.

Darius knew he wouldn't get a better chance than now to dispense with his brother. But no matter how his hand clenched at his sword to strike, he couldn't make his arm move to follow it. He exhaled in defeat, curiosity and hesitation overruling his need to do what he knew he had to, and instead he stepped nearer.

Extending from his brother's large frame was a smaller, shapelier figure that didn't move of its own accord. Only with the tremors of his brother's sobs.

"Oh no," Darius couldn't help but sigh out.

Dominus reacted at once to the sound like a reptile, eyes landing briefly on him before his neck fell back towards the dead figure of his mother, like it pained him too much to hold it upwards. "She told me to run." He sniffled, sliding his hand down her blood-smeared cheek. "She tried to stop him."

Darius moved towards his grieving brother and crouched low.

"*Don't touch her*," Dominus snarled as he held her even tighter to him. "Just don't. I don't want you to touch her. I don't want you to take her. I just—I just want to sit here with her. All right?"

"All right." Darius held up his hands. "I'm not going to touch her, Doma. And I'm not going to take her. You have my word." So he sat down next to his little brother as he snivelled and cradled his poor mother to him. And for a long moment he closed his eyes.

Vasilisa had not been his mother, but he had held a quiet respect for her. She did not deserve to be slaughtered in a misdirected attempt to claim Dominus. But such was the curse of reginas: they lived and they died by whatever face the coin of their rex happened to fall on, regardless of their choosing.

"Where is he, Dominus?" Darius asked.

"He's killing his guards." Dominus wiped his nose with the back of his hand. "He's killing everyone." He slid his hand down his mother's eyes, the same green as his own, and closed them. "I'm next."

"Help me stop him." Darius put his hand on his shoulder. "It doesn't have to be this way, Doma. You don't have to die. Help me stop him, and we can go back to Soleterea. Together. I can broker you a deal with the impératrice, and we can bury your mother. This can all end. Tonight. What do you say?"

Dominus swallowed thickly. "Do you think Laila would ever forgive me for what I've done?"

He didn't realise it was possible to feel such a chill in him until he heard her name on his brother's lips. *Come back to me,* her voice echoed in his mind. "I don't know, Doma."

Dominus lay his mother down to rest on the floor and crossed her arms over her chest. "All right." He rose to his feet and looked at Darius, holding out his hand. "Let's destroy the miserable bastard."

They searched high and low for him, following the bloodied trail of carnage he had left in his wake. Outside the sky was raging and lightning stuttered like a candle flame dwindling in and out of existence. Dominus trampled over body after body with little care for their dying gasps for release, a warrior on the warpath.

Darius had never seen such black anger in his brother as the one that possessed him at that moment. He leapt at shadows with his bone falcata drawn, ready to fight with the Citadel walls themselves.

"Come out, you coward," Dominus seethed between his gritted teeth. Then he upturned a row of bone porcelain he knew had belonged to their father's mother and let it burst into fragments against the nearby wall.

"Doma, calm down," Darius said, hiding the vial once he'd taken what he needed. He wiped the corner of his mouth. "The more of a racket you make, the more likely he'll hear us coming."

"I *want* him to hear me," Dominus growled back. "I want him trembling and fearful and in pain the way she was. I want him to know his moments are numbered. I want him to know I'm coming for him. And when I do—" He swung his sword and swiped off the bronzed head from a trophy. "Do you understand, Darius?"

"Yes, I understand. Do you think I'm not angry? Why in oblivion do you think I'm here in the first place? But we have to play this smart. We can't afford to go barrelling in like—*look out!*"

The lightning flashed, revealing his father's silhouette poised behind Dominus, falcata raised to strike.

Darius raised his blade to deflect. Their blades met with a hollow clank as they exchanged forceful blows before his father pressed his foot into the centre of Darius's chest and kicked him off-balance.

Darius fell back like a ragdoll, slowly righting himself back onto his feet.

Lanius chuckled. "Should've gotten your head out of those books a little more, boy."

"Then it's a good thing I'm here, isn't it?" Dominus said as he darted with quickness to swing at Lanius.

Lanius was prepared, however, and they engaged in a deadly swordplay. Darius took advantage of his distraction to leap into the fray, but Lanius managed to counter both of their attacks with diabolical precision. Then he struck the falcata from Darius's hand in one clean blow.

Darius had only moments to panic before his father's blade struck down with one brutal overhead sweep. He caught the falcata between his palms, wrestling it from Lanius's grip until his sword too was sent spiralling away with a clatter.

Then Dominus attacked from behind to stab his father in the gut.

Lanius grunted as he descended to one knee, but Darius knew the injury wouldn't have him down for long. Lanius tore himself free of the blade with near indifference before pivoting sharply to attack.

They engaged once more, dodging and weaving each other's impending strikes at unfathomable speed until Lanius struck the falcata from Dominus's hand.

"Well, well, fisticuffs it is, then," Lanius said, curling his fingers into fists. He went for a strike to Dominus's face.

Dominus dodged his punch and grabbed his father's attacking fist to snap his forearm.

Lanius growled out in pain, furtively glancing at his mangled bone as he cast a hex to mend it.

Darius barely left a millisecond for him to recover before he went for another strike. Lanius was prepared, however, and managed to counter with a blow so hard it knocked the colour from Darius's sight. Then Lanius came down on him with a cavalcade of even fiercer blows, flipping him onto his back with a leg sweep.

Darius rolled out of the way as Lanius's foot came down to stomp him, and Dominus picked him up, spinning his brother round to kick Lanius to the floor.

They leapt on him the moment he hit the ground, holding him down as he squirmed and struggled. Then Darius pulled out the vial of ætherald and shoved it forcefully down his throat. Lanius's face darkened as his veins burned with a divine glow exuding coils of steam. "What—" He clutched his throat, coughing up congealed lumps of black blood.

"It's ætherald," Darius explained, stepping close to him. "The crystal of the solarites. I thought there was a sort of poetry in that. If only you'd paid more attention to your books... perhaps you might have seen it coming."

"I should've—" Lanius coughed up another clot. "I should've gutted you for the snivelling little whelps you were over two hundred years ago.

You're nothing but failures to me, the pair of you." His throat gurgled. "Think you've won this? The greatest pleasure of all will be watching you tear each other to pieces." His breaths hitched as he exhaled his last before surrendering to unconsciousness, his heartless state keeping him preserved.

"It's all over," Darius said. He allowed himself to feel the brunt of the pain he'd been stifling as he bowed over in agony. But he'd become accustomed to tolerating toxicity. He could outlast this.

"Is it?" Dominus put a hand to his shoulder. "Let me look at you."

Darius let himself be taken into his brother's arms and leaned into his embrace. He closed his eyes, taking but a moment to savour it before he withdrew the bone dagger he kept hidden on his person and ran him through the chest.

Dominus gasped and staggered backwards, looking down to reveal the seeping rivulet of his blood. He descended to his knees.

"I'm sorry." Darius could barely speak above a rasp as he swallowed.

Dominus gave a wry chuckle as he observed the knife sticking out from him. "Serves me right." He hacked up a laugh. "I should've known you were here for me too. Makes it all easier for you in the end, doesn't it?"

"I didn't want this, Dominus." Darius's voice was a barely audible shudder.

"Yes, you did," Dominus said, throat bobbling. "All over that stupid fucking throne. I hope it is worth it for you in the end, Dara. I hope it gives you peace. That you don't turn out like him. All twisted and paranoid and bitter—" He started to cough.

"Doma." Darius's eyes misted over.

"I was dead the minute you came here, Darius. You don't have to lie to me anymore. I know you're good at it. I almost wanted to believe you, you know? You've always been so good at telling people exactly what they want to hear from you." Dominus swallowed once more, his chest hitching with a sob. "So tell Laila—tell her I'm sorry. Tell her something really pretty for me, all right?"

Darius closed his eyes, a hot tear sliding down his cheek. "I will."

Dominus nodded back. "Now kill me."

Darius hesitated, fingers flexing at his sides.

"You've already started." Dominus put a hand to the knife handle. "Don't let me die like this."

Darius took a deep, shaky breath as he sat down next to his dying brother. He always thought the thing he wanted most was to see him like this—pathetic, pleading and at his mercy. He looked into his brother's eyes for a final time before closing his own. "I'm so sorry, Doma."

He twisted the blade and let the life drain from Dominus with a sigh.

XXXI

LAILA HAD BEEN LEFT IN CHARGE OF THE VICTORY FEAST. She had spent days prepping the seven-course meal, picking out the finest porcelain and gilt cutlery, along with the procession of music and merriment to cultivate the triumphant spirit she wanted her attendants to feel.

There was little that offered her salvation like the planning of a party, for she could convert any form of unwanted emotional weight into fuel to generate merriment for the masses. Whenever she found herself plagued with bouts of heaviness, she could always count on a party to make it lighter.

On the night itself, Oriel dressed in a blue velvet ball gown reminiscent of the night sky, studded with more diamonds than there were stars. Then Astrid braided her hair with even more diamond-encrusted stars to rival her celestial counterparts.

"What do you think, madame?" Astrid said, holding up a mirror to the back of her head. "Are you pleased with our work?"

"Hm." Laila gave herself a critical glance in the mirror. "It's astounding work as always, girls. It's just—it feels like there might be something missing."

"There is."

Her pulse stuttered at the unexpected voice in the room and at the glimpse she caught in the mirror of the one who owned it. She stood at once from her vanity and turned to face him. "Darius."

Her knees gave out, just a little, when she saw him.

She kept thinking she should've had time to brace for it by now, the chemical way her body responded to his presence. How he made the ivory tower of her spine soften with carnal longing.

She knew that she should want to reach for more than him, *better*— higher rungs of virtue and self-improvement. There would be no light or truth in the place that he led. He would only ever be the unknowable void over the balcony ledge, two centuries worth of murder and mystery and mayhem. A dangerous height for a respectable lady like her to jump off without looking.

And yet she'd jump, every time.

"Hello, princess." He stepped towards her with a fiendish smile on his lips, and she noticed that he had a box in hand. "I was hoping you might wear this." He lifted the lid to reveal a large black diamond pendant.

Laila's lips parted with a gasp. "Where did you get this?"

"I might have swiped it from the castle on my way back."

Laila bit her lip as she slid her fingers over the large stone and its diamond setting. "You pilfered your own castle?"

"Well, I was thinking since we no longer have a regina to make use of it..."

"Darius." Laila sounded appalled. "How could you be so morbid?"

"I'm being pragmatic," Darius protested. "But if you'd rather not wear it—"

"That isn't what I said."

His smile returned, and it radiated such self-satisfaction that she couldn't help but share it. "Allow me."

She turned to face the vanity as he put the box down on the pale marble counter and fastened the necklace around her throat. The diamond lay heavily against her chest; it was blacker than coal with the lustre of ink.

"Perfect." He rested his hands on her shoulders before looking towards Oriel and Astrid. "What do you think, ladies?"

"Oh, it's wonderful."

"It's just what she needed."

"Dominus would've wanted for you to have it," Darius said. "He wanted me to tell you that he was sorry for not being the person that you needed him to be. That he couldn't have been better for you. And he hopes that you'll forgive him."

Laila clutched the diamond that much more tightly before turning to face him. "I do." Then she took him into her arms. "I'm so sorry about him, Darius."

"I am, too." Darius rested his chin on the crown of her head and, for the brief moment he was trapped in the safety of her arms with the scent of her hair on his nose, he allowed his legs to falter. He soon pulled back to hold out his arm for her. "Shall we?"

She locked her elbow with his and nuzzled into his shoulder. "I'll see you downstairs, ladies."

They made their descent into the waiting embrace of the festivities.

The Grand Ballroom was the pride of the palace—etchings of a marble frieze expanded over every wall depicting the solarites' fall from the sky and subsequent rise to regal prominence.

Dinner passed in a blur of rosé nectar wine and rose-dipped swan, both Laila's favourites. The soups were just the right amount of creamy, the desserts smeared in gold leaf, and the salads were all garnished with fragrant blossoms.

Her smiles came easier and her tongue grew looser the more she ate and drank. The chatter quieted as Amira stood to make a toast in honour of Lanius's capture.

"I would like to raise a glass to congratulate all you brave sprites and solarites for the diligent work you've done to rid our world of a murderous tyrant. Of course, none of it would be possible without the combined efforts of Lyra de Lis, our esteemed family Lightshield, and Darius Calantis, the as yet unseated Rex of Mortos. If you would please stand, Darius Rex."

Darius stood, more resigned than triumphant.

"Long live the king," Amira proclaimed, and thus she tossed the keys to his kingdom like toys to an unruly child. Yet it was she who seemed to be fixing to slot the ice blue diamond of Mortos into her imperial sceptre. Another jewel for her fine collection.

"Long live the king!" chorused the room.

After the toasts were made and the glasses clinked, the tables cleared to make room for a dancefloor. Laila saw a revolving door of partners throughout the night before Léandre approached to take her hand.

"I never received a chance to congratulate you on what a truly wondrous event you've put together," he said once they had drawn close, bodies moving in liquid rhythm.

Laila rested her head on his shoulder. "Thank you, Léandre."

"I mean it," Léandre continued. "I don't say it enough, but I am proud of you, Laila. Of what I have seen you achieve, of the maiden you are becoming. I believe you will make a fine impératrice one day. And I, for one, can't wait to see it happen."

Her throat squeezed and emotion moistened her eyes, but she put on a smile that she hoped shimmered brighter than her tears. She had to wonder if he would be so magnanimous with his praise if he were aware that she shared a bed with a monster and wore his jewels at her throat. If he would still smile upon her with such paternal pride.

"I'm so glad to have you home."

Léandre reached out to smudge the tear that stealthily escaped down her cheek. "Me too."

They took a moment to bask in the warmth of each other's smiles before a darker shadow intruded.

"Might I steal your princess for a dance?" Darius asked, hand outstretched.

"Is that all right with you, Laila?" Léandre asked, though his body had tensed with unspoken disapproval.

"You may." Laila took his hand and allowed herself to be shackled into his embrace. She propped her chin on his shoulder, inhaling the intoxicating musk of his cologne.

"I've been looking for an excuse to get near you all night." Darius murmured Mortesian low in her ear. "You are very high in demand."

"I know," Laila said. "I've been wanting to ask how you're doing."

"I'm as well as can be expected," he replied, "though I feel immensely better now that I'm holding you."

His hand glided leisurely down the small of her back, re-awakening the longing she'd tried hard to keep at bay. Her hips ghosted his in a sensual tempo to the music.

"I want to see you. Tonight. If you can manage to get away."

Laila glanced over his shoulder at Léandre, now in the midst of dancing with his niece. "Yes, of course," she said, for she needed it as much as he did. Perhaps even more. "But you don't have to put on a brave face for me, Darius. You can tell me how you really feel."

"Not here, not now," he said. "We can talk about it later. Just say you'll come, please?"

She drew back from his shoulder to nod at him. "I'll be there."

She slipped away to the Moon Tower once she'd had a moment to herself, content she could break free without too much questioning.

When she arrived, Darius was leaning against the fireplace, glass of whisky in hand and cravat loosened, watching the continuous leap of the flames. He made no move to acknowledge her entrance. He just kept watching the flames as they danced, the light fluctuating against his dusky skin.

He seemed solemn in a way Laila had not seen in him before, and she couldn't keep herself from reaching for him, sliding her arms around his shoulders to press a kiss to one of them.

She didn't understand how her body could still be so hungry for him even after the amount of times they'd touched each other. Perhaps that was why she let herself keep coming back, hoping that this would finally be the time she felt sated.

Her touch awakened him, and he put the glass down and took her face in his hands, leaning in for a kiss. She could taste the whisky on him as their lips met, smoky and smooth and strangely enticing.

He released a moan into her mouth, a vulnerable sound that travelled right between her legs. "Laila—" he began, and how was it that he was able to infuse *so much* into two syllables?

She shushed him, not wanting to confront more than the shallow surface lust that currently had possession of her. "Just kiss me."

He did as she asked, hands moving deftly to unlace her bodice. He pulled back to tug her dress away and let it puddle to the floor.

She re-joined their lips as she slid off his tailcoat and unbuttoned his shirt and waistcoat, her hands sliding down his sleek abdomen to undo his breeches next. Wood crackled in the fireplace, casting their bodies in radiant heat as they stripped each other bare.

"I'm so glad you're alive," Laila murmured as she kissed the sharp protrusion of his collarbone, sliding her lips down the plump bulge of his pectoral muscle.

Darius slipped his hand into her hair, tugging her to face him. "Then show me how much."

He brought his mouth down to hers into a kiss that left them both breathless. Then he lifted her to carry her over to the chaise lounge.

Laila sighed softly into Darius's mouth as their kiss deepened, finding it too easy to lose herself in this. The heat of his bare skin on hers, the thrum of his pulse assuring her he was here.

He pressed her upright against the back of the seat, her thighs against his as she braced her hands upon his chest. His hands roamed down the notches of her spine to her thighs, pulling her closer into his lap until the tip of his arousal was pressed against her. He was warm and sticky from his anticipatory spend, and she felt a throb of desire for how he might feel against her if she rubbed herself on him.

Laila found she couldn't resist the urge, and she moved his tip against her clit. With each motion there was a slight drag that went through her like static. She wrapped her hand around the base to hold him near, grinding against him as they kissed. She released a whimper from the delectable warmth of him pressed against her as his tip stroked her clit. Her hand tightened around him as she moved faster, coaxing a groan from him as she rocked her way to climax.

Once her shuddering subsided she circled his tip around her entrance, teasing him inside her, feeling herself edging towards release again from the movement alone.

He was remarkably placid during this, her exploration, engrossed just by watching her. There was something intoxicating about having this powerful creature literally in the palm of her hand, entirely obedient to her will.

"Are you going to tease me all evening?" Darius heaved a sigh in an amused and slightly exasperated fashion.

Laila dipped a hand between her legs to coat his shaft with slick, pressing the tip to her clit again. Her touches became bolder as his moans grew more laboured in the intensity, her grip getting rougher as he demanded.

Darius didn't flinch against the pain, liked it even, his hips moving to match the pace of her hand. He wanted, *needed*, to be inside her, to bask in the feel of her.

Laila tensed when he eased his way in, unable to keep herself from wincing in remembrance of the last time this happened.

He went still instantly, studying her expression. "Relax," he said, taking her cheek in hand. "I'm not going to hurt you."

She met his gaze and nodded, reassured.

"Would you like me to withdraw?"

She closed her eyes for a brief pause, trying to keep her body from seizing.

Darius tucked a strand of hair behind her ear, tilting her chin up to face him. "Laila?"

"You can continue."

He entered her slowly, taking it inch by inch, allowing her to grow accustomed to him. The sensation of her was sublime, like being enveloped in warm silk. He held back from taking a full plunge as she wrapped snugly around him, too fearful of harming her.

"How does that feel?" he asked on the edge of a moan.

Hearing how much he was enjoying it only aroused her even more. "It feels nice." She was unable to discover a more accurate term for something so unexpectedly pleasant. His girth was so prodigious she wasn't sure she could take him at first, but her body seemed to ache for more and accepted him until she was satiated. "Does it feel nice to you?"

"God, yes." His voice was hoarse, strangled. "You feel so good to me, Laila."

She smiled as she leaned in to brush his forehead with hers. She wanted to feel good for him, to bring him comfort and solace during this time.

"Good." She kissed him again, winding her arms around his neck.

That was all the enticement he needed, and he slung his hand over the top of the chaise lounge for purchase. He rolled his hips into hers at a languid pace, one hand gripping her waist to keep her still.

Laila surprised herself by how loudly she moaned into his mouth as he moved inside her, her toes curling in response. She was completely enraptured—it had been nothing like this with Dominus. Darius didn't approach her like a fort to be stormed by a battering ram, rather one whose doors should open for him on their own.

She wrapped her legs around him to hold him near, her confidence increasing in increments. "Stay still."

She nipped his bottom lip before gripping his shoulders. Then she circled her hips against him, moving one of his hands to cup her breast while guiding the other towards her clit to touch her the way that she wanted.

"That's it," he encouraged, his voice low in her ear as she writhed in his lap. His thumb traced lightly around her clit. "There's a good girl." The sound of him made the growing coil in her stomach tighten until she was pushed over the brink.

Laila cried out as she found release, her teeth bitten into his shoulder to muffle herself. There was something softer about the orgasm than the others she'd received—more muted. Yet the aftermath left her tingly all over.

Darius shuddered from the crackles of electricity shooting through his groin. Feeling Laila climax around him was a profound experience; a sensation so euphoric it almost provoked his own release. He couldn't quite reach completion in the depths of his sorrow, so instead he savoured the heady rush that came from working his way up to the edge.

"Do you want to finish?" she asked.

Darius hummed in refusal as he withdrew from her. "Just wanted to feel you."

They remained clasped around each other as she grew soft and malleable in his arms, their breaths hot and heavy, damp foreheads resting together in repose. He slid his hands through her hair, kissing her lightly on the nose, and she thought, *Perhaps I don't have to feel ashamed of wanting this*, because right now he was not two centuries worth of murderous monster to her. He was just a lover who held her tenderly in his hands.

"Come to Mortos with me."

She gazed up at him, her face quizzical. "What?"

"When all of this is over and I return to claim my throne, I want you by my side."

"Darius." She sighed softly as she traced the sharp contour of his cheek; she could pierce herself on the edges of him. "I can't."

"Why not?" he asked, releasing his grip in her hair to take her cheek in hand, ghosting his next words over her lips. "Come away with me."

"I have a country," she reminded him, "and I have a crown."

"I could give you all that and more," he told her, and there was nothing sweeter than the infinite potential of *more*. "I could take you to all the secret corners of the world that have been lost through time. The ancient cities, the sunken ships, the cursed vaults full of treasure that are spoken of only in myth." He pressed a soft kiss to her lips. "We'd visit tombs of all the great artists, and I'd raise their spirits to paint portraits in your likeness, then we'd go to the oldest library in existence and I'd read you poetry in extinct languages that only those with connections to the dead can master. We'd explore, you and I." He slipped a gold curl behind her ear. "You don't have any idea just how much I have to show you."

More, he promised to the one who has always had all she could want, and yet, how she still longed for these morbid offerings.

"If you want me to beg you Laila, I will," he vowed, "and I've never begged anyone before."

"It's not that I don't want this—" She sighed, weary in her rejection. For no matter how he might try to lure her to his underworld with the promise of forgotten culture and lost riches, she knew she must remain here. "I do want this, more than anything. But I can't just run away with you, Darius. And I'm not sure if this is truly what you want or if this is just you clinging to me in your fear of being left alone."

"It's not."

"How do I trust that?"

"Before I met you, I had fully resigned from life. There was so little joy to be found in it. Not much colour or hope. Every day was monotonous, and I felt... frozen. Then you came along and shattered your way through all of it. You set me free, Laila. Because of you I have a reason to hope again. And I can't stand the thought of losing that." He stroked her face with his thumb so carefully. "I can see that I've overwhelmed you. And you don't have to decide now. But at least promise me you'll consider it. Please?"

She closed her eyes before nodding. "All right."

He leaned in to kiss her once more.

XXXII

AILA PICKED A DANDELION FROM THE PALACE GROUNDS and blew on it, letting its downy tufts float off into the open air as she lay in the grass. Then she sighed as she sat up and hugged her knees to her chin, watching the fountain in the pond burble.

The sound of footsteps disturbed her from her serenity. She didn't need to look to know who it was.

"There you are!" Lyra said as she took a seat in the grass next to her.

Laila paused to take in the gentle wisps of air on the nape of her neck. "I needed a place to think."

"Corona for them?" Lyra asked, a small smile coming to her lips.

"Darius wants me to go away with him to Mortos."

"What?"

"He asked me after the feast, when we were... together."

391

"And you said no, right?" Lyra's brow contorted in concern. "Laila, tell me you said no to this."

"I told him that I would think about it."

"What is there to think about?" Lyra said in exasperation. "Are you honestly considering letting him drag you off to his evil citadel and make you his monster bride?"

Laila burst out laughing.

"Well, I'm glad you find this so amusing."

"You have to admit it is a little funny." Laila beamed brightly. "Just a little bit?"

"Perhaps," Lyra said. "Though to be perfectly honest I can't see why his offer would hold any appeal at all. He's so—" She threw her hands up in an encompassing gesture.

Laila cocked her head in amusement, having expected a full list of his misdeeds. "I know he's not good, Lyra. I've always known. But I also know that's not all there is to him. Darius... I've never met anyone like him before. I feel like I could sit there for hours trying to unravel the complex tapestry of his mind. Being with him feels exciting and unpredictable. He makes me want to challenge myself."

"You sound like you're falling in love with him."

Laila's lips parted briefly. The idea had never even occurred to her before Lyra mentioned it, and it terrified her. She concealed it behind a frivolous toss of her hair. "I'm always a little bit enamoured with anyone I take into my bed. My attention is a fleeting, inconstant thing; it takes a lot to keep it ensnared."

"I imagine you like us best when you can find a fragment of your own reflection."

"Is that not how we all form a connection with another being, by splitting them apart and finding the pieces that pair up well with our own, like matching shoes to jewellery?"

Lyra chuckled. "That makes some form of sense." She paused with a sigh. "And I won't pretend I don't understand the allure of a good rut with a beast. I admit I *may* have peeked at the regina a few times. But to go away with him—"

"I know," Laila sighed, picking up blades of grass to line them up along her thigh. "I'm going to have to let him down gently, aren't I?"

"Do you want me to come with you? Just in case he... doesn't take it well?"

Laila shook her head. "No, I'll be fine. I promise."

"Say the word if you change your mind."

"I will," Laila said, "but while we're on the subject. If you ever do find an occassella that fits your fancy. I highly recommend..."

"All right," Lyra exclaimed in horror. "I think this conversation needs to be put to a swift demise."

Laila giggled again and tackled her to the grass.

Darius sat upon the alabaster bench of the pavilion where he and Laila had decided to meet. He reached for one of the gold roses that had encroached upon the wrought iron structure to claim their hegemony, marvelling at its growth. His relationship with Laila had undergone a similar blossoming. He never would've thought before he'd come here just how indispensable she would be to him in such a short amount of time.

He heard her footsteps on the pavilion and stood as she approached in her ruffled pink gingham frilly shirt and matching culottes. The garment was a simple affair compared to the other ostentations of her wardrobe, but she was beatific in it as she greeted him with few adornments other than a radiant smile he couldn't believe was just for him.

"Glad you could make it," she said, rising onto her toes to peck his lips chastely. It was a gesture not out of sorts in the lands they now walked, but he longed to take her in for a deeper kiss. "Come on, we're going this way."

"And where are we going?" he asked as she locked their elbows together, guiding him through the grounds of the palace. Swinging on her other elbow was a wicker basket woven with flowers.

He did not have to wait long to receive an answer as the stables came into view, signalled by the euphonious whinnies of unicorns. However, as he approached, the soft, talkative murmurings of the mounts escalated into panicked screeches and cries.

"Hey, hey." Laila attempted to placate them in a caramel tone, approaching one unicorn, in particular, to grip his jaw and stroke his snout.

The animal would not be soothed, for it knew deep within the hindbrain, where all the rudimentary instincts of flight or fight linger, that something dangerous was near.

"I'm afraid it's my fault, princess," Darius said, head bowed in contrition. "Never was terribly popular with nature's creatures."

She turned to him over her bare brown shoulder with a disapproving look. "I don't suppose you have an off switch for that effect?"

He spread his arms out and shrugged.

She sighed, taking the basket off from her arm to clip it to the unicorn's saddle. "Well, this isn't how I imagined you would meet him but... Polaris was intended to be our steed for today. However, since he won't get anywhere near you, I shall have to be inventive."

She stepped towards Darius and cupped his cheek, speaking a few beguiling words before she stepped back. The screeching stopped.

"What did you do?" he asked.

"I cloaked your aura," she said, taking Polaris out by his braided mane adorned with wisteria. "Now they will no longer sense the occasso on you... whatever form of *essence* that happened to entail. I can't tell how long it will fool him, though, so we shall need to move quickly."

She hoisted herself onto the mount and then reached out her hand for Darius, helping him over the side so that he sat behind her.

"Are you going to tell me where we're going?" he asked, encircling his hands around her svelte waist and leaning his face into the glorious aureole of curls. He caught a whiff of gardenia and coconut oil, an indelible aroma that would forever leave its stamp upon his memory.

"On a picnic," she said brightly, and with a nudge of her ankles she sent Polaris galloping.

It had been so long since he'd ridden he almost forgot how much he missed Razer. Darius thought of the oily sheen of his hippogriff's wings and his taut, powerful muscles. The way he used to go for hours through the sky, always pushing faster and faster until the wind whacked Darius's face like a wall.

He'd had to leave him behind. Like Dominus. No doubt his father would've beheaded the beast, and the thought stuck to the back of his throat like tar. He clutched firmer to Laila's waist, thinking one day he might have to leave her behind too. The thought pained him more than he anticipated, and he longed to hear her soothe him of his worries, to not count her among the ever increasing spectres of those he'd loved and lost.

He'd been used to tearing out the pages of his past and leaving them to burn on a funeral pyre, remaking himself out of the ashes. When there was nowhere to belong to, there was nothing to keep, and so he had worn and discarded many aliases over time, finding them ultimately ill-fitting.

Brother. Lover. Son. Prefect. *Bastard.*

That last one he had scrubbed raw from his skin until he bled, but still it remained embedded in his scar tissue. He would never be free of that blight. It was hereditary, marrow-deep.

Being with Laila allowed him to erase these most loathsome aspects and rewrite himself into a storybook prince. One worthy of being the object of her desires and dreams. He liked the purity of affection that came of it—having nothing but the warmth of her smile when she saw him. He'd never think to sully it by having her know the body he'd stashed behind his bookcase. The sin he'd yet to confess.

Darius watched the wind carry the ringlets of her hair like streamers as they passed through the flanks of blondewood trees. Their branches were outstretched and swaying like an ovation—as though they had been waiting to usher her open-armed into their sylvan realm. He couldn't think of many places where she wouldn't be greeted, smiled upon; perhaps that was why it was so easy for him to smile with her, too.

They drew to a halt inside a field of chartreuse grass mottled with white daisies and salmon-pink poppies. The field sloped towards a blue lagoon, coruscant with dancing flecks of sunlight. Laila was the first to dismount, unclipping her picnic basket and setting it atop the velvet grass.

The first thing she pulled out was her floral-patterned blanket, unfurling it atop the field, and then she reached in to produce more of her hidden goods: strawberry shortcake, his much-favoured lemon pound cake, and vanilla crème éclairs topped with violet icing sugar. She produced a bottle of raspberry lemonade scented with lavender stalks, and then two glasses, pouring them each a cup.

Darius slipped down from her unicorn as the creature occupied itself by grazing the lush strands of grass.

"You mentioned you missed the sea," she said, handing him the glass. "Thought I'd bring it to you." She gestured towards the lagoon. "It's not quite the same, as the water here is secluded from the ocean. It comes through a little channel in an underwater cave. But we are completely alone here, no life around for miles."

He stopped to take in the gentle wisps of air on the nape of his neck. "It's breathtaking."

"I always thought so," she agreed, nostalgia edging into her smile. "Léandre and I used to hike here all the time. He always told me I should bring someone here myself one day. Someone special."

Her words rammed through him like a blade. How effortlessly she wielded that sterling silver tongue like a sword against his hardened black carapace. Slicing through him, flaying him of his impenetrable scales.

"Sure he won't mind you bringing an occasso to his special place?" he asked, taking a sip from his lemonade and sliding his tongue over his lips to savour it.

"Maybe," she said, clinking her glass against his before she sprawled out onto the blanket, her legs tented beneath the thin barrier of white cotton. "But Léandre isn't here."

His smile grew roguish as he sat beside her, and they helped themselves to a small feast of Soleterean pastries—an indulgent coating of sugar and crème.

As Laila bit into her third eclair in a row, he saw a small daub of crème had gathered at the corner of her mouth. He paused eating his lemon cake.

"You have a little crème—" He gestured to the corner of his mouth.

Her forehead crinkled delicately. "Where?" she asked, darting her tongue out to navigate in his general direction.

"There." He cupped her chin, leaning in to claim the crème for himself as he put his mouth to hers and lightly grazed his tongue over it.

Laila giggled wildly before his lips covered hers, and what started as an innocuous gesture grew into a passionate kiss as he drew her body to him.

She pulled away with a moan in protest. "Not yet." She grabbed his hands and returned them to his side. "I want to swim first."

She removed her clothes and undergarments, tossing them away with a saucy smile cast over her shoulder. The light teased across the star-flecks that constellated her body, her golden-brown skin glistening like a desert in midsummer. One could make themselves thirsty hiking their gaze up her sinuous miles, every generous curve and bend.

She ran down the slope of the hill and disappeared beneath the surface of the blue water. Darius watched her resurface, her hair now a curtain of dark gold plastered to her neck, burnished beneath the glow of the sunlight. He undressed himself and walked down to meet her, diving into the lagoon with an elegant pose.

The water was as warm and clear as it looked, no hint of salt in it. They swam alongside each other, chasing and splashing and laughing all the while, until eventually he dragged her to him by the arm to hold her close.

"Have an answer for me?" Darius asked, sliding a wet strand of hair away from her cheek.

Laila sighed as she strung her arms around his neck. "Can't we just enjoy today?"

"I'll be leaving soon, Laila. Once the trial of my father has been settled, that's it for me." He cupped her cheek in his hand. "I need to know what you've decided before then."

And though he hoped for otherwise, he could see the answer clear as day before she uttered it.

"I'm so sorry, Darius."

He closed his eyes and exhaled his disappointment. "It was always a gamble, princess." He slid his thumb down her cheek one last time, as though to memorise the impression, before he drew away. "I think it's time we left."

"Wait." She drew him back. "Please, let me explain."

"What is there to explain, Laila?" He took her hands and lowered them to her sides. "You've made your stance rather clear."

He made a turn to leave before she mirrored his movement.

"Please stay with me today, just one more day," she pleaded, reaching for him. "This isn't how I wanted things to end."

"Then why the charade? If you knew you had no intention of leaving with me, then why toy with me like this? Why give me hope?"

"I didn't do this to hurt you, Darius," she said, cupping his face in her hands. "I just wanted for us to—"

"I know what you wanted, Laila." He pinched his temples, massaging them with his fingers. "And I wish I could say I was charitable enough to give it to you, but I can't. I can't stay here with you a moment longer."

"So, that's it?" Her eyes shimmered in disbelief. "You're going to walk away from me after everything? Just like that?"

"Perhaps I'm simply unable to accept you will never return the same depth of feeling I have for you—"

"This isn't about what I feel or don't feel for you, Darius. You are asking a lot of me. You have no idea how much it scares me, the way I feel for you. A way in which I've never felt for anyone before in my life. It's too much. You're too much for me—"

He seized her by the face and kissed her, his hands sliding down her waist to pull her closer. He heard her moan against him as she pulled him in by the shoulders, her nipples stiffening against his chest as she returned the kiss with the same fervour.

Laila wrapped her legs around his waist as he pressed her up against the bank of the lagoon. This was both a plea and a punishment—a display of what she'd be giving up and a persuasion to keep it.

She broke away first, unable to bear continuing. "I can't come with you to Mortos, Darius. I can't."

He let himself exhale his disappointment, leaning wearily against her forehead before he pulled away. "Perhaps then it's best if we... stop this now. For both our sakes."

Then he walked away from her, not daring to look back as he dressed and wandered into a cluster of trees to brood.

The fate of Lanius Calantis was to be decided by a private trial at the Celestial Court. Among the attendees was the impératrice herself, joined by her Magisterium and a select few high-ranking Lightshields.

Darius's invitation was extended as a courtesy, and he was to act both as a witness and representative to the Mortesian branch of the law.

The matter of Lanius's danger was indisputable: what was then being argued back and forth was how best to neutralise him. His heart had been impossible to locate, and the court found themselves swiftly out of options.

"Your Luminosity, if I may posit," Lady Commander Cassia said from her seat, "I do not feel comfortable sentencing Lanius indefinitely to imprisonment. A prisoner of such high risk would be a constant hazard for escape, not to mention those he may have influenced enough to attempt to release him."

Darius couldn't be persuaded to disagree. In every trial of combat that was held in the past for Mortesian succession, the losing party was always killed. To leave him alive would forever be a lingering threat, one any sane rex would do well to dispose of.

"I hear your concerns, Lady Cassia, and I share them," Amira said. "However, I am afraid we do not have a reliable way of removing him as a threat."

"There is another alternative I might offer," said Léandre de Lis. "In the past, forest sprites have often used banishment to deal with particularly egregious monsters. I suggest we utilise this method to deal with Lanius."

"Banishment, as in eternal exile to an external dimensional realm?" Amira tapped her chin in thought. "It is worth considering; however, I recall that sort of magic does not come without great cost."

"To complete the spell for a lifelong hold would require a life to be given in exchange, yes," Léandre replied grimly.

"I don't imagine we'll see many willing volunteers for such an exchange, would we?" Amira asked, her tone ironic.

Her scepticism was validated by the soft murmurs of dissent.

"I would be willing to make the exchange, Your Luminosity," Léandre said, without even a hitch in his breath. The certainty with which he was willing to give up his life had even Darius sitting up in interest.

"Are you certain, Ser Léandre?" Amira asked, her expression as imperceptible as it ever was. "That is a large sacrifice for you to make on behalf of the country."

"I have lived three hundred years, Your Luminosity. More than enough time to see what I feel I ought to have seen of the world. I am ready to pass on to the celestial realm to be reunited with my sister in the knowledge that my niece, Lyra, will be prepared to take up my mantle."

"If that is the case, then you will be given a period of time to reconsider, during which you may make any final requests of the court to ease your passage."

"Only that I might have time with Lyra to prepare her," Léandre said. "And to say goodbye to Princess Laila."

"Your first request will be granted. However, I'm going to have to ask that you... suspend any farewell you wish to have with my daughter."

"You mean you would like for me not to tell her?"

Darius did not miss the slight undertone of accusation, nor could he prevent himself from sharing it.

"Not at all, Ser Léandre, only that I think it would be best to postpone it to prevent my daughter from making a scene. I think you understand well enough that Laila has a habit of getting into people's minds, supplanting their wills with her own." Amira's eyes flitted over to Darius upon the final point, and he realised with startling alarm that she must know about the affair. Though how long and for how much, he could not guess.

"I understand, Your Luminosity," Léandre said. "May I at least tell Lyra?"

"Considering the risk that the news might pass on to Laila through osmosis, I hesitate to permit it. However, I am willing to afford you the opportunity to do so provided you ensure she is sworn to secrecy."

"As you wish, Your Luminosity."

"Consider this meeting adjourned."

The attendees rose from their seats to depart. It was only when Darius made a move to leave that he heard her speak again.

"Please stay behind, Darius Rex."

His back stiffened, but he knew better than to refuse her. "How may I help, Your Luminosity?"

"I was hoping for a quick tête-à-tête between us." She stood to full height. "I was hoping you and I might discuss the status of our relationship when you return to Mortos."

"I would expect it would be a peaceful one, I hope." Darius allowed himself a wry smile. "What with my father now due to be safely out of the way and Dominus dispensed with, it seems everybody involved has gotten what they want."

"Now, see, that is precisely what concerns me, Darius Rex." She moved from behind her chair to close the distance between them. "I can't say I am sure what it is you want."

He met her imperious scrutiny with a smile of acquiescence. Though he might have an entire foot over her in height, there was no doubt she would enclose her teeth around his jugular to tear him open with little hesitation. They didn't call her the White Lioness solely due to the animals she kept.

"I'm an open book, Your Luminosity." He raised his arms in a blasé gesture. "Achieving the throne in Mortos is the only thing I could want."

"You see, it is just that I don't believe you," Amira said, "and I was wondering if you might do something to ease my mind."

His jaw flexed, and he braced himself for yet another display of her torturous illumination enchantment. "And what's that?"

"Allow me to have a little peek into your mind." She slapped her hands around his temples before he could move. Then she spoke a few soft words in a tongue he couldn't decipher and his vision was curtained in blackness.

When the blinds were lifted, he found himself inside a tower not unlike his own. There was the same spiral staircase, the same constricted walls of pristine marble. Only instead of one room there were several— locked doors varnished in a blue pigment that looked to have been stolen from the sky.

He neared the first step in caution, giving a quick glance around to locate any other exits before he called out: *Where am I?*

It took several moments for him to receive an answer: *This is known as the Dream Realm. It exists as a liminal space between the astral and physical plane. This tower is a gateway, and through these doors, you will find the thing that you most desire and the thing that you most fear.*

Darius chuckled dryly and shook his head in disbelief: *You know that was a rotten trick to play, Amira. If you wanted to see my wildest hopes and dreams, all you really needed to do was read my diary.*

Just step through a door and get it over with.

Seeing no other alternative to freedom, he decided he might as well do as she said.

When he stepped through the door, he knew little of what to expect. At first there was nothing but a simple blackness. But then he heard the orchestral tones of Mortesian music, the insidious, solemn, and soul-stirring resonance of it, as his shoes echoed atop floors of obsidian. The dancers appeared in a blink, pivoting in their well-timed circles, the men in their kaftans of velvet and gold-braiding and their feminine counterparts in their courtly gowns.

Something swelled in his chest at the sight of them, the mechanical clockwork rotation of their waltz, while ghoul servers weaved their way through the crowd, carrying their gleaming trays of whisky and wine.

"About time you got here," teased a voice from behind him. His shoulders tensed in an amalgam of delight and anticipation as he turned to face her. She was lovely, of course—when was she ever not? "I've been waiting for you."

She too was in a court dress—a deep wine velvet embroidered with foliate motifs in gold. He glanced at the diamond diadem atop her head, punctured through with rubies like congealed wounds.

"You look well," he said. "Mortesian fashion suits you."

"As it does you."

That was when he became aware of his own attire—the long coat embroidered with oak leaves in gold threading paired with a matching cloak with cream lapels. On his head rested the Mortesian royal crown he had seen many times on his father.

So, this must be his deepest desire, then. Fully decorous in Mortesian regalia. With Laila by his side.

"I must admit I am... shocked to see you here but not disappointed," he said, framing her cheek with the same reverence as if she were real to him at that moment. "I just wish you could see this for yourself, see how things could be between us if only you'd change your mind."

"Oh, Darius," she said softly, almost yearning, unless that was simply another trick of his mind. But then her expression distorted and her eyes turned cruel. "Did you really think I could ever love you?" She grasped his chin in her hand and whispered against his lips, "That hiding behind your princely airs would make me look past the horrors you've committed?" She stroked his cheek before shoving him with a laugh. "Don't be so silly. What makes you think I would ever see you beyond a body to warm my bed? What makes you think *anyone* could? What makes you think you even *deserve* to be loved?"

He swallowed, shifting his jaw. "Maybe I don't."

He let his hand fall from her instantly, his cheeks aflame and his throat clogged. Of course, he was foolish to ever think she would deign to lower herself to him other than for a few carnal moments in the darkness. Wasn't that what he had been for? Just a brute to mount for a nocturnal visit and then be sent away in the full brightness of day. She would never choose to stand with him, hand in hand, declaring her devotion to him before her country. And could he even blame her for that?

Perhaps it was he who had been wanting too high, reaching too far beyond his appropriate level. Perhaps, in the end, he was just... starstruck. Full of too much hope for what he could never attain.

Get me out of here, he called towards Amira. You've got what you wanted.

He saw the veil descend before his eyes again before it lifted from his vision and revealed him to be once more inside the courtroom with Amira.

"Well, I have to say," Amira declared, "I wasn't expecting that."

"Are you satisfied now?" he asked, eyes hardened in accusation.

"Slightly," she said. "You know, when my daughter's guard came to me and informed me you were carrying on an illicit relationship with Laila, she did it out of concern for her. She thought you might be planning to harm her. So I thought it best to take matters into my own hands and assess your danger."

"I would never hurt Laila."

Amira tilted her head to one side. "I can see why you might think that. But we both know better than to believe that to be true. Which is why I'm telling you to stay away from her from this moment forward."

"Our relationship has already been terminated, Your Luminosity," Darius said. "You have nothing to fear."

"But you still want her," Amira said, "and I have known occassi to be rather persistent creatures. I believe you call that hunter's instinct." Her face hardened into something smooth and impenetrable. "You can have your kingdom, Darius Rex, and you can have your crown. But you *cannot* have my daughter. Do you understand me?"

He swallowed thickly. "I understand."

"Then consider this the end of our discussion."

XXXIII

THE DAY OF THE BANISHMENT WAS HERALDED BY A GREY, dismal outcry from the heavens above. Never before had Darius seen such doleful weather in the lands that seemed permanently kissed by sun. The rain fell in a sepulchral parade of black ribbon, pummelling the earth and the flowers, beating all the animals into quiet submission.

The ceremony was subdued, observed by an exclusive few in one of the solarites' gilded temples. A priestess blessed her altar with the four elements—a chalice of rosewater, a lit candelabrum of consecrated sunflower oil, a loaf of honey bread, and rose incense in a brass censer.

Amira arrived looking resplendent in her long, flowing robes of gold and silver, sunlight rippling along them in soft fluctuations. On her head was a coronal of gold roses and a ringed band above set with stars—the symbols of the solarites. The train of her gown roused the film of dust that powdered the floors, causing it to coil around her in glittering tendrils—but not once did they sully her. Such was the proof of her anointed rank, for the dross of the earth could not touch her, while the light from the sky above sought to embrace her as a peer.

Lanius was led behind her in cosmic metal cuffs, his expression begrimed with hatred. At their approach, the solarites joined hands and began to chant the song of the sun. It rose and fell, slowly and rhythmically, the way the moon-guided ocean kissed the shoreline, rising alongside auspicious wisps of incense to the painted mural ceiling.

Amira withdrew the ceremonial golden dagger from its gem-encrusted sheath. The chanting intensified as she held it up to the sky to infuse it with divine light. Then she beckoned Léandre forth. He marched up the aisle in his robes of pure white silk, ready to selflessly relinquish his life to ensure Lanius's concealment.

Darius watched the scene with little sentiment other than pity for such a foolish display of martyrdom, before a loud wail pierced the procession and Laila burst through the doors.

"Stop," she cried out, darting with lightspeed before a Lightshield stepped forward to obstruct her path, picking her up off of her feet. "No, stop. Don't do this, Léandre, *please*. Let go of me! *Let go!*" Her body crackled with enough electricity to have the guard that held her crumple to his knees, but as soon as she slipped free, more arrived to restrict her.

Her pain penetrated right through Darius, in spite of his anger and resentment and his repression of both combined. He felt stirred to comfort her, whatever instincts he thought he'd suppressed towards wanting her becoming viciously roused.

"Keep her still," Amira instructed as she moved towards her daughter with ire in her step. There was almost a tenderness in the way she held Laila close as she spoke to her—right before she electrocuted her so violently she went limp.

Darius stood immediately in alarm. But what he noticed most prominently was the way the audience, minimal as it was, didn't even stir at the commotion.

Laila remained motionless for so long Darius worried she'd been killed. But then he noted with relief the little weeping tremors in her body before Amira had her escorted away, halting Léandre with a hand when he attempted to follow.

"She's just being emotional," Amira murmured as she went to resume the ceremony. "I've treated the issue."

Darius tried to soothe his emotions into slumber again as the ritual commenced.

During the crescendo of the chant, Lanius combusted into white flames, his primal cry echoing into nothingness. Then Amira stabbed Léandre through the heart with the dagger, causing whatever spark of life remained in him to be mercilessly snuffed.

Léandre's neck arched back with his dying gasp, his once pristine robes sullied red. Amira withdrew the dagger aglow with a pulsating heat, as though the metal were new from a forge. When the heat dissipated, she was left with a key in its place. She plunged the key through the flames surrounding Lanius and twisted it, causing them to burst into scattering embers until even they had faded. And the deed was done.

A few Lightshields escorted Léandre's body away on a pram as Amira approached Darius.

"It is done. Mortos is now fully yours to claim. Congratulations, Darius Rex."

He waited until the last of her clicking footsteps had fallen away before he let his chest shudder with the depth of this revelation. Because now there was just him. Dominus dead and his father exiled, there would only ever be him. He would return to a hall of phantoms.

He only wished he had someone waiting there for him to collect him into their open arms so he might unburden his troubles. But it was not to be. He would know no tender lover's touch when he stepped foot on the black sands of Mortos. Only judgement and suspicion and wariness. More than fully deserved.

He returned to the Moon Tower.

∞

He spent the next few days arranging his belongings to package away into a chest. These were the objects he'd procured from the country during his stay. All the books, the cosmetics, the clothing and souvenirs.

So distracted he was by his task that he didn't even notice Lyra when she slipped into his room, a potentially fatal error for which he immediately cursed himself when he heard her voice.

"I assume you'll be on your way, then."

His shoulders seized as he clutched onto one of the leather tomes he had been painstakingly arranging into alphabetical order.

"Yes, I will be. I'm sure you and the rest of your comrades will be satisfied to see the back of me."

"Oh, I will," she said, a touch more nasally than her usual tone. "Listen, I—I feel immeasurably foolish having to do this, but you have to believe me when I say I no longer know what else to do."

He stood to full height as he turned towards her and saw her opaline eyes had become clouded pink from tearfulness. She looked vulnerable in a way he had not seen her; it drew him like blood to a shark.

"What is it?" he asked, brow raised.

"Laila has not left her room for days," she said, and he tried to

410

avoid the way that rustled something in him. "All she does is cry since my uncle—they were very close, and... she won't let herself be seen by anyone. I've tried my best, but I can't give her what she needs right now, you understand. So, I've come to you."

"Laila and I are no longer in a relationship."

"I know," she said, "but I also know she regrets the way that you ended things. I think it would help her get closure to move forward if you went and said goodbye."

He exhaled sharply in a laugh, pinching the bridge of his nose. "You can't be serious."

"I just thought, seeing as you were purporting to care for Laila, you might want to do one thing to set her mind at ease." She raised her chin in disdain, her jaw set firm. "But now I see you truly are just monstrous."

Darius recoiled at the sheer venom in her tone as she pivoted and walked down the steps to the exit. Then he sent the book in his hand careening against the wall, watching it explode in a scattering of pages.

He massaged his temples and sighed before collecting the pages with a mental note that he would glue them back together at the earliest opportunity. He closed the lid to his chest and sat atop it, exhaling deeply, before he stood and marched down the steps of the tower.

He didn't know why he suspected she would have left the doors to her balcony open, but he was rewarded for his impulse when he saw the soft billowing of silk drapes yawning outwards into the breeze.

He scaled the unruly growth of climbing roses onto the landing, hauling himself with ease over the balustrade. He peered into the stagnant gloom of her boudoir. The only light that touched the room was whatever tendrils had snaked their way past the balcony doors before being shunned away.

Darius saw the amorphous lump of her silhouette through the

411

drawn drapes on her canopy bed and slowly inched forward to peel them back.

She did not rouse from her huddled position, her breathing a faint ebbing motion. She was clothed in one of her flimsy satin nightgowns, which rippled faintly with every exhale rolling in from the balcony doors.

He sped away to close the doors before rushing back to her and touching a few dried curls of her hair, brittle from dehydration.

She only made a soft sound in response, so meek and pitiful something in his chest drooped with it. "Léandre?"

"Laila," Darius said, dimpling the edge of the mattress beneath his weight as he sat on it.

She let out a snuffle as she turned to look at him, unravelling herself from the cocoon she'd made with her blankets. "What are you doing here?"

"Lyra sent me. I wanted... to apologise for your loss."

"Well, you came and you apologised," she said with a sniff, her red-rimmed eyes hollow. "Now you can go."

He clutched her arm before she could make a bid to escape him. "That's not all I came here for."

"Darius, please don't do this to me right now."

"I want to be here for you, Laila," he said, swallowing before he managed to cautiously add, "if you'll let me."

The words were enough to make her deflate for how little she could cope with it. That in her time of need he would be there, as he always had been, to offer her solace even after she'd hurt and disappointed him. Her chest spasmed with a hiccup, and he gathered her into his arms just as her face crumpled into a sob.

"It's okay," he said as she mewled her soft kitten cries. He cradled her to him with a shush as she trembled in his grip, resting his chin on her hair as he stroked it. "It's okay," he said again as her cries grew louder and more laboured. Then she rested her cheek on his chest, soaking his shirt.

He held her until her sobs quieted, raising her face to him as he brushed her tears away with his thumbs. "Is that better?"

She nodded weakly.

"Come on," he said, gathering her into his arms. "I'll run you a bath."

He carried her into the ensuite and set her on the edge of the cavernous rose quartz tub. Then he spun the swan tap, perusing her extensive collection of bath toiletries before he selected a few fragrant oils, slices of citrus, and wildflowers.

He unhooked the straps of her nightgown, peeling off the sheer garment with a strange sense of abashment for someone who had undressed her many times before now.

"Get in with me," she told him before unbuttoning his shirt.

He let her undress him as he slid down her undergarments, and soon they were bare before each other as she climbed in first to settle into the tub. He nestled in behind her as he surrounded her with his extensive arms and legs. Thankfully, the tub was such a size that it was not an uncomfortable fit for him. Darius stroked Laila's hair as she leaned back against him.

"This feels nice," Laila sighed in contentment, nuzzling into his chest.

He hummed in agreement as his arms encircled her waist to pull her near.

She stroked her fingers up and down his upper arm.

"I'm sorry about Léandre, princess," Darius said. "I know how much he meant to you. I can't say I understand what it means to lose a guardian in this manner, but—"

"It's okay," she said, pressing her lips to his biceps. "I'm just glad you're here with me now."

Darius swallowed, snuffing the sudden desire that perhaps, possibly, she meant it, *truly* meant it in the way he desired her to. That she had sought the ghost of his company outside her most carnal fantasies, as he had done her. But he knew better now.

"So am I," he said, "and I'm sorry to tell you this now, but... with my father out of the way, that means—"

"You're going back to Mortos."

"I'll probably have to depart within the next couple of days—"

"Don't," she told him, her fingers now clutching firmly into his biceps. "I don't want to think about you leaving me right now."

He buried his face into her hair and kissed the crown of her head. "I'm all yours until then."

"Thank you," she said, her hand sliding around his face to stroke his cheek before she drew him near. Their eyes met over her shoulder, her gaze intent, and though she knew she shouldn't she couldn't help but lean in to graze their lips against each other. The kiss was a soft, exploratory thing and dangerously tantalising.

It took every ounce of him to pull away from her, to take in a breath of air that wasn't stained with her scent. "We shouldn't."

"I don't care." She brought his lips back to hers to kiss him more intently.

He pulled away again. "Laila, please."

She turned herself around to rest her hands on his shoulders, pressing the warmth of her body against his in a way she knew enticed. "What's the matter, Darius?" She bit her lip as she searched his eyes. "Don't you want me anymore?"

Darius closed his eyes, heaving a sigh. "You know that isn't what this is about."

"Then what is it about?"

"You're grieving and you're vulnerable, looking for comfort wherever it comes, and I cannot—"

"I want you," she said, running her hands slowly down his chest. "I need you."

Though he fought against it, hearing her say she needed him was the crippling blow. He made a strained sound, as though wounded from it, and she seized his weakness.

"Laila—"

"Don't think." She put a finger to his lips, then moved her hands to palm his cheeks. "Just feel."

When she kissed him again he did not pull back. His mouth moved of its own accord as he deepened the kiss, wrapping his arms around her to pull her closer. As Laila moaned with relief, it made him realise how much he needed it too. Needed her. So he let himself succumb to her a final time.

Laila placed her hands on his shoulders, fingers digging deep as she pressed them closer. So close that it might have been impossible to pry them apart and leave them both intact. She was so needy and desperate that she could barely wait before mounting his lap, sliding up and down the length of his stiffened arousal until he was moaning into her mouth.

"Slow down," he told her, his fingers gripping her sides to keep her steady.

"Darius—" she said, throbbing all over with need to the point she thought she might die if she didn't find relief from it.

"Slow down." If this was going to be the last time they did this, then he needed it to last a while.

He pulled back from her to cup the side of her face, tracing his thumb along the plump softness of her bottom lip. He wondered how many would have the privilege to feel those lips long after him. How many it would take before the impression of his own was lost to her entirely. The thought made him both anguished and murderous, and for a moment he just looked at her, throat thickened, and found he couldn't bring himself to kiss her again. He couldn't bear the thought of the next kiss being their last, of every touch between them being tinged with loss.

That was, until Laila took his face in her hands, sensing his turmoil, and leaned in to brush their lips together ever so slightly. The soft heat of her hesitant breaths left a tickle on his lips and beckoned him nearer to close the gap between their mouths, his hand skidding down the small of her back as he lifted them both upright.

Then his lips were fixed to the sensitive spot beneath her jaw, lapping from it a rivulet of water tinged with the taste of floral and citrus. He migrated down the tender arc of her throat so he could memorise how smooth and delicate the skin was, how elegant its swanlike curve, before nipping the delicate protrusion of her collarbone.

Laila's head craned back with a moan as he left trails of bruisingly firm kisses along her neck and down her breasts, sucking a glistening droplet from the edge of her nipple. She could sense the heat growing between her thighs as he skimmed the sensitive underside of her breast with his shapely mouth.

His fangs scraped along her skin with just enough of a bite to send shivers through her, and he continued to focus on how to coax those weak little sounds from her lips as she entangled her fingers in her hair to draw him nearer.

"Darius—"

The sound of his name made him shudder, a possessive growl muted into the crook of her neck. He couldn't get enough of it. That light, breathy pitch and the sheer *need* it exuded. When he was through with her, he wanted to make it so she forgot how to pronounce any other name but his.

416

He picked her up by the hips, rotating her so that her back was splayed against his chest. Then he put his fingers through her hair, kneading her scalp and teasing through the luscious locks he realised he might never feel again. He set that thought aside as he massaged her shoulders, moving down to cup the fullness of her supple breasts, squeezing them and thumbing over the nipple, skidding his fingers over the dampness of her stomach, so lightly and reverently, collecting all the petals that clung to her from the bath water.

All the while Laila was growing more restless against him, her breaths getting shorter and shorter apart. Her hand clenched the edge of the bath as she rocked on his lap in a bid to stir him to action.

Darius suppressed the groan that followed as his cock became nestled in the cleft of her buttocks. "Steady." He pressed his hand against her stomach as his other slid up her thigh before stroking inwards with his thumb. He circled her clit with the slowness he knew she liked to start with, just to provoke that flex of anticipation.

Laila moaned, her toes already curling from the precision of his movements as he followed it with the slow glide of his finger inside her to tease a hypersensitive spot. She couldn't help but give an involuntary buck of her hips as he added another finger, gyrating on his lap with hypnotic rhythm. Then they were teasing and taunting each other, their moans staining the air with a heady resonance as their bodies moved in tandem, melding together as water splashed liberally onto the floors from the bath.

Darius exhaled hotly into the nape of her neck before placing his lips against it. "Do you like that?"

She whimpered in response.

"Laila." He'd taken on a commanding tone. "Tell me."

"I—I like—" She'd lost coherency. The way his hand stroked her clit

417

was so languorous, so attentive, that she couldn't take it for long before she was crying out with her orgasm.

His own left a trail up her spine as a few rougher, more insistent pumps from her hips brought him to climax with a grunt. They slumped together in the aftermath, breathless and spent. Until Darius swiped her hair from her shoulder to latch his fangs into her neck, biting her hard enough to leave a mark.

Laila sighed gently at this and inclined her head to him over her shoulder. "Why do you do this to me?" She turned to burrow her lips on his chest as he drew her nearer, his other hand rinsing clean her slippery back. The gesture was enough to make her hum in contentment. She felt warm; comforted. But as his fingers slid further up her spine she could feel the fever renew in her blood.

He paused to look at her inquisitively.

"You make me ache for you so much," she explained. "Even after all the times we've—"

"I know." His expression turned to something carnal and hungrier. "Perhaps it's a sign we haven't finished."

She bit down on her bottom lip. "Take me. Please."

He finally stopped taunting her enough to show her mercy, carrying her out of the tub to the bed as he brought her into a kiss. Their lips didn't once part even as they both tumbled onto the mattress, their legs entwining, her wrists pinned above her head.

He went all over her body with his lips, like he did the first time they were in this bed together, like he was discovering her anew.

Laila scrabbled at his back with her nails as her hips arched, one leg slung over his waist to urge him on, her toes curling against the back of his calf.

There was a conjoined gasp from them both when he sank into her, their pelvises pressed together, and then he went still. The entire world seemed to go still as they shared a kiss, their breaths shaky in each other's mouths before he started to grind on her in smooth and continuous motions for what seemed like an age. He kept that unhurried pace along her swollen clit until Laila felt those delicate quivers travelling up inside her, and then she started to move back against him, gripping and tightening her interior muscles.

Warmth spread in the pit of her stomach the more the weight of him glided along her, stroking against that elusive spot, and she could tell that she was reaching the brink. And from the creasing of his forehead, he wasn't long behind her. She kept swivelling her hips against him, pressing his buttocks in her hands to move him as she needed, trying to aid them both along.

Darius whispered something indistinct in Mortesian as he quickened the rhythm of his hips, building up the excitement until he slowed once more to those soothing, quiet movements. She claimed his face to touch their lips together, their sighing measured as they rested their foreheads atop each other. She wasn't sure when it would end, and she didn't want it to. She just wanted to be close to him, to feel him rooted within her so deeply that she felt certain he would never leave.

Darius found himself wanting to scar her, mark her, leave his impression so deep within her bones she would be able to feel him rustling beneath her skin long after he'd left.

"Laila," he groaned against her ear in a way that made her shudder. He scraped his enlarged canines underneath her jaw. "I need—"

"Bite me," she said.

Darius kissed a trail down her neck before he embedded his fangs into her. The bite felt just as good as entering her and his body trembled with a powerful climax, marked by a long sigh. He soothed the wound with the wet massage of his tongue, sampling the sublime golden nectar that was her ichor as he released his venom into her veins.

419

"Harder," she insisted as her body wilted into bliss. Then the tranquilising secretion of his venom seeped into her bloodstream, coaxing her to the brink of ecstasy. It was mind-shattering. No mortal body could hope to survive something this ruinous. Her orgasm surged with such exquisite pleasure-pain she thought she might expire.

Darius rocked his hips through the throes of his own before finally going slack. He unlatched his teeth to look down into her venom-blissed face, stroking away the damp strands of hair from her forehead. He could see she had taken on that roseate afterglow he so favoured, her sweetly heart-shaped face having ascended to levels of unreality through her ecstasy.

He watched the glow of her like he'd captured the sun in his arms. His own personal midnight light. And though he knew she was not his to keep, he still desired to contain her, to bottle her up and secrete her away beneath his pillow like some newly discovered trinket.

Wasn't it the height of arrogance in all beasts to think they might ever conquer the sky?

She reached out lazily to touch his face, sliding her fingers down his jawline. "That was—"

"Beyond words." Darius's voice was thick with meaning as he slid his thumb down her moistened cheek. He wanted to kiss her again, but he withheld; instead he just gazed at her, his thumb easing up and down. "How do you expect me to find the strength to leave you after this?"

It was spoken with such an earnest sense of wonder, edged with pain, that she couldn't help but feel her throat swell from it.

"By putting one foot in front of the other," she replied, steeling her voice. "Just like before."

"Laila—" He wanted to plead for her to come with him, run away with him, but he knew his words would be wasted. So he swallowed them back.

"Nothing has changed." She fought to keep the tremors at bay. "You know it has to be this way."

Darius closed his eyes, heaving a deep exhale before he nodded and drew back from her.

The cold air attacked her body the instant he left her. She grabbed the sheets to cloak herself in the aftermath. Her stomach bottomed as she watched him prepare to make the final walk out of her life, and before she knew it she had seized his arm. "Wait." She clutched him tightly. "Please." She moistened her lips, tilting her head to shield the tears that varnished her eyes. "Don't—don't go yet."

It was selfish to demand so much of him after all she'd taken already. Selfish and rotten. But whatever it was in her that kept on reaching for him decided it had not had its fill yet.

Her plea caused a monstrous part of Darius to rustle awake. The same part of him that wanted to pull away and leave her there, desperate, and begging for him not to go. Feeling rejected. But one look into her sad, pleading eyes and he couldn't do it. His expression softened and he gathered her his arms. "I'll stay until you fall asleep."

Because of course, he hadn't been ready to let go either. Not for a very long time.

XXXIV

AUTUMN SLOWLY CREPT ONTO THE PALACE GROUNDS and announced itself with a few wet shakes. Laila observed the spatter of it against the glass doors to her balcony, now kept closed to hinder the fat droplets that showered profusely from the heavens above.

She had been longing for a decent storm, but the weather now was disappointingly tame and mournful. So it was with a heavy sigh that she tied back her curls with a pink ribbon and practised smiling before the mirror.

There were still times when she woke up and expected Léandre to walk through the door.

She would be lying in bed in her depressive stupor, listening to the continuous *dripdripdrip* against her window pane, and she would think: this was it, this was the day he lost patience and came into her room. This was the day he would walk in with his brisk soldier's stride, peel the covers back from her bed and command her to face all the harsh grey interludes between the rosy parade of her existence.

But now she was forced to face them all without him. And how could he just *leave* her here when she was still floundering to keep herself afloat in her mind's oppressive tide, when she still needed him to guide her, to be the beacon she swam to when she was left hopelessly adrift?

She let her forced smile fall as tears came to her eyes before she blinked them back. She knew he would want her to be stronger than this. That he would not have left her if he didn't think she had the capability to learn to swim without his aid.

She just wanted a little while longer with him. She wanted to climb to the pinnacle of her potential with him still there to cushion her falls. Yet here she was all the same, putting one step in front of the other, breathing easy as she presented herself before her mother's company in her solar.

"Well, isn't this a surprise," Amira declared over a delicate bite of her cinnamon-scented fried toast. "I was starting to think I'd need to send someone to drag you out of your room."

"Good morning, Maman," Laila said with grace as she took a seat beside her at the table.

"Good morning." Amira raised her cappuccino to her lips. "Finally decided to stop sulking, did you?"

Laila knew that was bait and so she did not rise to it, instead helping herself to a cup of drinking chocolate and a lavender-almond croissant. "It would've been appreciated if you and Léandre had discussed it with me before making your decision, but I respect that you both felt you were doing what was best."

"That's a far cry from your earlier response, when you were

screaming the temple down like a banshee, but I am pleased that you eventually came around to my way of thinking."

Laila clenched her fist as a violent pulse of electricity surged through her veins and held it until it passed. The last thing she desired was another shock from her mother if she believed her daughter to be getting too unruly. She picked up her cup with a steady hand and sipped, closing her eyes in pleasure from the silken texture of her chocolate.

"But you are looking... presentable now, at least." Amira bit into her toast with a punctuated crunch. "Any particular reason you decided to finally grace me with your company?"

A warmth flooded Laila's cheeks as she remembered the feel of Darius's lips and hands along her skin. "No reason." She sniped the memory before it could continue.

She had thought it would help to be in his arms again, but after he left she only grew more aware of the emptiness in her room. And so she'd decided to depart from it. Even Amira and her barbed wire quips were preferable to being tormented by her longing.

"Well, your timing is impeccable, all the same. You've just missed Darius Calantis as he left for Mortos."

She tried and failed to stop the lurch in her chest from emerging. "Oh? Already?"

"Just this morning." Amira slathered her croissant with broad strokes of cornflower butter. "I know how fond you became of him, so I thought that you might like to know."

Laila reached deep within herself for the whimsical starlet who let her lovers go without a fuss, casting them off with the rest of her jewel-encrusted trinkets to be replaced anew. It didn't work as well as before, for the polish was chipped and the smile was dimmed. But Amira didn't expect an immaculate performance.

"Thank you, Maman. It was kind of you to let me know." She rose from her seat, dropping her croissant unfinished on her plate.

"And *where* are you going?" Amira demanded in affront.

"Not hungry all of a sudden," Laila answered as she drifted out of her mother's solar and into the hallway. To walk out on her mother, mid-meal no less, was an impulse so impossible to fathom it was a wonder lightning did not strike her just for thinking it. Yet the sheer outpouring of grief that filled her upon news of Darius's leaving was enough to eject everything else. She collapsed against the wall and slid her hands into her hair. She could feel a scream rising in her throat but she obstructed it, biting down hard on her lip until she bled and the desire deflated.

Outside, the rain had faltered to a pitiful sputter, so she thought nothing of rushing out into the drizzle in her peach chiffon blouse and white pleated skirt—the scant needles of rain dissolving into beads against her skin as she ran to the tower.

Under the dimmed gloom of the sky, the marble bricks had adopted a grey surliness that seemed especially unwelcome to visitors. Laila craned her neck up towards the lone window and found it blackened, no signs of any life stirring inside it.

She climbed the myriad steps and entered the room to find all of it, everything, pristine—as though he had never disturbed it. Seeing that confirmation only sent her mother's earlier words hurtling to the forefront of her mind, and Laila released a soft gasp as though backhanded, a few hot tears rolling down her cheeks.

She closed her eyes and let herself slip down the wall onto the floor as the first of her sobs rolled through her in waves.

She wandered out to the rose garden shortly after.

Upon discovering the alabaster bench still damp, she cast an enchantment to dry it before slumping wearily on top of it. Even in autumn, the gold roses were still vicious in their vibrancy, and she let her fingers trail across the lustrous petals with a smile and a little lift in her chest, something telling her it would all be okay.

"Thought I might find you here."

Her head whirled, loose curls batting against her face as she saw him standing there, his broad figure eclipsing the opening of the pavilion.

She blurred her way into his arms in an instant, clutching him to her as she flattened her cheek against his chest. "My mother told me you left," she said, pausing to inhale the scent from his shirt as she clutched him tighter.

Darius rested his chin against her hair, kissing it briefly. "Not yet." He took her face in his hands and brought it up to him. "I wanted to see you first."

She exhaled in relief, a smile broadening her lips as her hand enclosed around his wrist. "Thank you."

He smiled back at her, hesitancy flickering across his features. "I admit, part of me wondered if I still couldn't convince you to leave with me."

She nuzzled his palm as he stroked his thumb against her cheek, finding herself wanting to tell him so many things. But when she opened her mouth to speak, her tongue only tripped itself over the barrage of words unspoken.

Her silence, however, told him all he needed to hear.

"I know you're not ready to come with me, Laila. But perhaps one day, a decade or so down the line, you will be. I have to hope."

He leaned in to kiss her forehead before letting his hand drop from her cheek with a parting smile.

She watched him leave without a word in response, a sheet of tears clouding her vision.

"So he's gone, then?"

She heard Lyra approach to sit beside her on the bench. Close, but not too close. She knew neither of them were ready to take that step.

"Yes," Laila answered, wiping her tears with the edge of her finger. "He's gone."

Lyra nodded, and for a moment they sat together, the silence between them spanning a conversation on its own.

"Why didn't you tell me he was going to do it?" Laila asked, puncturing the silence when she could take it no longer. "I know why he wouldn't have told me, because I would only try to convince him not to go through with it. But I know he would've at least told you. So why didn't you warn me? Why keep this a secret?"

She knew Lyra did not need elaboration to know which *he* she meant. "Because from the moment my uncle became your Lightshield, I have watched as he bent over backwards to protect you. Often at the expense of everything else. Including me. So when he told me what he was planning to do, I thought... I thought about how *nice* it felt to have something between us that was only ours for once. And so I kept it from you."

To that, Laila could say nothing. Though her heart was still heavy with the loss of those final days, days she knew she could never reclaim, it was nothing compared to the abundance of years she'd had before them.

Yet she'd always been greedy, even for the crumbs.

"Did he tell you why he did it?" Laila asked.

"He said that it was his time, that he had lived a long life and it was time for me to take up the mantle while he protected the weak and innocent."

Laila snorted with derision. "What a foolish, foolish thing."

"It's not foolish, Laila," Lyra said, her eyes going hard. "It's our way."

But she was tired of hearing that. Tired of being told continually about tradition as though it was some immovable stone in the path to progression. "Then change your ways."

Lyra raised her shoulders in affront before sighing heavily. She took one of her sprite braids between her fingers to trace the labyrinthine pattern and the miniature blossoms tucked within. "You know, my people have always taught me that there are monsters and there are the people you protect from monsters. No in between. I consider you the person that I protect. I also consider Darius Calantis a monster. Tell me, then, why I stood aside and let you have your heartfelt goodbye rather than slaying him where he stood? I think my ways have changed enough."

"It's because they're not all bad, Lyra. They deserve a chance to prove to us that they can be reformed."

"And suppose they can't be, are you ready for that?" Lyra asked, genuinely desiring to know.

"I don't know," Laila replied honestly. "All I know is it would be wrong of me not to at least try to believe in their betterment."

"Well, you're more hopeful than I, in any case."

Laila sighed, resting her head on Lyra's shoulder. "What do you say we take a break from all of this, then? I've been aching for a decent holiday for months now. Somewhere warm and tropical, the furthest thing away from a northern climate that you can think of. We can warm ourselves on the beach and drink from coconuts and have muscular merfolk give us massages."

Lyra chuckled, resting her head atop Laila's. "That sounds marvellous."

EPILOGUE

LAILA TOOK AN INDULGENT SIP OF WHITE RUM and mint leaves, the ice clinking against her lips. This would be her third glass, enough for the languorous haze of alcoholic stupor to set in. She draped her long, lean legs across the small bar table.

Such a gesture did not go unnoticed by onlookers, and she felt more than a few eyes become magnetised to the opulent display of her golden brown skin—a hue gifted to her by copious amounts of sun.

"You're certainly not short of admirers this evening," Lyra noted over the edge of her glass of sorrel. Malakia's finest. Her skin, unlike Laila's, had rebuffed the sun's enriching rays to maintain its pristine pallor.

Laila crushed the mint leaves to a pulp with her cocktail stick, wiping her tongue along the crystallised flecks of sugar on her plump bow lips. "Oh? I hadn't noticed."

"That's certainly not like you." Lyra set down her own glass and fiddled with her fingers. "Usually when an open buffet makes itself available, you're first in line for pickings."

"I'm just not feeling that sort of appetite right now, Lyra," Laila admitted, tilting her chair back onto its hindlegs. "I guess I'd rather let you have your pick of the lot uncontested."

"How magnanimous!" Lyra exclaimed in mock amusement. "And quite out of character."

"Oh, come now." She tilted her chin to reveal violet eyes hidden beneath oversized sunglasses, then downed the contents of her glass and gave a sharp exhale. "I rather would've thought you would be grateful for the lack of competition."

"Implicit humble bragging aside, I happen to *enjoy* a little healthy competition on these trips of ours. After all, it is our holiday tradition." Lyra gave one of Laila's legs a playful nudge. "Come *on*. Sure I can't tempt you? You did, after all, promise me fun and sun."

"I remember." Did she ever.

It had been the parting vow that had led them south of the continent to the shores of the tropics—the furthest thing possible from any whiff of winter. Yet while Laila's intent was to flee the cold, it had never quite left her. And it was in her bed she often felt the draft most of all.

"So, when are we going to talk about what's really bothering you?" Lyra's voice lured Laila out of her thoughts and back to the immediacy of Malakia's molten air.

"Hm?" Laila enchanted a shrimp from a nearby cocktail glass to dip into sauce and levitate towards her waiting fingers.

"The stampeding elephant in the room?" Lyra continued to coax. "You haven't said his name since we've landed here."

Laila took a large bite of shrimp, the sour-sweet tang of the sauce suddenly ashen in her mouth. "I didn't think you would've wanted to—to talk about it. You know. After. But if that's what you need, Lyra, then—"

"I wasn't talking about my uncle, Laila." Lyra's interjection was sharp as a dagger, a pin in the cushion of a subject she had no desire to broach.

"Y-yes, of course," Laila said, rushing to sip from her glass only to realise it'd become all ice. "I won't bring him up again."

"And yet, you knew precisely who I meant."

Laila met Lyra's gaze, the full accusatory righteousness of it, and knew she'd need a dozen more drinks if they were to finish this night without coming to blows.

"You have your subject to avoid, Lyra," Laila said, gesturing for a server to approach them, "and I have mine. Let's not sour what has the makings to be a pleasant evening, all right?"

The server arrived within moments of her summons. "Is everything to your liking, madame?"

The switch to princess performance triggered with immediate effect, and she turned to him armed with her best and brightest smile. "Yes, everything is wonderful. It is only that I believe my guard and I will require something a little more... potent for the evening. A bottle of your finest starshine, perhaps?"

"Starshine?" That certainly had Lyra's brow raising, for the liquor was quite infamous for its intoxicating influence.

"Right away, madame," the server said, then scurried off.

"What are you playing at, Laila?" Lyra asked once the server was out of earshot.

Laila turned the beacon of her smile to her guard next, though it had

431

notably sharpened at the edges. "You wanted fun and sun, didn't you? Well then, the fun is just getting started."

⁓〰⁓

In the end it took her three and a half bottles to relieve Laila of her senses.

With the first bottle, she loosened just enough to begin dancing on the tables. With the second, she fell into the ocean of hands outstretched for her, riding the wave of their love. Lyra could hear the peals of her laughter as Laila's body rippled along the surf, and she sighed in amusement. At the very least Laila was smiling. She never seemed happier than when she was basking in adoration.

By the time she reached her fourth bottle, Lyra had the sense to make good on her guardianship duties, and she carried a severely drunk and soon to be quite regretful Laila back to the safety of her room.

Lyra nudged the door open with her back as she carried her princess across the threshold, then gently laid her to rest upon her myriad of pillows.

Laila flopped onto the lace-edged silk with the limpness of a ragdoll, her arms raising with a catlike languor to shield her face from the light. "Mmph—too bright, too bright."

"Yes, you'll certainly be feeling that in the morning." Lyra sighed, flipping the switch to the ætherald lamps to darken the room. She unlaced Laila's sandals and tugged the ribbon straps of her dress, stripping her of both. "The things you make me do for you."

She shook her head in disapproval as she hooked the dress over the door of Laila's wardrobe, but her tone stopped short of unkind.

She'd never had a temperament suited to caregiving; that had always been one of her uncle's natural gifts. Lyra tried to imagine the tone of gentle disapprobation he might have taken with the scene unfolding between niece and charge and wondered if perhaps he might have handled tonight a sight better than she had.

She'd wondered that a lot recently.

Léandre always knew when the time called to be a calm stream to wear away the stone or the strong current to crash through it. But Lyra. Ah. Lyra approached conflict with the subtlety of a tidal wave and blundered through apologies with the same unceasing force.

Calmness was not a virtue that came easily.

Yet there was a tenderness that eased over her in seeing Laila so vulnerable, so undeniably in pain, and she couldn't help but tug the silk sheets over Laila's unclothed body and smooth them carefully over her shoulders before she turned to leave.

"Lyra..."

The soft slur of her name on Laila's lips gave Lyra pause. She turned to see that Laila had risen from the pillows, hair mussed and sprouting wild spirals in every direction like yellow dandelions.

"Yes?"

"I love you."

And though Lyra knew it was likely the result of Laila having drunk herself senseless, she'd be lying to herself if that didn't make her swallow just a little bit harder.

"Get some rest," she said, opening the door and closing it behind her. They both knew and understood the unspoken reciprocity implied beneath.

Laila stretched out on the beach towel, *lazy and feline. Above her, the palm trees lulled with a faint susurrus of the leaves, intermingled with*

the smoothly overlapping skirts of seafoam rolling in from the tide—a soft summer harmony.

Her back was painted gold with the wedges of sunlight that squeezed through the palms' green canopy, the leaves having formed a valiant shield to prevent her from experiencing the fullest extent of solar fury.

Though she was grateful for the buffer, something in her would always long for fierce climes and passionate temperatures. Thus her body angled towards the heat softening all the strength in her limbs—starting in surprise when instead she was met with the foreign bite of winter chill.

She moaned softly as the cube of ice eased its way along her spine, between the wings of her shoulder blades. Her back arched to the cold, strangely soothing in the mercurial heat.

Darius continued trailing the ice cube secured between his lips across the nape of Laila's neck until it melted, culminating in a cool kiss pressed into the base of her skull.

"Does that feel nice?"

His voice was like silk along tile. Her stomach clenched in response to it. Though she had heard it in her dreams several times before now, she didn't think the sound of him would ever not hit her.

"Very nice." She rolled over onto her side and into his waiting arms; the transition seamless. She nuzzled her chin against his biceps as his fingers grazed through her hair. "Why do I keep dreaming of you?"

Darius pulled back a curtain of curls to expose her shoulder to him, kissing it. "Because in the privacy of your own mind, there is no longer any place to hide from what you truly feel. What you truly want."

Laila swallowed thickly as she turned to look at him, drowning in the depthless blue of his stare. That was too much for her; she had to close her eyes. She took his hand and brought it to rest on her cheek, hiding herself in it.

"I miss you," she whispered meekly into his palm, a secret she couldn't

434

bear to admit to herself even now. "I tried so hard not to, but I just can't stop."

"Then don't," he said, stroking his thumb down her cheek. "You never have to stop, Laila. I'll be here for as long as you need me to be."

She scoffed a bitter laugh. "You're not even real."

"I'm real enough." He reached to tuck her hair behind her ear. "In all the ways that matter."

She kept her eyes on his hand during the gesture before she inhaled, as if to do just that. Then, slowly, she raised her eyes to look at him. He was just as beautiful as she remembered, every angular plane of his face perfect. She reached out to trace his jawline, trailing her fingers up to his cheekbone's sharp peak.

He reached up to cover her hand with his own, kiss the inside of her wrist. And that was enough to have her leaning forward to brush their lips together. Cautiously, at first, almost scared to rush it lest he vanish. But the moment their lips met in earnest, she couldn't hold herself back.

She slung her arms around his neck to pull him closer, kissing him with all the pain and longing and desperation for touch she'd had mounting up inside her since he left. She made a timid sound as Darius enclosed his hand around the small of her back, fingers roving down the notches of her spine and curving around the underside of her thigh before he tugged her swimming briefs down to her ankles.

She kicked them off to free herself, hooking one leg over his hip to draw him in. Closer. Though he could never be close enough, never be real enough. Not like this. But her loneliness had grown chronic, and she was willing to take what she could.

Darius gripped beneath her knee to drape her leg over his, massaging the crook with his thumb before his hand skirted upwards to slip between her thighs.

Laila cried out in relief the instant he touched her clit, not realising how badly she needed it until then. She kept grinding herself against the flat of his palm as his fingers leisurely explored the slick folds of inner skin.

"So eager," he marvelled as he teased back and forth with his thumb, circling her entrance. "How long has it been since you've been touched like this?"

"Far too long," she sighed, bringing him back in for a kiss as his fingers slipped inside her and crooked forth, soothing a much neglected ache.

Tangled in the silken sheets of her hotel bed, Laila had begun to overheat. Her skin was inflamed with a radioactive fever, little starbursts of white-hot energy dappling her constellated body. Celestial patterns struck their reflection along the ceiling—an enclosed cosmic vault of ever-shifting stars that danced across Laila's writhing limbs.

She clutched the pillow between her legs with a sense of possession, thrashing vigorously against it to chase the release lurking so tantalisingly over the brink. So deep was her yearning and so intense the relief that the moment she crossed the threshold to victory, she experienced a violent expulsion of her astral body. It hovered long enough in suspension for her to watch the shuddering convulsions and pearlised sheen of sweat signalling the finale of her climax.

She floated back into herself during her awakening in the aftermath, the closing images of her dream dispersing into hazy flecks the moment she opened her eyes.

"*No,*" she whined in refusal as she squeezed her eyes shut, burrowing her face into the pillow as if this alone would coax her back into her slumbering state. But she was alone.

She had *always* been alone.

Her throat hiccupped with a sob as hot tears slid down her cheeks.

436

She felt sated but empty, already plummeting from her pleasurable peak, leaving behind a body still touch-starved and a mind aswarm with the heavy smog of alcohol.

∞

Darius had become accustomed to locking the door twice behind him.

Each night, when he sealed himself in his quarters away from the rising chords of chatter, he made certain. Two locks. Once by key, and once by curse. That way there would be no witness to the sight of his eventual crumbling—the moments where he could do nothing but sink mournfully in his chair and palm his face in his hands, willing away his anguish. Then he'd pop open a bottle of polugar, drowning himself in it until he could no longer taste the sorrow in the back of his throat.

The tears would come by the third glass. The fourth, if he was lucky. And he hated himself for it each time. How he still felt the puncture of his grief months later, like a wound that wouldn't close. And what made it worse was knowing the true source of it. Not the kin he'd slain by driving a dagger through his heart. But the maiden who'd done so to him with just a word.

How pathetic, to mourn someone who was still alive and well and simply did not want him.

Just like his mother.

That revelation was enough to make him snort derisively into his glass as he knocked back the last of it. He massaged his dewy eyes in the aftermath, feeling the burn of tears emerge. This time he let them fall. Just to unleash them. He knew if he didn't let them out now, the anguish would come out of him in some other form, and he couldn't afford it. He couldn't allow his prefects to scent that kind of blood in the water. Not if he wished to rule.

And isn't that what I wanted? he thought bitterly. *To rule?*

He simply hadn't factored in the toll of having to do it alone. He knew he did not have to. With one snap of his fingers, he could have a lineup of occasselle all willing and waiting to be chosen as his bride. Then he could have a regina at his side, someone to rule with and seek comfort in during nights like these when the silences had grown too empty. But in the end, he knew it wouldn't be enough. It wouldn't be *her.* With the smile and touch and voice he so craved.

So he put aside his delusion and stumbled over to his desk, opening it to reveal the ribbon-bound stack of love letters he had not sent. He traced his fingers along the diaphanous pink silk, remembering how immaculately it once adorned her golden curls, before he pulled up a fresh bit of parchment and prepared to pen a new missive. He knew that, as with the others, he wouldn't muster the courage to send it. But the process of spilling the contents of his heart to her and imagining her reading them was enough to give him comfort.

"I have gathered you all here under the aim of transparency."

Darius stood with his hands behind his back. His quick gaze darted over the occupants at his table in an attempt to glean their expressions.

"I recognise many of you have concerns over my ascension, and so, to dispel your doubts, I have decided to share with you my immediate aims for the kingdom."

With this, he made a gesture for the copies of parchment he'd been labouring over for months to be distributed. Though he'd been dreaming of the contents for far longer. Even now, he could scarcely believe his luck at being able to share his plans somewhere other than in the confines of his own imagination.

He took a seat and raised two fingers to his lips, awaiting the question likely poised on the edge of everyone's tongue.

"What precisely is the purpose of this text, Your Majesty?" asked one of his father's prefects, the manner of address just about getting past his throat. It was a wonder he didn't choke on it.

"I'm very glad you asked." A satisfied smile crawled across Darius's features. "This document shall encompass all my plans of action for the reformation of Mortos and how to nurture our country to the greatness my father withheld from it."

They didn't like that. Not one bit. Already he could see the impression of a sneer lurking from within many austere faces. But that had been Darius's intent, after all. To lay the bait and watch them gobble it. Those who still held allegiance to his father and his primitive ways would have no further place in his world.

"Please read thoroughly and without prejudice." Darius spread his arms in welcome. "I encourage all to air their view unfiltered."

And so he watched and he waited as the prefects scoured the text with faint murmurs of commentary and interest.

"As you can see, I have put together a list of many directives I plan to implement." Darius rose from his seat to circle the table. "I find our spending on training, arming, and maintaining warriors to be at our personal service to be immensely wasteful and indulgent. This practice shall be phased out, and a more centralised local enforcement shall take its place. As seen on page five, these enforcers will handle local disputes as well as patrol roads and slay the feral beasts that plague them." A way to resolve the petty turf wars throughout the country. "While in the meantime, I prepare my chimeras to be our primary defence."

The complaints came as expected.

"You wish to *outlaw* the practice of retaining personal warriors?"

"You expect us to divert our taxes from furthering the martial glory of our kind to... *farming*?"

"You intend to make us sit *exams* in order to hold our position as prefects? I've never heard of such nonsense. Occassi are creatures of might, not pompous and pampered intelligentsia!"

"Times are changing, my good fellows," Darius replied in a smooth, honeyed tone. "I suggest you march with them or risk being pummelled underfoot."

"Well, I refuse!" A disgruntled prefect slammed the parchment on the table. "I refuse to allow our country be run into the ground by the likes of a worthless bastard—"

Darius muttered an ancient phrase, and the prefect's tongue halted mid-word. Then his limbs followed, going stiff and rigid as a plank before he collapsed backwards into his chair.

The others could only watch with frantic eyes as their own limbs ceased to work, an invisible force keeping them pinned to their chairs.

"What?" Delanus cried out, the sole guest in the room still ambulatory. "What is the meaning of this?"

"It's just a little contingency I put in place in case things were to get heated." Darius waved it off in dismissal. Then he gave a roll of his eyes when Delanus's accusatory gaze strengthened. "I cursed the wine."

Delanus spun round to look at his goblet with a shiver.

"Not to worry, I made sure yours was skipped—I want you to witness what comes next."

Raspy breaths sounded as the remnants of what was once Emica Hariken emerged from the shadows. Her limbs were so long and gangling she could scarcely do anything but skitter along the floor like a spider. Her face could not be seen behind the curtain of limp, oily hair, but it was clear from the dangling threads of drool and harsh, panting breaths that the creature had only one thing on her mind—hunger.

"Darius, what..." Delanus had gone white from shock. His mere fear was enough to paralyse him better than the wine ever might have.

"It's like I said, Delanus—" Darius's voice was deceptively soothing as his creation drew nearer and nearer to her defenceless prey.

His prefect gibbered as she sniffed him and then opened wide for her first bite.

"Times are changing. You can either step towards the future with me... or be devoured by the past."

"Please, no—"

Delanus thought it came from his own lips until he realised it was the prefect who screamed as the chimera savaged him before leaping towards the others. He whined softly as she detached one prefect's head from his shoulders and squelched it loudly between her jaws before making quick work of the others. Crunching their bones. Peeling skin away from muscle with a cold curiosity to gorge herself on their innards, splattering blood and viscera.

Darius watched with an unflinching focus, his head cocked to one side. "Shame." He heaved a sigh once the feast was done, and then glanced down at the lone survivor. "Now I'm going to have to fill all those empty seats."

THANK YOU FOR READING! WHAT'S NEXT?

Please do remember to leave a review on your website of choice if you'd like to support me further. Every little helps, even just a rating or sentence.

You can also enjoy a free first chapter of the sequel if you subscribe to my newsletter on **aninkwellofnectar.com** as well as exclusive content, snippets, and release updates for all future novels.

ACKNOWLEDGEMENTS

This book owes a great deal to the endless support, praise and passion of many individuals I've collected through social media over the years, some of whom are still with me and some of whom are not. I don't know all of you by legal name but if you're reading this now I want to thank you all from the bottom of my heart for following me for so long on this journey. It means the world to me to have you champion this book whether it be from the very start or whether you'd hitched a late ride on this crazy train to self-publishing.

I never expected to find people who would hold this book with as much esteem and enthusiasm as I do, and without your feedback and love, I doubt I'd be in the position I am today. So, thank you, once again, from Tumblr to Twitter to Discord. Another thanks goes to my ko-fi members: Han, Tyler, Lau, Valmont, DC and Nix. Your additional support goes a long way keeping me afloat.

I also want to give a shout to Molly Rookwood for her diligence in editing this book. You've been a joy to work with, and it warms my heart that you considered this project among your favourites.

To Eeva Nikunen, whose work I have been a secret admirer of for years, being able to hire you was a dream and I couldn't think of a better person to bring my artistic vision for this book to life.

To Megan Wyreweden, thank you for creating the beautiful drop caps for that extra fantastical flourish.

Finally, a heartfelt thanks to any readers, old and new, who have decided to take a chance on this passion project of mine. It's been a labour of love for years and it both frightens me and thrills me to send it off into the world. I hope you find it worthy.

ABOUT THE AUTHOR

Camilla Andrew lives in a leafy English town that sounds remarkably like a fairytale setting with talking animals in suits. She spends her days writing, reading, drinking tea and working diligently at her (remote) office job in a local government council. Her works also feature in Cloaked Press and midnight & indigo.

www.aninkwellofnectar.com

BES - #0032 - 021024 - C0 - 216/142/25 - PB - 9781739308902 - Gloss Lamination